PROPHECY

THE FRACTURED KINGDOM

PROPHECY

M.L. FERGUS

tundra

Tundra Books, an imprint of Tundra Book Group,
a division of Penguin Random House of Canada Limited

Library and Archives Canada Cataloguing in Publication

Title: Prophecy / M.L. Fergus.
Other titles: Gypsy king
Names: Fergus, Maureen, author.
Description: Series statement: Fractured kingdom ; 1 |
Substantially revised edition of: The gypsy king.
Identifiers: Canadiana (print) 20240357191 | Canadiana (ebook) 20240357213 |
ISBN 9781774886076 (softcover) | ISBN 9781774886083 (EPUB)
Subjects: LCGFT: Fantasy fiction. | LCGFT: Novels.
Classification: LCC PS8611.E735 G96 2025 | DDC jC813/.6—dc23

Published simultaneously in the United States of America by Tundra Books
of Northern New York, an imprint of Tundra Book Group, a division
of Penguin Random House of Canada Limited

Library of Congress Control Number: 2024936358

Edited by Lynne Missen (original) and Margot Blankier (updated)
Designed by Sophie Paas-Lang
Cover art: croisy /Adobe Stock
Typeset by Daniella Zanchetta
The text was set in Adobe Caslon Pro.

Printed in Canada

www.penguinrandomhouse.ca

1 2 3 4 5   29 28 27 26 25

Penguin
Random House
tundra | TUNDRA BOOKS

*For my beautiful family, who never
stopped believing in this story—or me*

You are about to enter a dark and dangerous kingdom. Over the course of your journey, you will encounter or hear mention of sexual situations as well as the abuse, kidnap, murder, enslavement, imprisonment, brutal torture, illness, death and grief of people of all ages. The mistreatment and death of animals are also a part of this harsh world. Readers who may be sensitive to these elements, please take note before joining the adventure.

Prologue

THE LAST SURVIVING Methusian Seer struggled to her feet.

An ancient crone, she'd sat alone beneath the banyan tree for a day and a night and another day. Not eating, not drinking, not sleeping—only emptying her mind and waiting to be shown the truth about things past and the promise of things yet to come.

Now, filled with wonder and confusion at what she'd been shown, the old woman gathered up her charcoal and scrolls. Groping in the darkness for her cane, she hobbled toward the hidden camp where her beloved people were dancing, singing and feasting to honor the memory of the many who'd lately been murdered in the healing pool massacres.

When she was nearly there, the mouth-watering scent of roast mutton caused her shriveled stomach to clench painfully. As she stumbled and fell to her knees, the thin, high-pitched scream of a small child pierced the night.

As one, the Methusians before her turned toward the sound, which ended with chilling abruptness.

The next instant the horsemen were upon them, slashing and cutting. Dressed in darkest black from head to toe, to a man they resembled Death, though none were as merciful or discriminating as Death. Even as the heartsick old woman watched, a tiny, toddling infant was trampled beneath pounding hooves, and a heavily pregnant woman was gutted as though her swollen belly was nothing more than a piece of ripe fruit.

While most of her beautiful, brightly clad people took up arms and began to fight, a handful of the women grabbed the children and ran into the forest. One of these—a girl carrying a child in one arm and dragging another by the hand—almost tripped over the old woman kneeling in the darkness.

Stifling a scream, the girl gasped, "Run, old mother! The fighters will not be able to hold the Regent's soldiers off for long!"

The distant crash of cooking pots being overturned made the girl jump and the children whimper. The old woman did not even blink.

"I am too old to run, Cairn," she said.

"But they will kill you!"

"Then I will die—but first you will hear that I have Seen a king! A great king, a Methusian king! A king whose coming will unite the five clans of Glyndoria and set things to right for all people!"

"I care *not* about all people or about uniting the clans," hissed the girl as she tightened her grip on the children she'd just seen orphaned. "I care only about our people and our clan—what is left of it, anyway. Why could you not have had a vision of the healing pool found, that we might once again have power over death itself?"

"Balthazar swore he'd found the sacred pool and it did not give him power over death. Indeed, it brought Death to his very doorstep—and to ours," reminded the old woman. "The Pool of Genezing is more a curse than a blessing in these dark days, Cairn. But perhaps it will not be ever so. Perhaps the coming king is meant to see our people safely settled on its shores once more. But if that is true, it is more than the Fates saw fit to share with me this night."

The girl started to say something more, but her throat closed in terror at the sound of someone large crashing through the bushes nearby.

Swiftly, the old woman pulled two scrolls from the pouch at her waist. Unrolling the first, she handed it to the girl, who barely glanced at it before asking, "Who is she?"

"I do not know. I know only that you must find her, for it begins and ends with her. As for the second scroll," said the old woman, passing it over without unrolling it, "you are not to look upon it until the first anniversary of this night that follows the discovery of the girl. Only then will the words have any meaning at all."

Tersely nodding her understanding, the girl shoved both scrolls down the front of her shift. Then she hoisted the younger child higher on her hip, grabbed the hand of the older child and prepared to run. "I will come back for you if I can," she said.

"Do not come back for me," said the old woman. "Only promise me that you will carry my last and best prophecy onward to those of our people who survive this night."

"But—"

"Promise!" commanded the old woman, as the large, crashing someone drew nearer still.

"I promise!" blurted the girl, with a terrified glance over her shoulder.

"Now, go," said the old woman, giving her a shove. "They are coming!"

Without another word, the girl turned and fled into the darkness. Desperate to give her and the children a few precious extra moments to escape, the old woman moaned loudly to attract the attention of the crashing someone.

Almost immediately, she heard a gruff voice shout, "I've found another!"

And then he was looming over her, a flickering torch in one hand, a bloody blade in the other. For half a heartbeat, he gazed down at her with the blank, soulless eyes of one who murdered infants and old women for profit. Then he casually set the tip of his sword against her belly and ran her through.

As the old woman felt the cold steel pierce her flesh, she smiled at the thought of the Methusian who would be king.

Then, still smiling, she walked without fear into Death's cold embrace.

Fifteen Years Later

One

PERSEPHONE AWOKE WITH A START.

Even so, she moved not a muscle, having long ago learned the usefulness of controlling the twitches and fidgets that gave others away. Taking care to keep her breathing deep and even, she half opened one violet eye. Through the thick tangle of dark lashes, she scanned the dirty stall in which she lay for some sign of whatever it was that had jarred her from sleep. She couldn't see much by the light of the moon that bled through the cracks in the barn walls, but she could see enough to know that danger didn't lie within gutting distance. Nevertheless, her fingers slid to the hilt of the stolen dagger in the makeshift scabbard strapped to her bare thigh. It was a good knife—well balanced, well pointed and razor sharp. It could be used to skin a hare as easily as to kill a man, which suited Persephone just fine. She enjoyed hare stew and had no use for men whatsoever.

SNAP.

There—at the far end of the barn. A sound that didn't belong!

Quick as a cat, Persephone tossed aside her thin blanket and rolled off the pile of old straw that served as her bedding. Too late, she remembered the heavy chain that hung between the cuffs of her leg irons. As it clinked and clattered to the hard-packed dirt floor, she gritted her teeth against the urge to curse aloud. What a fool the owner was to have clapped her in irons! True, she'd run away again after promising not to do so, and true, the ill-humored old sow had used the opportunity to escape her pen and wreak havoc in the bean field again, but how could Persephone possibly be expected to protect the livestock if she could neither sneak up on thieves nor give chase to them?

She listened now for the sound of this particular thief fleeing in panic. When she heard nothing, she unsheathed her dagger and listened harder—this time for the sound of the thief trying to sneak up on her that he might slit her throat or force himself upon her or both. When she *still* heard nothing, she lifted the chain at her feet to prevent it from dragging, tiptoed toward the opening of the stall and cautiously peered around the rotting wooden half wall.

So confident was Persephone that the thief would be cowering behind a goat somewhere that she nearly bumped noses with him before realizing that he was, in fact, crouching motionless before her in the moonlit darkness, looking almost as startled as she felt. Actually, he did not look startled as much as he looked utterly astounded. With a gasp, Persephone let go of the chain in her hand, jumped backward and whirled around to press her back against the half wall. On the other side of the divide, she heard an abrupt clanking sound—as though the thief had dropped something heavy—and then an anxious squawk. Persephone scowled as alarm gave way to indignation. So! He thought he would help himself to one of the chickens, did he?

Not if he wanted to live to see another sunrise, he wouldn't.

"Put down that chicken!" she ordered, her voice ringing with authority.

"No," said the thief.

"Yes!"

"No."

He sounded young but annoyingly self-assured, and not at all frightened even though he had to know that one shout from her would bring the owner running, useless though he was.

"Who *are* you?" asked the thief wonderingly. "Where did you come from? What is your name?"

Persephone's heart nearly stopped when she realized that these words had issued from high above her head. Flinging herself forward into the shadows, she rolled to her feet with surprising speed and grace for one so heavily fettered.

The thief continued to comfortably balance upon the narrow half wall for a few seconds more. Then, without taking his eyes off her, he leapt lightly to the floor of the stall. The chicken tucked under his arm squawked once and then fell silent.

Persephone dropped into a fighting stance. She'd been right—the thief was young, probably not much older than she, though certainly of an age to do the work of a man. Strong enough to do the work of a man, too, judging by the long, lean look of him. A white silk shirt open halfway to his waist revealed a smooth ridge of pectorals and a hard, flat belly; tight black breeches accentuated powerful legs. High boots and a dark headscarf knotted over long, unkempt curls completed the look, which was that of a pirate clutching a chicken.

The thought brought a faint smile to Persephone's lips, but it died the next second when her gaze drifted to the thief's face, and she realized with a start that he was staring at her even more intently than she'd been staring at him. Worse, there was a strange, rapt look in his eyes—a look that made her instantly, uncomfortably aware of the fact that beneath her thin nightshift, she was wearing nothing at all.

Wordlessly, the thief took a step toward her.

Heart thudding madly, Persephone stepped farther back into the shadows. "I have a knife," she warned.

"So do I," said the thief. "Now, tell me who you are."

Shaking her head, Persephone tried to take another step backward, but stumbled over the chain of her leg irons. When the thief reached out to steady her, she jerked her arm away with such vehemence that she accidentally struck herself in the face.

The thief didn't smile, but Persephone could tell that he *wanted* to smile, so she slashed the air with her dagger and snapped, "I'm not afraid to use this, you know!"

"And I'm not afraid to use *this*," he replied genially as he reached over his broad shoulder to pull a much larger dagger from the scabbard that was evidently strapped to his back. "In fact," he added, in an almost nostalgic voice, "I've seven corpses to this blade."

"Really?" sniffed Persephone, feigning indifference. "I've ten to this one."

The thief grinned at the lie. "Excellent!" he said. "We'll be well matched, then. Come, step out of the shadows. Let us fight to the death. If I win, I get myself a fine, fat chicken dinner, and if you win—"

"You will leave Mrs. Busby alone and depart at once!" said Persephone fiercely.

There was a long moment of silence. Then, in a rather mystified voice, the thief asked, "Who is Mrs. Busby?"

Without thinking, Persephone gestured toward the chicken in his arms.

"I . . . see," said the thief. He looked to one side and then to the other before tilting his head toward her and solemnly inquiring, "Tell me, mistress, do you name all creatures or just the ones that taste good with gravy and potatoes?"

Persephone's cheeks burned with embarrassment as the thief began to chuckle. "Stop laughing," she muttered. "It's not funny."

But the thief wouldn't stop laughing, and the longer he laughed, the more irritated Persephone became. Finally, heedless of the danger and not knowing how else to get him to shut up, she lunged at him with her dagger. She was quick, but he was quicker. Dropping his own knife and flinging the startled Mrs. Busby to one side, the thief deftly sidestepped Persephone's attack and grabbed the wrist of her knife hand. Yanking her forward, he spun her around, caught her around the midsection with his free arm and dragged her back until she was pressed against him.

"Never attack in anger," he whispered, his lips so close to her ear that she could feel his breath on her skin. "And never start a fight you can't win."

"Let . . . go . . . of . . . me," she panted, as she twisted and struggled in his arms.

"That's quite a temper you've got there," the thief continued, in a voice that was almost a purr. "Is that why you're in irons? Because I must say, I never expected—"

Persephone cut him off with a heel stomp to the foot.

"Ow!" cried the thief. Angrily, he spun her back around so that she was facing him. Forcing her knife hand behind her back, he pulled her so close that she could hardly breathe.

Persephone glared up at him in defiance. Then, as though in a swoon, she let her head fall back and her body go limp. The instant the thief loosened his grip on her in order to accommodate the sudden shift in her weight, she drove her knee upward into his groin with all her might.

He didn't let go of her knife hand, but his eyes did bulge alarmingly. Slowly sinking to the ground, he clutched his mangled vitals with his free hand and wheezed, "I cannot believe . . . that you . . . of all people . . . did that . . . to me! It would bloody well . . . serve you right . . . if I . . . if I . . ."

Persephone watched with some apprehension as the furious thief cast about for something truly terrible to do to her.

"If I up and gave you a good, sound spanking!" he finally exploded.

For a moment, Persephone just gaped at him.

"A spanking?" she finally spluttered. "A *spanking*?" She started to laugh. "That is the most absurd thing I've ever heard in my life. A spanking? You wouldn't dare!"

"Oh, wouldn't I?" cried the thief, who suddenly looked more like an outraged boy than a powerful stranger.

Persephone continued to laugh as he staggered to his feet.

"Stop laughing!" he ordered, giving her knife hand a little shake. "I warn you—I'll do it, I'll spank you! I don't care who you are, I'll—"

Before he could finish his sentence, from the threshold of the stall there came a wet snarl.

It was Cur, back from the hunt. The fur on the back of his thick neck bristled menacingly, his jaws were dark with fresh blood and his fearsome canines glinted in the thin shaft of moonlight.

A dead hare lay at his feet.

"My dog," said Persephone, by way of introduction.

"Oh," murmured the thief, who hesitated before casually adding, "I . . . don't much like dogs."

Cur snarled again and snapped his teeth.

With comical swiftness, the thief moved to put Persephone between him and the beast. "He, uh, looks vicious."

"He *is* vicious," said Persephone with relish. "Moreover, he is *extremely* protective of me."

"Humph," said the thief.

"If I order him to attack, he'll rip out your throat," she confided as she wrenched her knife hand from the thief's grasp. "He's killed dozens of men at my behest."

"Ten with the blade, dozens with the dog," muttered the thief. "You're a likely wench, aren't you?"

Persephone smiled humorlessly. Then she lifted two fingers to Cur, who immediately stopped snarling, trotted to her side and lay down at her feet.

"Well," said the thief, with a darting glance at the dog, who silently bared his teeth. "It seems you've bested me."

"It seems I have," said Persephone.

The thief eyed her speculatively. "I don't often get bested," he said.

Persephone shrugged to hide her almost-intoxicating sense of triumph. She'd spent her entire life being bested; it was a powerful feeling to be on the other side for a change.

The thief frowned now and muttered something under his breath about having made a poor start of things. Then he cleared his throat and said, "I don't suppose I could convince you to come away with me?"

Persephone stared at him. "Come away with you?" she said incredulously. "Are you mad? Why on earth would you think that I would ever agree to come away with you?"

"Because," he replied, "I think it is possible . . . that is to say, I'm coming to believe . . ."

"Yes, yes?" said Persephone. "What are you coming to believe?"

"That I have been looking for you for as long as I can remember."

Two

PERSEPHONE WAS SO STARTLED by the thief's reply that for an endless, breathless moment she stood transfixed, unable to break eye contact with him. In fact, it wasn't until she felt his fingers brush against hers that she returned to her senses.

"No," she said abruptly, jerking her hand away. "No, of course I won't come away with you."

The thief looked disappointed but not surprised. "Very well," he said resignedly, "I guess I ought to bid you good night, then."

"I guess you ought," agreed Persephone.

"May I retrieve my knife?" he asked.

"No."

"May I have the chicken?"

Persephone rolled her eyes. "No."

"Please?" he said. "I haven't eaten in three days."

Something about the way he said it made Persephone believe that he was telling the truth. This, combined with the fact that she knew what it was to go hungry and had the power to make him go hungry yet, is perhaps what prompted her to pick up the hapless, squawking Mrs. Busby (who was, after all, a farm chicken destined for the dinner platter) and hand her over.

The slow, considered smile the thief gave Persephone made her stomach do a funny kind of flip-flop and left her with the distinct and intensely annoying impression that she'd just passed some kind of test.

"Thank you," murmured the thief. He sighed deeply. "The problem now, of course, is that I'm going to have an awfully hard time carving up this chicken unless you allow me to retrieve my—"

Persephone threw her dagger without warning. It flew so close to the thief's head that it nicked his cheek before slamming into the wall behind him.

"Bloody hell!" he yelped. "You could have killed me!"

"If I'd wanted to kill you, you'd be dead," said Persephone flatly. "Now take Mrs. Busby and get out of here before I change my mind."

As soon as she was certain that the thief was gone for good, Persephone retrieved her dagger and slipped it back into the scabbard on her thigh. Then she hid the thief's knife beneath the straw and lay down next to Cur. He immediately snuggled closer and began to snore. Persephone threw her arm across his matted fur and stared into the moonlit darkness before her, replaying the encounter with the thief over and over in her mind—smiling when she recalled his dismayed expression at her triumph, frowning when she recalled the unyielding strength of his arms around her. She wondered what would have happened if Cur hadn't shown up. Would the thief really have tried to spank her? She couldn't help but chuckle at the thought. What kind of criminal believed that the most effective way to deal with uncooperative damsels was to *spank* them? Then again, perhaps he'd been something more than a common criminal. Though he'd clearly been no nobleman, he *had* been wearing a silk shirt and good boots. Moreover, he'd carried himself with the bearing of a battle-tested young lord. To say nothing of the strangeness of his words—*I have been looking for you for as long as I can remember. . . . I don't care who you are. . . . I cannot believe that you, of all people. . . .* Whatever could he have meant by these things? Who had he thought she was that he should say them? And asking her to come away with him? Though the night was far from cold, Persephone shivered once, violently.

Then, resolutely pushing the chicken-eating pirate thief with the slow smile and the quick hands from her thoughts, she squeezed her eyes shut and yanked her thin blanket up to her chin, certain that sleep would elude her.

The next thing Persephone knew, Cur was gone and a gruff but familiar voice was ordering her awake. Instantly, her eyes snapped open to see the dark silhouette of the owner looming over her, framed by the blinding light of full day that poured in from the open barn door.

"Why are you still abed, you shiftless, good-for-nothing lay-about?" he demanded. When she didn't answer, he hurled a shovel at the ground by her head. "And what is this?"

Lifting a hand to shield her eyes from the sunlight, Persephone squinted at the shovel for a very long moment before declaring, "It's a shovel."

"Don't get smart with me, girl!" the owner shouted. "I know it's a shovel! I found it lying on the ground beyond your stall, out of place. And do you know what else? By my count, one of my chickens is missing. You know what that means, don't you?"

Instead of answering, Persephone gazed up at him with a bland expression on her face.

He scowled. "It means that I've once again been robbed by some thieving piece of scum and that you've once again done nothing whatever to prevent it!"

Persephone looked at the owner as though *he* were a piece of scum. "Perhaps the chicken *was* stolen," she said levelly. "Then again, perhaps she left of her own accord. Everyone knows that chickens are a faithless sort. I tell you what: remove my leg irons and I shall seek her out. Upon finding her, I shall drag her back here so that you can give her a good beating and fix her with a tiny set of leg irons of her own. That should not only strike fear into her tiny chicken heart but also prevent her from ever again attempting to flee your tender mercies."

His fleshy face mottled with fury, the owner lifted his heavy boot and aimed a kick in Persephone's direction. She rolled away unharmed and was on her knees facing him in a single fluid motion. Her fingers itched to reach for the dagger at her thigh, but she didn't dare. Much as she despised the owner, she wasn't prepared to kill him over a chicken, and inflicting a non-mortal wound would only enrage him further. Moreover, the dagger in question used to belong to him, and if he were ever to discover that she was the one who'd stolen it, he'd give her a beating the likes of which she'd never known. Worse, he'd take the knife away from her, and though she now had the thief's much larger knife in her possession, she'd become rather attached to her own little dagger.

The owner eyed her now with a mixture of wariness and dislike. "You think you're so quick and clever," he sneered. "Well, I warned you what would happen the next time your sloth cost me a chicken."

"You did," agreed Persephone.

"Ten lashes is what I said," he reminded.

Persephone nodded.

"And you know what will happen if you resist."

Persephone nodded again, her eyes cold.

Seemingly dissatisfied by her lack of terror, the owner added, darkly, "No amount of begging is going to spare you."

Persephone nearly laughed aloud. Enslaved though she might be, she'd never begged for anything in her life, least of all from this pig on two legs.

"No begging," she said gravely. "I understand."

The owner waited for her to say something more. When she didn't, he gave his head a jerk to indicate that she was to follow, then he turned on one heel and stomped toward the open barn door. Slowly, Persephone got to her feet and fell into step behind him.

They hadn't gone more than a few paces when the owner paused. Reaching down, he picked up the dead hare that Cur had brought home the previous night. Persephone sighed inwardly at having forgotten to hide it after the thief had departed, for she'd have liked to have made a nice hare stew for her supper that evening, after the day's many chores were done.

As though he'd heard her sigh and understood the cause of it, the owner gave Persephone a spiteful, rotten-toothed grin, shook the furry little corpse at her and said, "You will prepare it for *my* supper, along with gravy and potatoes."

Shrugging as though the loss of the hare was neither here nor there to her, Persephone reached out and touched the soft, spotted fur between the dead creature's ears. Then she cocked her head to one side and said, "I believe I shall call him Lord Pirate."

The owner's mouth dropped open at this startling statement. "Why would you call the hare Lord Pirate?" he blurted. "Why would you call the hare anything?"

"Don't you know?" she said, pushing past him with a faint smile. "I name all creatures—most especially those that taste good with gravy and potatoes."

Moments later, Persephone stood in the yard with her shift pulled down to her waist, clutching the whipping post and gritting her teeth so that the owner wouldn't have the satisfaction of hearing her cry out. He wasn't hitting hard enough to peel the skin from her back, for such injury might result in her many chores having to be done by his own lazy self. But he was applying the whip with a will, hitting hard enough to raise welts that were sure to weep and sting for days. Still, Persephone moved not a muscle. When she'd first come to the owner, small and undernourished though she'd been, she'd openly scorned his attempts to punish her. Her defiance had been so absolute that in order to get her to turn around and stop laughing at him, he'd had to resort to binding her wrists to the post—something he'd never managed to do without earning himself at least a few well-deserved kicks, bites and scratches.

Then one day, after happening upon Persephone companionably chatting with several sheep, the owner had come up with a far cleverer idea. For every kick and scratch that Persephone directed at him, for every drop of her spittle that flew in his direction, for every lash that she refused to take on bended back, one of the barnyard animals would get two lashes—even if it meant flogging the unfortunate creature to death.

Persephone had not believed for a moment that the owner would purposely flog one of his own animals to death, since he himself would be the poorer for it. But as she'd ever been unwilling to see any creature suffer harm on her account, she'd thereafter always submitted to her beatings without protest, regardless of how unfair she felt they were.

Of course, she thought now, grunting quietly as the whip whistled through the air and landed yet again across her bare back, *some beatings are fairer than others*. In spite of the pain, she smiled at the thought that she'd purposely given away one of the owner's chickens. Then she gave herself over to imagining the hungry thief squatting before an open fire, his silk shirt stretched taut across his muscular shoulders, his mouth watering at the sight of a plucked and spitted Mrs. Busby browning nicely over the leaping flames.

Something about the image sustained Persephone through all ten lashes. When it was over, she was breathing hard and relieved to still be in complete control of herself. Leaning against the post, she was about to ease her shift up over her injured back when:

CRACK!

"One for luck!" sang the owner, staggering as he delivered this final blow.

Unprepared to receive it, Persephone gave a loud cry. The owner laughed when he heard it. Furious, Persephone yanked up her shift to cover her nakedness, wincing as the rough material scraped across her fresh welts. Then she spun to face him and shouted,

"You said ten!"

With some difficulty, the owner tore his gaze away from the front of her shift, which was yet unlaced. "I said ten for losing me a chicken," he corrected thickly as his eyes drifted back to the front of her shift. Swallowing hard, he dragged the back of his filthy hand across his mouth. "That last one was for luck, like I said."

Noting the wanton look in his eyes, Persephone turned away in disgust, her leg irons clanking in sympathy. *Pig*, she thought savagely, as she tugged the laces of her shift tight. She knew the owner wanted her—he'd wanted her ever since he'd first set eyes on her when she was nothing more than a desperate little starveling. However, *he* knew—as he'd always known—that if he ever laid so much as a finger on her, he'd have to kill her or he was a dead man. Whether she slit his throat while he slept, burned his thatch-roofed cottage to the ground with him inside it, buried a carving knife in his turned back or poisoned his dinner, one thing was certain: if he touched her, she would be damaged—though not broken—and he'd be a walking corpse.

The grim smile this brought to her lips was wiped off when the owner grabbed her by the arm, jerked her around and pushed his sweaty face into hers.

"It occurs to me that none of the other gentleman farmers lose half so many chickens as I," he breathed, his small, mean eyes glittering with unfulfilled desire.

Persephone's only reply was to slowly turn her head to avoid his foul breath.

The owner gave her a shake that made her teeth rattle. "If I ever discover that you are one of those traitorous slaves that sympathizes with the lowborn scum who skulk around the countryside, stealing and rioting and refusing to adapt to changing times—"

"Changing times have brought them low," said Persephone, as though in agreement.

The owner's face turned very red. "Not as low as a stinking Erok slave like you," he sneered, "who could only sink lower if you were a branded tribal barbarian!"

"And not as low as an upstart New Man like *you*," she flashed back recklessly, "who could only sink lower if the dirty work you did for the Regent was first dipped in mud and then rolled in *pig shit*."

"What do you know about the work we New Men do?" bellowed the enraged owner, giving her a vicious backhand across the face. "What do you know about anything? You are nothing but an ill-bred, ignorant little nobody. So keep your mouth shut, do your work and know that if I ever discover that you have aided or abetted a thief on my land, I shall drown that mangy dog of yours before your eyes. And then I shall drown you!"

Persephone stared after the owner as he stormed across the yard and into the thatch-roofed cottage. Her face throbbed where he'd hit her, but she was savagely pleased for having said what she had.

"He thinks he's so much better than me, but he's just a lowborn thug who was raised up because he's willing to do things that would turn a decent man's stomach," she muttered a short while later. "Beating, burning, kidnapping, murdering, stealing—I may be ill bred and ignorant, Mrs. Foster, but when that pig signed up for the Regent's New Man army, he sold his soul to the *devil*!"

Mrs. Foster was so surprised to hear this that she mooed.

"It's true!" insisted Persephone as she leaned her forehead against Mrs. Foster's warm flank and continued to milk her. "You might be tempted to pity the Regent Mordesius for having been all but burned alive as a boy in the fire that killed his family, Mrs. Foster, but save your pity, for he is the very devil himself! Do you remember me telling you about Cookie, the cook in the manor house belonging to the merchant who owned me when I was very young? Well, she told me that the things the Regent ordered his New Men to do were *nothing* compared to the things he himself has done. You'd think that such a great man would leave torture to his underlings, but Cookie said her cousin's husband's sister by his father's third wife—his half sister, really—knew a man who mucked the royal stables at the palace in the imperial capital. And he said that the Regent often descended into the dungeon to take care of business himself. This man even saw *children* delivered to the dungeon—delivered but never released. Can you imagine? And Cookie always said that it was surely no coincidence that old King Octavio died within weeks of appointing Mordesius regent of the unborn prince—now our young King Finnius. Nor did she think it a coincidence that the queen died within days of delivering her child and that all who attended the birth later disappeared. All but the Regent, that is . . ."

Mrs. Foster shifted restlessly, as though, dead monarchs and mysterious disappearances notwithstanding, she'd begun to find Persephone's chatter a bit of a bore.

Admonishing the cow for her ill-bred, ignorant behavior, Persephone stripped the last of the creamy milk from Mrs. Foster's teats, slipped the rope from around her neck and gave her a push in the direction of the barnyard.

"You, too," she said to the goats, shooing them out of the barn.

As she followed them to the threshold of the open barn door, Persephone's thoughts drifted back to life at the merchant's manor house. To the long, hard days spent scrubbing floors and scouring pots; to the long, cold nights spent serving the merchant and his companions as they gambled and drank. To the sound of them gleefully recounting stories of Methusian camps destroyed and hulking Panoraki warriors fighting to the death; to the sight of them laughing at tales of Gorgishmen trying to wheedle their way out of imprisonment in the mines that once belonged to them. Closing her eyes, Persephone saw the gentle smile of the sad, old Marinese artisan who'd taught her to swim and throw a knife, and she felt Cookie's warm, plump arms holding her close. And she remembered how she'd believed that life at the manor would go on forever, how she'd never dreamt that one day her world would be torn apart by a toss of the dice—

A shrill, horsey squeal jolted Persephone out of her reverie. Opening her eyes, she saw a broken-down old gelding by the name of Fleet careening across the yard toward her, whinnying with heartfelt joy and rudely bashing other creatures aside in his haste to reach her. She laughed aloud and was just about to turn her pockets inside out to prove to Fleet that she was not hiding a treat within when a shadow passed over the yard, sending the chickens running in all directions, squawking and flapping their wings in panic.

The hawk circled the yard once before swooping down to settle on Persephone's shoulder.

"Ivan," she smiled.

The hawk looked down at her with a haughty expression on his proud face, as though thoroughly offended that his lowly perch had had the temerity to address him.

"I've asked you before not to scare the chickens," Persephone reminded.

If hawks could sniff and roll their eyes, Ivan would have done both. As it was, he had to settle for gently digging his talons into Persephone's shoulder and pointedly looking away from her.

"Well, anyway, it's nice to see you," she said.

At this, Ivan screamed and took flight once more.

"Troublemaker!" she called after him, as she watched a thoroughly terrified chicken run headfirst into a fence post.

Like Cur, Ivan had found her a couple of years back. He'd obviously been trained for the hunt by some young lord, though apparently not trained well enough to return to his master on command.

Smiling at the thought that Ivan had broken free from those who'd thought to master him, Persephone tossed a handful of grain to the traumatized chickens and scrounged a piece of cut turnip for Fleet, who noisily gobbled it down without once taking his adoring eyes off her. Then she headed back into the barn to milk the other cow, muck the stalls, tend to the other horses and slop the ill-tempered old sow. When she was finished there, she fetched enough water to last for the rest of the day before heading over to the garden where, in spite of her various aches and pains, she managed to pass a rather pleasant few hours hoeing, weeding and thinning out the weaker plants to make room for the stronger ones.

Late in the day, the owner appeared in the doorway of the thatch-roofed cottage, calling for her to come make his supper.

"I'll be right there," she called back. Lifting the chain of her leg irons, she picked her way out of the bean garden, taking care not to damage any of the tender young shoots as she passed. Then she walked down to the stream, rolled up her sleeves and knelt to wash. As she dipped her dusty hands into the cool water, she examined for the thousandth time the vivid scar that crisscrossed the outside of her left arm almost to the elbow. She'd always thought of it as her "whiplash scar" because it reminded her of the lash marks left by a whip, but Cookie used to say that it looked more like a burn, most likely inflicted by some monster when Persephone was but an infant. The world being what it was, Persephone knew that Cookie was probably right, yet she'd never entirely let go of the childish fantasy that her scar had been caused by nothing more sinister than an accident—and that the baby she'd been had afterward been comforted in the loving arms of the mother she'd never known.

Sitting back on her heels now, Persephone twisted her long, dark hair into a loose coil, tossed it over her shoulder and leaned forward to wash her face. At the sight of her reflection, she hesitated. This was what the young thief had seen the previous night—well, this less the faint bruise around the eye, that is. Leaning so close to the water that the tip of her nose got wet, she stared into her own thickly lashed violet eyes, idly wondering if—

"My supper!" bellowed the owner from up the hill.

Startled, Persephone plunged her hands beneath the surface of the stream, obliterating her reflection. Hurriedly splashing some water on her face, she rubbed it dry with her grubby apron and scrambled up the hill as best she could in her leg irons. Ducking into the owner's cottage, she silently set to work. After boiling the potatoes and setting them on the hearth to keep warm, she skinned, bound and spit Lord Pirate, hung him over the fire and set a pan beneath him to catch the drippings for gravy. As she crouched at the hearth, turning the spit and sweating from the heat of the flames, she was aware of the gaze of the owner on her whipped back, but she ignored it. Instead, she smiled again at the thought that Ivan had broken free from those who'd thought to master him—and she dreamt of escaping those who thought to master her. *Someday*, she promised herself, as Lord Pirate sizzled merrily and her empty stomach growled, *someday I will—*

KNOCK! KNOCK! KNOCK!

Persephone was so startled by the sound that she'd knocked over the pan of drippings, spun to her feet and reached through the torn pocket of her shift for the dagger at her thigh almost before she realized what she was doing. Luckily, the owner didn't notice any of this, having accidentally toppled backward in his chair at the sound of the knocks.

Crawling out from under the table on his hands and knees like the pig he was, he wrinkled his nose at Persephone and whispered, "Who could it be?"

Persephone had no idea who it could be. The owner's farm was at least a day's ride from the nearest well-traveled route, so unexpected visitors were as rare as snow in June. "I expect it is soldiers sent by the Regent to turn you out so that the farm can be given to one more elevated than yourself," she whispered back promptly. "Changing times, you know."

The owner scowled and huffed and shook his head, but Persephone was pleased to see that she'd unnerved him.

Another round of impatient knocks unnerved him further. With an undignified squeak of terror, he scrambled to his feet. "Well, don't just stand there, girl," he hissed. "Answer the door!"

Persephone hesitated for only a moment. Then, with the hand in her torn pocket firmly clutching the hilt of her unsheathed dagger and her belly steeled to gut the unexpected visitor at the first sign of trouble, she walked over to the door, flung it open and gasped to find the laughing chicken thief standing before her dressed like a gentleman of means.

And no longer laughing.

Three

MANY MILES AWAY, at the southernmost tip of the kingdom, in a sumptuously appointed room in a splendid seaside castle, a man slouched before a blazing fire.

He didn't slouch because he was tired or lazy or old, he slouched because the contracture scars that had twisted his back made it impossible for him to sit straight and tall like other men. They also made it impossible for him to square his uneven shoulders, throw out his thin chest and hold his head high with ease. Sometimes, if he drew upon every last drop of his formidable willpower, he could temporarily keep from bending his neck and bobbing his head like a turkey vulture, but after only a short while the strain of doing so made him want to scream in agony. This was particularly true if he was trying to walk at the same time, for the legs that protruded from beneath the hem of his luxurious, fur-trimmed robe had likewise been grievously injured. One foot was turned in and one leg was considerably shorter than the other, its growth having been stunted by the burns that had nearly killed him. Together, they accounted for his awkward, lurching gait, which he had ever despised for being so utterly lacking in dignity.

Yet for all of this, the man's greatest torment came from the fact that above his ruin of a body, two fathomless eyes stared out from a staggeringly handsome face. Eternally youthful and framed by hair as thick and dark and glossy as a sable pelt, he knew it was a face that radiated power and magnetism, a constant reminder to all that he would have been a man among men—lusted after by women, admired by all!—but for an ill-timed gust of wind.

The slouching man was the Regent Mordesius: the power behind the Erok throne. The visionary who'd conquered the four lesser clans to bring all of Glyndoria under Erok rule; the man who could only have been more powerful if he'd been king.

The high-backed chair in which he sat was grand enough to be a throne; the well-worn cushion upon which he sat had been painstakingly embroidered by the long-dead queen herself in the final days of her confinement. She'd intended the cushion as a gift for the child who'd been got upon her by a spoiled tyrant old enough to be her grandfather when she was hardly more than a child herself. But it hadn't worked out that way, and Mordesius had always taken pleasure in the memory of how decisively he'd acted on the fateful night she'd given birth—and how helpful she'd been to thereafter expire of childbed fever, thus sparing him the inconvenience of having to silence her himself.

Smiling at how neatly things had fallen into place in the ensuing years, Mordesius dismissed the past as inconsequential and once more turned his thoughts toward the all-important coming Council meeting. As he reviewed his strategy for the thousandth time, he lifted his scarred hand and began idly stroking the impossibly soft fur at his collar. Seeing the movement, one of the liveried servants who stood against the wall took a hesitant step forward, a questioning look on his face. Without taking his eyes from the fire, Mordesius waved him away impatiently. Instantly, the servant melted back into the shadows and resumed staring straight ahead and trying not to shiver. The room was icy cold but Mordesius had ever been impervious to both the cold and to the discomfort of his inferiors.

Suddenly, he heard the sound of running feet in the hallway outside, followed by a brisk knock at the door.

"Come," he said.

At once, the door flew open and a member of his personal guard announced that a messenger had arrived.

"Send him in," ordered Mordesius, wincing slightly as he tried to sit up straighter.

The guard bellowed the order to enter and the next instant a breathless, bedraggled man with the look and bearing of an ordinary foot soldier stumbled into the room. Snatching the cap from his head, he clutched it to his heaving breast and dropped to one knee.

"My Lord Regent," he murmured, bowing his head.

"Yes, yes," muttered Mordesius as he sourly eyed the breadth of the man's shoulders. "You have news?"

"Yes, Your Grace!" cried the man. "I have ridden all the way from the southern edge of the Great Forest! Four days and nights without rest, changing horses whenever—"

"I don't care about any of that," snapped Mordesius. "Was the lowborn revolt stamped out?"

"It was, Your Grace," said the soldier, bobbing his head, "even though it was the biggest one yet, by my reckoning. Ignorant, ungrateful wretches, they were. Why, when General Murdock offered those who'd been turned off their land a chance to join the next transport of lowborns being shipped north to work the sheep farms in the foothills of the Mountains of Pan, they jeered him! Jeered *him*—General Murdock himself!" exclaimed the soldier, as though he still couldn't believe it.

"And how did General Murdock respond?" asked Mordesius, smiling slightly in anticipation of the answer.

"He invited the rebel leaders to share their grievances over a sizzling joint of beef," said the soldier. "Gave them his word of honor that no harm would befall them, and when the ingrates suggested that the General's word alone was an insufficient guarantee of their safety, he offered as hostages his two finest lieutenants."

Clever, thought Mordesius. "Go on," he said softly.

"The leaders came, then. They were wary at first, but the General greeted them as equals, sat them at his own table and poured their wine with his own hand. As the night wore on, they grew comfortable and began to speak freely. Then," continued the soldier, dropping his voice a notch, "nigh about midnight, when the evening had descended into shouts of drunken laughter and lustily sung refrains, General Murdock invited the rebel leaders to take a view of the night sky from the topmost tower of the castle. The boldest among them leapt from his seat, threw his filthy arm about the General's shoulders and bellowed for him to lead the way. General Murdock threw back his head and laughed, and when they reached the top of the tower, he shoved the man to his death." Here, the soldier paused. "The others were quickly overcome."

"And their families?"

"Were barricaded inside their shelters and burned alive, Your Grace," said the soldier, faltering for the first time. "Even . . . even the children. The screaming was . . . terrible. And then there was silence."

Without warning, Mordesius heard the shrill, long-ago screams of his own family being burned alive by his hand, felt the sudden gust that blew the roaring flames back at him, smelled his own flesh begin to sizzle. Grinding his teeth against the urge to vomit, he waited for the assault on his senses to end. When, at last, it did, he raggedly asked after the General's lieutenants.

"Torn to pieces by the mob," said the soldier. "General Murdock answered by hanging the first hundred lowborn men who crossed his path, selling their widows into servitude and transporting their children to the Mines of Torodania."

Mordesius nodded, well pleased. In spite of his best efforts to educate them otherwise, some Erok lowborns continued to believe that they had some right to the air they breathed and the land upon which their families had squatted for centuries, just as some surviving members of the conquered clans continued to fight Erok rule even though their mountains of dead should have been proof enough that resistance was futile.

Luckily, General Murdock—that shining example of all that a New Man should be—had always proven himself singularly adept at handling the problems caused by such troublemakers.

Of course, Mordesius saw no need to share his satisfaction with the well-built wretch who yet knelt before him, so he merely muttered, "I'd have hanged a thousand," and asked when he could expect to receive the valuable prisoner whose delivery had been delayed by the need to put down the revolt.

"Oh, uh, well, I'm not exactly sure, Your Grace," said the soldier uncomfortably. "See, um, the night after the hangings, someone set fire to the General's tent. Normally, o'course, an intruder wouldn't have been able to get within a cat's throw of the General's tent without losing some vital piece of his filthy, good-for-nothing person. But . . . but on this particular night . . . well, uh, for s-some reason the sentries . . . they, uh—"

"Stop this foolish babbling or I will have you beheaded!" bellowed Mordesius. "*Tell me what happened to the sentries!*"

"They fell asleep!" blurted the soldier with a spasm of fear. "All of them, all at once! And what a strange sleep it was—after failing to detect liquor on their breath, the duty sergeant kicked my younger brother nearly to death trying to revive him, to no avail. He and his fellow sentries were as dead to this world as . . . well, as the dead! And when they awoke the next day, they were sick enough to wish they were dead. And that is all I know!"

By the flickering glow of the fire's light, Mordesius stared at the soldier in silence for so long that the blood drained from the man's face and the chill of the room penetrated his core.

"I see," said Mordesius at length. "So am I to understand that you and the other men will be delayed in delivering my prisoner to me due to the need to bury the charred remains of your general?"

"N-no," stammered the soldier. "General Murdock escaped the fire unharmed."

"Ah," crooned Mordesius. "Then you will be delayed owing to the need to soothe and care for your dear, sick brother and the other negligent sentries?"

Mutely, the soldier shook his head.

Mordesius gripped the arms of his throne-like chair and leaned forward as far as his twisted back would allow.

"Then tell me," he said in a dangerously soft voice. "What . . . is the cause . . . of the delay?"

"Sabotage!" cried the soldier, who was, by this point, visibly quaking. "While we were busy trying to rescue the General and douse the first fire, the scoundrels who'd set it stole through the camp setting other fires. By the time we realized what was happening, half the camp was ablaze! Such was the chaos that the filthy ne'er-do-wells were able to lurk undetected for some time afterward, slicing our tacking to ribbons, stealing weapons, destroying food stores and somehow ensuring that every last one of our supply wagons was fed to the inferno. And forgive me, Your Grace, for this is the very worst of it: by the time anyone thought to check on the prisoner, he was gone!"

For a long moment, Mordesius said nothing, only eyed the soldier malevolently, as though he was personally responsible for the disaster.

"Forgive me, Your Grace," repeated the soldier in a pleading voice.

Instead of answering him, Mordesius nodded in the direction of one of the liveried servants pressed against the wall. Instantly, the man strode forward and, without a flicker of expression on his face, dealt the soldier a vicious blow—the kind of blow that Mordesius himself would have dealt if he'd been able. The soldier, having made no attempt whatsoever to defend himself, was knocked backward by the force of it. When he was finally able to drag himself back into a kneeling position, Mordesius was pleased to see that the blow had knocked out the man's two front teeth.

"This news displeases me," he said, smiling broadly to display his own perfect teeth. "I dislike excuses and I grow tired of hearing them. Lately, I can't seem to turn around without finding myself subjected to the insufferable babblings of some untried New Man who has failed in his duties." Mordesius steepled his fingers and frowned as though thinking hard. "I cannot believe that after all these years General Murdock has suddenly grown incompetent, so I am forced to conclude that the men under his command are the problem. Perhaps my problem would be solved if I sent General Murdock different men—and shipped you, your brother and the other incompetents onward to the mines."

At this, the soldier grew even paler—so pale that the blood that continued to stream from his ruined mouth looked as red as rubies by contrast. "No, Your Grace, please," he gasped, his voice garbled both by the blood and by the loss of teeth. "My battalion is already tracking the scoundrels responsible for the theft of the prisoner, and I swear to you that we'll find them. And when we do, we'll take them apart piece by piece and deliver the prisoner here to you in Parthania or die trying!"

Beneath the brittle veneer of bravado and shining optimism, the man's terror was clearly visible, and the air was thick with the stench of it. Mordesius was seized by a sudden urge to have the wretch beaten to death for being such a cowardly waste of a healthy body, but he forced himself to resist the temptation.

It had already been a long day, after all, and if he overexerted himself with entertainment tonight, he would pay dearly for it tomorrow.

"Oh, stop your sniveling," he finally muttered, "or it will be you who is taken apart piece by piece. Return to General Murdock and tell him that if the scoundrels turn out to be kinsmen of the prisoner and he manages to slaughter them all, I will pay double the normal rate for each verified kill," said Mordesius as he absently resumed stroking the soft fur at his collar.

"Yes, Your Grace," gulped the soldier. "I'll leave at first light."

"You'll leave now," said Mordesius, pulling his warm robe tighter about his thin shoulders.

The soldier—who was wet, hungry, bleeding and exhausted from having ridden four days without rest—staggered to his feet, bowed and murmured, "Yes, Your Grace."

Mordesius said nothing. The soldier lingered in awkward silence for a moment or two longer until he was certain that a formal dismissal was not forthcoming, then he pulled on his cap and fled the room.

After the soldier had departed, Mordesius slouched low in his chair and let his head fall forward in order to relieve the strain on his aching neck.

Then, in a sudden fit of fury, he snatched up a nearby goblet of wine and hurled it into the fire. As he watched it shatter, he cursed the loss of the prisoner whose dungeon accommodations had been prepared for a fortnight, ever since Mordesius had first learned that a family of Methusians had been discovered masquerading as Erok lowborns in one of the northern prefectures. The report he'd received had said that only a single member of the family still lived— a child too young to have yet taken the mark of his clan. The mark had been plain to see on the stripped corpses of his parents and older siblings, however, so when General Murdock arrived in the village, he'd paid the family's neighbors handsomely for their efforts and set out to bring the child—a boy—back to Mordesius so that he could attempt to tap into the fabled healing power of the child's blood.

Now the child was gone, and while it was possible that low-borns had attacked the camp in retaliation for the hangings and whatnot, the "strange sleep" described by the soldier smacked of Methusian trickery. Moreover, Methusians alone had a reason for wanting to save the child.

Methusians.

Oh, how Mordesius *hated* the Methusians.

Though they were sly, they were not as sly as the repulsive Gorgishmen of the west, the former lords of the Mines of Torodania, many of whom now toiled deep within the mines' dark and dangerous shafts. Nor were they as uncouth as the hulking Panoraki of the mountains with their long, dirty hair and the stink of their precious woolly sheep ever upon them. And they certainly weren't as despicably meek as the Marinese, who'd delivered their most gifted artisans into servitude in exchange for peace only to be driven from their ancestral village on the eastern seaboard anyway.

No, the reason Mordesius hated the Methusians was that every last one of them was blessed with preternatural health and vitality. That, and the fact that their long-dead clansman Balthazar had refused to reveal the location of the Pool of Genezing.

Like every child in Glyndoria, Mordesius had grown up hearing some version of the legend of the pool. On frigid winter nights as he'd huddled in the lowborn shack in which he'd been born to the mother who'd ruined his childhood by dying in the act, he'd often listened to his peasant father speak of it to his dull yet better-loved brothers. He'd heard how the Methusians believed their kind had once lived a settled life on the shores of a miraculous pool whose waters could cure any ill. How one among them had spilled the blood of a trusted companion at the water's edge; how the tainted pool had dried up upon the instant. How, ever since, the Methusians had been a wandering people—an echo of the healing power of the pool coursing through their veins, the belief that their sacred pool would one day reappear burning in their hearts.

Like most people, Mordesius had thought the legend nothing but a story dreamt up by the insufferably proud Methusians to set themselves above the other clans. In the terrible months following the fire, however, as he lay feverish and shivering, his body a mess of charred flesh and weeping wounds, he'd convinced himself that it was something more. And so, once he'd grown to manhood and, against all odds, clawed his way into King Octavio's glittering inner circle, he'd begun secretly kidnapping Methusians in order to question them about it. Over and over they'd told him—first in terrified babbles, then in wailing screams—that while their kind almost always survived infancy and thrived thereafter, the heartiness that allowed them to withstand the illnesses that cut down others was nothing they could control or share. Incensed and certain that they were holding out on him, Mordesius had eventually turned to seeking answers within their flesh and blood itself, and while he'd found the blood of the very young to have certain rejuvenating qualities and the ability to speed the healing of minor flesh wounds, he'd never found a way to harness this power to cure his own great and terrible injuries.

Then the mercurial old Erok king decided to invite ambassadors from the four other clans of Glyndoria to Parthania so that they might all come to know one another better and thus see trade and relations among them improved. The Methusian ambassador Balthazar had been the first to arrive and settle into the unimaginable luxury of the imperial palace. Mordesius had done his best to befriend the big, bluff Methusian in the hope that as a clansman of some prominence he might know something of the healing pool that the others had not. But Balthazar's response to these overtures of friendship had been decidedly lukewarm, and then one day—in front of the entire court!—he'd loudly told Mordesius to go away and to stop pestering him.

To stop pestering him!

Even now, the memory filled Mordesius with a murderous rage.

He'd felt no less murderous back then, but before he'd had a chance to act upon his feelings, Balthazar had disappeared. Following a night of drunken debauchery, he'd commandeered a ship and sailed away to points unknown. Mordesius had prayed that he was dead or, better yet, fatally wounded, in terrible pain and too weak to beat off the carrion birds that sought to get an early start on dinner. As the days slipped by without any word of the Methusian ambassador, it had begun to seem that Mordesius's dark prayers had been answered.

Eventually, the grieving King Octavio had commanded the entire court to attend a funeral service in honor of his dear, lost Methusian brother. As though all of nature was affronted by the sight of noble heads bowed in memory of a tribal dog, halfway through the service a terrible storm had struck, battering the imperial capital with torrential rains and gale-force winds. The storm raged for three full days, and when it finally abated on the morning of the fourth, none other than Balthazar himself bounded into the palace courtyard. Wet, muddy and grinning with excitement, he'd initially refused to say where he'd been. Eventually, however, he could not resist confessing that he'd discovered the reborn Pool of Genezing. In carefully evasive terms, he'd described journeying far across the water, suffering a shipwreck and making it to shore only to find himself chased by a great, frothing beast into a place of nightmares. He'd explained how the beast had chased him through the darkness without tiring—indeed, how it had seemed to gather strength and fury with each passing second. With flailing arms, he'd pantomimed how, in his haste to escape the monster, he'd stumbled and suffered a terrible fall.

Dropping his voice to a dramatic whisper, he'd told of landing hard upon the jagged rocks at the edge of a glowing pool. Of being helpless to prevent his shattered, bleeding body from toppling into the pool; of slipping beneath the glowing surface believing that he'd breathed his last . . . only to have the waters of the pool instantly heal his catastrophic wounds and restore him to perfect health.

At first, King Octavio and the other ambassadors had been skeptical, for Balthazar was a renowned storyteller. But after Balthazar showed them the torn, bloodstained doublet he'd been wearing at the time of his fall and the faint but unmistakable scars on his back, some among them had begun to wonder if perhaps he wasn't telling the truth, after all.

Mordesius hadn't wondered if Balthazar was telling the truth— he'd *known* that Balthazar was telling the truth. His twisted back, withered limbs and melted skin had tingled with the knowledge of it; he'd hardly been able to breathe for the excitement of it! The Pool of Genezing had sprung up once more. It was out there somewhere and Balthazar knew where it was. All he, Mordesius, had to do to rid himself of his terrible injuries was to convince Balthazar to lead him to it.

But Balthazar would not be convinced. He reminded Mordesius, King Octavio and everyone else at court that the healing pool was sacred to his people. He said that while he could not imagine them wishing to live by its shores given its present location, until he'd met with his clan, he would not reveal its whereabouts to anyone else, not even upon pain of death.

Seeing that Balthazar would not be persuaded by reasonable means, a seething Mordesius had set about trying to convince the Erok king to put the Methusian ambassador's bold declaration to the test.

As it turned out, it had taken almost nothing to turn King Octavio against Balthazar and the rest of the useless Methusians— just a few carefully chosen words hinting that Methusian trickery had somehow rendered all of Octavio's previous wives barren and the thinly veiled suggestion that Balthazar would use the powers of the pool to become richer and more powerful than King Octavio himself. With dizzying swiftness, brotherly love had turned to hate, Balthazar and anyone he may have confided in had been arrested, and the roundup and slaughter of the Methusians had begun.

Balthazar had gotten down on his knees in the filth of the dungeon and begged King Octavio to stop the killing. Like the liar he was, he swore that his silly story about the beast, the fall and the pool had never been anything more than that: a silly story. It was a lie that he stuck to right up until the moment of his rather gruesome demise, but hadn't made a whit of difference. King Octavio had continued the indiscriminate slaughter of the Methusians out of anger, resentment and fear that they knew of a magical healing pool that could topple him from his throne. Indeed, such was his paranoia that Mordesius had eventually been able to convince him to withdraw the hand of friendship from the other clans and begin persecuting them as well.

About a year later, King Octavio died—agonizingly, of slow poison, no doubt wishing with every fiber of his being that he'd kept his dear Methusian brother alive on the off chance that he *had* found the pool and might be persuaded to procure a vial of its waters to save a dying friend.

In the seventeen years since, Mordesius had been consumed with the demands of running the kingdom—stamping out the last of the Methusians, quelling the lowborns, controlling the clans, currying the favor of the nobles and managing the king. Yet through it all, he had never stopped seeking the pool.

And though he'd never found any sign of it, and though he often despaired of ever being the man he might have been, on the balance, the Fates had served him well.

He'd risen from the foulest gutters in Parthania to stand behind the throne of the infant king whose days had been numbered from the moment of his birth.

He was but a single Council meeting away from greater glory still.

Nothing could stop him now.

Four

FINDING HERSELF FACE-TO-FACE with the thief again so shocked Persephone that she did something she'd never done before in her life: she let the dagger slip from her fingers. It fell to the hard-packed dirt floor at her feet and spun toward the thief.

"What was that?" barked the owner, striding forward now that it was clear that the unexpected visitor posed no immediate threat.

"What was what?" asked the thief in a slightly baffled but deeply cultured voice.

Deftly placing his gleaming black boot lengthwise over top of the dagger so that it was hidden from sight, he looked at Persephone in a way that made her feel completely exposed, as though he'd once again caught her wearing nothing but her nightshift. Scowling slightly, she began to shut the door on him. He put out a hand to stop her even as the owner shouldered her to one side so hard that she stumbled. Jerking the door wide again, the owner scanned the ground in search of whatever it was that had made the noise he'd heard. When he saw nothing, he planted his fists on his hips, puffed out his chest and glared at the thief.

The thief stared back, one eyebrow raised in the perfect imitation of a gentleman unused to being challenged by his inferiors.

Instead of using the standoff as an opportunity to develop a strategy to deal with this most unexpected and precarious of situations,

Persephone found herself studying the thief. He was taller than she remembered and even more finely muscled. Handsomer, too—if one cared about such things—with blue eyes that seemed almost too beautiful for his face and a wide, sensuous mouth. The long, unkempt hair from the night before had been brushed as smooth as the rippling curls would permit and secured in a pigtail at the nape of his neck by a bejeweled clasp. Persephone gloated to see the spot on his cheek where her dagger had nicked him the night before, until she noted with a flash of irritation that it gave him a rather dashing air. All in all, he looked so fine, standing there in the doorway of the house where she cleaned out the chamber pot full of piss each morning, that Persephone had a sudden urge to tell him that she thought he looked like a pompous, overstuffed peacock, just to see what his reaction would be.

Before she could succumb to temptation, however, the owner cracked under the pressure of being stared down by a supposed nobleman. Releasing the air from his lungs with an audible *whoosh*, he allowed his chest to deflate and dropped his hands from his hips.

The thief acknowledged his capitulation with an elegant nod of his head. "Allow me to introduce myself," he said, plucking at the tips of a pair of fine riding gloves that didn't quite seem to fit him. "I am Lord Damon Bothwell of the Ragorian Prefecture."

At this, Persephone laughed aloud.

"Shut up, you insolent brat!" shouted the owner, rounding on her at once. He shook a dirty fist in her face before anxiously turning back to the thief. "Lazy, useless good-for-nothing has a mouth on her the likes of which you've never seen. You'd think a slave born and bred would know her place, wouldn't you, m'lord?"

"I would indeed," said the thief, giving Persephone a penetrating look, which she pointedly ignored.

"Yes, well, not this one," whined the owner. He faked a swipe at Persephone, who didn't even flinch. "You see? You see that? No respect. I tell you, this one is more trouble than she's worth."

"Is that so?" said the thief. "Well, in that case, we have much to discuss."

Something about his words—and the way he said them—caused Persephone's heart to give a sudden lurch.

"Yeah?" said the owner, sucking at a piece of old meat caught between his rotting teeth. "How's that?"

The rascal posing as Lord Bothwell looked mildly offended. "I'm afraid I am not in the habit of conducting business on door-steps, sir."

Slack-jawed, the owner looked blankly at him until compre-hension hit him like a hoof to the side of the head. "Oh!" he cried. "'Course you're not, 'course you're not!" He glared at Persephone as though the gross breach of etiquette had been her fault. "Well? Don't just stand there! Go draw two tankards of ale and set out some bread and cheese for Lord Bothwell and me!"

Persephone hesitated. She didn't believe for one single moment that this scoundrel in the fancy doublet was a lord from a distant prefecture. He was a thief and a liar, and he was up to something, and it almost certainly had something to do with her, and whatever it was, it couldn't possibly be good. Moreover, the very idea that she should have to lay out food and drink for him—the one she had bested!—well, it was enough to make her want to—

"Go!" bellowed the owner. Raising his hand, he was about to cuff her when the thief's hand shot out and grabbed his grimy wrist, holding it fast.

"What do you think you're doing?" demanded the owner in amazement, wincing slightly.

"Holding your wrist," replied the thief in the tone of voice most people reserved for children and fools. "You see, I'd rather you didn't strike her."

"You'd rather . . . *you'd* rather," spluttered the owner indignantly, trying to yank his arm away. "She's mine—what's it to you if I strike her?"

"If you'll allow me to come into your home and sup with you, I believe I'll be able to provide you with all the answers you're looking for," said the thief smoothly.

At this, Persephone's heart gave another wild lurch. What answers did the thief have? What answers could he *possibly* have? Things were moving too quickly for her. She needed time to think— to figure out what the thief was up to and to decide how much danger she was in. To weigh the risk of blurting out that "Lord Bothwell" was, in fact, the chicken thief from the previous night against the risk that he'd reveal that she'd handed over the chicken of her own free will. Her accusation would see him imprisoned or executed; his accusation would, at the very least, see her beaten and her dog drowned.

But she didn't have time to think, because the owner—whose wrist was still trapped in the thief's iron grip—winced again and muttered, "Very well. I promise I shan't strike the girl until I know what you're about."

"Excellent," said the thief. Releasing the owner's wrist, he deliberately wiped his hand across the front of his doublet. Then he turned to Persephone, touched his throat and murmured, "I thirst. Might I trouble you to fetch me that tankard of ale now?"

Persephone wanted to kick him in the shins to show that she wasn't afraid of him, that she didn't think him clever and that whatever he was up to, if it caused her grief, discomfort or distress, she'd make sure he paid dearly for it. However, feeling that—for the moment, at least—a more circumspect approach was warranted, she bobbed him a stiff curtsey, said, "Right away . . . *my lord*," and stepped past him, taking care to tread heavily upon the toe of his boot as she passed.

When she got back from the shed where the ale and other provisions were stored, the thief and the owner were seated at the rough-hewn table in the corner, their heads bent in conversation. Surreptitiously, Persephone's eyes darted to the floor in search of her dropped dagger, but it was gone. Looking up in confusion, she saw the thief gazing at her with an inscrutable expression on his handsome face, and she knew—she *knew!*—that he'd somehow managed to pocket her dagger without the owner noticing.

Persephone was so affronted by his audacity that she forgot all about her resolve to take a more circumspect approach. Stomping across the room as best she could in her heavy leg irons, she slammed the two tankards of ale down on the table and snapped, "There's your ale!"

Predictably, ale foamed up and spilled over the brims of the tankards.

"Clumsy!" cried the owner, slurping frantically to avoid spillage.

"Thank you," murmured the thief.

Ignoring them both, Persephone removed the badly charred Lord Pirate from the fire and stormed off to fetch bread and cheese. When she got back, she was surprised to hear the owner praising her.

". . . terribly strong," he said, giving Persephone's biceps a squeeze, "though you wouldn't think it to look at her."

"No, you wouldn't," agreed the thief. "She looks rather scrawny."

Setting the bread and cheese down on the table, Persephone smiled pleasantly at the thief, then calmly cast about for something to plunge into his eye.

"Not scrawny," protested the owner hastily. "Wiry. Like a plow horse."

"A plow horse," mused the thief. His eyes wandered over Persephone. "Yes, I see what you mean."

I don't need something to plunge into his eye, Persephone corrected herself. *I need something to plunge into his heart.*

"Plus, she don't eat much," bragged the owner. "And she knows her way around animals, and you can set her to almost any task and she'll do it twice as good as you ever could have done it yourself and—"

"I thought you said she was a lazy, useless good-for-nothing," interrupted the thief.

The owner began to laugh so hard that his whole head turned the color of a blood blister. "Oh, ho!" he blustered. "I said that—yes! But . . . but . . ."

"But you didn't mean it?" prompted the thief.

"Exactly!" exclaimed the owner. "I only said it because . . . because . . ."

"Because you're in the habit of insulting her?" suggested the thief.

"Yes!" cried the owner, clearly relieved to find himself so well understood. "Yes, it's nothing but a habit! The truth is, I'm terribly fond of the girl."

Persephone watched in amazement as the owner punctuated this remarkable statement with a sniffle. In the five years since he'd acquired her, he'd never once asked her name nor anything else about her. She was his property—more important than his goats and chickens, less important than his cows and horses. If there was one thing she was sure of in this world, it was that the owner was *not* fond of her.

"In fact, I don't know what I'd do around here without her," he mumbled now as he gazed up at Persephone with what he obviously believed was a kindly expression on his ugly face.

It was like being ogled by a demented hog.

"Even so," said the thief, "you must be reasonable."

"Reasonable!" said the owner, flinging his arms into the air so that the ripe smell of unwashed armpits wafted through the low-ceilinged room. "What is reasonable, m'lord, when we're speaking of such a jewel?"

Casually, the thief took a small velvet bag from the front of his doublet and tossed it onto the table.

At the sound of clinking coins, Persephone froze. She'd seen purses like that change hands before, and she knew what it meant when they did. The blood in her veins turned to ice as she realized what a fool she'd been to listen to the men's conversation but not to hear it, and to have forgotten for the briefest of instants that, like the owner's horses and cows and chickens and goats, she could and would be sold if it suited his purposes.

As it did now, it would seem.

Biting the inside of her cheek to keep from immediately crying out in protest, Persephone desperately sought a way to prevent this from happening. It wasn't as though she liked the owner—she didn't, she hated him. But she knew him, and, more importantly, she knew how to control him. Moreover, this farm was the closest thing she'd had to a home since the merchant had lost her in a game of dice on that terrible night so long ago. And she knew and loved all the animals—even the ill-tempered old sow—and if she sometimes didn't get quite enough to eat, and if she suffered the occasional beating, well, she knew from hard, personal experience that it could be worse.

Much worse.

"Coin of the realm," said the thief now, as he nudged the little velvet bag toward the owner.

The owner eyed it greedily but made no move to pick it up.

"You could buy two fine slaves for that price," encouraged the thief.

The owner licked his lips. "Well, then, so could you," he said.

The thief shrugged. "Yes," he agreed. "But I'd not be able to do so until I reached a town with a decent-sized market, and it suits my purposes to purchase one immediately. My other died three days past, and I've some ways to go before I rejoin my retinue on the road to Parthania—"

"No!" blurted Persephone.

Both men looked up at her.

Persephone cleared her throat. "No," she repeated, more calmly this time. Focusing her full attention on the owner, she continued in a low, persuasive voice. "You need me. You *know* you do. I tend to everything about this place—everything!—and your wealth and circumstance have improved immeasurably since I came here. Perhaps you could buy two slaves for the price this man would pay to acquire me, but you know as well as I that two slaves would eat twice as much and work half as hard."

"Perhaps," retorted the owner sourly. "But at least I would have a hope that they would behave like slaves instead of disrespecting me and running away and sympathizing with the scum who would rob me blind given half a chance!"

Studiously avoiding even the tiniest glance in the direction of the "scum" who'd most recently robbed the owner, Persephone swallowed hard and murmured, "I . . . I know I haven't always behaved *exactly* as I should have. However—"

"You really want to stay here?" interrupted the owner in an almost-kindly voice.

Persephone could feel the thief's eyes upon her as she nodded.

"All right then," said the owner, who waited until he saw Persephone sag with relief to add, "beg."

"What?" she said, stiffening at once.

The owner leaned forward. "You heard me, girl. You want to stay here?" he asked with a slow, mean smile. "Get down on your knees and beg for it."

For the merest fraction of an instant, Persephone actually considered making things easier on herself by doing as he'd asked.

Then she had a vision of herself on her knees before the owner—head bowed, back bent, hands clasped in supplication—and she decided on a different tack altogether.

Throwing back her shoulders, she lifted her chin, looked him straight in the eye and calmly said, "I'll see you in hell first, pig."

Then, to make absolutely certain that he understood how she truly felt about him, she spat in his face.

With a mighty roar, the owner leapt from his seat, but the thief got to him before he got to her. Lifting the owner right up off the ground, the thief hurled him back into his seat so hard that the owner grunted with the force of it.

"Hasn't anyone ever told you that it's bad business to mishandle the merchandise?" asked the thief, who sounded as though he was trying not to laugh.

"Did you see what that . . . that stupid cow did to me?" ranted the owner as he furiously wiped Persephone's spittle off his face. "She spat at me! At *me*! I'll kill her. I swear it! I'll drag her down to the stream by her hair and drown the life out of her! I'll wring her scrawny neck! I'll—"

"I'll throw in this pendant if you'll sell her to me," offered the thief, throwing the piece on the table.

"Done!" screamed the owner.

"Of course," continued the thief, "for that price, I also expect to take ownership of any possessions belonging to her."

"Fine!"

"And the leg irons—"

"You may have them as well!" snarled the owner. He fumbled inside the pocket of his dirty breeches for a moment before snatching out a rusted key and practically hurling it at the thief, who deftly slipped it into his own pocket. "And on top of all that, I'll give you a piece of advice for free, m'lord: keep this one locked down tight and beat her hard and often. As you can see, I was clearly too soft a hand!"

"Clearly," said the thief, with a glance at Persephone's bruised eye. "Now, have you the original bill of sale as proof of ownership?"

The owner stopped thrashing and frothing at once. "Well, now," he said, looking as shifty as a fox in a henhouse. "I'm, uh, not quite sure where—"

Persephone's heart leapt as she saw her chance. "He doesn't have it," she said quickly, "because he never bought me. He caught me after I'd run away from . . . from another place. He gave me the choice of being sent back to that place or staying here."

"And you decided to stay *here*?" asked the thief in a voice that sounded almost pitying.

Persephone ignored the question—and the tone. "The point," she continued, "is that I am stolen property and if my true owner were ever to happen upon me in your possession, you would not only hang for it but your family name would be ruined forever—a fate, *as you well know*, that would be far worse than death for any nobleman worth his salt, *my lord*."

The owner—who was now clutching the pendant and purse to his chest as though in terror that "Lord Bothwell" would suffer a sudden attack of conscience and snatch them both back—immediately began babbling protestations, but the thief silenced him with an elegantly raised hand.

Then he turned to Persephone.

"You make a good point," he said gently. "However, as I've never much cared for the name 'Bothwell' and as I've yet to meet the man who could force a noose around my neck, I'm content to take my chances. The deal is done, mistress, bill of sale or no. Come, let us collect your possessions and be on our way."

Five

IT DIDN'T TAKE LONG to collect Persephone's meager possessions. The dried-up tail of the rat who'd once been her only friend; the comb she'd painstakingly whittled out of a single piece of wood three summers past. Her blanket and her nightshift; the braided, berry-dyed twine she used in place of ribbon to tie back her hair. The scrap of lace she'd torn from the hem of Cookie's apron the night she'd been dragged, screaming and crying, from the merchant's house.

And, of course, the knife she'd stolen from the thief the previous evening.

"That's mine," announced the owner as soon as he'd recovered from the nasty shock of seeing Persephone draw such a formidable weapon from beneath her straw bedding. "I've been searching and searching for it these last months. I am so pleased to have found it! It belonged to my grandfather, you see, and—"

"You lie," said the thief absently as he tugged the knife from Persephone's resistant grasp.

The owner gasped at the insult. "Now, you listen here, m'lord!" he blustered. "You've no right to say such a thing to me! I said you could take ownership of the girl and her possessions—"

The point of the thief's knife was at the base of the owner's throat with frightening speed. "And I said you lie," said the thief in a voice that was all the more menacing for its softness. "Do not test my patience, sir, for I find I like you not at all, and if you push me, you will find that I have as little fear of the noose when it comes to bloody murder as I do when it comes to purchasing stolen property."

The owner was so stunned by this outburst that his only response was to stare at the thief with his mouth hanging open. The thief glared back at him for a long, tense moment before removing the knife from his throat with a great show of reluctance.

"Come," he said to Persephone, through his teeth. "Let us leave this place before I commit yet another hanging offense."

Mutely, Persephone looked around "this place." At the spot where she'd laid her head for five years' worth of nights; at the rotten boards and rusted implements that were as familiar to her as her own hands. At the grumpy old sow and her rooting piglets; at the silly cock who preened and strutted before the magnificently uninterested chickens. At the half-grown kittens wrestling in the hay; at the spindly-legged kid who bleated and butted anxiously at his mother's teats before finally managing to latch on.

Riveted by the sight of the suckling kid, Persephone held her breath and stared as he drank greedily of his mother's warm milk, and when his eyes began to roll in contentment, her own began to sting.

"Are you all right?" murmured the thief, touching her elbow.

Persephone blinked once, and the sting was gone. "Fine," she muttered, jerking her arm away from him. "Come. Let us leave *this place*."

His horse was nothing like dear, broken-down old Fleet, who'd begun charging about the yard kicking at the fence boards and whinnying in panic the instant he'd caught sight of his beloved Persephone walking away from him. Rather, the thief's horse was a beautiful, high-bred bay that was expertly shod, with a finely groomed mane and exquisite leather tacking polished to a soft shine. The thief had just made a show of pulling on his ill-fitting riding gloves and unwinding the reins from the hitching post when Cur came dashing across the yard, snapping his teeth and snarling fearsomely. With an undignified yelp and all the grace of a drunken ox, the thief scrambled atop the horse, who whinnied her displeasure at this oafish behavior and reared up on her hind legs. Cursing mightily, "Lord Bothwell" flung himself forward to keep from sliding off the back of her. It worked, but it also caused his pigtail to come loose, setting free his auburn curls and instantly giving him the look of a pirate thief once more. The owner—who'd thus far been standing well back of volatile "Lord Bothwell" and his knife—narrowed his piggy little eyes in sudden suspicion and took a step forward.

"All is well!" called the thief cheerily, waving him back. "It was, uh, just your dog—"

"He's my dog," interrupted Persephone, dropping to her knees and burying her face in Cur's smelly fur. "And he's coming with us."

"What? No!" exclaimed the thief. "Absolutely not. I categorically forbid it!"

"He's coming," repeated Persephone. Rising to her feet, she tucked her bundled belongings under one arm and gestured with her free hand—first to Cur and then to the owner. When she was certain that the latter had understood her gesture and been suitably insulted by it, she turned and began striding purposefully away from the thief, the chain between her leg irons rattling with defiance.

Cur bounded after her, barking with joy.

With significantly less joy, the thief chirruped his still-skittish horse into motion and cantered after them both.

"I understand how difficult this must be for you," he said as he drew alongside Persephone, "and I am not without sympathy. However, for reasons that will reveal themselves in time, I'm afraid I must stand firm on my decision that the dog cannot accompany us."

Instead of answering him, Persephone called a greeting to Ivan, who swooped down and landed on her shoulder.

"You can't bring the hawk, either," said the thief with a trace of complaint in his voice.

Ivan regarded him with almost as much respect as one would afford a particularly disgusting slug. Persephone kept walking.

"Oh, all right," grumbled the thief at length, throwing one hand in the air. "You may bring them both. But they must fend for themselves, and if they cause us any delays whatsoever, we will leave them behind. Agreed?"

"No," said Persephone.

She flinched inwardly as soon as she said this, worried that perhaps she'd pushed her luck too far, but to her surprise, the thief threw back his head and laughed unreservedly. She watched him warily, just in case this sudden laughter was a sign that he was becoming unhinged.

It wasn't, apparently, because the only thing he did after he'd recovered from his fit of mirth was to look down at her with a strangely exultant expression on his handsome face and say, "Your former owner was right—you really aren't a very good slave at all, you know that?"

"Yes," said Persephone, taking care not to look back at poor, heartbroken Fleet. "I know that."

The thief didn't say anything more until they got over the first hill, at which point he reined in his horse, dismounted and took a long, hard look to the east.

When he was done looking, he turned to Persephone. "We're going to have to set a good pace," he declared, shrugging out of the tight-fitting velvet doublet in much the same way that a small boy might wriggle out of his Sunday best. "But first, I want to take a closer look at you."

Instinctively, Persephone shrank away from him—rounding her shoulders and folding her arms across her chest—but the thief wasn't talking about her body. Gently taking hold of her chin, he carefully examined her face first from one side, then from the other.

"I cannot believe . . . it is truly remarkable," he murmured after a long moment of study. Gazing down at her with an intensity she found unnerving, he said, "I want you to know that I mean you no harm whatsoever. In fact, I would gladly die before seeing you harmed in any way."

"Strange words from a slave owner," observed Persephone.

At this, the thief jerked his hand away from her chin. "I am no slave owner," he protested, clearly stung by the suggestion. "I would never be a slave owner!"

"No?" said Persephone. "So, you did not just buy me for the price of a fat sow?"

"Well, I—"

"And you are not forcing me to leave behind all that is familiar and dear to me?"

"Yes, but—"

"And I am free to leave you at any time—to find my own way in the world, to seek a destiny that belongs to none but me?"

"No," he admitted reluctantly. "But not for the reasons you think."

"Well," said Persephone sarcastically, "that makes all the difference, doesn't it?"

"It doesn't—but I believe that, in time, when you understand more, it will," murmured the thief with conviction. "For now, would you be kind enough to tell me your name?"

"My name?"

"You know—the particular handle by which people address you," he explained solemnly but with a glint in his eye.

Persephone scowled and told him her name.

"And what manner of creature would call himself your 'true owner,' Persephone?" he asked. "Who holds the slip of paper that names you a slave?"

"What does it matter?"

"It matters to me, for I would know who or what I might one day be forced to face in defense of you," said the thief. "However, as you've recently suffered the shock of being unexpectedly uprooted, I'm content to let it be for the moment. Now, go sit on that rock."

"Why?" she asked.

The thief threw his hands in the air. "Tell me true, Persephone—is there even the *faintest* hope that you will ever simply do as you're asked rather than questioning or defying me outright?"

He sounded so exasperated that Persephone felt an unwilling smile tug at the corners of her mouth. "Not even the faintest hope," she replied. "Why do you want me to sit?"

"Because," he said, pulling a key from his pocket, "I want to remove your leg irons."

Though this was not the answer Persephone had expected, it was the most welcome answer the thief could have given. She'd been in irons for nearly three months now, ever since she'd last tried to run from the owner. Having saved up a few old potatoes and some strips of dried hare meat, she'd waited for a cloudy night and then set out. She hadn't had much of a plan, really—just that she'd run until she'd put time and distance enough between her and the owner that she could safely join the throngs of displaced lowborns scrounging for work as day-laborers in the hope of earning a crust of bread and a reprieve from transport onward to the mines or somewhere almost as bad. Unfortunately, the Fates had not been inclined to grant Persephone even this dreary dream, for at the exact moment she'd made her desperate dash to freedom, the moon had burst out from behind the clouds and the bleary-eyed owner had looked up from his seat on the chamber pot to see her slipping over the crest of this very hill. It had been a simple enough matter for him to saddle a horse and give chase, but the very fact that he'd been forced to do so had so enraged him that when he'd caught her, he'd beaten her nearly senseless and clapped on the irons for good.

Hastily now, Persephone put her bundled belongings to one side and sat down on the rock. Cur, having just returned from chasing a fox through the nearby meadow, bounded over, skidded to a halt beside her and stared at the thief as though he'd like nothing better than to take a juicy chunk out of his backside.

The thief gave a long-suffering sigh. "Send the beast away," he said.

"He's harmless," said Persephone as she carefully teased a burr out of the fur on Cur's ear.

The thief pursed his lips. "I thought you said he'd killed dozens of men at your behest."

"I exaggerated."

"Oh?" he said, arching an eyebrow at her. "How many has he killed in truth?"

"In truth?" she said. "None."

"I see," said the thief, making a face at Cur, who responded with a growl. "Well, as long as we're sharing truths, Persephone, I'm afraid I have a rather shocking confession to make."

"What is it?" she asked, steeling herself for something unpleasant.

The thief squinted up at the sky, then looked down at his hands and sighed. "It's just that . . . well . . . although there is a 'Lord Damon Bothwell' and although he does come from the Ragorian Prefecture, I'm afraid . . . I'm afraid that I am not really him," he mumbled.

Persephone stared at him. "Well, for heaven's sake, I knew that," she said tartly. "What do you think I am, some kind of simpleton?"

The thief burst out laughing. "No, of course not!" he protested. "I'm sorry, it's just that . . . I rather thought you'd react the way you did and I'm afraid I couldn't resist. Forgive me, and allow me to introduce myself. I am Azriel."

"Azriel what?"

"Just Azriel."

"I see," said Persephone disapprovingly. "And what am I to call you?"

"Well . . . um . . . I thought you could call me 'Azriel'," he said. "You know—since it's my name. The particular handle by which—"

"It's your given name," she interrupted.

"Yes," said the thief—Azriel—looking at her as though he wondered if perhaps she wasn't a simpleton, after all.

"You want me—your *slave*—to call you by your given name," said Persephone.

Azriel flinched at the word "slave" but all he said was, "Well, I intend to call you by your given name. It seems only fair, doesn't it?"

He's a lunatic, thought Persephone.

"Yes, *Azriel*," she said loudly, to humor him. "I suppose it does only seem fair."

"Excellent," he grinned. "I'm glad that's settled. Now, before I remove your fetters, I have one more confession to make."

"What is it?" she asked suspiciously.

He hung his head. "Last night, in the barn, before I saw you, I was planning to bash you over the head with a shovel," he admitted. "Not hard enough to hurt you, mind, just hard enough to render you unconscious."

"Really?" she replied airily. "Well, Azriel, last night, in the barn, before I saw *you*, I was planning to slit you from bow to stern and feed your still-warm innards to the ill-tempered sow three stalls over."

Azriel looked rather taken aback by this news. "In that case, Persephone," he said mildly, "I must confess that I no longer feel quite so guilty about almost having gently bashed you over the head with a shovel."

For the second time in as many moments, Persephone felt an unwilling smile tug at the corners of her mouth.

Then, without warning, Azriel stepped forward and sank to his knees before her.

Something about the gesture caused Persephone to inhale sharply—though not nearly so sharply as when he reached for her. Sliding one hand under her skirt halfway up the back of her bare calf, he used his free hand to ease her skirt up over her knees. Then, without releasing his hold on her leg, he reached into his pocket, took out the key, slipped it into the lock of the iron cuff at her ankle and gave a sharp twist. The cuff fell away with a clatter.

Feeling somewhat short of breath, Persephone tried to pull her foot away, but Azriel held it fast.

"Wait," he murmured. With the lightest of touches, he began to run his fingers over her damaged skin—tracing the outlines of old bruises, skirting the places where the heavy cuff had rubbed her skin raw. Mesmerized, Persephone watched as he leaned forward and slowly ran his fingers over the delicate bones along the top of her foot, down to the very tips of her toes and back again, then up past her ankle, until—

Abruptly returning to her senses, she jerked her foot out of his grasp so spasmodically that she kicked him right in the face.

"Ow!" he cried, reeling backward.

"Sorry," she said, not sounding sorry at all.

"What did you do that for?" he demanded irritably as he checked his nose for blood. "For pity's sake, I was just making sure that the fetters had done no serious damage!"

Persephone didn't believe him for a second. "Of course you were," she said, tugging down her skirt. "Unfortunately for you, Azriel, I don't particularly like having my feet touched."

"*Noted*," he replied moodily.

After quickly removing the second cuff and storing both the leg irons and Persephone's meager belongings in his pack, Azriel mounted the horse and invited Persephone to ride with him. She refused. For one thing, she was reveling in the sensation of walking without irons for the first time in three months. For another thing, there were only two places for her to sit on that horse: astride behind Azriel, in which case she would be forced to wrap her arms around his waist to keep from slipping off, or in front of him, in which case she would be all but nestled in his arms, her back pressed against his well-muscled chest, her buttocks pressed up against his—

"No," she repeated, with a vehement shake of her head. "I'll not ride with you under any circumstances."

"Don't be foolish," he said impatiently. "We've a very long way to go before we make camp for the night, and you don't look as though you'll make it to the crest of the next hill."

"I'm stronger than I look," she said.

"Like a plow horse," he suggested, with a hint of a smile, "or a mule."

She ignored him.

He sighed heavily. "*Please*, Persephone. I don't want to frighten you, but the fact is there are some rather . . . unpleasant individuals following me at the moment, and though I was making a fine job of leading them on a merry chase prior to meeting you, it is exceedingly likely that the time it took to secure your release from your previous arrangement has given my pursuers an opportunity to draw somewhat closer than I now find comfortable."

"How unfortunate for you," she said drily.

"How unfortunate for *us*," he corrected, "for I assure you that it will go badly for both of us if they catch me."

"I can't see how it will go badly for me," she countered. "As I recall, you said you'd gladly die before seeing me harmed in any way."

"Hmm. Yes, well, perhaps 'gladly' was overstating it slightly," admitted Azriel. "Truth be told, I'd rather *not* die, Persephone. At least, not today."

Persephone shrugged, as though his death was neither here nor there to her. "I'm not riding up there with you," she said flatly. "So if you want me to ride, you'll have to walk."

Azriel made a noise that was somewhere between a laugh and a snort. "By the stars, I'll not walk to humor a stubborn little fool, no matter who she might be!" he exclaimed. "Walk if you wish, Persephone, and take comfort in the knowledge that when you begin to falter, I'll show myself to be a true and noble gentleman by giving you the choice between riding up here with me—or being dragged behind my horse."

"I won't falter," she sniffed, "and if I do, I can assure you that I'll insist on being dragged, thank you very much."

Azriel laughed again. Then he shrugged, dug his heels into the flanks of his horse and was off.

For all his smiles and laughter, Azriel set a brutally punishing pace. Up one hill and down another, through woods and streams, west then east then west again, on and on and on he rode, until Persephone had to bite her lip to keep from clutching at his leg and begging him to stop. She was proud and fiercely determined, but also weakened by hunger and abuse. Several times, she fell back, breathing hard, but a single questioning look from those very blue eyes was all it took to make her dig in and keep going.

Long after the golden sun had set and the silver moon had risen to its rightful place in the night sky, they arrived at a shallow creek. Without stopping or even looking back, Azriel led his horse into the middle of it, turned and began quietly splashing upstream. Persephone followed mindlessly, not hearing Cur barking from shore, not seeing Ivan gliding soundlessly overhead, her entire world reduced to keeping the glossy hindquarters of Azriel's horse in her sights and putting one torn foot in front of the other, come what may.

After a moment or an eternity, the hindquarters turned and climbed up out of the creek. Persephone followed, stumbling against them when they stopped without warning.

Swaying back and forth, she felt her knees slowly give way.

And then Azriel's strong arms were around her, lifting her off her feet.

She wanted to push him away, but she was too exhausted to do more than whimper—even when she felt him carry her into the shadows, lay her down on a bed of moss and gently brush her hair from her face. The nearness of him, so close in the darkness, was making her dizzy. She parted her lips to whisper a warning that she'd make a corpse of him if he tried anything, but before she could breathe a single word, she tumbled over the edge of consciousness and was lost in sleep.

Six

PERSEPHONE AWOKE EARLY the next morning. Out of habit, she did not stretch or yawn or do anything else to give herself away. Instead, she recalled the events of the previous day—everything from the shock of seeing the chicken thief again to the clink of money changing hands to the feel of him cupping her bare calf in his hand. And later, sweeping her exhausted body into his arms. Kneeling by her in the darkness—close enough to touch, but not touching.

Not even trying.

In spite of herself, Persephone gave a soft sigh.

"You're awake at last," declared a voice at her feet.

With a gasp, Persephone's eyes snapped open. Instinctively reaching for her missing dagger, she made a valiant attempt to roll into a kneeling position but fell back almost at once as her stiff, aching muscles gave way beneath her.

Azriel, who was squatted with his elbows resting on his knees, watched with interest her undignified collapse and listened to the accompanying groans.

"Has anyone ever told you that you have all the grace and poise of a natural dancer?" he finally asked.

"As a matter of fact—yes," grunted Persephone as she laboriously pushed herself into a sitting position. "I'll have you know that I was once invited to the imperial castle to dance for King Finnius himself."

"Really!" exclaimed Azriel, feigning amazement. "How did it go?"

"Exceedingly well," she replied smoothly. "In fact, if my chicken-feeding talents hadn't been urgently required elsewhere, I expect I would be dancing there yet."

Azriel threw back his head and laughed. When he was done, he leaned forward, tweaked her bare toe, then laughed again when she scowled and snatched her foot away. "You're a surprise in more ways than one, Persephone," he murmured.

Then he stood and held out his hand to her. "Now, come. Break your fast, that we might be on our way at once."

Ignoring his proffered hand, Persephone got to her feet and followed him across the small, sheltered clearing to the edge of the stream through which she'd slogged the previous night. Wincing slightly as her dress peeled away from the welts on her back, she knelt, rolled up her sleeves and quickly washed her hands and face.

"What happened to your arm?" asked Azriel, when he noticed her whiplash scar.

Instead of telling him the truth—which was that she didn't know—she told him it was none of his business.

"I don't know how this happened, either," he confided, showing her the little finger of his left hand, which appeared to have been cleanly amputated at the first joint.

When Persephone sniffed as though his measly mutilation was hardly worth the breath it took to mention, Azriel chuckled and said nothing more until she'd finished her ablutions and perched herself on a nearby rock. At that point, he reached into the leather pack at his side, pulled out a chicken leg wrapped in a large leaf and hesitantly handed it to her.

"I should warn you that this is—or rather, this was—your, uh, Mrs. Busby," he said, cringing slightly as though in anticipation of a noisy storm of tears.

Pouncing on the bundle in his hand, Persephone flung the leaf to one side and reverently sank her teeth into the succulent meat. With a sigh of obvious relief, Azriel reached back into the pack and withdrew a large hunk of dark bread and a wedge of cheese. "I borrowed these from your previous owner the same night you gave me the chicken," he explained. "Perhaps it was wrong of me but I fear I cannot regret it, for this bread and cheese are by far the finest I've ever eaten."

Though Persephone felt an unexpected rush of pride at his words, she kept her tone light when she told him that it was she who'd made them.

"Is that a fact?" said Azriel, who seemed very impressed. "Well, then, once you've learned to curb your tendency to verbally attack, openly defy and hurl knives at your betters, I'm sure you'll make some lucky man a fine little wife."

Persephone bristled like a hedgehog. "You're not my better," she said through gritted teeth.

"Truer words were never spoken," he agreed cheerfully.

Irritated by his reply for reasons she couldn't quite put her finger on, Persephone picked up the cheese and muttered, "I don't suppose you'd like to give me back my dagger so that I can eat this like a lady instead of gnawing away at it like a half-starved sailor?"

Wordlessly, Azriel reached back into his leather pack, pulled out her dagger and casually offered it to her.

After a moment's hesitation—as though fearing that the dagger would be snatched back if she made any sudden movement—Persephone slowly reached for it.

"Thank you," she murmured as her fingers closed around the hilt.

"You can thank me by promising never to slit me from bow to stern," he said.

"I promise," she said absently as she tossed the dagger from hand to hand, rejoicing in its familiar weight and balance, "provided you never give me cause to slit you from bow to stern."

"Not exactly the response I was hoping for," sighed Azriel, "though I am encouraged to learn that I have at least some hope of escaping disembowelment."

Persephone smiled faintly and shook her head at his silliness. As she did so, something caught her eye. Or rather, the absence of something caught her eye.

"Where is your horse?" she asked with a frown.

"I don't have a horse."

She folded her arms across her chest. "You had one yesterday."

"It was only a borrowed beast," he explained. "Last night, after you'd fallen asleep, I decided to let her find her way home to her true master so that the gentleman in question had no need to come looking for her . . . or me."

"A borrowed beast, was it?" said Persephone, arching an eyebrow. "What about the money and pendant you gave to the owner?"

"Borrowed."

"And the gloves and the doublet?"

"Also borrowed, I'm afraid," he admitted with an air of contrition that didn't fool Persephone for an instant. "Though the doublet suited me remarkably well, don't you think?"

"Not really," she sniffed. "To be honest, I thought it made you look like a pompous, overstuffed peacock."

Azriel laughed loudly. "Perhaps it did, at that," he agreed, still smiling. "Now, enough talking. Eat, for time grows short."

"Because you have unpleasant individuals following you," recalled Persephone as she lifted the wedge of cheese to her lips and took a bite that was hardly in keeping with her passionately expressed desire to eat like a lady. "Soldiers?" she guessed through her enormous mouthful of cheese.

Azriel paused for a fraction of a second before nodding. "Yes," he said.

Persephone swallowed. "Hunting you," she guessed again, waving the half-eaten cheese at him, "because you're a *thief*."

Azriel gave her a hard smile. "I'm a good deal more than a thief, Persephone."

She opened her mouth to ask him what he meant by this, then closed it again at once. It didn't matter to her what he was except for the fact that he was stupid. Stupid because he thought he could endear himself to her with his jolly laugh and his pretty eyes; stupid because he thought she would dutifully cleave to him just because he'd removed her fetters, given her back her own dagger and fed her bread and cheese made by her own two hands. If she lived to be a thousand years old, she would never cleave to him or any man who'd paid coin for her, whether he called himself owner or not. In fact, the sooner she got away from this particular man the better, for the soldiers who pursued him were likely filled with bloodlust and boiling over with unquenched appetites, and she knew that if they were to get their hands on her, nothing in the world could save her.

That said, unless she wanted to escape him only to starve in the wilderness, she needed a plan. "So, where are you taking me?" she asked, since this seemed as good a place as any to begin formulating one.

Azriel opened his mouth to reply, but before he could utter a word, they both heard the unmistakable sound of something approaching quickly through the tall, scraggly bushes behind them. With lightning-fast speed, Azriel was on his feet with his sword drawn. Grabbing Persephone by the wrist with his free hand, he yanked her off her perch and hurled her headlong into the cover of the thick reeds at the water's edge. Then he spun to face the threat.

The next instant, Cur burst from the bushes and crashed into Azriel with such force that he nearly knocked him over.

There was no time for anyone to breathe a sigh of relief, however, because it was obvious that there was something else charging through the bushes toward them.

Something bigger.

Much bigger.

Seconds later, it came crashing into the clearing in a flurry of torn leaves and snapped branches and skidded to a halt almost nose to nose with Azriel.

There was a moment of stunned silence. And then:

"Fleet!" shrieked Persephone.

Excitedly clawing at the thick reeds in an effort to pull herself to her feet, she lurched out of the water like a drunk on a bender. Shoving Azriel to one side, she flung her muddy arms around the sweaty neck of her beloved, broken-down old horse, who responded by whinnying and stamping his hooves with joy.

"Look—it's Fleet!" rejoiced Persephone, throwing Azriel the first unguarded smile she'd ever given him.

"That's . . . terrific," he said in a slightly stunned voice, his gaze so drawn to her beaming face that he hardly seemed to notice the way her thin, sodden shift now clung to her every curve.

"You don't really think it's terrific," said Persephone, turning back to the horse. "But I don't care and neither does Fleet. Do you, boy?"

The horse peeled back his lips and neighed rudely at Azriel. Evidently wanting to make it clear that he also didn't care what Azriel thought, Cur chimed in with a wet snarl.

"Oh, that's nice," muttered Azriel, sheathing his blade.

Just then, Ivan swooped down and settled on Persephone's shoulder.

Jamming his fists on his hips, Azriel jutted his chin forward and scowled at the hawk. "I suppose you don't care what I think, either?" he asked in a crabby voice.

The hawk screeched once—loudly—then flew at Azriel's head and beat upon it with his wings until he grew bored of the indignant cries of the hopping human beneath him and flew off in search of more entertaining sport.

In between pushing tangled auburn curls out of his blazing blue eyes and picking feathers out of his mouth, Azriel—who plainly found the entire situation an unspeakable outrage—shook his fist in the air and shouted oaths after the departing bird.

"Azriel?" gasped Persephone, who was laughing harder than she could ever remember having laughed in her entire life. "Let me give you a piece of advice for free: in the future, do not ask questions unless you are fully prepared to receive honest answers."

Azriel could not get over the fact that Fleet's deep affinity for Persephone had allowed him to effortlessly follow a trail intended to confound dogs and trained trackers; Persephone could not get over her joy at being reunited with a friend she'd thought lost forever. Even so, she knew that Fleet's careless, trampling hooves and tendency to emit sudden, noisy declarations of affection made him a less-than-ideal traveling companion for two people on the run for their lives—or for one enslaved girl making a desperate bid for freedom.

But if she could not take him with her when she made her escape, neither could she abide abandoning him to fend for himself. That is why, after she and Azriel finished wiping the foam and sweat from Fleet's heaving flanks, she asked Azriel to promise to take care of her animals if anything should happen to her. When he didn't answer immediately, she took a deep breath and tentatively laid her hand on his bare forearm.

"Please?" she asked, hoping she didn't sound as breathless as she felt.

For a moment, Azriel just stared down at the hand resting upon his arm. Then he flicked his eyes upward to meet hers and, placing his free hand over hers, said, "Very well, Persephone. I promise to take care of your animals, provided that you promise you won't ever try to run from me."

Startled though she was by both his request and the feel of his hand upon hers, Persephone didn't hesitate or even blink.

"I promise," she lied. "Of course I do."

The going was hard but not quite so hard as it had been the previous day, for Azriel no longer had the luxury of a mount. For the most part, they walked single file—Azriel followed by Persephone, who was, in turn, followed by Fleet and Cur. From time to time, Cur attempted to slip forward so that he could walk at Persephone's heels. Each time he did so, however, Fleet neighed shrilly and attempted to trample him in a fit of jealousy, so a visibly disgruntled Cur eventually resigned himself to bringing up the rear. Azriel was also visibly disgruntled by Fleet's behavior, because each time he tried to lead the group into a stream in order to obliterate their scent trail, Fleet not only refused to follow but galloped to and fro along the bank beside them, whinnying in panic, destroying great swaths of vegetation and leaving deep hoofprints in the sucking mud.

"He's never liked getting his feet wet," explained Persephone in confidential tones. "He'll pass through water if he absolutely has to, but he won't stand or walk in it for any length of time. I think he must have experienced some sort of water-related trauma as a foal."

When Azriel responded by muttering darkly that Fleet was about to experience a boot-in-the-arse-related trauma, Persephone gave him a reproachful look.

"You promised to take care of him," she reminded.

"But he is the most willful, disruptive, irritating bag of horsemeat it has ever been my misfortune to look upon!" exploded Azriel. "He will be the death of us all!"

"Nevertheless," said Persephone, unruffled by his outburst, "you promised."

If anyone had pointed out to Persephone the irony of the fact that she fully expected Azriel to hold to his promise to care for her animals when she had no intention of holding to her promise not to run from him, she'd have told them that she had no choice in the matter. For more than anything in this life, she longed to be free to seek a destiny that belonged to none but her, and if she was true to her word, she would remain enslaved until she was dead or sold, and that was simply not an option.

And that is why, once they stopped for the night, she was going to undertake a few simple preparations and then, as soon as Cur left to hunt and Azriel and Fleet were soundly sleeping, she was going to make her escape.

Her plan was not to just steal away and run as fast and as far as she could in the treacherous, unfamiliar dark, either.

No, she was going to do something far cleverer than that.

It was nearly dusk before Azriel finally announced that it was time to make camp. While he went down to a nearby stream to fetch water and catch fish for supper, Persephone hastily carried out her preparations for escape. When she was done, she swept the campsite, built a fire and helped to clean and cook the fish. Then, after hastily gulping down her supper, she lay down and closed her eyes—or pretended to, anyway. In truth, through the thick tangle of her lashes, she watched Azriel and wondered about him. Wondered what it was that made her believe that this handsome rascal really *would* die before seeing her harmed in any way; wondered what he'd meant when he'd said that he was a great deal more than a thief. Wondered why he hadn't even asked if she wanted to lie with him that night. Asking was not the same as forcing, after all, and everyone knew that many desperate women acquiesced to such arrangements. Even though Persephone probably would have tried to knife Azriel if he *had* asked, it seemed odd that he hadn't. Unless, of course, he found her repulsive or beneath him, or had a beautiful sweetheart to whom he wished to stay true. For he was the type to stay true, Persephone was sure of it, and it suddenly struck her that she could have done worse than to remain in the ownership of this particular man—wherever he was taking her, for whatever purpose.

But she wanted a good deal more than to avoid the worst that life had to offer, and so it wasn't long before she found herself clinging to the fragrant trunk of a nearby evergreen tree, panting wildly and looking down at the still, sleeping figure by the fire who, from that great height, resembled nothing so much as a small, tousle-haired boy clutching a gleaming, much-favored toy sword.

The next day dawned with the promise of rain.

Feeling as indecent as if she was on her knees with her eye pressed up against the keyhole at a gentleman's bedroom door, Persephone watched breathlessly as Azriel awoke, languidly stretched and rubbed his sleepy eyes. Slipping his hand inside his shirt to scratch his chest, he slowly turned his head and looked past the cold fire to where Persephone should have been sleeping. Almost before she realized he was moving, he was on his feet with his sword in hand, scanning the forest. He called her name once, twice. When there was no reply, he muttered something she couldn't hear and roughly jammed the sword into his scabbard. The noise woke Fleet, who took one look at the empty spot where Persephone had been lying and began charging around the campsite, whinnying in panic and trying to trample Azriel. *That* noise brought Cur flying out of a thicket of waist-high ferns. He didn't even bother to look at the empty spot where Persephone had been lying but instead ran straight at Azriel and bit him. Persephone felt rather bad about this but consoled herself with the knowledge that Cur probably hadn't been able to get a very good hold of her former owner's leg, given the energy with which he was jumping and dodging in an effort to stay ahead of Fleet's deadly hooves.

Just as Persephone was beginning to worry that they'd never get down to the business of dashing off to look for her so that she could climb down and run away, Ivan swooped down and settled on a branch directly in front of her. She quickly put her finger to her lips to quiet him, but he was so incensed to find her—a mere human!—perched in his domain that he dropped the dead ferret in his beak so that he could squawk crabbily at her before taking to the gloomy skies once more. Persephone watched anxiously as the ferret hit branch after branch before finally landing on Azriel, who bellowed in shock and nearly leapt out of his skin at the feel of the dead furry thing hitting him squarely on the top of the head. Glaring up into the tree in which Persephone was huddled, hidden from sight by the prickly boughs, he scanned for some sign of the vile ferret-dropper. Then, as though suddenly remembering that Cur and Fleet were trying to kill him, he whipped around so fast that he tripped over a tree root and went sprawling. Evidently satisfied by the sight of his nemesis so humbled, Cur barked once, turned and put his nose to the ground. He spent several fruitless moments following the scent trails Persephone had purposely left around every tree in the vicinity (including the one in which she was hiding) before bolting along the scent trail she'd made walking into camp. Azriel looked to see if Fleet would tear off in the same direction, but Fleet had just discovered the sugarberry juice that Persephone had rubbed all over Azriel's traveling cloak and he was too busy happily chewing on it to tear off in any direction. Visibly disgusted, Azriel wrestled the cloak out of the horse's mouth, slung it over one shoulder and slung his pack over the other. Then he took off after Cur at a run with a salivating Fleet galloping close behind him, his eyes fixed upon the delicious cloak.

Persephone heaved a great sigh of relief. Then, quite without warning, she began to laugh—softly at first, then harder and harder, until her whole body was shaking and she had to hug the tree to keep from tumbling, ferret-like, to the ground. She'd done it! She'd really done it! Her daring plan had succeeded.

All I have to do now, she rejoiced as a chill rain began to fall, *is to wait for Azriel to give up the search and continue on his original path so that I may head back toward civilization—and freedom.*

Seven

DEADLY POLEAX CLUTCHED TIGHTLY in one hand, a liveried guard with a wine-colored birthmark on his cheek hurriedly tiptoed across the floor of the high-ceilinged chamber. He halted a respectful distance from his silk-and-velvet-clad king, who sat absently munching on a golden pear as he studied the well-worn playing cards in his hand and cast intermittent brooding glances across the table at the stalwart opponent who'd beaten him so mercilessly and so often.

The air was thick with tension: Who could say what would happen next?

Suddenly—recklessly!—King Finnius pushed the entire fortune with which he was gambling (a modest pile of dried white beans) into the center of the table. With his head held high, he slowly sat back in his ornately carved mahogany chair, folded his arms across the front of his gem-encrusted doublet and waited for his opponent to crumble before his breathtaking daring. The guard, who had no idea what game the young king was playing nor if his gamble had been a wise one, smiled inwardly at his theatrics. Then he remembered his purpose and quietly cleared his throat.

"Yes?" asked the king, who seemed only mildly annoyed at being interrupted during the very moment of his triumph. "What is it?"

"Sorry to bother you, Your Majesty," murmured the guard, ducking his head, "but the Regent Mordesius is come to see you."

"Oh!" cried the king. Leaping to his feet with a distinct lack of majesty, he tossed the golden pear to one side and flung the cards across the table at his opponent. "Quick, Moira, hide these! And the beans!" he hissed. Without waiting for an answer from the woman who'd mothered him since infancy, he rifled madly beneath a messy stack of parchment for the Latin text that he was supposed to have been translating—a text that he'd gladly shoved to one side to make way for more entertaining pursuits.

The woman—Moira—deftly swept the beans into the deep pocket of her apron, but before tossing the cards in after them, she took a moment to examine those that the young king had been holding. "Looks like I'd have won again, Your Majesty," she informed him in a pleased voice.

Grimacing at this most unwelcome news, the king flapped his hands to shush her, then flopped back into his seat, took a deep breath and regally nodded at the guard, who'd since hurried back to his spot at the door. Tugging at the hem of his tunic, the guard smartly rapped the butt of his poleax on the richly polished floor and bellowed, "The Regent Mordesius!"

Almost before the words were out of his mouth, the door banged open and the Regent slouched into the room. He glowered evilly at the idiot guard who'd left him waiting in the king's outer chamber as though he were some sort of commoner, then turned a charming smile upon the king himself.

"Majesty," he murmured, bowing as low as his twisted back would permit.

With a flick of his hand, the king bade him rise and approach. "Good day, Your Grace," he said.

"Good day, Your Majesty," said Mordesius. "How goes the translation?"

"Wonderfully well, thank you for asking," replied the king heartily. He paused to give the Latin text a look of deep fondness before inquiring as to the purpose of the Regent's visit.

"Well, Majesty, there is a meeting of the Council this afternoon—"

"And I'm to attend at last?" interrupted King Finnius, gripping the arms of his chair and leaning forward in his eagerness.

"*Majesty*," chided Mordesius, his head bobbing slightly. "We've discussed many times how unwise it would be for you to attend Council meetings before you're ready to fully assume your duties as king. The men on your Council are noblemen from ancient families, but they are also hard men who need to be ruled with an iron fist."

"They would have to obey me," insisted the young monarch, holding an index finger high in the air, "for I am their king. They have sworn fealty to me—loyalty unto death, upon pain of death."

Across the table, the servant woman, Moira, placidly nodded her head. The Regent felt his blood rise that such a low creature would not only dare to sit in his presence but would also presume to offer any kind of opinion on a private exchange between a king and his Lord Regent. Not for the first time, he thought how he'd like to see that head of hers separated from her revoltingly sturdy peasant body by a drunken blind man wielding a blunt ax.

Forcibly pushing this most-satisfying image from his mind, Mordesius took a deep breath and turned his attention to the king.

"Of *course* they've sworn fealty to you," he soothed. "But as we've discussed many times, Majesty, a great king commands obedience and respect because of who he is as a man, not because of a few words uttered at the feet of a royal infant many years past. I fear—as I have always feared—that if you were to take your seat at the head of Council before such time as you were a man fully grown, the members of your Council would ever see you as the boy king, and you would ever rule in the shadow of your long-dead father, the great and powerful Octavio who came before you."

At the mention of his dead father, the young king loosened his grip on the arms of the chair and slowly sat back. "Well, it won't be long now," he consoled himself in a subdued voice. "My eighteenth birthday fast approaches and thereafter, the men on the Council will have no choice but to recognize me as a man fully grown. And I shall prove myself to be a ruler the likes of which this kingdom has never known!"

Moira nodded as solemnly as a sage. Blinking once to rid himself of the vision of blood spurting from her ragged, headless neck, Mordesius asked the king if he might have a word in private.

"Of course, Your Grace," said the king. Turning to the servant, he said, "Leave us, Moira . . . please."

Moira rose to her feet at once, curtseyed with surprising grace for a woman of her age and bulk, then backed out of the room with all due deference to His Majesty the King and not so much as a glance at the Regent Mordesius.

Mordesius watched her go, hating her every step of the way. When at last she spun around and bustled through the great doors at the entrance of the chamber, he turned to the king. "She is as dear to me as she is to you, Majesty," he murmured, "but it is obvious to all that she doesn't know her place, and I fear that the noblemen of your Council will have a hard time respecting you if you cannot even rule your own servants with a firm hand."

King Finnius laughed aloud. "No one rules Moira," he said with obvious affection.

Mordesius, who had hoped that his words would be enough to goad the young king into putting that troublesome and interfering creature in her place, felt his blood rise higher. "Her overly familiar behavior is not the worst of it, Majesty," he said, dropping his voice a notch. "I'm afraid there has been . . . talk."

"Talk?" frowned the king.

"The court doesn't understand why you spend so much time with her, why you treat her as . . . as a *companion*," said Mordesius, who could hardly spit the word out. "They whisper, they wonder if . . ."

"If what?" demanded the king. "What do they wonder?"

Mordesius bowed his head as though he could hardly bear the shame of what he was about to say. "Forgive me, Majesty," he whispered, wringing his badly scarred hands, "but they wonder if you and that servant woman are lovers."

For a moment, the king was so silent that Mordesius, to his horror, thought there might actually be some truth to the ludicrous rumor he'd invented for the sole purpose of pushing the king to do his ill will.

Then the king was laughing so long and so loud that he drove himself into one of his coughing fits. When he finally recovered, he wiped the tears of mirth from his eyes and said, "Good lord, Your Grace, you do say the most amusing things sometimes."

"There is nothing whatsoever amusing about these accusations, Majesty!" flared Mordesius, his entire withered body shaking with indignation.

The Regent seemed so terribly upset that out of kindness, King Finnius tried to appear terribly upset as well, but after only a few seconds of frowning and clucking he couldn't help dissolving into helpless giggles once more. The enraged Regent said nothing, only stared at the handsome, laughing young monarch in a manner that would have seen any other man in the kingdom executed for treason.

But the young king never noticed his Regent's murderous expression. Indeed, such was his faith that Mordesius was a true and loyal councilor that the man probably would have had to snatch up the silver fruit knife and plunge it into the king's throat for the king to notice that something was amiss. Sighing contentedly, the grinning monarch reached over, plucked a fresh pear from his fruit bowl, took a large bite and said, "Your Grace, I laugh only because the accusations are so preposterous that they can't possibly do me any harm. You have my word of honor that there is nothing untoward going on between me and Moira."

"And yet she looked very guilty when I first arrived," said Mordesius darkly, even though this was not true at all.

King Finnius gave a long-suffering sigh. "Well, if you *must* know, she was playing cards with me."

"Cards?" spat Mordesius, sounding as disgusted as he dared. "Majesty, *commoners* play cards. Kings play chess."

"You're right, of course," agreed the king easily. "But Moira doesn't know how to play chess."

"Who cares what she knows how to play? She is a servant!" cried Mordesius in frustration. "You have an entire court full of young noblemen who would like nothing better than to spend time with you, to say *nothing* of the young noblewomen. Their sole purpose in life is to keep you entertained and happy! Surely you could find one among them with whom to play chess, rather than lowering yourself to playing cards with a *servant*."

"Have a care how you speak about Moira, Your Grace, for I believe that, in truth, she is dearer to me than she is to you," said the king, taking another bite of his pear. "As for the courtiers who live to please me, they are well enough, I suppose, though I do not like the way they laugh when I laugh and frown when I frown. I know the stronger, more vigorous young men hold back so that I may win in games and tournaments, and as for the young women—well, there's not one among them who has not made it abundantly clear that she would gladly crawl into my bed at the crook of a finger."

"And . . . this is a bad thing?" asked Mordesius raggedly—he, who would have given almost anything to have a tender piece of noble flesh willingly lie down beneath him.

King Finnius waved the pear around. "It is a tiresome thing," he said. "I wish to be desired for who I am, not what I am. Moreover, I do not want everything handed to me. How am I ever to prove myself a great ruler if I never have to fight for any victory I achieve? And then, of course, there is the fact that these young nobles and their families are always after something—more land, more money, more titles."

"You are the only one who can grant such favors," murmured Mordesius, even though everyone but the king knew that the Regent himself was the greatest giver of gifts in the realm.

"Nevertheless," said the king, "it annoys me and leads me to feel as though I cannot count any among them as true friends. That is why I enjoy spending time with Moira. She will trounce me soundly when my poor card playing warrants it and she never asks anything of me but that I listen to the advice of my doctors, be kind to others great and small, be just and wise in all my dealings and find what happiness I may in a life of duty to my kingdom."

Mordesius was so disgusted by this little speech that he thought he might vomit up his guts, right then and there. Instead, he smiled like a snake, spread his hands wide and murmured, "Now that you've explained it to me in such eloquent terms, Your Majesty, I understand perfectly why you occasionally feel compelled to seek entertainment among those of inferior birth. Moreover, I feel much grieved that I failed to consider your need to spend time with true and trusted friends—so much so, in fact, that though I already toil tirelessly tending to Your Majesty's business, I will gladly set aside some time each day so that you and I may play . . . cards."

The king laughed—a careless sound that Mordesius had heard more and more of late, one that he was rapidly growing to despise. "That is a very kind offer, Your Grace," chuckled the king. "But I think there is no one in the realm who can play cards like Moira. Now, was there anything else?"

It took Mordesius a moment to recover from the staggering insult of having been so casually passed over in favor of an ill-educated, lowborn servant woman. "Yes, Majesty, there is something else," he said, when he was finally able. "I wish you to approve a proposal to raze the slum that encroaches upon the north wall of the palace so that when the matter is discussed at Council this afternoon, I may advise the lords that it has royal assent."

The king frowned. "Why do you want to raze the slum?"

Mordesius did not tell the true reason, which was that the slum was a smelly eyesore, that the choking smoke from its many cook fires obscured his view of the great city and, worst of all, that it was a constant reminder of his own low beginnings.

Instead, he said, "I fear disease, Your Majesty. The slum is over-crowded and filthy, and of late, the death carts have been more overloaded than usual at the end of their daily rounds. It is rumored that this is due to an outbreak of the Great Sickness—an outbreak that has been wickedly covered up for fear of reprisals."

The king sat up straighter. "The Great Sickness is come to the slums once more?" he said, his blue eyes filled with concern. "If that is so, we must act at once, Mordesius. We must dispatch physicians to treat the sick and spiritual men to give comfort to the dying. We must send in women with food and drink for those who are too ill to feed themselves!"

The Regent sighed. "Would that we could, Majesty, would that we could," he said mournfully. "However, we cannot take the chance that while we are busy tending to the sick, the dread disease will somehow creep over the palace walls and find its way through halls and passageways to Your Majesty's very own sleeping chamber. After all, you're not yet married and therefore have no legitimate child to name as heir to your throne. Until such time as you do, you cannot afford to take chances with your already delicate health, for—heaven forbid—if you were to fall sick and die without an heir to follow you, the great lords would surely tear the kingdom apart in their quest for power."

The young king nodded reluctantly, for he knew this to be true. Even Moira said it was so.

"Of course," continued the Regent, straightening his back and lifting his head high, though the pain of it made him want to scream aloud, "if you were to name another as your heir in the absence of a true begotten child, and if you were to compel the great lords to swear fealty to this man in the event that—heaven forbid—you were tragically and unexpectedly struck down, perhaps we'd be able to show some mercy to the unfortunate residents of the lowborn slums. Perhaps we'd not have to burn their homes and scatter them to the winds." Redoubling his efforts to keep his perfect head high and his body from trembling, Mordesius inhaled deeply so that his sunken chest expanded ever so slightly. "Perhaps if you named an heir, we wouldn't need to be forever making such terrible sacrifices to guard Your Majesty's person."

"I know you speak the truth," said the king, with a brooding toss of his dark curls. "But who would I name? To choose the son of one of the great families over the son of another would cause strife as surely as naming no heir at all."

At these words, the Regent's chest deflated, his back seemed to curve of its own volition and his head drooped and bobbed. "On this matter, I fear I can provide no counsel, Your Majesty," he said, "except to say that I agree that it would be unwise to name as heir the son of one of the great houses."

"Truly, you are a councilor among councilors, Your Grace," said the king solemnly but with a glint in his eye, "for even when you profess to have no counsel to provide, I somehow find myself receiving your most valued opinion anyway."

Unsure as to whether or not the king was teasing him, Mordesius smiled tightly. "Yes, Sire," he said through his teeth. "Now, if it pleases Your Majesty, do I have your approval to raze the lowborn slum to the north?"

For a long moment, the young king looked down upon the half-eaten pear in his hand, as though the answer lay in its sweet and perfect flesh. "For the sake of the kingdom, you have my approval to proceed," he said at last, in a troubled voice. "But instruct the soldiers to show the people who dwell within what kindness they can, for low and filthy and sick though they may be, they are still my subjects, and it is my duty to care for them."

"Of course it is, Majesty," said Mordesius smoothly, bowing as low as he could. "Do not trouble yourself further with this matter. Rest assured that I will see to it that these, the least of your subjects, receive all the consideration they deserve."

Eight

SEVERAL HOURS AFTER Persephone watched Azriel, Cur and Fleet dash off in search of her, she watched them slip and slide back into sight.

Even from her cold, wet perch high in the tree, she could tell that Cur and Fleet were deeply distressed by her disappearance, but she steeled herself against the temptation to think that abandoning them was a mistake. How could it be a mistake when it was the only way she could ever be free? Besides, even as she watched, Azriel tentatively reached out and gave Cur a comforting pat on the head, and he only shouted a little bit when Cur rewarded his kindness by trying to bite off his fingers.

Feeling somewhat cheered by this evidence that the handsome chicken thief would keep his promise to take care of her friends, a shivering Persephone watched Azriel stamp his foot in apparent frustration, then kick a tree so hard that he started hopping about, cursing and clutching his toe. When he was done having his little tantrum, he threw up his hands and resignedly trudged onward into the forest. After a moment's hesitation, Cur and Fleet trotted after him.

Persephone followed their departure with her eyes and ears, and when she could no longer see or hear them, she blew on her fingers to warm the stiffness out of them, carefully climbed down out of the tree and began to run in the opposite direction.

It didn't take her long to figure out why Azriel had returned to camp covered in mud. The dirt trail along which they'd walked into camp the previous evening had been turned by the rain into a long, slick ribbon of slippery mud, and no matter how carefully she ran, every few steps her feet flew out from under her and she landed hard on some part of her body that was already aching.

Frustrated, Persephone stepped off the trail in the hope of finding firmer footing a little farther into the bush. Unfortunately, she'd walked less than half a dozen paces when she promptly fell again.

Only this time, she didn't lie where she fell.

This time, the earth gave way beneath her and she found herself sliding toward the river down a hidden, mud-slick embankment. She was gathering momentum so fast that she probably would have screamed if her heart hadn't been lodged in her throat. Desperately, she tried to grab hold of something that would slow her down, but there was nothing to grab on to and nothing to dig her heels into. She just slid faster and faster, until she was going so fast that she didn't even see the lip of the embankment until she was already flying over it.

Instinctively windmilling her arms, she whipped her head this way and that, trying to judge how far she was going to fall and how hard the landing was going to be, but it was all a blur. She heard an irate squawk from high above and an ominous burp from far below and a truly horrible stench rose up to meet her and the next thing she knew—

GLUG.

She landed headfirst in a deep pool of warm mud so smelly that she started retching the instant her head broke the surface. In between heaves, she slogged to the edge, dragged herself up out of the pool and collapsed.

After she caught her breath and checked her pocket to make sure that she'd not lost the rat tail and lace she'd taken from Azriel's pack the night before, Persephone assured Ivan that her brief, graceless flight had not been an attempt to challenge his dominion over the skies. Then she turned to inspect the strange pool into which she'd plunged. The first thing she noticed was that she'd been lucky, for if she'd landed even a foot to the left, she'd have hit her head on the edge and dashed her brains out. The second thing she noticed was that beyond the pool was the fast-moving river, but before that were several more of these small, belching mud pools.

And one large bubbling pool of what looked to be clean water.

Leaving muddy, squelching footprints on the smooth, black rock, Persephone eagerly made her way to this pool. Dipping her toe in, she was delighted to find that it was not just warm, but as hot as any bath Cookie had ever had her prepare for the merchant. Hotter, even! With a sigh, Persephone thought back to the endless pails of steaming water she'd had to lug to the merchant's room, and how she'd always yearned, in her childish way, to be allowed—just once!—the unimaginable luxury of bathing with warm water, in a tub, in private, instead of standing in the yard trying to clean herself as best she could with a rag and a pail of ice-cold well water.

Well, here was her chance.

Feeling almost giddy, she looked around to make sure she was truly alone. Then she hastily peeled off her filthy shift, rinsed it so that she wouldn't muddy herself again after bathing, flung it onto a nearby rock and eased herself into the pool.

"Ooooooh," she breathed, closing her eyes in ecstasy. "*Ahhhhhh.*"

The water stank like rotten eggs but it was gloriously hot and clean. Pinching her nose shut, Persephone dunked her head below the surface over and over just for the thrill of being completely submerged. She floated on her back; she clung to the sides and kicked her feet. Pretending she was a grand lady in a private bath, she called to her imaginary servants to bring more hot water, perfumed soaps, a goblet of fine wine! Then she laughed at her own silliness and paddled at the water with her hands. She'd never felt so free in her entire life—she'd never felt so clean.

As the clouds parted and the sun began to shine, Persephone thought what a wonderful way this was to begin her new life as a free woman.

Then she heard it.

The sound of something big, noisy and clumsy approaching fast.

CLIP, CLOP, CLIP, CLOP, CLIP, CLOP.

"Oh, *no!*" she wailed.

There was no time to escape—no time even to grab her shift—for the next instant, Fleet rounded the corner at the bend in the river and spotted her. Neighing joyfully, he fixed his loving eyes upon her and clip-clopped across the rock toward her as fast as he could, pausing only once to try to kick Cur in the head to prevent him from reaching her first.

After greeting them both with all due affection and watching them wander away to explore the nearby bush, Persephone warily turned her attention to Azriel. He was just as filthy as he'd been the last time she'd seen him—filthier, perhaps—and his expression was inscrutable. As he slowly walked toward her, she saw him make note of the fact that her shift was lying some distance from the pool, and she flushed hotly when she saw his gaze briefly drop from her face to the water in which she crouched with nothing but her hands and a few bubbles to cover her nakedness.

Neither of them said anything until he walked right up to the edge of the pool, dropped his pack, unbuckled his sword and began unbuttoning his shirt.

"How's the water?" he asked.

Persephone didn't answer him because she *couldn't*. All she could do was stare up at him with her mouth hanging open. He couldn't think that . . . he couldn't *possibly* mean to . . .

"I hope it's nice, because I could use a good soak. As it happens, I've not had a very pleasant day thus far," he said as he peeled off his shirt.

Persephone inhaled sharply at the sight of him wearing nothing but boots and breeches.

Then he pulled off his boots. And stood up.

And reached for the laces at the front of his breeches.

"*Stop!*" she cried.

"Stop?" he echoed, looking down at her in mild surprise.

If Persephone's hands hadn't been gainfully employed trying to cover up her private parts, she'd have buried her face in them. She'd never seen a half-clothed man before and for some reason, the sight of this particular half-clothed man was making her feel very confused. She knew she shouldn't be looking, shouldn't be letting him see her gaze sweep across his bare skin, but she couldn't help it. With his broad shoulders and taut stomach he just looked so . . . so . . . *strong*, and she felt an unexpected, unwanted thrill of excitement uncurl in her belly at the memory of their first meeting, when he'd pulled her close and she'd felt his long, lean body against hers. Squeezing her eyes shut, she gave her head a desperate shake. Even the thought of him completely naked was enough to shatter what was left of her composure.

"I'm sorry I tried to run away, all right?" she blurted, her words coming in a breathless rush. "I'm sorry! Just . . . just hand me my shift and—"

"Your shift?" interrupted Azriel. Frowning, he cocked his head to one side as though deeply confused. Then he gave a scandalized gasp, leaned very close and murmured, "Why, Persephone, do you mean to tell me that at this very moment you are wearing nothing at all?"

She scowled and dropped lower in the water. "I'm wearing my dagger," she muttered, doing her best to sound threatening. "So . . . you'd better just back away and . . . and hand me my shift."

Wordlessly, Azriel walked over, picked up her shift and walked back to the edge of the pool.

"Here you go," he said, dangling it so high above her that she'd have had to climb out of the pool to reach it.

Persephone scowled again. "Are you enjoying yourself?" she snapped.

"Not as much as I could be," he replied.

The sudden heat in his voice sent a shock wave through her, but before she could react to it, he smiled disarmingly and set down the shift. "Get dressed," he said. "We'll discuss the matter of your broken promise—and its consequences—once we've made up some of the time that your willfulness has cost us."

"I'm not getting dressed until you turn around and . . . and go away," she muttered.

Though it briefly appeared as though Azriel might refuse—might insist upon watching her climb naked out of the pool—in the end, he gave a gentlemanly bow, picked up his shirt and boots, turned and headed down to the river. Persephone waited until she saw him wade in and start rinsing off. Then, her mind brimming with thoughts of the many hideous and painful things she would do to him if he dared to sneak a peek, she scampered out of the pool, snatched up the wet shift and tugged it on so fast that she tore one of the sleeves half off the bodice.

She started to swear but broke off at the sudden sound of Fleet whinnying in panic.

"Persephone, *wait!*" bellowed Azriel from his spot in the river.

But it was too late—she was already sprinting, dagger in hand, through the bush toward her beloved horse. Seconds later she found him trapped at the river's edge by three enormous, barking black dogs. They were sinewy, evil-looking creatures with cropped ears and amputated tails, and when Persephone burst upon the scene, the nearest and largest of them turned and stared at her with glittering yellow eyes.

Instinctively, Persephone took a step back. Tripping over a fallen branch, she fell and landed so hard that her teeth snapped down on her tongue. The dogs leapt at her and as they did, three things happened at once. First, Fleet's horror at seeing his beloved Persephone under attack instantly overcame his terror of being drowned or eaten. Eyes rolling and deadly, trampling hooves flying, he galloped full force at the dogs and caught the largest one with a kick to the hindquarters that sent him sprawling face-first into the dirt. Second, Cur burst from the trees beside Persephone and slammed into the smallest dog. Finally, Persephone—one arm flung over her face to protect her from the dog that was still bearing down on her—stuck out her dagger and locked her elbow so that when the dog landed, he found himself not burying his teeth in the tender flesh of her neck, but impaled upon her dagger by the force of his own momentum.

In the stunned silence that followed, the dog that had been kicked in the hindquarters struggled to his feet and awkwardly slithered into the far bushes. Fleet—whose brains, guts and nerves had been entirely used up in his one shining moment of bravery—noisily trumpeted his terrible grief at the apparent demise of his adored mistress and galloped off in the opposite direction.

One heartbeat later, a dripping, shirtless Azriel burst into the clearing. At the sight of Persephone struggling feebly beneath the limp dog as blood poured down the side of her shift and pooled on the ground below her, he let out a hoarse cry. Sprinting over to where she lay, he heaved the dog aside, dropped to his knees and began frantically searching her blood-soaked shift for the fatal wound.

"I can't find it," he cried desperately as he ran his hands up and down her body. "I can't find it!" Leaning over her, he gripped her shoulders hard and gave her a shake. "Persephone, please—I may be able to help you but you must tell me where it hurts!"

"My . . . tongue," she replied thickly, shoving him away with what Azriel must have thought was surprising strength for a girl who'd lost that much blood.

"Your tongue?" he said blankly, staring at the front of her blood-soaked shift as though trying to figure out how such a minor wound could have resulted in such a gruesome mess.

Determined to put up a brave front even though she was trembling so hard she could barely keep her teeth from chattering,

Persephone rolled her eyes and said, "Really, Lord Common Sense, I should think it obvious that the blood isn't—"

Her throat closed abruptly when she saw the skid marks in the dirt. They could only have been made by Cur and the beast he'd attacked—and they clearly showed that the two grappling animals had not slid to a halt at the river's edge, but had gone right over it. Jumping to her feet, Persephone ran to the riverbank. When a quick scan revealed no sign of Cur, she stepped back, took a running leap and would have flung herself into the chill, fast-moving water to swim off in search of him if Azriel had not managed to grab a handful of her hair.

"Ow!" she shrieked, stumbling backward against him.

"Sorry," he said, as he deftly transferred his grip to her biceps.

"Let go of me!" Persephone demanded, giving her arm a sudden yank in the hope of putting him off balance.

"No," he said, unmovable as a monolith. "Persephone, you must listen—"

"No, you must listen!" she cried as she drove her heel downward toward his foot. "I have to go after Cur! He saved my life!"

"And lost his own in the bargain," said Azriel, moving his foot at the last second so that Persephone's heel landed on a sharp pebble instead of her intended target.

She grunted in pain. "You cannot know that for a certainty," she said as she leaned backward in a vain attempt to drag Azriel into the water with her.

"No," he agreed, "but I do know these things for a certainty: if your dog is not a strong swimmer, he is already dead. If he has somehow managed to survive, he will find you. If I allow you to jump into this river you will drown, succumb to the chill of the water or hit your head on a submerged rock. I cannot allow that to happen because you are—"

"Your property?" she said scornfully, thrusting her chin out at him.

"My responsibility," said Azriel, who seemed to be getting annoyed.

"Well, so is Cur," she reminded swiftly. "You promised you would take care of my animals, remember?"

"You promised me something, too, Persephone—*remember*?" said Azriel.

"You said we'd discuss that later," she said with a dismissive wave of her hand. "Cur requires your help now. So unless you are a faithless liar on top of being a no-account thief with an extraordinarily high opinion of his own good looks, you had best get a move on and—"

"E-*nough*!" growled Azriel, whose eyes were suddenly blazing like blue flames. Ignoring the way that Persephone shrank from him as though she were afraid of getting burned, he grabbed her by both arms and roughly pulled her close. "I may be a no-account thief, Persephone, but you are a reckless little fool," he hissed. "For your information, that dead beast over there was an army tracker, and if he is here, it means that those who seek us are dangerously near at hand. So unless you have an especial desire to find out for yourself what a gang of bloodthirsty New Men will do to a piece of fresh meat like you, we must go—now."

"But I can't just leave Cur—"

Evidently deciding that the time for discussion was over, Azriel took hold of Persephone's arm so that he could drag her along behind him whether she liked it or not. Quick as an angry cat, she sank her teeth into his bare forearm. When he released her with a bellow of pain, she turned on one heel and tore headlong into the bushes. With another bellow, Azriel tore after her. Veering back toward the river, Persephone threw a quick glance over her shoulder to see if she had enough of a lead on him to be able to—

"Oof!"

She ran smack into a soldier. He was dressed in black from head to toe, stank of old sweat and held a bow in one hand. For an endless moment, the two of them stood open-mouthed, staring goggle-eyed at the other. Then, a fraction of a second before the

New Man recovered his wits, Persephone recovered hers. Whirling around, she blindly pelted back in the direction from which she'd come. She hadn't gone three steps before she ran right into a still-shirtless Azriel.

"Soldiers!" she cried as his arms instinctively closed around her. "Run!"

Her directive was really not required, for the next second, the New Man behind her gave a shout and an arrow flew past Azriel's head. Spinning around with Persephone still in his arms, Azriel set her down, placed his hand on the small of her back and shoved hard. She needed no encouragement to run. Another arrow flew past them, and another, and now she could hear dogs barking and other men shouting, their voices filled with excitement, their weapons clanking. The noises got closer with each thudding heartbeat and somehow, they seemed to come from all directions at once.

"They . . . have us surrounded!" panted Persephone as she and Azriel burst into the clearing. "What . . . what are we going to . . . to do?"

Instead of wasting his breath on an answer, Azriel grabbed her hand and, as two black terror dogs burst out of the bushes behind them, he ran full tilt toward the water's edge and launched them both into the chill, fast-moving waters of the river below.

Nine

"YOU'RE SURE IT'S HIM?" asked General Murdock, taking another dainty nibble of the fresh liver the steward had prepared for his dinner. A military man through and through, General Murdock nevertheless insisted upon the trappings of fine society. Simple things, like clean stockings, a comfortable bed, linen hand towels with supper. Meals served on fine china, at the proper hour, no matter what the circumstances.

"Oh, it's him all right, General Murdock, sir!" bellowed the excited young soldier. "He killed two of our tracking beasts, but the one what got away caught the scent sure and clear. It's him from the night you was nearly roasted alive, sir. And now he's in the river! And he's got a girl with him! A *girl*, sir!"

"Interesting," said General Murdock, half to himself. Above his weak chin and small mouth, his long, thin nose twitched as he chewed and chewed and chewed. "And is the man a Methusian?"

"Big and bluff enough to be, sir!" replied the soldier, who was still bellowing. "'Course, he jumped into the river afore we could catch him and properly examine him for the mark."

"I see," said General Murdock, nodding thoughtfully. "And where are the others?"

"The others, sir?" asked the soldier eagerly.

Swallowing the mouthful of liver, General Murdock tore a small piece of bread from the loaf before him and took a nibble. "The others who were with him on the night in question," he clarified.

A little of the excitement drained from the soldier's face. "Sir?" he said.

With his unusually small hands, General Murdock carefully brushed the crumbs from his thin lips. "Before we set out, I explained to all of you new recruits that it was inconceivable that the destruction wrought upon our camp could have been effected by fewer than half a dozen men. I explained that our objective was to find and finish them," he reminded. "You have thus far reported having located one man, but I must assume that you've also found the others, for I cannot imagine that you would be so foolish as to interrupt my dinner to report with such enthusiasm that you have failed in your ultimate objective."

The soldier suddenly looked unsure of himself. "Ah. Well, sir, as . . . as I've said, there is, um, also a girl."

"Even if she is something more than a plaything," interrupted General Murdock, turning his attention back to the liver on his plate, "do you think it likely that she is capable of doing the mischief of five men?"

"Well, uh—"

"And where is the prisoner?" asked General Murdock dispassionately, as he sawed off another tiny piece of liver and placed it in his mouth.

"I . . . I don't know," stammered the now-miserable soldier.

"Mmmmm," said General Murdock, closing his eyes.

The soldier didn't know if his general was savoring the taste of the liver or musing over his incompetent responses, but he did know that he'd blundered badly and that his only hope of escaping a punishment as torturous as the one those sleeping sentries had endured was to keep his foolish mouth shut.

Determinedly, he clamped his lips together.

At length, General Murdock swallowed and opened his eyes. "So," he said as he carefully smoothed a long, thin lock of mousy hair off his forehead. "What do you think we should do?"

The soldier's mouth popped open at once. "Do?" he blurted.

"If, in fact, this man is one of those who set fire to my tent, and if he is in the company of no one but a girl," said the General, "then I should think it obvious that we've been deliberately deceived."

The soldier nodded knowingly, but it was clear that he was completely mystified.

General Murdock sighed and pressed his lips together. "Obviously, the man in the river has been purposely leaving a trail— initially a scent trail that the dogs could easily follow and later a trail of trampled vegetation and hoofprints that anyone with a pair of eyes could follow," he explained. "The question is, why would he do this?"

"Because he's a fool!" cried the soldier, with more than a hint of his previous enthusiasm.

"No," said General Murdock patiently, "because he is clever. By leading us on, he drew us away from his clansmen in the hope that they would be able to reach safety."

The soldier's face fell, but he lifted his chin. "Well, anyway, his head should bring a fair price from the Regent," he said with the indefatigable air of one determined to find something positive to say about the situation.

"One head to the six I might have had," sighed General Murdock. "And what if those six were spiriting the child to a Methusian nest somewhere? They still exist, you know, though obviously not in the numbers they once did, thanks to my efforts. A Methusian nest might have yielded a dozen kills or more, along with any number of Methusians too young to have yet been branded with the mark of their clan—Methusians whose rejuvenating blood is so coveted by our Regent. Forgive me, but compared to the bounty that could have been, I find it difficult to be excited by the prospect of a single dead Methusian."

"A single dead Methusian *and* a girl," reminded the soldier, who could not seem to keep his mouth shut. "And perhaps the one in the river knows the way to a nest and . . . and perhaps if we, you know, pretend to leave, we could follow him in secret and see where he goes or else . . . or else perhaps we could drag him from the river before he drowns and hang him by his feet over a hot fire until he tells us everything he knows!"

General Murdock shook his head. "If the one in the river is really a Methusian—and I happen to believe that he is—we'll never learn anything from him. Have you never heard the stories of the Methusian ambassador Balthazar and the things the Regent did to him in an effort to get him to reveal the location of the Pool of Genezing? Suffice it to say that Balthazar left the dungeon very gradually, in very small pieces. Even so, our beloved Regent never got the answers he sought. Methusians are stubborn, and no clan in Glyndoria will fight more fiercely to protect its own. The man in the river is a lost cause. Now that he knows he's been found, he'll never risk endangering his clansmen by returning to the nest. No, following him would be a waste of valuable time." General Murdock pressed his small hands together and thought hard for a moment before continuing. "Here are your orders: search the riverbanks for this man and his woman. If you find them, kill the man and bring both his corpse and his woman to me. You have one hour. After that, whether they have been found or not, we will turn around and go back the way we came in the hope of discovering the spot where the man in the river separated from his clansmen. The trail will be cold, yet we will endeavor to follow it. Though the messenger has not yet returned from Parthania with orders from His Grace, I am sure he would approve this course of action, for it is our best hope of finding the nest."

"Yes, sir!" cried the soldier. "Shall I go and relay your orders now, sir?"

Tearing off another small piece of bread, General Murdock dipped it in the bloody juice of the liver and took a tiny bite. "You may," he said thoughtfully as he began to chew. "And then you may report to my steward. Inform him that you are to be hung by your feet over a hot fire. Explain to him that you are being punished for failing to do your duty and for failing to understand that you were failing to do your duty. Tell him that you are to hang until your face is well blistered from brow to chin—unless you unman yourself by screaming, in which case you are to hang unto death."

The young soldier was aghast. "What? No! I beg you, sir, *no*! Please! I'm sorry! I didn't know! This is my very first hunt, sir. *Please*!" he babbled, his voice rising in terror. "I didn't mean to make you angry, I just—"

"I'm not angry, soldier," interrupted General Murdock gently, as he used a fine linen napkin to daintily wipe a dribble of liver juice off his chin. "I am merely trying to maintain discipline among my troops. Now go, and don't forget to tell the men to bring the girl to me alive, if possible." He belched softly. "I do so enjoy an after-dinner treat. . . ."

Ten

PERSEPHONE HIT THE ICY WATER with such force that it drove half the air out of her lungs. The other half was driven out by the shock of the cold, which began leaching strength from her limbs even before her feet hit the rocky bottom of the riverbed. Glancing upward through her own floating mass of hair, she thought the surface of the water looked very far away indeed, but she did not give in to the panic that threatened to overwhelm her. Fighting against the current, she bent her knees and drove upward with all her might. The first thing she noticed after her head broke the surface and she'd sucked in a great, gulping breath was that the high riverbank off of which she and Azriel had jumped was now lined with shouting, black-clad soldiers.

The second thing she noticed was that Azriel—whose hand had been torn from hers when they hit the water—was floating face down by the far riverbank, some distance downstream.

Paying no mind to either the soldiers or the heavy clumsiness of her own weakening limbs, Persephone kicked hard in Azriel's direction. Somehow, she managed to avoid smashing into one of the jagged gray rocks that reared above the surface—or worse, lurked right beneath it. In seconds she was clutching the fallen log on which Azriel's breeches had become snagged. The bloody water swirling around his head gave her cause to suspect a head wound, but there was no time for tender ministrations. Grabbing a handful of Azriel's sodden auburn curls, she heaved his face out of the water and, grunting and straining, rolled him onto his back. Then, one arm still wrapped around the fallen log, she maneuvered his head onto her shoulder, wrapped her other arm across his bare chest and started shouting at him.

"Wake up! Wake *up*! You say you'd gladly die before seeing me harmed in any way, but what possible use is that to me, you great useless oaf?" She gave him as fierce a jostle as she could manage under the circumstances. "You'll be dead and *then* I will be harmed, and in the worst possible way!"

Desperately, she pulled herself a little farther out of the water and craned her head for a glimpse of his mouth so that she could check if he was breathing. The movement caused his head to roll toward her so unexpectedly that their lips brushed. The shock of it probably would have caused Persephone to dump him face-first into the icy water (and hold him there) had the soldiers on the riverbank not suddenly started heaving rocks at them. Realizing that she had no other course of action, Persephone adjusted her grip on the now-breathing-but-lucky-for-him-still-unconscious Azriel, pushed away from the fallen log and swam as hard as she could toward the center of the river. The soldiers jeered at the foolishness of her actions, which were bringing her and Azriel ever closer to capture or caved-in skulls, until the faster current in the center of the river abruptly caught hold of them. As the suddenly mute soldiers watched their quarry sweep past, the identical expressions of dismay on their faces were comical indeed, but Persephone was not laughing. With each passing second, she was finding it harder to keep afloat and away from the rocks. Coughing and choking, she strained to protect Azriel and to keep his head above water even as her strength began to fail and she was unable to keep her own head above water.

She went under once . . . twice . . .

Then, just as she was going under for the third time, someone grabbed the collar of her shift and hauled her to the surface. She cast a terrified look back, expecting to see the leering face of a soldier, and nearly fainted with relief at the sight that greeted her.

"Cur!" she spluttered.

Untangling his teeth from her collar, Cur ducked under her free arm and when he was sure that she was securely supported by his powerful body, he took a moment to bare his teeth at Azriel.

"Not now," admonished Persephone breathlessly. She could hear the soldiers charging angrily along the riverbank just around the bend behind them. Any moment, they would have her, Azriel and Cur in their sights, and when they did, it would be all over.

That was when she saw it: a cluster of toppled willow trees at the river's edge. Having bravely taken root in a thin patch of soil at a low spot on the riverbank, they'd half fallen into the river some time ago but hadn't yet been washed away. If she, Azriel and Cur could make it to the fallen trees, they might be able to conceal themselves within the shelter of the dripping leaves.

Using her head, she nudged Cur in that direction. He immediately turned and began paddling harder. By the time they reached their destination, Azriel had come out of his stupor. Groggily taking stock of their situation, he pulled Persephone farther back into the leafy green shadows. The next instant, soldiers stormed past them. Up and down the riverbank they ran, beating the bushes near the river's edge and shooting arrows into likely hiding spots—including the spot where Persephone, Azriel and Cur crouched motionless and shivering. Some soldiers snarled threats of torture if Azriel and Persephone failed to reveal themselves at once; others called out sweet promises of mercy and a hot meal. All searched with unflagging zeal and determination, stopping only once when a sudden, high-pitched scream rent the air—a sound so hideous that Persephone was almost grateful when Azriel pulled her closer still.

The search went on and on until, just as Persephone was beginning to fear that she and Azriel were in real danger of succumbing to the chill of the icy water, a hunting horn sounded and the soldiers abruptly stopped shouting and departed.

Unable to believe their good luck, Persephone did not move or speak until long after the birds' song and rushing water were once more the only sounds to be heard. Then she half turned her face toward Azriel and whispered, "D-do you think they're really gone?"

"I . . . do," he said haltingly.

"Good," said Persephone. Wriggling out of his lingering embrace—which she thought his precious sweetheart probably wouldn't appreciate overly much—she was about to duck out from under the willow boughs so that she could follow Cur onto shore when she noticed that Azriel wasn't moving and that his face was bathed in a fine sheen of sweat. "Does your head hurt that much?" she asked with some consternation.

"Difficult to say," he replied with a rather ghastly attempt at a smile. "As luck would have it, I find that my attention has been most effectively drawn away from that particular wound."

"By what?" asked Persephone.

"By the arrow in my arm," he replied weakly.

Persephone's gaze, which had thus far been intently focused upon Azriel's head and face, dropped at once to his arm. There, half-hidden by the dripping willow leaves, she noted the long shaft of an arrow, the tip of which was buried deep in Azriel's biceps.

"Oh, *no*," she gasped.

"Oh, yes," he said, biting back a groan. "And what's more, the arrow isn't the worst of it."

Wildly, Persephone's eyes roved over Azriel's body in search of some other grievous injury she'd somehow failed to notice—a gaping chest wound, perhaps, or a missing limb. When she could find none, she looked up at Azriel in bewilderment and said, "What could be worse than the arrow?"

"The poison on the tip of the arrow," replied Azriel, who hesitated for only a moment before adding, "for you see, Persephone, when the Regent's soldiers come hunting Methusians, they almost always shoot to kill."

"You're a *Methusian?*" she said incredulously.

"Still not the worst of it," warbled Azriel in a feeble attempt at humor.

"*Well, for pity's sake!*" cried Persephone, who could not take much more of this. "*What on earth is the worst of it?*"

"Judging by how quickly the poison is taking effect," gasped Azriel, "if I do not get help by sundown, I will almost certainly be dead by morning."

With Persephone's assistance, Azriel managed to haul himself out of the water and prop himself up against a rotten tree stump. He nearly passed out when the arrow snagged on a weed and dug deeper into his already-inflamed flesh, but Persephone slapped him hard across the face to bring him back to his senses. When he woozily protested that a kiss would have worked just as well, she threatened to slap him again. Then she sat back on her heels and tried to figure out what to do. Her mind was reeling with the revelation of what he was. A Methusian! The thought had never even occurred to her. Well, why would it? To her knowledge she'd never seen one, and it was a well-known fact that between them, the old King Octavio and the Regent Mordesius had all but wiped out the clan. It wasn't just a matter of soldiers hunting them down, either—any person in the realm who assisted in the capture or death of a Methusian was handsomely rewarded. Why, if an enslaved Erok girl—even a runaway!—were to hand a Methusian over to the Regent's soldiers, by law she would be granted her freedom forthwith. And if the Methusian she handed over was notorious—as Persephone could well imagine the one before her to be—such a girl might even be given a few coins with which to start her new—

"Well?" Azriel's voice interrupted her thoughts. "Are you going to do it?"

"Am I going to do what?" asked Persephone with a start.

"Trade my life for your freedom."

She flinched at the sudden image of Azriel dead at her feet. "Of course not," she said irritably. "If I wanted you dead, I'd have let you drown, wouldn't I?"

"Not necessarily," said Azriel with a wan smile. "You may have saved me without entirely thinking through the great advantage to yourself of having me dead."

"Don't be ridiculous," snorted Persephone, who *had* saved him without entirely thinking through the great advantage to herself of having him dead.

Azriel gave a strained chuckle. "Spectacular," he wheezed. "Then if we're agreed that you don't want me dead, perhaps you'd be kind enough to remove the arrow from my arm?"

Judging by the way he said it, he clearly assumed that he'd have to cajole Persephone to act, but without speaking, hesitating or flinching she leaned forward. Firmly pressing one hand against the already burning-hot skin of his arm, she grabbed the exposed base of the arrowhead with the other hand and carefully pulled.

Azriel groaned horribly as the arrowhead slipped free, then started retching. When he was done, he asked Persephone to rip a strip of cloth from the hem of her shift and tie it tight above the wound to slow the progress of the poison. She did as he asked, all the while silently eyeing the foul-smelling, greenish ooze that continued to trickle from the wound.

"Aren't . . . aren't you going to do something about that?" she finally asked.

He looked at her uncomprehendingly for a moment before understanding dawned upon his face. "Ah," he croaked. "I see you've heard stories of the healing power of Methusian blood."

Persephone, who was still kneeling between his splayed legs, nodded breathlessly and glanced at the wound again as though expecting it to miraculously close up before her very eyes.

Azriel swallowed hard. "Come close and I'll tell you a secret, Persephone," he whispered.

Unable to even begin to speculate what marvelous or terrible thing he might be about to tell her, she leaned as close as she could without toppling forward.

"Closer," urged Azriel.

After a moment's hesitation, she gingerly placed her hands on either side of his body and slowly leaned so close that they were a hair's breadth away from touching.

Azriel took a deep breath, so that for a brief, electrifying instant Persephone felt his hot skin through the thin, clinging fabric at her chest. "The secret," he murmured, "is not to believe half of what you hear about anything."

After giving Azriel a pinch on the leg to show him what she thought of both his secret and his suspiciously timed deep breath, Persephone listened as he explained that while Methusian blood did have healing power, this power diminished dramatically with age and even at its most potent, it was only strong enough to speed the healing of minor flesh wounds.

"But there is an antidote for the poison," he explained, wincing as he tried to get more comfortable. "Some years back, our healers concocted it and those of us who venture forth into settled parts of the kingdom try to keep several doses on hand at all times. Unfortunately, I gave away the last of my supply several days before I found you and now my only hope lies in reaching my clan. They are camped several hours away from here at the edge of the Great Forest. Will . . . will you help me reach them, Persephone? Please?"

Persephone looked south toward freedom, then north toward the Great Forest, then straight ahead into the feverish eyes of the Methusian outlaw to whom she owed nothing. Then she huffed loudly and shook her head in frustration.

"Is that a 'yes'?" he asked with a lopsided grin.

"It is," she grumbled, "though I'll have you know that no one of consequence would have blamed me if I'd decided to leave you to die in agony."

"Spoken like a true angel of mercy," murmured Azriel.

Persephone scowled. "Do you want another pinch?" she asked.

"No," he coughed, bowing his head to hide his smile, "but I thank you kindly for the offer."

Persephone helped Azriel stagger to his feet, then led him and Cur back to the pool of hot, smelly water. Fleet was nowhere to be seen, but Persephone was confident that he'd find his way back to her once he'd recovered from the trauma of his own bravery. Azriel's shirt was gone, as was his pack, but his weapons—which he'd taken care to hide among the grasses at the water's edge—were still there.

"Help . . . help me on with these," he panted as he fumbled with the knife and the sword.

"I'll do no such thing," she replied.

"But if the soldiers return, I . . . I need to be able to defend you!" he protested.

"As ever, your willingness to lay down your life is a tremendous comfort to me," said Persephone as she effortlessly plucked the weapons from his shaking hands, strapped the knife in its scabbard to her back and belted the sheathed sword around her waist.

"However, given that you appear barely able to stand on your own two feet, I expect that if there is any defending to be done, it will have to be done by me."

"Well, all right," muttered Azriel, leaning over to catch his breath. "But . . . I feel it is my duty to warn you that this situation has the potential to cause irreparable harm to my manly pride and . . . and if that happens, well, let me tell you, madam, the consequences could be *truly dire*."

He spoke with such utter solemnity that Persephone nearly choked on the bubble of laughter that welled up inside of her. "I thank you sincerely for the warning, sir," she said with equal solemnity. "But between you, me and your manly pride, I think you'll live."

Three and a half hours later, she wasn't so sure. Azriel had fought the evil that coursed through his body with dauntless courage—battling his way through the cramps and seizures, refusing to complain about the unnatural thirst that parched his throat and the waves of pain that racked his muscles. But as he once again stumbled and fell, a despairing Persephone had to admit that the poison was winning.

"How much farther?" she demanded after she'd prodded him to his feet once more. When he didn't answer but only stood there swaying, she reached up and cupped his hot face in her hands. "Azriel," she said urgently. "Azriel, look at me!"

With agonizing slowness, his bleary, unfocused gaze shifted from the horizon to her face.

"You," he croaked, as though amazed to find her standing before him.

"Yes, me," she said. "It's been three and a half hours, Azriel, and I've seen no sign of a camp—Methusian or otherwise. Are you sure this is the way?"

He opened his mouth to speak, but before he could do so, his eyes rolled into the back of his head, white froth appeared at his lips and he fell to his knees.

"No!" cried Persephone frantically. Dropping to her own knees, she made a valiant attempt to prevent him from falling to the ground face-first. But he was so much heavier than she was that she only managed to steady him for a moment before his greater weight and momentum overcame her and she found herself pinned to the forest floor beneath his outstretched body.

"You know," he whispered weakly, his lips soft against her ear, "if you'd wanted to avail yourself of my lovemaking skills, Persephone, you had only to ask."

Persephone was so shocked by his impertinence that she actually squeaked. "How dare you even suggest such a thing!" she cried. "I would *never* ask—"

"Never ask?" interrupted Azriel, chuckling in spite of the terrible pain. "But . . . hasn't anyone ever told you that . . . that it isn't seemly to take advantage of a gentleman against his will, Persephone?"

"You, sir, are no gentleman!" she huffed. "Now, get off me before I am forced to cause you further injury!"

Still faintly chuckling, Azriel laboriously did as she asked and then promptly suffered another racking fit. This one caused him to gag wretchedly and his back to arch so far that Persephone truly thought his spine would snap in half. When the fit was over, she wiped the sweat from his brow and begged him to get up, but it was useless. She was losing him.

"At least tell me where the camp is," she pleaded. "Cur can stay here with you and I'll go for help."

"No . . . use," he slurred, as his red-rimmed eyes fluttered closed once more, "you'd . . . never get back in time. I'll be dead if I don't reach it by sundown . . . remember?"

Persephone pressed the heels of her hands against her eyes. This Methusian was nothing to her and yet for some reason, she could not bear the thought of watching him die. There had to be some way to get him to his clansmen in time, there just had to be.

Then she heard it.

The unlikely sound of salvation.

CLIP, CLOP, CLIP, CLOP, CLIP, CLOP.

Springing to her feet, Persephone whirled around just in time to see Fleet canter over the ridge behind her.

"Fleet!" she shrieked as she jumped up and down and waved her arms. "Over here! We're over here!"

With a whinny of joy, Fleet launched himself down the ridge at a death-defying gallop and skidded to a halt in front of her. After giving him a quick hug to show that she was just as happy to see him as he was to see her, Persephone coaxed him to lie down next to Azriel so that she could more easily maneuver the unconscious man onto his back. She held Azriel in place while Fleet lumbered back into a standing position, then tore a few more strips from the hem of her shift and tied Azriel's hands and feet together beneath Fleet's belly to prevent him from sliding off. Finally, panting and sweating with exertion, she dropped to her knees beside Azriel's dangling head and used shouts, slaps and pinches to prod him back to consciousness one last time.

"Azriel, *how do I get to the Methusian camp?*"

"Water—" he croaked.

"Water won't help a poison thirst!" shouted Persephone in frustration. "The only help lies in reaching your clansmen and we'll never get there if you won't—"

"Water," breathed Azriel as his eyes rolled back into his head, "fall."

"He said 'waterfall'," reminded Persephone loudly.

Fleet whinnied in distress and probably would have started trampling in circles if Persephone hadn't had a firm hand on his mane.

"I know," she shouted over the din of the crashing water. "I don't understand, either."

They'd found a waterfall, all right, but Persephone couldn't see any sign of a camp. To her right was the river, to her left was wilderness and ahead was an imposing rock face. As she struggled to quell her rising panic so that she could figure out what to do next, Ivan appeared with a bloody rabbit in his talons. He swooped low enough to dangle his prize just beyond the reach of Cur's snapping teeth, then soared out over the river, folded up his wings and dove for the foot of the falls. Just before hitting the water, he made a graceful landing on a narrow ledge Persephone hadn't noticed before. As he did so, Cur charged toward the rock face, made a sharp right and disappeared only to reappear seconds later *on the ledge at the bottom of the falls!* The unexpected appearance of his teasing victim understandably ruffled Ivan, who took to the air so fast that he nearly flew headfirst into the falls, but Persephone hardly noticed.

That had to be it—the way into the Methusian camp.

"Come on!" she shouted, urging Fleet forward as fast as she dared given that Azriel was only haphazardly slung over his back. When they reached the overgrown dirt path that led to the bottom of the falls, Fleet started snorting and tossing his head. Hoping to stave off a complete nervous collapse, Persephone dashed forward and slashed off a fistful of branches from a nearby sugarberry bush. Whirling around, she waved them at the horse.

His demeanor changed instantly. The wild panic in his eyes was replaced with a hungry gleam, he stopped frothing and started drooling, and, most importantly, he began eagerly cantering toward her. Persephone hurried down the path ahead of him, her heart in her throat every step of the way. In places, the path was so narrow that she could barely keep her footing, but Fleet—whose eyes had not once left the sugarberry branches in her hand—seemed to be paying no attention at all to where he was going. Twice, Persephone actually saw the path crumble beneath his hooves, but he always seemed to be one step ahead of disaster and in no time at all he'd somehow managed to get himself *and* Azriel safely down to the ledge at the bottom of the falls.

Persephone saw at once that the rock face jutted back just enough to allow a person (or a horse) to follow the ledge behind the falls, so without pausing to give Fleet a chance to consider the thousand tons of falling water that were crashing down a whisker from his knobby shoulder, Persephone plunged behind the falls with Fleet and Cur hot upon her heels.

The next minute she found herself standing in a small cave. It did not extend very far back, but there was a large tunnel in the right wall. A cool, piney breeze issued from it, ruffling Persephone's mist-drizzled hair. After giving Fleet his tasty reward for a job well done, she stepped up to the threshold of the tunnel and tentatively poked her head into it. Over the din of the pounding falls, she heard the faint but unmistakable sound of music.

The idea of venturing forth into the tunnel brought back nightmarish memories of her months in the mines, but Persephone hadn't come all this way to see the handsome chicken thief die for her lack of courage. So, she took a very deep breath and tentatively started forward. After a mere dozen steps, she found herself swallowed up by a darkness so deep that she was utterly blind. Dread washed over her, clammy and cold as death, but she resisted the urge to turn back. Running one trembling hand along the stone wall of the tunnel and waving the other in front of her face, she forced one foot in front of the other, always bracing for the moment that the ground would give way beneath her or the roof would cave in on top of her or something feral would dart out and attack her.

But none of these things happened, and almost before she knew it, she, Cur and Fleet had reached the other end of the tunnel. Now, in addition to music, Persephone could hear voices, clinking cooking pots and cooing pigeons. An enormous, flame-haired Methusian stood with his back to the mouth of the tunnel, his sword at the ready and his foot tapping in time to the music. In the forest clearing beyond him, Methusians dressed in faded purples, yellows and reds bustled to and fro in the throes of preparation for something that appeared to have them all very excited.

Persephone didn't care or even want to know what it was, so long as it held their attention. Turning away from the opening of the tunnel, she silently unsheathed her dagger and dropped to her knees at Fleet's side. With infinite gentleness, she brushed Azriel's tangled curls from his face and pressed the palm of her hand to his hot, dry cheek. He was alive, but only just barely. The thought of him dead and cold brought a lump to Persephone's throat, but she forced herself to swallow past it. Impulsively cutting off a lock of Azriel's beautiful hair, she slipped it into her pocket. Then she reached for the cloth strips that bound his hands to his feet. Her plan was to cut him loose, lay him on the ground, retreat with Cur and Fleet as far back into the tunnel as she possibly could and then hurl a rock at the red-headed monster standing at the entrance. When he lumbered in to investigate, he would find his deathly ill clansman and call for help. Persephone had to assume that he'd thereafter pursue her, of course, but with luck, she, Cur and Fleet would have enough of a head start by that point that they'd be able to make good their escape.

It was a plan that meant she'd never see Azriel again—or even know if he lived or died—but there was no help for that. Nor, she told herself fiercely, any reason to mourn it.

Unfortunately, at the very instant she took hold of the strips of cloth, Azriel's dead weight shifted without warning and the strips jerked so tight around Persephone's fingers that she couldn't pull them free. Nor could she simply cut the strips with her dagger, for if she did so, Azriel's now-precariously dangling body would crash headfirst to the ground and his neck would surely be broken.

Even more unfortunately, before Persephone could come up with a solution to this dilemma, Fleet noticed that several of the Methusian women in the clearing were cutting up turnips.

With an enthusiastic whicker, he began to trot forward.

"No!" hissed Persephone as loudly as she dared. "No! Stop! *Bad boy!*"

But Fleet appeared to be deaf to anything but the juicy sound of his favorite tuber being sliced and diced, and though Persephone twisted and turned and dug her torn heels into the rocky floor, it was no use.

She could not stop him, and she could not get free of him.

All she could do was cringe as he bashed aside the exceedingly startled, flame-haired giant at the entrance of the tunnel and merrily trotted into the heart of the Methusian camp.

Eleven

AS MORDESIUS SLOUCHED through the narrow, torch-lit stone passageway toward the chamber where the Council was about to meet, he glared at one useless nobody after another. Most of the men in the crowd were petitioners hoping to be noticed by someone who could give them money, land, position or a satisfactory ruling against a particularly irksome neighbor. Mordesius despised petitioners—despised the unwashed smell of them and the way they clamored for the attention of their betters, always jostling and pushing and shoving ratty pieces of parchment under the noses of lords, dukes and earls. They never dared to shove anything under his nose, of course, but that was hardly the point. The point was that they were like an unruly herd of farm animals, and if it had been up to Mordesius, he'd have had them all slaughtered where they stood. But, of course, the king indulged them like spoiled children.

The king, the king . . .

Not for the first time, Mordesius cursed his own folly at having sent the king from court immediately following his coronation. Touting the benefits of fresh air and country living, Mordesius had shipped him off to a royal estate at the northern edge of the Primus Prefecture, along with a large household of his own and all the goods and furnishings befitting an infant king. He'd thought it a clever way to get the child beyond the reach and influence of the noblemen of the great houses, but what he'd not anticipated was that in the absence of a true family to care for him, the little king would turn his sunny, dimpled smile upon the servants around him in the hope of receiving the love he craved—and that they would respond by treating him with such tender affection that it would ruin him utterly. Indeed, by the time Mordesius realized what was happening, the boy was nearly ten years old and had enough of a mind and will of his own that he could not be made to see that he should not be thinking about servants, much less developing affection for them. "They are like pieces of furniture, Your Majesty," Mordesius had patiently tried to explain not long after he'd ordered the boy king brought back to Parthania. "They serve their purpose and then they are discarded or replaced. Does one talk to a chair? No. Does one consider the thoughts and feelings of a chair? No. One sits on it. And that is all." In response, young King Finnius had given him a cheeky grin and whispered, "Don't let Moira hear you talk that way, Your Grace, for I should think you've never met a piece of furniture with a will to speak its mind like she has!"

Since then, it had always been more of the same—or worse. Still, Mordesius could not be entirely disappointed with the way the boy had turned out. Over the years, he'd grown to have the look of both parents, a fact that seemed to have quelled at least some of the rumors that had dogged Mordesius since the night the queen had given birth and nearly ruined everything. The boy was tall and lithe and, despite his slight build and delicate health, he was a passable swordsman and a fine dancer. He was well educated despite his tendency to laziness when it came to his studies, and he could charm the warts off a toad by doing nothing more than being his own handsome self. He had enough natural poise and strength of character to hold the promise of becoming a strong king—something the great lords needed to see if they were to remain true to both the king and to Mordesius's regency—but he trusted Mordesius completely and almost always took his counsel.

Until lately, that is. Lately, the king kept his own counsel almost as often as he took Mordesius's, he laughed at things Mordesius did not find funny, and he spoke with increasing eagerness about the day he would sit in Mordesius's seat at the head of the Council table and become a true ruling king at last. In truth, if Mordesius did not have long-standing plans to see the boy cold and dead in his grave before he ever had a chance to rule, he probably would have found the young monarch's selfish and disloyal behavior very upsetting indeed.

Pausing now before the final turn in the passageway, Mordesius reached up and tried in vain to massage the knots out of his aching neck muscles so that he could hold his head high without pain. He then carefully smoothed down his glossy dark hair, gave the golden crest of his office a quick polish and adjusted his long, ermine-trimmed robe. No one else at court wore robes as everyday wear— not even the king himself—but Mordesius knew that his withered, uneven legs looked so ridiculous in tight-fitting silk hose or breeches that he would not suffer to wear them, not even for the sake of fashion. Robe adjusted, Mordesius lastly withdrew a silken handkerchief from his sleeve and carefully mopped the sweat from his smooth brow, for it would not do to enter the Council chamber looking anything other than utterly composed.

Today of all days, Mordesius must look like a king in all but name, for half a lifetime of planning had led up to this moment.

Taking a deep breath, he threw back his narrow shoulders, strode purposefully around the corner of the passageway and promptly collided with a young liveried page who was barreling down the passageway on some errand of great urgency. Though no more than twelve, the lad was already so sturdy that he somehow managed to stand his ground while Mordesius bounced off his chest and went sprawling across the flagstone.

Dazed by his fall and spitting with fury, Mordesius savagely tugged his robe back down over his bare legs and was about to snarl an order to have the offending page dragged to the dungeon when he looked up to see that the wretch had vanished.

"Gone, Your Grace," came an impassive but deeply dignified voice from high above. "Poor little lad took one look at whom he'd knocked over and lit off down the passageway as though the beasts of hell itself were nipping at his heels."

Choking back the venomous threats he'd been about to spew at both the wretch who'd humiliated him and at the goggling, whispering imbeciles who'd witnessed his humiliation and were staring at him still, Mordesius awkwardly staggered to his feet. Adjusting his badly rumpled robe, he attempted to rearrange his perfect features into an expression other than murderous rage.

"Lord Bartok," he said, bowing low (but not too low) to the second most powerful man in the kingdom, after himself.

Lord Bartok smiled thinly and gave a barely perceptible nod in return. The Bartok Dynasty had been around since the beginning of time. Relied upon by Erok kings and so noble that they themselves were almost royal, the Bartoks were forever plotting the rise of a favored son or daughter, or the downfall of some enemy or friend who'd risen too high for comfort. From the first, Mordesius would have liked nothing better than to crush them utterly—starting with the smug, silver-haired patriarch who now stood before him. But since he'd always known that he was going to need noble support for his daring plans to come to fruition, he'd instead chosen to lavish the Bartoks with such land, riches and titles that even they could not dispute that they owed him.

"Shall we, Your Grace?" Lord Bartok asked now, tilting his head in the direction of the Council chamber.

"Of course, my lord," murmured Mordesius with the dignity of a nobleman bred and born.

Together, they walked into the Council chamber, with its high, beamed ceiling and painted walls hung with exquisite tapestries and gloomy portraits of dead Erok kings. Sparing not even a passing glance at the portrait of the old royal fool who'd died of slow poison administered by his own trusted hand, Mordesius strode as smoothly as he was able to the head of the long table that dominated the room. When he got there, a waiting servant silently pulled out the ornately carved high-backed chair that was reserved for the king or his representative. Without looking at the servant, Mordesius slowly sat down and placed his shiny pink hands flat on the table before him.

"My lords," he breathed.

From around the table came respectful nods and murmurs of "Your Grace." Mordesius accepted their greetings with an air of polite distance, then bid them be silent with a nonchalant flick of his fingers.

The great lords of the kingdom fell silent at once. Mordesius's dark heart swelled with satisfaction.

"There are several matters I would like us to address," he began. "First, earlier this day I spoke with my ward, His Majesty the King. Among other things, we discussed the need to raze the slum that encroaches upon the north wall of the palace. It is a veritable stew of filth and disease, and the king agrees—as I know you will, my lords—that we cannot risk his precious health by its proximity."

The noblemen nodded dutifully.

"Excellent," said Mordesius. "Since we are all in agreement, I shall see to it that within the week, soldiers are sent into the slum to roust the population and burn their pestilent shacks to the ground."

"And what then, Your Grace?" asked Lord Bartok, stroking his trim silver beard. "Surely you don't mean to allow the slum's *lowborn* inhabitants to roam the streets of our fair city, begging for food and searching for another place to set up housekeeping, such as it is?"

Mordesius managed not to flinch at Lord Bartok's emphasis of the term "lowborn"—but only just barely.

"Of course they shan't be allowed to roam the streets," he said evenly. "They shall be sent where they are needed."

Or else they shall be raised to New Men, that they might pledge loyalty to me alone and thereafter join the ranks of my personal army, he added in his mind.

"Your Grace, do you not fear another revolt like the one so recently put down?" inquired a troublemaking minor lord by the name of Pembleton. Having recently come to court after having inherited his seat at the Council table from his dead father, he did not as yet appear to grasp either the subtleties of court politics or the importance of showing due deference to the Regent.

"I fear nothing," replied Mordesius flatly. "I do not doubt for a moment that the slum's inhabitants will consider making trouble, but the simple fact is that they will comply or be killed. In all the long years I have ruled this kingdom on behalf of His Majesty King Finnius, I have found that those sorts of terms generally have a calming effect on even the most base and recalcitrant of subjects."

Most of the noblemen chuckled at this, but not Lord Pembleton.

"I cannot believe that this was His Majesty's idea," he said with a frown.

"As ever, His Majesty is content to take my counsel," replied Mordesius coolly.

"He'll need to do more than take your counsel if he's to be a true ruling king someday," volunteered the fatally foolish Lord Pembleton.

"Indeed," rumbled Lord Belmont, a good-natured glutton who labored under the delusion that having ridiculously enormous shoulder pads sewn into his doublets somehow camouflaged his ponderous belly. "To be a true ruling king, His Majesty will need to settle upon a fertile wife and get down to the business of getting down to the business. After all, the first job of any king is to do his duty between the sheets as well and as often as is necessary to give his loyal subjects a healthy heir. And, of course, to see to it that his beloved queen is too exhausted to complain when he starts plowing other bean fields."

The noblemen chuckled again, winking lewdly and nudging each other.

Mordesius's heart beat faster.

It was the opening he had been waiting for.

"As it happens, my lords," he said lightly, "the question of succession is another matter that the king and I discussed at some length this day."

The men around the table instantly fell silent and eyed one another speculatively. The possibility that the king might name one of their sons as heir—or marry and get a child upon one of their daughters—was never far from their minds.

Pretending not to notice their darting glances, Mordesius licked his lips before continuing. "Unfortunately, the king has not yet expressed a willingness to marry, and I regret to inform you that he remains reluctant to name as heir any one of your sons for fear of offending the other great families and precipitating a battle for power in the event of his untimely demise."

Some of the lords looked disappointed, but Lord Bartok stuck his aristocratic nose high in the air and haughtily said, "Such a thing would never happen, Your Grace. The men you see before you are of noble blood. We would all of us pledge our unquestioning loyalty to whomever the king chose to name as heir."

Mordesius's heart beat faster still. He knew perfectly well that Lord Bartok believed his own son, Atticus, was most likely to be named heir in the absence of a true-begotten royal child and that he therefore thought he was laying a clever trap for the other great lords. The truth, however, was that he, himself, was about to become as ensnared as they.

"Is this true, my lords?" asked Mordesius doubtfully. "Would you truly pledge unquestioning loyalty to whomever the king chose to name as heir?"

Since most of them suspected that they were being led into a trap by the more powerful Lord Bartok, most of them hesitated.

But in the end, there was no help for it. They could not openly suggest that they were unwilling to support the king's choice, for to do so would be tantamount to treason.

Reluctantly, they all nodded.

Mordesius had to bite his lip to keep from shouting out in triumph. "In that case," he said, "I feel compelled to advise you that, as it happens, the king has repeatedly spoken to me of the one he wishes to name as his heir."

Breathlessly, all the lords sat forward, eager as hounds on point.

"Who is it?" demanded Lord Bartok, clenching his hands as though trying to resist reaching across the table and shaking the information out of the Regent. "Who does the king wish to name as his heir?"

"Me," lied Mordesius.

For a long moment, the lords just stared at him.

"But . . . but you're not of royal birth," that insufferable buffoon Lord Pembleton finally blurted. "You're not even of noble birth!"

Mordesius swallowed hard to keep his rage in check. "I, of course, am aware of that," he said calmly, "but as His Majesty *insists* upon reminding me, for almost seventeen years I have ruled this kingdom on his behalf, and there is not one among you who has not profited from my efforts. The king seems to feel that this should inspire in each of you a personal loyalty to me quite beyond the loyalty you have all vowed to unquestioningly pledge to whomever he chooses to name as heir." Mordesius shrugged as if to say that it was difficult to argue with the king's logic in this regard. "Add to this the fact that I have a large and powerful army of loyal New Men at my disposal, and I suppose that I begin to see why the king feels it would be in the best interest of the realm to name me as heir."

Most of the lords continued to stare at him blankly.

Not Lord Pembleton.

"But you're not of noble birth!" he repeated, as though Mordesius had somehow missed this vital fact. "And forgive me, Your Grace, but you're much too old to be named the heir of such a young king. What's more, you . . . you . . ."

He broke off then, but Mordesius knew full well that he'd been about to make some vile reference to Mordesius's terrible injuries—to say that he could never be king because he didn't *look* like a king.

"Your Grace," interjected Lord Bartok smoothly, before the blundering Lord Pembleton could do any further damage, "I am sure that I speak on behalf of my fellow lords when I say that I would be honored to pledge my loyalty to you as heir to the throne."

Mordesius was so surprised by this unexpected declaration of support that his outrage melted like butter in the sun. Thrilled quite beyond words and more touched than he would have thought possible, Mordesius placed his withered hand upon his heart and nodded graciously to all the lords except Pembleton.

"However," continued Lord Bartok, after Mordesius had finished nodding his thanks to all, "the unfortunate truth is that the Erok people have never had a king of . . . shall we say . . . less than noble birth." He smiled apologetically at Mordesius, as though the subject of his low birth was an embarrassment to them both. "That is not to say that it would not be *possible*, of course—it is merely to say that we will need to do much research and studying on the matter in the hope of finding precedence or other support for what the king proposes."

As he was speaking, some of the other lords nodded importantly and tugged at their beards; others smiled imperceptibly and whispered among themselves. Lord Pembleton looked utterly baffled, as though he'd just woken up and discovered himself sitting on the moon. Mordesius slowly took his hand away from his heart, feeling like a fool and hating them all. "I am sure that the king will be shocked and disappointed by your unwillingness to pledge your loyalty as he sees fit," he said tightly. "I know he had hoped to settle this matter promptly."

"Perhaps," said Lord Bartok silkily, "if I was able to speak with the king privately on the matter of succession—"

"No," said Mordesius flatly. "As Lord Regent, I forbid it. The king's cough has worsened of late. I will not have him pestered."

"But he is the king," said Lord Bartok, spreading his hands wide. "It is his duty to make a decision in this matter."

"He has made a decision!" bellowed Mordesius, slapping the table so hard that his scarred hand sang with pain. "What remains is for this Council to agree to honor it!" Then, abruptly realizing how very *common* he sounded when he let his temper get the best of him, he took a deep breath, smiled as disarmingly as he knew how and added in a murmur, "Of course, if you believe it necessary to undertake research in order to feel comfortable honoring the king's decision, my lords, you have my blessing to proceed with all due haste."

Many of the noblemen exchanged inscrutable sideways glances as they nodded and waited for Mordesius to dismiss them. After he'd done so, they pushed back their chairs, stood and began filing from the room. Mordesius sat rigid and unmoving in his high-backed chair, watching them go and wishing he could cut them down to size right there and then. But he couldn't, of course, because without their declared support the king would never dream of naming him heir. Instead, he had to content himself with calling Lord Pembleton back to congratulate him heartily for having had the courage to speak his mind during the Council meeting and to ask him how his only son was faring. Lord Pembleton beamed and said that the young man was faring very well indeed, his wife having recently been delivered of their first child, a healthy boy.

"Ah," crooned Mordesius, smiling faintly. "How sweet."

Twelve

THE SHOCK OF BEING unexpectedly bashed aside by a drooling horse dragging a kicking, cursing girl didn't prevent the flame-haired Methusian giant at the tunnel entrance from sending up a shrill, warbling cry of alarm. Instantly, every other Methusian in the clearing sprang into action—drawing weapons and taking up defensive positions, cutting loose tethered livestock and flinging open cages and coops, scooping up startled children and fleeing toward the cover of the forest at the clearing's edge.

As an oblivious Fleet came to a clattering halt in front of the pot full of cut turnips and a high-pitched yelp told Persephone that Cur had been captured—or worse—the commanding voice of a woman cut through the chaos: "Hold! Do not yet loose your arrows. Look—there, on the back of the beast. It is our own Azriel!"

Do not yet *loose your arrows?* thought Persephone. Frantically—and with great difficulty, owing to the fact that her now-aching fingers were still hopelessly caught in the cloth strips—she struggled to her freshly scraped knees that she might explain her business.

Before she could utter a word, however, something impossibly heavy landed on top of her, driving her face forward into the dirt and wrenching the shoulder of her trapped arm.

"Where are the others?" bellowed a voice in her ear. "What trap is this?"

Out of the corner of her eye, Persephone saw a lock of flame-colored hair; at the tender flesh of her throat, she felt the sharp point of a dagger. "There are no others!" she protested, her voice muffled by the dirt. "It is no trap! I've done nothing wrong!"

"You enter our camp through a secret passageway with a dead Methusian slung over the back of your horse and tell me you've done nothing wrong?" roared the giant on her back.

"He's not dead!" insisted Persephone, struggling as fiercely as she dared. "But he *is* dying! He hit his head . . . and nearly drowned . . . and took a poison arrow to the arm and—"

"You did these things!" accused the giant. "You and the New Men for whom you work!"

"No! You're wrong! I did none of those things! I am . . . I am an angel of mercy!" gasped Persephone, recalling the words that Azriel had spoken in jest. The sudden memory of him slumped before her, grievously wounded but still smiling, caused something inside of her to snap. Heedless of the dagger at her throat, she curled the fingers of her free hand into claws, reached over her shoulder and took a vicious swipe at her captor's eyes. "What kind of Methusian are you that you would let your own bloody clansman die, you over-grown redheaded lump?" she shouted. "Get off me and tend to him this instant or I'll . . . I'll—"

The words "up and give you a good, sound spanking" came to mind, but they caught in her throat when the giant—who still had her pinned to the ground by the back of her neck—gave a menacing growl and reared up behind her. Squeezing her eyes shut, Persephone waited to feel the cold steel of his dagger in her back, but it never came. Instead, she felt the cloth strip around her poor fingers drawn excruciatingly tight before suddenly falling free. And instead of hearing the sound of Azriel crashing headfirst to the ground, she heard the sound of him being lifted off Fleet's back and hastily carried away.

"So," boomed the giant, "I'm an overgrown redheaded lump, am I?"

Before Persephone could reply, the giant picked her up by the scruff of the neck as effortlessly as if she were a half-stuffed rag doll. Slamming her onto her feet with such force that her knees almost buckled, he grabbed her by the arm and spun her around to face him.

Tossing her hair out of her face, Persephone was about to spit at him when he gave a strangled cry and released her so suddenly that she nearly fell over. Persephone instinctively ducked down and looked around for the cause of the giant's startling behavior, but the only thing any of the Methusians seemed to be looking at was *her*. And the expressions on their faces caused a wave of goose pimples to ride up one side of her and down the other. Halfway between terror and amazement, every single one of them looked as though they'd seen a ghost.

As if by mutual accord, the awestruck crowd parted and a woman slowly stepped forward. Neither young nor old, she wore a leather canister on a cord around her neck and was possessed of a beauty that seemed to have less to do with her fine features than with the strength that radiated from her like a desert heat wave. When she spoke, Persephone recognized her as the one who'd earlier saved her from being turned into a bloody pincushion.

"Who *are* you?" asked the woman searchingly.

"That is none of your business," said Persephone, folding her arms across her chest. "Where is my dog?"

"With our dogs," replied the woman. "What is your name?"

"What is *your* name?" said Persephone, glad to hear that her voice wasn't shaking half as much as her knees were.

"My name is Cairn. How did you come to be with our Azriel?"

"What does it matter?" said Persephone, who had no intention of revealing that she'd been bought and paid for, even if it was by a

Methusian outlaw who swore he was no slave owner and was forbidden by law from owning anybody in any event. "I should think that all you need to know is that I risked my life and the lives of my animals to bring your clansman to safety."

"You might think that is all I need to know, but it is not," said Cairn. "For you see, whoever you are, your presence here on this night is a complication the magnitude of which you cannot even begin to imagine."

"I see," said Persephone as she felt a trickle of perspiration snake down her back. "Well, release my dog and my horse and order your people to stand aside, and I will leave at once so that your evening may continue . . . uncomplicated."

An agitated murmur rose up from the crowd. Cairn cocked her head to one side and gave Persephone the kind of look one might give a favorite chicken just prior to wringing its neck. Sympathetic, but resolute. "That is a most generous offer," she murmured, "but I think we both know that is impossible."

"I don't see why it should be so," blurted Persephone, uncrossing her arms so that she could slip her hand through the hole in her pocket and take hold of her dagger. "I never meant to cause trouble. I didn't even want to come here! If you feel a need to exact revenge on anyone for the complications caused by my presence here on this night, exact it on *your* Azriel. I tried to get away from him, but he is most infernally persistent, and after he cornered me in the hot spring—I'll not go into details but suffice it to say that he walked *dangerously* close to the line of ungentlemanly behavior—well, after that we ran into soldier trouble, and then he went and got himself shot with an arrow and—"

"You could have left him to die of poison," Cairn pointed out.

"Well, yes, I suppose I could have," said Persephone in a slightly exasperated voice, "but I really cannot believe that you would punish me now for failing to have done so."

"No, of course we wouldn't," agreed Cairn. "On the contrary, we would ask you to remain here as our honored guest."

"And if I don't want to remain here as your honored guest?" asked Persephone, gripping her dagger a little tighter.

"Then you will remain here as something other than our honored guest," said Cairn softly.

When Persephone withdrew her dagger to show that she was not inclined to remain as either, Cairn leaned forward and murmured something to the redheaded Methusian and another man. Persephone watched with the darting, glittering eyes of cornered prey. And when the men turned toward her—as she'd known they would—she began making gutting motions in their direction. Unfortunately, they were not the least bit intimidated by her ferocious display. With humiliating ease, they stripped her of her weapons, escorted her across the clearing, opened the door of a small, thatch-roofed hut and deposited her inside. Frightened and furious, Persephone pivoted on one foot and was about to hurl herself against the closing door when she heard a noise directly behind her. Heart in her throat, she dropped to a crouch, spun around with her fists raised high and came face-to-face with—

Herself.

Time froze. Everything froze.

Her hair, her brow, her eyes, her nose, her chin.

THUD . . . THUD . . . THUD . . .

Someone's heart was beating unnaturally loudly, but whose? Persephone's? The Other Persephone's? It was impossible to say. Or was it?

Perhaps it was not one heart beating unnaturally loudly at all, but rather two hearts beating in perfect unison.

For some reason, the thought made the real Persephone shudder. *No, not the "real" Persephone*, she corrected herself wildly, *the only Persephone!*

Slowly, she straightened up from her crouch, made a sign to ward off evil and whispered, "Who—or what—are you?"

The Other Persephone (for Persephone simply could not stop thinking of her in this way) whispered back, "I am a girl. Who—or what—are you?"

"I am also a girl," said Persephone in a hushed voice.

"A girl who looks like me," said the Other Persephone in a similarly hushed voice.

Persephone nodded, then inhaled sharply as a breathtaking possibility occurred to her. "Do you think . . . is there any chance that . . . that we are twins?" she asked.

The Other Persephone shook her head. "We do not look *that* alike—your features are finer than mine, and I see that your ears do not stick out at all whereas mine are like a pair of open barn doors. Besides, the women who attended my birth were such frightful gossips that I assure you that I and every other person in the village would've heard if a second infant had been born that night and later spirited away to parts unknown."

"Oh," said Persephone, trying not to sound disappointed. "Well, then, perhaps we are sisters?"

The Other Persephone shook her head again. "I'd have known if my parents had had and lost another child," she said. Frowning, she reached out and gave Persephone's hand a sympathetic squeeze. "From your questions, am I to understand that you know nothing of your origins? That you were orphaned as an infant?"

"I was enslaved as an infant," replied Persephone, pulling her hand away.

"Oh," murmured the Other Persephone, flushing. "I'm sorry."

"Don't be," said Persephone brusquely, "for someday very soon I shall have my freedom, you may depend upon it." Then, wanting to change the subject, she said, "What is your name, anyway? I am tired of thinking of you as the Other Persephone."

The girl smiled. "I am enjoying thinking of you as the Other Rachel," she said. "It makes me feel as though I am not really alone in the world, after all."

Persephone noted a faint but unmistakable echo of pain in the girl's words but did not press to know its source. Instead, she said, "So that is your name? Rachel?"

"Yes," said the girl, tucking a lock of dark hair behind one admittedly prominent ear. "I come from the Marinese village of Syon on the northeastern coast."

"You're Marinese?" said Persephone in surprise, having thought that all members of that clan were fair skinned and flaxen haired.

"Of course not," smiled Rachel. "I'm Erok; the lowborns of my ancestral village in the south were transported north when I was a small child. After the Marinese were relocated to the Island of Ru, the Erok nobility who took up residence in their village needed household servants, fishermen, dock workers and the like."

"And how long have you been here?" asked Persephone, gesturing to the little hut in which they stood.

"Since about midwinter," replied Rachel. "One morning, a beautiful noblewoman approached me as I was scrounging for scraps behind the fishmonger's stall. She offered me a position as a lady's maid at her husband's great estate in the country. I should have suspected something was amiss. After all, I was filthy, starving and stinking of fish—hardly what the average noblewoman looks for in a lady's maid. But I'd been so lonesome since my parents died and I was so worn down by the struggle to survive that I fairly leapt at the prospect of daily bread and a safe place to lay my head at night. Of course, as it turned out, the woman who'd approached me was not a noblewoman, and she did not have a husband *or* a great estate. She was a Methusian and she brought me here."

"Did she tell you why she'd done so?" asked Persephone, leaning closer.

Rachel shook her head. "She said only that her people had been searching for me and that my destiny would be revealed to me in time."

"The Methusian rascal who persuaded me to bring him here told me much the same thing," said Persephone, her heart clenching unexpectedly at the thought that the "rascal" might even now be dead of poison. "Do you have any idea what they meant by it?"

"No, but I gathered that I was meant to find out this night," said Rachel.

As if on cue, the music she'd heard earlier started up once more.

Persephone shivered. "Well, do you think they mean us harm?" she asked.

Before Rachel could reply, the door of the hut banged open. Instinctively, Persephone jumped in front of her doppelganger and reached for her dagger.

"I got your little knife, remember?" boomed the red-haired giant, seeing the movement.

"I remember," scowled Persephone. "What do you want?"

In response, the giant stepped aside to reveal a very small child. He was hardly more than a baby, with firm, rosy cheeks and a head full of downy curls. In his pudgy arms, he carried a loaf of dark bread that was almost as big as he was.

"Me and Tiny brung you thupper!" he shouted, toppling over backward in his excitement.

Persephone watched blankly as the little boy laboriously hauled himself to his feet, toddled over to where she stood and proudly laid the loaf of bread at her feet.

"Do you like hare thtew?" he asked, beaming up at her.

"What? Oh. Uh, yes," she stammered. Out of the corner of her eye she saw the red-haired giant named Tiny set two mugs, two bowls, one jug and a good-sized copper cauldron on the floor just inside the door.

"Hareth gotth four feetth," said the child, holding up three fingers.

"Yes, they do," agreed Persephone distractedly. "But the thing is—"

"Thum of them gotth thpotth on their fur."

"Spots on their fur . . . yes," nodded Persephone, trying not to sound impatient. "But what I want your clansman to tell me is—"

"Eat your supper," boomed Tiny as he stepped forward, scooped up the child, tucked him under one meaty arm and turned to leave. "The hour for questions—and answers—fast approaches. Honored guest or no, you'll just have to be patient until then."

Persephone looked past him through the open hut door. Outside, twilight was rapidly giving way to night. She could see Methusians in faded finery excitedly seating themselves around a roaring bonfire; she could see drummers drumming and beautiful girls with bells at their wrists and ankles leaping and twirling.

And she could see the Methusian woman Cairn sitting silent and straight-backed with her leather canister in one hand and a gleaming dagger in the other.

Slowly, Persephone brought her gaze back to Tiny's big face.

"Very well," she said placidly as she picked up the loaf of bread and tore off a chunk. "I'll be patient until then."

Thirteen

"BUT YOU SAID 'VERY WELL'!" whispered Rachel in alarm as she watched Persephone hurriedly tear chunks of bread off the loaf and stuff them into her pockets. "You said 'I'll be patient until then'!"

"I lied," said Persephone tersely. "We have to get out of here. Now."

The sudden clash of cymbals made them both jump.

"Why?" cried Rachel, wringing her hands. "We've no proof that the Methusians mean us harm!"

"None except that they kidnapped us without explanation, that they consider me a complication and that the woman who appears to be their leader currently awaits us with knife in hand."

Rachel brought her knuckles to her lips. "But . . . but if they truly mean us harm, why would they trouble themselves to shelter and feed us?" she asked desperately as the cymbals clashed again and again.

"Why does one shelter and feed a calf or a pig?" said Persephone in a hard voice.

Rachel bleated with fear. Then, without warning, she flung her arms around Persephone and hugged her hard. "I'm so afraid!" she whispered. "But if you really think we should go, we'll go. Just tell me what you want me to do!"

Persephone was so startled by the unexpected feel of warm, friendly arms holding her close that for a handful of seconds, she could hardly breathe, let alone speak. When she finally recovered, she awkwardly untangled herself from Rachel's clinging embrace, told the trembling girl the plan and made her promise not to follow until she'd heard the all-clear signal.

Then, turning toward the back wall of the hut, Persephone began to climb, digging her fingers and toes into the cracks between the logs. When she reached the ceiling, she began burrowing her way through the thick thatching. At length, her head popped free; a bit more wriggling and the rest of her was free. After pausing just long enough to take a deep breath of the crisp, fragrant breeze that blew out of the forest, she slowly began sliding down the roof. She was nearing the bottom edge and about to leap for the ground when she suddenly noticed a shadowy figure standing motionless by the wall of the hut. With a muffled yelp, she twisted onto her stomach and desperately clawed for a handful of thatching to stop her fall. It was too late for that, however, and the next thing Persephone knew she was on the ground in an ungainly heap with her skirt up around her ears.

Grunting and flopping around, she yanked down her skirt, jumped to her feet, gamely raised her fists and prepared to confront the shadowy figure. Even as she did so, however, she found herself pushed up against the hut with both wrists pinned above her head. She immediately tried to drive her knee into her captor's groin. He managed to evade her (though just barely), then stepped forward so that she had no room to try again—so that she was unable to squirm or even move without feeling some part of her brush up against some part of him. Just as she was about to drive her head forward in the hope of smashing her captor's nose with her forehead, an unsteady but infinitely warm and familiar voice murmured,

"I see that you still have the grace and poise of a natural dancer, Persephone."

Her heart leapt into her throat even as her knees went weak with relief. "And I see that you still have the irksome habit of showing up in the dead of night unannounced and unwelcome, *Azriel*," she said coolly. "Feeling better, are we?"

"Yes," he said, "the healers' antidote is wondrously effective, though I admit that I'm still rather weak."

"And rather hot," she added distractedly as her skin began to tingle in response to the waves of heat that radiated off every part of him.

"Rather hot?" he echoed.

Persephone could hear the smile in his voice. "I meant *feverish*," she said as she tried without success to jerk her hands free of his grasp. "Why are you here, Azriel?"

"Two reasons," he said, grunting softly as he shifted his weight from one leg to the other. "First, I wanted to prevent your inevitable escape attempt as I did not wish to spend the better part of tomorrow collecting the pieces of you and Rachel that would have been strewn about by the ravenous night beasts of the forest had you ventured therein."

From inside the hut there came a small whimper.

"Second," continued Azriel, who was wheezing ever so slightly, "Cairn wanted me to prepare you for what you will see and hear when you join my people at the fire this night."

On the far side of the clearing, the music suddenly grew louder, making Persephone's blood run so hot and so fast that she wanted to slap Azriel hard across the face and kiss him hard on the mouth, all at the same time.

"Azriel," she whispered, "Cairn said my presence here is a complication. Is that because your people need a girl who looks like me— but only *one* girl who looks like me?"

"Yes," he whispered as he slowly released her hands but made no move to step away. "The night I met you I told you I'd been looking for you for as long as I could remember. We'd all been searching, and when Fayla discovered Rachel scavenging for scraps behind the fishmonger's stall, we thought we'd found her. But after I met you and saw how dauntless you were, I started to believe that you were the girl—"

"What girl?"

"The girl at the heart of a prophecy made long ago," replied Azriel, leaning against the wall of the hut as though for support. "A prophecy made by the last surviving Methusian Seer—an old woman murdered fifteen years ago this very night."

On the other side of the wall, Persephone could sense Rachel holding her breath, and she found that she, herself, was also hardly daring to breathe. "What did this prophecy say, Azriel?" she asked.

"That there would be a great Methusian king whose coming would unite the five clans of Glyndoria and set things to right for all people," he said, his voice tinged with excitement. "And that a girl who looks like you—and Rachel—would have something to do with bringing this king to power. And that maybe—just maybe!— this king was meant to rediscover the Pool of Genezing and see my people safely settled by its waters' edge once more!"

For a moment, Persephone could only stare at Azriel, indignation swelling in her breast at the fact that her whole world had been turned upside down on account of some ridiculous *fantasy*.

"So," she finally said, "this is the reason Rachel was kidnapped and I was bought like a mule on market day and dragged halfway across Glyndoria?"

"Persephone—"

Pressing her palms against Azriel's burning chest, she shoved him away with such force that in his weakened state, he actually staggered backward a few steps. "You had no right," she said flatly. "Moreover, it makes no sense at all. Rachel and I are both penniless orphans— how could either of us ever play the kingmaker? And how could a Methusian ever rule Glyndoria? The Erok have all but conquered the kingdom and their nobility would never bow to a Methusian king. Never! Neither would any of the other three clans! As for the healing Pool of Genezing—well, everyone knows it is the stuff of fairy tales."

"It is *not* the stuff of fairy tales," insisted Azriel. Taking her wrist, he pulled her close once more. "It *is* real and a Methusian king *will* come and tonight we will finally find out what part you—or Rachel—will play in bringing him to power."

"Oh, really?" said Persephone, managing to sound sarcastic in spite of her sudden breathlessness. "And how, exactly, will you decide which of us is expected to do this impossible thing?"

"I don't know."

"Well, what will you do with the girl who is not the one you seek?"

"I . . . don't know that, either."

The truth—which was that the Methusians could never risk releasing someone who could lead the Regent's New Men to their secret camp—hung between them. But Persephone already had a plan to deal with that, so all she said was, "Even if all you say is true, Azriel, the path to setting a Methusian upon a throne recognized by all clans would be a dangerous and bloody one, indeed. What on earth makes you think that either Rachel or I would be willing to follow it?"

Azriel slid his free arm around her waist so that he could pull her closer still. "The girl who is meant to follow the path will have no choice but to do so, for it is her destiny," he whispered. "Now come. Let us fetch Rachel so that we may join my clansmen by the fire and learn the answers my people have waited fifteen long years to know."

A few heartbeats later, Persephone was standing by the fire next to Rachel, the eyes of every Methusian in the clearing upon them. Directly before her sat Cairn, still holding the canister and the dagger; beside Cairn sat an exceptionally beautiful Methusian girl. Asleep in the arms of the girl was the little boy who'd earlier "brung them thupper."

To hide her sudden nervousness, Persephone lifted her chin and threw a cool look at Cairn. The older woman returned her look with an equal measure of coolness. For a long moment nobody moved, and the only sounds were the crackling of the fire and the whisper of the wind through the trees.

Then Cairn began to speak.

"A week ago, we received a message by carrier pigeon that this boy and his family had been discovered masquerading as Erok," she said quietly, gesturing toward the sleeping child. "The family's neighbors—people with whom they'd shared many years of good and hard times alike—had sent word to the Regent Mordesius, murdered the parents and older siblings and shut away the child until the New Men could arrive to transport him back to Parthania and such horrors that his certain death, when it finally came, would seem a great mercy indeed." Here she paused. "The Methusian who sent the carrier pigeon could not intervene for fear of endangering his own masquerading family, so Azriel, Tiny and the others tracked the New Men, set fire to their camp and liberated the child." She paused again. "It is our hope that it was one of the last such rescue missions we shall ever have to undertake." Reaching into a small wooden chest at her feet, she brought forth an ancient-looking scroll. With painstaking care, she unrolled it and held it up so that Persephone and Rachel could see it. Drawn in charcoal, the bold, confident lines of the sketch were remarkably few, but the likeness to her and Rachel was so unmistakable that it made the hair on the back of Persephone's neck stand on end.

"While deep in her final trance, our last Seer drew this sketch," said Cairn. "One of you is this girl, while the other is—"

Persephone held up her hand. "Before you go any further, you should know that Rachel and I have sworn a blood oath that if harm should come to one of us, the other shall immediately impale herself upon the nearest sharp implement," she lied.

This announcement made Rachel gasp aloud and set the Methusians to muttering among themselves.

Cairn quieted her people with a sweep of her hand, then raised a fine, soot-colored eyebrow at Rachel and asked, "Is this true?"

Mutely, Rachel bobbed her head up and down even as her eyes darted about wildly as though in search of the implement upon which she might be forced to impale herself forthwith.

Leaning forward slightly, Cairn gave Persephone a penetrating look and said, "You inspired her to lay down her life for your cause."

"It was she who inspired me," corrected Persephone, who had no intention of letting Rachel be viewed as the "complication."

Half of the Methusians nodded emphatically at the news that the blood oath had been Rachel's idea; the other half frowned as though this made no sense at all. Azriel, who'd just eased himself down onto a seat beside the beautiful girl holding the sleeping child, looked at Persephone as if to say that he wasn't fooled by her tricks for an instant.

She ignored him.

"As you can see," said Cairn, "my people are divided on the issue of which one of you is the girl we seek. Since we've not been able to agree upon a suitable manner by which to resolve our dilemma, for the time being, you are both safe, blood oath or not."

"For the time being," echoed Persephone. Out of the corner of her eye, she saw Azriel lean over and whisper something to the girl beside him. *Probably his beautiful sweetheart*, she thought irritably, before turning her attention back to Cairn.

"There is no use trying to cross bridges before we come to them," said the older woman, as though plans to indefinitely detain or dispose of one girl or the other was an issue of minor importance. "Tonight, there is but one bridge to cross."

The flames of the bonfire seemed to leap higher with these words. Somewhere in the darkness, an owl hooted.

Persephone said nothing, but her gaze darted to the leather canister clutched tight in the older woman's hand. Obviously, it contained a message from the long-dead Seer explaining how the girl in the sketch was meant to fulfill her destiny. What the message was going to say, Persephone could not imagine—except for imagining that it was going to spell grave danger for her and Rachel.

Suddenly fearful of where this madness was about to lead, Persephone cast a desperate glance at Azriel, but he was too busy listening to the whispered response of his beautiful sweetheart to notice. Before she could even begin to resent this, the drums began to beat once more. Rachel whimpered softly and reached for Persephone's hand. Cairn slowly rose from her seat and held the stiff leather canister aloft for all to see. With trembling hands, she lifted the dagger she'd been holding, cut through the wax that sealed the canister and pried off the top. Eagerly, she removed and unrolled a scroll. When she read the words written upon it, however, the eagerness in her eyes abruptly faded. Frowning, she gazed up at the night sky for a long moment before handing the scroll to Azriel. With a puzzled expression, he, too, looked up. Then he held the scroll out to Persephone, who took it and studied it very closely before showing it to Rachel.

"I don't understand," said Rachel, after she'd laboriously sounded out the words under her breath. "What does this mean?"

The beautiful Methusian girl stood up. "What does what mean?" she asked impatiently. "What does it say?"

"I think . . . I think it says 'Look up'," said Rachel doubtfully.

The Methusians stared blankly at her for a moment. Then they all looked at each other. Then, rather uncertainly, they all looked up.

Even as they did so, there came a loud screech from high overhead. The next instant, Ivan swooped down, dropped a bloody bundle of feathers at Persephone's feet and did several spectacular loop-the-loops before finally alighting upon her shoulder and moodily glaring at the Methusians as though he would gladly peck out the eyes of every last one of them.

"Is that your hawk?" asked Tiny in a hushed voice.

"No," said Persephone. "He is my friend."

"He has killed one of our pigeons," observed Cairn, who was staring fixedly at the bloody bundle of feathers on the dusty ground at Persephone's feet.

"He only wanted to bring me a gift—he didn't know it was one of your pigeons," said Persephone quickly, before anyone could think to punish Ivan for his misdeed. "I'm sure if he'd known, he never would have attacked her."

Azriel started to snort in disbelief, but stopped in a hurry when he noticed Ivan ruffling his feathers threateningly.

Cairn was paying no attention to any of them. Walking over to where the murdered pigeon lay, she picked up the unfortunate creature with such gentleness that Persephone wondered if perhaps it was still alive and that Cairn meant to use Methusian magic to somehow heal its terrible wounds. Then she saw the older woman carefully removing something from the pigeon's little stick leg.

"Of course," whispered Rachel, giving Persephone's hand a squeeze. "It was a *carrier* pigeon."

Persephone said nothing, only watched as Cairn unfolded a scrap of paper so tiny that Persephone could not imagine how anyone could have written anything at all upon it. But apparently someone had, for after she'd read its contents, Cairn sighed deeply and looked around the clearing, her expression an odd mixture of exultation and dread.

"It is a message from Parthania," she announced. "Another family has been identified as Methusians; another set of parents is dead. Three of their children were murdered alongside them; a fourth child, a boy, happened to be in the care of trusted friends at the time of the attack. He is being hidden still, but the family that hides him grows too fearful of their own safety to keep him."

Rachel gave Persephone's hand another squeeze. Persephone said nothing, only watched as Ivan took flight and disappeared into the night.

The beautiful girl glanced down at the little boy in her arms. "What do you think this means, Cairn?" she asked. "Do you think this means that Rachel is meant to go to Parthania to rescue the child?"

"I do not think that Rachel *or* Persephone is meant to rescue the child, Fayla," said Cairn thoughtfully, "for I cannot believe that we are meant to risk a child's life on untried rescuers. I do believe, however, that whichever one of them is the girl in the picture is meant to accompany you and the others to Parthania. I cannot guess what she is meant to do there nor how she is meant to do it, but now, more than ever before, I have faith that the answers we seek will be provided as they're needed."

Almost all of the Methusians nodded in emphatic agreement: they'd looked up as they'd been bidden by a long-dead Seer and a clear message had been delivered from the heavens. Their faith had been affirmed in the most unequivocal terms; their hope that better days lay ahead had been renewed.

Only Azriel looked troubled. "Are you sure about this?" he asked, as the Methusian girl Fayla edged forward to stand near his side. "Parthania can be a treacherous place."

"That is true," agreed Cairn, turning her dark eyes on Persephone, "but it is also the glittering imperial capital and the seat of all power in Glyndoria. Where better to forge the first link in the chain of events that will, at long last, see the great Methusian king set upon his throne?"

Fourteen

IT WAS SEVERAL DAYS after the disastrous Council meeting, and Mordesius was still beside himself with fury.

In a dreaded place deep within the bowels of the castle, he raged on about the meeting and about the great lords who dared to think themselves better than he.

"Their objection to my being named heir wasn't just a matter of my low birth, either," he snarled as he hurled an oversized pair of rusted pincers at the iron cage that hung from the low ceiling. The inhabitant of the cage, having long since sunk into madness, grabbed the bars of its tiny prison, bared its crowded teeth at Mordesius and hissed loudly.

General Murdock, who'd always felt oddly at home in the foul, smothering darkness of the dungeon, nonchalantly pointed the glowing-hot tip of a poker in the direction of the cage. The cage's inhabitant hissed once more, then abruptly let go of the bars, shrank back and covered its milky eyes with its hairless arm.

Mordesius's sunken chest heaved beneath his robe. "I know what Pembleton was thinking—"

"He is the nobleman whose only son will soon be found guilty of treason and beheaded, is he not? The one whose newborn grandson will shortly thereafter fall ill and die?" said General Murdock, his ratlike face half-hidden in the shadow beyond the light from the fire that never stopped burning.

"You know he is," spat Mordesius. "And I know what he was thinking during the Council meeting—what they were all thinking! They were thinking that even if I bled purple, they would never in a thousand years allow me to be named heir because I do not *look* the part of a king! They were thinking that I would never be able to lead an army into battle, never be able to get a son upon a noble young wife. They were thinking that the proud, *proud* Erok would never accept a king whose body was a scarred, twisted wreck—would never line the streets of Parthania to cheer for a king whose head ducked and bobbed beneath the weight of the crown!"

"The people would do as you bid, Your Grace, else your army would destroy them," offered General Murdock as he used the long, thin nail of his little finger to delicately pick a shred of old meat from between his long, yellow front teeth.

"But I want them to worship me as they would a prince of the blood," cried Mordesius in an almost plaintive voice as he slumped against the bloodstained butcher block before him. "I want them to bow to me and know in their hearts that I am greater than the very greatest among them!"

Another of the inhabitants of the room laughed hoarsely at this—a fearless sound for which he would later suffer the violent loss of another small piece of himself. General Murdock briefly trained his beady eyes upon the hulking wretch chained to the glistening wet wall, then flicked his gaze onward to yet another cage. Shoved into the darkest corner of the low-ceilinged room, past the dusty remains of one who'd long since withered in the darkness, this particular cage was currently empty but for a thin scattering of dirty straw, one filthy hair ribbon and a hastily discarded rag doll.

The General then flicked his gaze back to Mordesius. "Surely you've not lost hope that your old injuries will one day be healed," he murmured. "After all, one only has to look at how remarkably well your facial treatments work to know that true healing power courses through the veins of Methusian whelps. Surely it is just a matter of time before you discover the key to unlocking its power for greater uses."

"I have spilled an ocean of the most potent Methusian blood in the kingdom and have discovered nothing but that Methusian infants squirm and squeal like piglets when stuck," snapped Mordesius. "Yet it is true that I have not lost hope of growing well and strong, Murdock, because liar though he was, I know Balthazar spoke the truth when he spoke of discovering the Pool of Genezing. It is out there somewhere, Murdock. I know it is! And you must find it for me!"

General Murdock gave his nose a dainty scratch. "Of course I and my men will continue to search for it," he said diffidently, "but I must remind Your Grace that no Methusian, nor any of the tribal animals who knew Balthazar"—here, he nodded casually in the direction of the hulking wretch, the mad caged creature and the corpse—"has ever been persuaded to reveal what, if anything, Balthazar told him about the location of the pool. Moreover, in all our long years of searching Glyndoria, neither I nor my men have ever come across any trace of it."

"Oh? And how can you be sure that one of your men has not found it and kept the information to himself?" demanded Mordesius.

General Murdock smiled thinly. "The men have no idea what they are looking for, Your Grace," he reminded. "There has never been any reason to tell them, for they are all so greedy and lacking in discretion that if one were to find something as miraculous as healing waters, he would fall all over himself in his haste to tell me of his amazing discovery and receive his just reward."

"And what would be his just reward, Murdock?" breathed Mordesius, who already knew the answer.

"Death, of course," replied the General with a gleam in his eye. "Death to him and to every man he told, so that none but you and I would ever know the true location of the pool."

"Very good," murmured Mordesius.

Not for the first time, he marveled at what a perfect henchman he'd found in General Murdock. Murdock himself wasn't perfect, of course—as his most recent failure to guard against the escape of the Methusian prisoner had proven—but he was strong, loyal, ruthless and, amazingly, he never sought any reward but to be allowed to continue to serve. Plus, he was so repulsive to look upon that, burned body notwithstanding, Mordesius always felt more gloriously handsome by contrast.

All in all, he was such a perfect henchman that if Mordesius were someday strong and well and capable of leading the New Man army himself, he thought it possible that he might even keep General Murdock around.

It was unlikely that he would, of course—but it was definitely possible.

"You will redouble your efforts to seek out the Pool of Genezing, Murdock, and you *will* find it," ordered Mordesius now. "In the meantime, I will show the great lords that a king is not the only one who can ride among the people like a majestic young god."

Absently, he picked up an odd-shaped implement from a nearby tray and began tenderly fingering its razor-sharp edge.

In spite of his great bravery, the wretch chained to the wall gave a small moan.

"I will show them," continued Mordesius softly, as he turned and began slouching toward his unfortunate victim, "that though I am yet crippled by my terrible injuries, I am stronger than they think."

Fifteen

PERSEPHONE AWOKE EARLY to the quiet sounds of the Methusian camp slowly coming to life.

As she stared into the predawn gloom of the hut, listening to the crackle of kindling catching fire, the muted clink of cooking pots being set to simmer and the slosh of water being hauled, she thought back to all that had transpired the previous night. Though she had to admit that the arrival of Ivan and the dead pigeon at the exact moment that the Methusians had looked up had been a rather remarkable coincidence, she refused to believe it had been anything more than that. The idea that a Methusian king was coming and that he was somehow meant to lead the Methusians to their mythical healing pool was preposterous. That said, while she'd initially balked at Cairn's presumptuous announcement that she and Rachel would accompany the orphan rescuers to Parthania, she'd quickly come to realize that the journey to the imperial capital would be the perfect opportunity to escape. After all, she and Rachel would be well provisioned and heading toward settled country where even a pair of nearly identical runaways might find a way to get lost in the crowds. Moreover, they wouldn't need to suffer a moment's guilt over abandoning an orphan to his death because the Methusians didn't expect them to have a hand in rescuing the child. Best of all, since Persephone knew the way to the Methusian hideout, there even existed the possibility that she might someday, somehow, be able to return for Fleet and Cur—if they didn't manage to track her down first.

Jostling Rachel awake, Persephone quickly explained all this, then sat back and waited for Rachel to clap her hands with excitement at the prospect of freedom.

To her surprise and dismay, however, Rachel only frowned and said, "I don't know."

"What don't you know?" asked Persephone, trying not to sound impatient.

"I don't know if I want to escape," said Rachel. "Last night, when I overheard Azriel speaking of the destiny of the girl who looked like us, I thought . . . well, I thought that I should like to have a destiny such as that."

Persephone stared at her blankly.

"I want my life to matter, Persephone," explained Rachel. "My father died of the Great Sickness when my mother was with child, but before he did, he told me that he believed I was meant to do something important with my life. When my mother came to her time, I thought that perhaps helping to deliver her baby was the important thing I was meant to do. But the child—my brother—was born dead. So then when my mother fell ill, I thought that perhaps saving her was the important thing I was meant to do. But she died, too, and since then I have done nothing but survive. I do not know if the prophecy of the Methusian king is a true one or not, but I think that I would happily lay down my life in the pursuit of it."

Before Persephone could muster an argument to these exasperatingly selfless sentiments, the door of the hut opened to reveal the smiling faces of Azriel and the little boy from the night before. Azriel was carrying a brimming basin of water; the boy was carrying soap and towels. They were halfway across the room when a sound outside the hut made Azriel glance over his shoulder. The next instant Cur burst through the doorway, and such was his eagerness to reach Persephone that he apparently felt he had no time to run around obstacles in his way but must run straight through them. As it happened, the only obstacles in his way were Azriel's legs, and before Azriel could jump, dodge or even curse, they were violently swept out from under him and he crashed to the hard-packed dirt floor with a thud, a splash and a clatter.

Biting her lip to keep from laughing, Persephone peeked past Cur (whom she was hugging tightly in spite of his tremendously naughty behavior) to see Azriel looking pained, outraged and *wet*. The little boy wasn't nearly so concerned with sparing Azriel's feelings. Pointing one chubby finger at his drenched clansman, he clutched his belly and laughed heartily.

"Um, are you all right?" asked Rachel timidly.

"Fine," growled Azriel, flicking his dripping auburn curls out of his eyes so that he could better glare at Cur, who promptly started barking at him.

At this, the child clapped and laughed harder.

"It isn't nice to laugh at people, Sabian," grumbled Azriel as he clambered to his feet and shook like a wet dog.

"Oh, he wasn't laughing *at* you, Azriel—he was laughing *with* you," protested Persephone, who was still struggling to keep a straight face. "Isn't that right, Sabian?"

"No," said the little boy solemnly as he reached up to scratch his nose. "I wath laughing at him."

Several moments of unrestrained hilarity followed this guile-less confession, and Azriel suffered them with an air of severely injured dignity.

"We leave for Parthania within the hour," he finally huffed. "I'll fetch more water, and after you've washed, you may join me to break your fast and discuss plans."

A second basinful of water was delivered without incident, and after Persephone and Rachel had scrubbed their hands and faces and tidied their hair, they headed outside in search of Azriel. They found him seated at a table set beneath a sturdy canopy of thatching; across from him sat the redheaded Tiny and the beautiful Fayla.

His injured dignity seemingly having made a complete recovery, Azriel gallantly jumped to his feet and indicated to Persephone and Rachel that they should sit on the bench next to him. "There is sausage, porridge, boiled eggs, pie, ale and leftover hare stew," he said, gesturing to the bounty spread across the table. "Eat and drink as much as you like."

Rachel did not need to be told twice. Eagerly, she ladled an enormous portion of thick, steaming porridge into the bowl before her, laid five sausages over top of the porridge, piled three eggs on top of the sausages and gave the pie and the stew a look that promised she'd be back for them in due course. Smiling broadly, she sat back down, poured herself a large mug of ale and dug in.

Persephone ate, too, but with significantly less gusto, owing to the looks that Azriel's beautiful sweetheart was giving her. The previous evening, he'd left for bed immediately following the great reveal, and even though he'd looked *perfectly* capable of taking off his own boots and pulling the blankets up to his own chin, the beautiful Methusian girl had *insisted* on accompanying him to give him what assistance she could. Objectively speaking, even now Persephone thought that the two of them had made a rather disgusting spectacle of themselves, what with Azriel limping along (even though it was his *arm* that was injured) and Fayla glued to his side, tenderly crooning and fussing over him (even though he was a grown man and not some ridiculous overgrown baby). Not that it mattered to her, of course, but—

". . . the matter?" Azriel was saying.

"What?" blurted Persephone.

Azriel leaned so close that she felt the warmth of his uninjured arm pressed against hers. "I asked if something was the matter," he murmured, gesturing to her barely touched plate.

"No," she mumbled with a darting glance at Fayla, who was staring fixedly at their touching arms.

Azriel did not seem to notice Fayla's stare. With a frown he pressed even closer to Persephone—so close that she could feel his warm breath tickling her neck. "Are you sure there's nothing the matter?" he asked.

Persephone nodded, not trusting herself to speak.

Across the table, Fayla narrowed her eyes and folded her arms across her chest.

A blissfully oblivious Azriel proceeded to explain to Persephone and Rachel that the journey to Parthania would take about five days. They'd all be disguised as Erok lowborns for the first four days, he explained; after that, Fayla would dress as a noblewoman, he and Tiny would play her armed escort, and the two of them would play her servants.

"Her *servants*?" exclaimed Persephone with ill-disguised dismay. "Why do we have to play her *servants*?"

"Because we need someone to play a noblewoman," explained Azriel, "and noblewomen always travel with servants."

"Well, *fine*, but . . . I mean . . . I just don't see why she gets to play the part of the noblewoman," spluttered Persephone, cringing to hear how childish she sounded.

"Acting the part of a noblewoman is harder and more dangerous than you might think, Persephone," said Azriel. "The slightest gesture or turn of phrase can give you away, as can the inability to answer simple questions upon the instant. Do either you or Rachel know enough about any noble family in this realm to pass yourselves off as a distant—and thus safely obscure—relation? Could either of you comfortably speak at length about this noble family's long and distinguished history, or give me the name of the eldest brother of your so-called noble father's second wife? Could you tell me which nobleman sits next to your so-called great-uncle at the Council table, or describe in detail the most recent execution you attended? Could you spit in the eye of a New Man soldier who was accusing you of imposture and demanding that you get down on your knees and beg for a swift death? You may think you could—and you could be right—but Fayla *knows* she could, for she has done it before and done it well enough to save lives."

"You've spit in a soldier's eye?" Rachel asked Fayla in a wondering voice.

"The wretch is lucky I didn't have him flogged to within an inch of his life," said Fayla, sounding as haughty and cold and noble as could be.

Rachel laughed aloud at her cleverness.

Irritably wondering why Azriel's sweetheart had to be beautiful, brave *and* clever, Persephone shoved a whole sausage into her mouth and muttered, "Very well. Fayla will play the noblewoman. What else do we need to know?"

"For the first four days we'll be traveling through sparsely settled country where our greatest danger will be bandits," explained Azriel. "That is why we'll be dressed as lowborns, for to have Fayla dressed as a noblewoman in the wilderness would attract those who would think nothing of robbing and forcing himself upon a noblewoman, slitting her throat and the throats of all those in her company and dumping their bodies where none but wild beasts would ever find them."

Rachel covered her mouth with her hand but said nothing.

"Once we are within a day of Parthania, the countryside will be more populous," continued Azriel. "There, having Fayla dressed as a noblewoman should protect us from being rounded up by New Men and also from the bored sons of nobility who enjoy making sport of lowborns almost as much as they enjoy hunting and carousing. It will also help get us into Parthania, for lowborns, enslaved persons and other so-called undesirables are not allowed passage through the gates of the imperial city unless they can prove that they are on the business of someone more important than themselves. While we could almost certainly come up with a convincing story in that regard, it is a safer and more desirable thing by far to walk through the gates unmolested."

"What happens once we're inside?" asked Rachel.

"We find somewhere for Fayla to change back into her lowborn clothes so that she can make her way into the slum and retrieve the child," explained Azriel.

"Why not send him to fetch the child?" asked Persephone, pointing at Tiny. "Or you? I would think that a big, strong man would stand a better chance of success than a mere girl."

"You would think so," growled Tiny, who did not appear to appreciate hearing the beautiful, brave, clever Fayla referred to as a "mere" anything. "But among the Erok, hauling children around is women's work, so if a man was seen carrying a child it would instantly raise suspicion."

Azriel nodded. "After Fayla returns with the child, she will change back into her gown and we'll begin the return journey at once. If all goes well, we should be back here within a week of rescuing the child."

For a long moment, there was only silence around the table as the five of them contemplated the many reasons why things might not go well.

Then Rachel said, "And have you any idea at all how we're to go about finding and crowning the Methusian king, Azriel?"

Smiling slightly, Azriel shook his head. "I'm sorry, Rachel, I don't. However, if Cairn can have faith that the answers we seek will be provided as they're needed, then so can I."

Plans discussed and their fast broken, Persephone and Rachel returned to the "guest cottage" to change into the disguises Azriel had provided. In addition to identical drab, shapeless smocks that hung half-past the knees, there were identical dirty head wraps and identical pairs of soft-soled ankle boots that looked (and smelled) like old men's crusty stockings.

"I cannot believe that we have to wear these horrible things and *she* is going to be dressed as a noblewoman," complained Persephone as she picked something sticky, brown and *disgusting* off one of her "boots."

"Not at first, she isn't," comforted Rachel as she gamely tied a length of limp cord around her waist. "And consider this—these items are far more durable than our threadbare old ones."

Persephone, who admired beauty and elegance in clothing infinitely more than she did durability, merely grunted and adjusted her smelly head wrap. She then ripped a large hole in the right pocket of her ugly new smock so that she would have easy access to her dagger, which had been returned to her by Tiny. Finally, she transferred to the left pocket her bit of lace, her rat tail and, after promising herself she'd throw it away later, the auburn curl.

After she and Rachel were finished dressing, they went back outside to find Azriel, Tiny, Fayla and the rest of the Methusians waiting for them at the opening of the tunnel that ran beneath the waterfall. Persephone was trying to figure out how Fayla was managing to make her lowborn disguise look charming and rustic (instead of ugly and disgusting) when she heard the familiar sound of a much-beloved horse losing his mind with joy at the sight of her.

As she turned to greet Fleet, she noticed that he was wearing a saddle and panniers as well as several large packs. "What is this?" she asked Azriel in amazement.

Azriel gave a long-suffering sigh. "Well, since we *are* going to need a horse and since we *know* that this particular beast will find some way to follow you and make a complete nuisance of himself anyway, I decided to bring him along from the start."

"I'm amazed that he stood still to be saddled," marveled Persephone.

"I've never seen a horse eat so many carrots," grunted Tiny, by way of explanation.

"Even so, he's always felt that doing the bidding of humans is beneath him," confided Persephone.

Azriel rolled his eyes. Then he, Tiny and Fayla bade farewell to Cairn and the other Methusians, who responded with heartfelt cries of goodbye and good luck.

"And good luck to you," said Cairn as she watched Persephone peel Sabian's chubby little arms from around her legs. "I shall look forward to our next meeting."

If good luck is with me, you shall never see me again, thought Persephone.

But, of course, she didn't say this. Instead, she murmured something to Cairn about sharing her sentiment, whistled for Cur and followed Azriel and the others into the darkness of the tunnel.

Sixteen

THAT FIRST DAY of the journey, Azriel set such a pace that by the time they finally stopped for the night, Persephone was almost indecently excited by the thought of a few bites of hot food and some much-needed rest. Most unhappily, before they could even pluck the two fat grouse that Fayla had brought down with her bow, it started to rain.

"Oh, *no*," groaned Persephone as the light sprinkling rapidly gave way to a torrential downpour.

With a cry of dismay, Azriel shouted for them all to run for the shelter of a nearby rocky overhang. Though Persephone was fairly certain that Fleet was not included in the "all," he insisted upon joining them anyway. Unfortunately, his steaming bulk took up most of the shelter provided by the overhang, so his human companions were reduced to crowding around him while they supped on strips of dried meat, soggy cheese and biscuits hard enough to crack teeth. After washing down their meager meal with a few sips of tepid water from their waterskins, they huddled together waiting for the chill rain to ease up so that they could lay out their bedrolls with some hope of not having them instantly drenched.

"This reminds me of the night afore we found Azriel," said Tiny gruffly.

"Found Azriel?" said Rachel in surprise.

"That's right," said Tiny. "Found him huddled at the edge of our cook-fire pit. A well-fed, comely lad of about seven years, he was dressed better than an Erok lowborn but not so well as a nobleman. He was mute for the first year or so, and once he started talking, he couldn't tell us a single thing about himself. It was as though he hadn't even existed before the morning we found him! Isn't that right, Azriel?"

"That's right, Tiny," agreed Azriel impassively as he stared out into the darkness.

Persephone, who'd long believed that memories were the only things that *couldn't* be stolen away, felt an unexpected rush of sympathy for Azriel. Reaching out, she laid a hand on his arm. As she did so, something occurred to her.

"But if you don't know who you are or where you came from," she said, "how do you know you're a Methusian?"

At her words, Tiny gasped and began choking on a sip of whatever it was he'd been sneaking from his hip flask, and Fayla threw Persephone a cold look.

"He has the look of one, and whoever left him knew how to find us," said the beautiful Methusian girl. "Moreover, he came to us as a child, was adopted and willingly received the mark as a man and that's the same as blood to us."

Stung by Fayla's rebuke and feeling as though she owed Azriel something for having questioned whether he really belonged among the only people he'd ever known, Persephone mumbled, "Well, uh, as it happens, I don't really know who I am or where I came from, either. I lived in a manor house near the slave markets of Wickendale until five summers past when my master lost me in a game of dice."

"A game of dice?" said Azriel softly, turning his gaze upon her.

Looking up at him, Persephone nodded. "He lost me to a tavern owner who insisted upon collecting payment that very same night. I . . . did not go quietly," she faltered.

"So the 'true owner' you spoke of was a tavern owner," murmured Azriel.

"No," Persephone told him. "The tavern owner sold me after just six months. Well, he gave me away, actually. To the man I stabbed."

"Oh, Persephone, you *stabbed* a man?" squeaked Rachel, her eyes wide and her breath a frosty cloud.

Having forgotten that there were others listening besides Azriel, Persephone started at the sound of Rachel's voice. "I only stabbed his hand," she clarified as she hugged herself for warmth, "and only after he tried to stick it up my skirt."

"So the 'true owner' you spoke of was this disgusting beast," growled Azriel.

"No," she replied. Now it was her turn to stare out into the darkness. "The man I stabbed sold me to an overseer at the Mines of Torodania. I was locked in one of the restricted sections of the mine. The other children and I were not allowed aboveground at all, and we were only given food and water if we delivered our quota of gemstones. Many were unable to do so, of course. Some of them died and rotted where they fell, while others grew feral. They were vicious and they would eat . . . anything." She looked down at her hands. "They ate my only friend."

"They *what?*" exclaimed Rachel.

Persephone smiled thinly. "F-F-Faust wasn't a human being, Rachel," she explained as a sudden, violent shiver racked her body. "He was a rat."

At the memory of the clever creature who'd kept her from descending into madness in the mines, Persephone's throat closed up without warning. As though sensing how close she was to tears, Azriel chose that moment to announce that he thought the rain had eased up enough for them to unpack their bedrolls. Giving him a quick, grateful smile, Persephone hurriedly fetched hers, curled up next to Rachel on the cold, soggy ground, closed her eyes and tried to stop remembering—and shivering. Moments later, she felt someone tucking something heavy firmly about the two of them.

Her eyes popped open at once. "A-Azriel?" she whispered through chattering teeth. "What is this? Is this your cloak?"

"Yes," he whispered.

"I c-can't let you give us your cloak," she protested. "You'll freeze to death!"

"If you're sincerely worried, perhaps I could slip in there next to you," he suggested as Rachel stifled a giggle. "As you, yourself, have noted in the past, Persephone, I *am* rather hot, and I'm quite sure that our combined body heat would—"

"On s-second thought, it is exceedingly unlikely that you'll freeze to *death* without y-your cloak," interrupted Persephone, who was feeling warmer already. "But I thank you for your generous offer."

"You are most welcome," murmured Azriel as he reached down to brush a lock of hair off her cheek.

Without meaning to, Persephone smiled at the touch of his hand. Then she yawned hugely, snuggled closer to Rachel and fell asleep at once.

Over the next three days Azriel set an even more punishing pace than he had on the first day. But if the going was hard, at least they were not set upon by bandits, and though the tranquility of the days was occasionally disrupted by Persephone's animals, even Fayla had to laugh at the sight of Azriel cursing and shoving his broad shoulder against Fleet's rump in an effort to get the traumatized horse to ford even the shallowest of streams.

The only downside to their uneventful travels was that there hadn't been a single moment of distraction in which Persephone could try to convince Rachel to run away with her. This was doubly troubling as she had a bad feeling about what lay ahead. She knew that the actual rescue of the orphan would be fraught with danger, of course, but it was more than this. Something deep inside her told her that things were about to go very wrong, very soon—and that she and Rachel would best be gone by the time they did.

As she gnawed on some cold roast venison on the morning of the fifth day, Persephone was so wrapped up in trying to figure out a solution to the problem of escape that it took her a moment to realize that everyone but Azriel had left the campsite and that he was perched on a nearby rock eyeing her speculatively.

"What are you looking at?" she asked as she tossed her half-eaten breakfast to Cur and self-consciously wiped her mouth with the back of her hand.

"You," he said. "I am looking at you, and I am wondering why you want to leave us."

Persephone stared into his very blue eyes for a long moment before deciding that there was no point lying to him. "It is not so much that I want to leave you," she explained. "It is that I want free- dom—for me and for Rachel."

"Is that what Rachel wants?" asked Azriel.

When Persephone didn't reply, Azriel nodded. Then he reached into the front pocket of his breeches, withdrew the key to her dis- carded fetters and pointed it at her. "I told you before that I am no slave owner, Persephone," he said. "I told you that I would never be a slave owner."

"That does not mean that I am free."

"Why would you say that?" asked Azriel as he absently slipped the key back into his pocket.

Persephone stared yearningly after the bitter symbol of her enslavement until it dawned on her that Azriel probably thought she was staring at his crotch. Jerking her gaze upward, she scowled at his smile, then tossed her head and said, "I would say that because freedom isn't freedom if it doesn't include the freedom to refuse to join somebody else's outrageous quest."

"And what if the quest is not so outrageous?" said Azriel. "Has it ever occurred to you, Persephone, that the child we are trying to rescue might be the Methusian king?"

"Even supposing that he is—even supposing that you manage to rescue him—how, exactly, do you intend to supplant the Erok king?"

"Who says Finnius is the rightful king?" said Azriel. "Some people say the true prince was born dead and that Mordesius arranged for a changeling to be placed in the royal cradle in order to preserve the power of the regency. Others say the true prince was born alive and that Mordesius had him strangled so that he could secretly put his own newborn son in the cradle. Still others say there never was a true prince at all and that the Regent somehow forced the queen to fake a pregnancy so he could hoodwink the old king into handing over power."

"Rumors," said Persephone.

"It is a fact that all who attended the birth—including the queen herself—died or disappeared before they had a chance to discuss the details of it with anyone," said Azriel. "You are a great fan of coincidences, Persephone. Does that sound like a coincidence to you?"

When she didn't answer, he got to his feet, took two steps and sank to his knees before her. Ignoring her gasp, he reached for her hand and pressed it against his beating heart. "All I am asking, Persephone, is that you consider the possibility that things aren't always what they seem. Our quest seems outrageous to you now; give us a chance to prove that it is not."

"And . . . if I refuse?" she stammered as she tried not to notice the firm contours of his chest muscles beneath her fingertips.

Without releasing her captive hand, Azriel placed his free hand high upon her thigh and slowly leaned so close that he could have kissed her without leaning closer. "May I tell you a secret?" he whispered.

She nodded mutely, hardly able to think for his nearness.

"I do not believe that the Fates will allow you to refuse. I believe that a path stretches out before us, Persephone, and though I cannot say exactly where it will lead, I would stake my life on the certainty that we are meant to walk it together, come what may." Then, before she could even begin to think of a response, he smiled, gave her thigh a friendly pat and said, "Now, be a good girl and go help Rachel dress Fayla in her gown and other things, will you? We'll be traveling through heavily settled country today, and if all goes well, we'll reach Parthania by nightfall."

Feeling distinctly unsettled—both by Azriel's troubling words and by the lingering feel of his hand on her thigh—Persephone reluctantly made her way toward the sound of Rachel cheerfully chattering away to Fayla. She was just wondering what the Methusian girl would have made of Azriel's wandering hand when she rounded a thicket of sugarberry bushes and beheld a sight that caused her to give a heartfelt cry of anguish. For when Azriel had referred to Fayla's "gown" Persephone had never imagined that he'd meant a gown like *this*, with its innumerable snow-white petticoats edged in finest lace, cunningly embroidered silk skirts and bodice encrusted with seed pearls and tiny gemstones! And when the pirate thief had referred to Fayla's "other things" Persephone had never *dreamt* he'd been referring to rings of real gold, ruby pendants, crystal hairpins, a velvet riding hat adorned with three snow-white pheasant feathers, a matching traveling cloak with an actual fur collar, impossibly soft kid gloves that fit like a second skin and gleaming riding boots without a mark on them!

At the sound of Persephone's cry, Fayla turned. "Is something the matter?" she asked in her haughty, cold, noble voice as she wiped tiny beads of sweat from her upper lip with her gloved finger.

"Nothing is the matter except that you look completely and utterly *exquisite*!" lamented Persephone.

"I do?" said Fayla uncertainly.

"You *do*," said Persephone, so woefully that the other girl couldn't help smiling.

"Show her how the skirts swirl when you twirl, Fayla," said Rachel, who was already grinning in anticipation of Persephone's reaction.

Still smiling slightly, Fayla began to twirl, but before she was halfway around, her knees buckled. Persephone and Rachel just managed to catch her before she hit the ground.

"Fayla, what's wrong?" cried Rachel.

"It is . . . nothing," gasped Fayla.

"You're flushed," said Persephone in alarm, noticing the girl's unhealthy pallor for the first time.

"And warm," added Rachel, putting the back of her hand against the Methusian girl's forehead.

"I am a little feverish but it is nothing," repeated Fayla, jerking away from Rachel's touch. "And since it is nothing, I would ask that you not concern Azriel and Tiny with mention of it. A child's life depends upon me playing my part and nothing short of death shall stop me from doing so."

With Azriel and Tiny in the lead, Fayla on Fleet in the middle, Persephone and Rachel bringing up the rear and Cur alternating between loping alongside their little train and diving into the brush to terrorize something small and furry, they set out. Before long the dirt path along which they were trudging emerged from the woods, widened and finally met up with a well-traveled road. The land rapidly grew replete with signs of humanity—vast agricultural fields and neatly fenced pastures, haystacks and signposts, wagon tracks and hoofprints, great castles and mean huts, bridges and other roads. By midmorning, they arrived at the first of several hamlets. Most of its inhabitants were in the fields, but a few tired-looking women with scrawny babies on their hips and even scrawnier toddlers clinging to their dirty skirts stood in the door-ways of their hovels and stared dully at Fayla as she rode by in her finery. Persephone was acutely aware of the fact that even one of the gemstones sewn into the bodice of the Methusian girl's lavish gown would have paid for food enough to fill all those empty bellies for a year, but there was nothing to be done about it. For an Erok noble-woman to acknowledge the presence of a nobody was an unheard-of thing—had Fayla gone so far as to offer charity, the villagers would have known beyond a doubt that they were not who they appeared to be and they could not risk letting that happen. Hard as it was, the only thing to do was to keep walking.

No one had to tell this to Fayla, of course, though Persephone couldn't even be sure that the Methusian girl had noticed the women, the children or even the hamlet itself. She'd said not one word since they'd first set out, and though the way she held herself in the saddle could easily have been mistaken for a noble bearing, something about her ramrod straight posture gave Persephone the impression that she was fighting for control. She could tell that Rachel had the same impression, and that she, too, was torn between telling Azriel and Tiny the truth about the girl's ill health and respecting her request for silence. It was a terrible decision to have to make, and as she watched the growing stains of fever-sweat darken the fine cloth at Fayla's back and beneath her armpits, Persephone was so consumed by it that she all but forgot her earlier fears that something was about to go very wrong, very soon.

Then, nigh about noon, the sound of galloping horses and barking dogs brought her sense of foreboding flooding back with a vengeance.

Seventeen

LOOKING WEST, Persephone saw half a dozen colorfully dressed horsemen appear at the far end of a fallow field. They were riding parallel to the road and for a happy moment, it looked as though they might continue to do so. Then one of them must have noticed Fayla and her entourage because with a loud whoop, all the horses veered left and began galloping across the field, dogs baying and barking at their hooves the entire way. The dogs were hairless, gray-black beasts like the ones that had attacked Persephone by the river, and they slithered beneath the nearby fence rails like eels while, one after another, the horsemen urged their steeds over the fence and reined up beside Fayla.

"Well, now!" cried one.

"What have we here?" cried another.

"Marry me!" cried a third.

"Yes, do marry him!" shouted a fourth. "Then take me as your lover!"

At this, the horsemen all guffawed raucously, and several drank deeply from silver hip flasks. Persephone, who'd kept her head down thus far, took the opportunity to risk looking up. One glance at the horsemen told her that they were all young, all noble, all drunk and all looking to make the kind of mischief that could mean terrible trouble—even for a noblewoman.

Azriel and Tiny obviously saw the same thing Persephone did, but before they could move to place themselves between Fayla and the drunken noblemen, a soft-featured young man with close-set eyes and a fleshy pink pout offhandedly issued a command. At once, the dogs surged forward. Slinking around and around Azriel and Tiny, they snapped their teeth and whined so hungrily that there was little doubt as to what would happen if either Methusian moved so much as a hair.

With the "armed escort" thusly taken care of, the fleshy-lipped nobleman nudged his horse forward until his knee brushed Fayla's thigh. Bowing in his saddle so that his face was mere inches from Fayla's, he deliberately dropped his watery gaze to the swell of her breasts.

"I am Lord Atticus Bartok, future duke of these parts," he said thickly. "My friends call me Lord Atticus, so as not to confuse me with my father, Lord Bartok, the all-powerful current duke."

Fayla drew herself up with what Persephone was sure must have been the last of her strength. "I am Lady Elwin of the Nicene Prefecture," she said haughtily, using the name Azriel had said she always used in such situations—that of an actual living noble-woman, but one from such a distant branch of such a minor family that though the name would sound familiar to most, few would have met the lady in question or been able to recognize an imposter.

After introducing herself, Fayla held out her gloved hand, as was custom among the Erok nobility. With an intimacy that made Persephone's skin crawl, Lord Atticus took it in both of his hands and pressed his fleshy lips against her glove until his saliva left a mark on the soft leather. "You are exceedingly beautiful, Lady Elwin," he murmured without letting go of her hand. "And yet I can feel that you wear no wedding ring. Can I therefore assume that you are as yet a maid, untouched by any man?"

"No, you cannot," said Fayla. "As it happens, I am a widow."

"Ah," said Lord Atticus with a sudden leer. "A young, noble widow—my favorite kind of diversion. Rich, proper, experienced in the ways of the flesh and hot with pent-up desire."

At this, the other young noblemen laughed lewdly and nudged each other. Lord Atticus grinned over his shoulder at them.

"You embarrass yourself, m'lord," said Fayla icily. "Kindly order your men to stand aside so that I may continue on my way."

"Brrrr," said Lord Atticus with a mock shiver. "Fear not, m'lady, I've just the thing to warm you up."

"Your jests demean us both, m'lord," murmured Fayla, who was clearly fading fast. "Once again, I ask you to kindly—"

Without warning, Lord Atticus thrust his soft-looking hand forward and clamped it around Fayla's biceps. Almost before she realized what she was doing, Persephone had lunged forward and shoved her shoulder hard into the muscular hindquarters of Lord Atticus's horse. The horse was so startled that he reared up on his hind legs. With a cry, Lord Atticus let go of Fayla's arm and grabbed wildly for his horse's mane in an effort to stay mounted—a task made doubly difficult by the fact that Fleet had chosen that exact moment to begin aggressively nosing at the already-panicked creature's left saddlebag.

Predictably, the other drunken young noblemen were, by this point, quite helpless with laughter. In a rage, Lord Atticus raised his riding crop high in the air and yanked his horse around so that he could punish the interfering wench who'd diverted him from his diversion and made him look the fool.

Just before he delivered the first stinging blow, however, Persephone saw his eyes flick sideways from her face to Rachel's and then widen in surprise.

Ever so slowly, he lowered the riding crop.

"Twins," he murmured in wonder. Abruptly, he slapped his blue-velvet-clad leg and started laughing—a shrill, unpleasant sound. "Twins!" he repeated, louder this time. "Filthy, lowborn twins, to be sure, and not nearly ripe enough for my taste, but I'm not especially fond of green apples, either, yet I'll eat them when I'm hungry enough."

Fayla, who was already white as a sheet, grew paler still. "You . . . you'll leave my servants be," she said hoarsely, "or I'll—"

"You'll do nothing, m'lady," said Lord Atticus absently as he tossed the riding crop to a nearby companion and slid out of the saddle, "for I am the eldest son of the great Lord Bartok and you are the widow of an unknown minor lord from the middle of nowhere. I will do as I please and you will do nothing at all."

Without taking his eyes off Rachel and Persephone, he snapped his wormy white fingers at the other young noblemen, who promptly slid, jumped or fell out of their saddles, depending on their state of drunkenness.

On the other side of Fleet, the noblemen's beasts began barking with such vigor that Persephone somehow knew that Azriel was attempting to make good on his "solemn vow to protect her with his life" in spite of his rather endearing terror of dogs. Unfortunately, she also knew that he was never going to be able to fight his way past the dogs and the leering noblemen in time to save her and Rachel from Lord Atticus, who was even now advancing upon them.

It was going to be up to her.

And so, forcibly shoving Rachel behind her, Persephone reached for her dagger. She did not unsheathe it just yet, however, for she could not risk having it knocked from her grasp before the young lord was close enough that she could be sure of spilling his guts. Instead, she squared her shoulders and readied herself to attack.

Lord Atticus scowled and started to say something, but Persephone never found out what it was because he was suddenly struck in the side of the head by something fast, furious . . . and feathered.

"Ivan!" breathed Persephone.

"What the devil?" shrieked Atticus, who'd begun to bleed copiously from a vicious scratch above the eye.

Whirling around, he was just able to catch a glimpse of the hawk before he was once again at the mercy of those powerful, beating wings and deadly talons.

Seeing his leader under attack, one especially drunken nobleman clumsily unsheathed his sword and staggered forward as though he meant to slash the offending bird to bits. Whether he'd have been able to accomplish this without also removing large pieces of Lord Atticus's head and upper body was destined to remain a mystery, because before he could deliver the first blow, Ivan abruptly took flight. Grunting in dismay, the drunk but determined young man flung his sword aside and fumbled for his bow so that he might shoot the hawk out of the sky. Unfortunately for him, before he could remember where he'd put his arrows (they were in the quiver on his back), Lord Atticus unsheathed his own sword and, using the flat edge, hit the man across the forehead so hard that he dropped like a sack of potatoes at Persephone's feet.

"Gods' blood, Atticus," cried a squat, giggling nobleman in green and red hose. "You've rendered him quite unconscious!"

"Never mind him! To the horses—quickly!" ordered Lord Atticus as he hastily re-sheathed his sword, retrieved his riding crop and ran back to his own mount. "We must keep Faldo in sight!"

"Who is Faldo?" called a nobleman who'd been matter-of-factly holding back the hair of a vomiting companion but who had now joined the others in running for his horse.

"My hawk, you fool!" bellowed Lord Atticus as he swung up into the saddle without taking his eyes off Ivan, who was flying loop-the-loops some distance away. "Stolen from the nest as a fledgling and trained by my own hand . . . until the day he willfully ignored a pheasant in plain view, shat on my doublet and flew off to destinations unknown. I never thought I'd see the feathered devil again but by the gods he's come back to me—and I mean to recapture him at once!"

At this, Persephone gasped and might have said or done something very foolish if Rachel hadn't grabbed her hand and given it a painful squeeze.

"Stealing a fledgling from the nest is one thing, my lord," gasped the reeking vomiter, who'd somehow managed to haul himself back onto his horse. "Capturing a full-grown hawk is . . . a bird of a different feather altogether."

Several of the other noblemen chortled at his cleverness. Lord Atticus flung his riding crop at them.

"A clean shot through the wing will bring him down without crippling him," he snapped. "And as long as the dogs don't get to him before we do and the wound doesn't fester, there is a chance he'll mend almost as good as new. And if he doesn't—well, we'll call it payback for his lack of loyalty."

"And also for shitting on you," offered the squat nobleman with mock solemnity.

The other noblemen laughed again. With a scowl, Lord Atticus turned away from them and dug the heels of his riding boots deep into the flanks of his horse. As his steed leapt forward, all the other mounted men dug their heels into the flanks of their horses. The air was momentarily filled with dust and the sound of trampling hooves, and then the horses were gone. An instant later, a shrill whistle sounded and the hairless, gray-black dogs lit off after them, barking and baying like the hounds of hell.

In the stunned silence that followed, Persephone wrenched her hand free of Rachel's grasp, whipped out her dagger and would have bolted after the noblemen in the futile hope of catching and gutting them all before they had a chance to harm Ivan, if two things had not happened.

The first was that, anticipating exactly this reaction from her, Azriel stepped forward to block her way so quickly that she nearly gutted *him*.

The second was that Fayla mumbled something unintelligible, gave a thin, shuddering gasp and slowly toppled sideways out of the saddle.

Eighteen

LUCKILY, TINY CAUGHT FAYLA before she hit the ground—but a cursory examination of the unconscious Methusian girl revealed that the luck ended there.

"It is the Great Sickness," gasped Rachel, her nose pressed into the rough cloth of her sleeve to prevent her from breathing in the sickness.

Even Tiny recoiled at the dread pronouncement.

"We can't be sure of that," said Azriel without conviction.

"The instant we removed her gloves I was sure of it," said Rachel. Without taking her nose out of her sleeve, she gestured toward the blackened tips of Fayla's now-bare fingers, and to her swollen hands, which had the look of being severely bruised. "If you were to remove her boots her feet would look the same—for now. A short while hence," she continued, her voice taking on the faraway quality of one reliving a powerful memory, "her hands and feet will be entirely black and the bruise-color will begin creeping up her arms and legs. If the fever continues to rage on, she will suffer violent fits and her entire body will become bloated and begin to smell like—"

"Enough!" blurted Persephone, who could feel her gorge rising. Turning to Azriel, she said, "Can you help her?"

He hesitated. "Our healers may be able to do something if we return to the camp at once, but . . ."

"But?" prompted Persephone impatiently. "But what?"

"But if we turn back now, it is unlikely that we'll be able to get to Parthania in time to rescue the child," he said quietly.

Persephone's heart sank like a stone. "So we must choose between Fayla and the child?" she asked, swallowing hard.

Azriel gave her a bleak smile. As he did so there came a distant screech and the sound of men cheering. Startled, Persephone looked around to see Ivan—dear, brave, funny Ivan!—plummeting from the sky with an arrow through his wing.

Oh, Ivan, thought Persephone, squeezing her eyes shut so that she wouldn't have to watch the dogs tear him to pieces. Shoving aside her grief, she angrily thought how Ivan would still be alive if not for the Methusians and their ridiculous prophecy, and how they had no right to expect anything from her but resentment and bitterness and a desire to flee from them at the first opportunity!

Then she opened her eyes and saw the beautiful, brave, clever, well-dressed sick girl lying at her feet. And she thought of the child awaiting rescue—the child who, in her mind's eye, had somehow come to look very much like jolly, lisping little Sabian.

And she knew that however angry she might be, freedom wouldn't be freedom if it didn't include freedom from the guilt of knowing that she hadn't done what she could to save them both.

In view of this rather irksome truth, she said, "Well, what if we were to split up?"

"Split up?" said Azriel, who'd been watching her closely the whole time she'd been thinking.

Persephone nodded. "You, Rachel and I carry on to Parthania to rescue the child," she explained without much enthusiasm. "Tiny takes Fayla back to the camp."

"I don't know—" began Tiny doubtfully.

"It is . . . a good plan," came a hoarse whisper from the ground.

Startled, Persephone looked down to find Fayla awake and staring at her with glittering, red-rimmed eyes. She motioned for Persephone to kneel beside her.

"You will save the child?" she gasped, clutching at Persephone's arm with her cold, blackened fingers.

"I will try," replied Persephone, trying not to show her fear and revulsion at being touched by those awful fingers.

Fayla nodded jerkily and mumbled something else. Unable to make it out, Persephone held her breath and leaned as close to the sick girl as she dared.

"Azriel is . . . as a brother to me," Fayla mumbled again, even more faintly than before. "Do not . . . break his heart."

Persephone's own heart leapt at these unexpected words. "What are you saying? Fayla, listen to me—"

But the Methusian girl had lapsed back into the tormented slumber of her sickness and was beyond listening to anyone.

The plan agreed upon, it did not take long to change Fayla back into her lowborn smock and settle her upon the hastily fashioned sledge that Tiny had attached to the horse belonging to the now-gagged, bound and blindfolded unconscious nobleman who'd been left behind by Lord Atticus.

After the two of them had departed, Rachel and Persephone returned to the place where Fayla's sweat-soaked noble clothing had been laid out to air. Seeing Rachel's terror at the prospect of donning garments worn by someone afflicted with the disease that had killed her parents, Persephone insisted upon playing the part of the noblewoman. Rachel protested feebly for only a few seconds before capitulating with a grateful hug and then quickly helping Persephone dress and fix her hair.

"*Oh,*" she sighed after she'd set the last crystal hairpin in place. "You look beautiful—and nobler than the very noblest of noblewomen!"

Pleased in spite of the fact that she was wearing grim Death on her back, Persephone smiled, picked up her skirts and gracefully made her way back to discover Cur returned from the hunt and thoroughly enjoying the spectacle of Fleet refusing to stand still for Azriel. When the irritated Methusian finally managed to wrestle the last pannier closed, he turned, caught sight of Persephone and stopped short so abruptly that it was as though he'd slammed into an invisible wall. Knees trembling, Persephone waited for him to say something but he only stared; the expression on his face was hard to look at yet she could not look away. A fleeting moment stretched into an eternity as his gaze wandered over her. It was so warm that she could almost feel the heat of it upon her skin, and she stood paralyzed, wondering if she might faint, feeling as vulnerable as if she were standing utterly naked before him.

"Is . . . is something wrong, Azriel?" she finally stammered.

"Persephone . . . I . . . you . . ."

"She looks terrific, doesn't she?" prompted Rachel, when it became clear that Azriel had temporarily lost the ability to form intelligible sentences.

Nodding, Azriel wordlessly held his hand out to Persephone. She slowly glided over to where he stood and then inhaled sharply when he slid his hands around her waist. Refusing to look up at him for fear of what might happen if she did, Persephone raised her hands and rested them lightly on his powerful shoulders.

"Ready?" he asked as he prepared to toss her into the saddle.

For anything, she thought wildly. "Yes," she said primly.

It turned out that being tossed into a saddle was not as easy as Fayla had made it look. When Azriel tossed Persephone up, in addition to smacking her tailbone on the hard edge of the saddle, she lost her balance and very nearly toppled over backward. Azriel smiled and made some comment about her still having the grace and poise of a natural dancer, but Persephone was too focused on remaining mounted to reply.

Fortunately, it didn't take her long to get used to the rhythm of Fleet's movements and begin to feel comfortable in the saddle, though she was surprised to discover that in many ways, riding in the guise of a noblewoman was actually less comfortable and more tiring than walking. Regardless, she kept her back straight, her chin up and uttered not a single word of complaint. Indeed, she uttered not a single word at all until shortly before sunset, when they crested a hill and the great black walls of Parthania loomed in the distance. Silhouetted against a sky streaked orange and red with the last light of the dying day, the walls seemed to stretch from one horizon to the other and all the way up to the heavens.

It was the most awesome sight Persephone had ever seen in her life.

"Oh, *my!*" she exclaimed, gaping like—well, like an ignorant, ill-bred nobody on her first trip to the imperial capital.

"Parthania," offered Azriel unnecessarily.

Persephone nodded and closed her mouth. Her weariness had vanished at the sight of those great walls, but now nervousness rushed in to take its place. Over the course of the day, she'd deigned to nod at a few fellow travelers who looked to be about "her" station but she'd not been challenged or even had to speak. Now, suddenly, she was going to have to pass through the gates of the imperial capital under the scrutiny of soldiers who had the authority to execute her on the spot for a traitor if they discovered her deception. Rachel would be lost and the child, too. And if they discovered that Azriel was a Methusian? They would force him to his knees right in front of her . . . they would grab his hair . . . they would put a knife to his throat . . . they would—

"Steady, m'lady," urged Azriel, gently but firmly.

With a start, Persephone looked down to see him gazing up at her with a calm, expectant expression on his handsome face. As though it had never for a single instant occurred to him that she wasn't brave and strong and clever enough to do what had to be done; as if he was just waiting for her to get on with it.

For a long, quiet moment, Persephone concentrated on slowing her breathing and letting Azriel's unshakable confidence in her wash over her soul, lifting her up and restoring her own faith in herself.

When the moment was over, a remarkable change came over her. Eyeing Azriel coldly, she said, "The next time you address me without permission, you filthy mongrel, I will have you flogged to within an inch of your life."

Giving Persephone the same slow, considered smile that had made her stomach do a funny kind of flip-flop in the owner's barn on that night that now seemed so impossibly long ago, Azriel dutifully bowed his head, turned on one heel and led them all onward to the gates of Parthania.

As it turned out, passing through the city gates was no trouble at all.

The trouble started shortly after they got inside.

"Something is wrong," said Azriel softly as Fleet clip-clopped through the nearly deserted street with Cur at his heels. The door of every narrow dwelling on the street was closed and the windows were shuttered tight. "It is not yet so late—there should still be people about," he continued. "They should be returning from their daily business, tending to the evening chores, visiting with their neighbors. Children should be playing—there should be noise and bustle and instead there is nothing. I do not like it."

Persephone nodded but said nothing as Azriel warily continued to lead Fleet onward in the direction of the imperial palace. With each passing moment, the stout turrets and glittering spires loomed larger. Even as they did so, the streets grew narrower, the dwellings smaller and the air less sweet. At length, Persephone realized that she'd broken into a cold sweat. Fervently, she hoped that it was not a sign of fever but rather the result of the increasingly uncomfortable feeling that behind these shabbier closed doors and shuttered windows, many eyes were watching her—and waiting. Waiting for what, Persephone did not know, but she had a strong sense that she didn't want to find out.

"We must find a place to temporarily stable the horse," Azriel murmured.

"Why?" whispered Persephone, leaning forward so that she could hear him.

"We shall shortly reach the slum that encroaches upon the north wall of the castle, where the child is being hidden," he explained in a hushed voice. "You need to change back into your smock and we need to find an alley in which you can do so. Even if we were able to convince your beast to voluntarily join us there and stand quietly while you go for the child—which I highly doubt, given his unnatural attachment to you and unwavering determination to make life difficult for me—if a passerby was to notice a horse standing in an alley, he would almost certainly come to investigate. And I would be forced to kill a man for nothing more than ill-timed curiosity."

Looking about the deserted, rapidly darkening streets, it did not seem likely to Persephone that anyone would happen by. Nevertheless, she did not want to risk the slaughter of an innocent man, so she nodded and attempted to climb out of the saddle. As she did so, she became hopelessly tangled in her skirts, lost her balance and would have tumbled to the cobblestone street if Azriel had not been there to catch her.

"You and Rachel stay here," he whispered in her ear as he ever so slowly set her down. "I'll be back in a moment."

Nodding wordlessly, Persephone watched as Azriel pulled a handful of something edible out of his pocket, held it under Fleet's nose and started walking. With a soft whicker, Fleet eagerly began trotting after him and whatever was in his hand. A moment later, the night swallowed them both. Cur let out a soft whine. Suddenly feeling very alone, Persephone reached for Rachel's hand just as

Rachel reached for hers. Together, the two girls and the dog waited in tense silence for Azriel to return.

A moment later, he was back with Persephone's lowborn smock tucked under one arm.

"Best luck," he panted. "I found an untended stable with a bin full of turnips in one corner. There were sufficient to keep all the horses in the king's own cavalry well-fed for several long winters, so there just might be enough to keep your beast distracted for the next half hour or—"

He stopped speaking abruptly and cocked his head to one side as though listening hard. Alarmed, Persephone did the same thing and that's when she heard it: the distant but unmistakable murmur of a large crowd gathering.

"Come!" ordered Azriel tersely. "There is no time to waste!"

Reaching for Persephone's free hand, he nearly wrenched her arm out of the socket in his haste to lead her and Rachel onward. The farther they ran, the louder the murmuring became. Soon, they were able to distinguish voices—hard male voices intermingled with pleading female ones.

Then, just as they reached the entrance of a dark and altogether unpleasant-looking alley, they heard the first scream.

"What was that?" exclaimed Persephone, as the first scream was joined by another and then another.

"*What is going on?*" wailed Rachel softly.

Instead of answering either of them, Azriel turned and plunged into the alley. Cur bounded after him. Persephone and Rachel stumbled blindly after him, slipping in unseen puddles of muck, tripping over repulsively soft things that stank of rot and trying not to hear the squeaks of vermin scuttling ahead of them. Suddenly, Azriel stopped so abruptly that Persephone bounced off his back and had to throw her arms around him to keep from falling. Without thinking what she was doing, she held on tighter and leaned into the warm, solid strength of him.

"Wait here," he said, pulling away from her.

Shocked by how empty her arms felt without him in them, Persephone shivered and watched as he silently and swiftly navigated around the precariously stacked crates, barrels and piles of old hay that cluttered the alley. He paused only briefly at the edge of the alley before turning and hurrying back with an urgency that set Persephone's heart pounding.

"The square is swarming with soldiers," he whispered grimly. "They are driving people from the slum—it looks as though they mean to torch it!"

"Torch it!" gasped Persephone, even as she caught a whiff of smoke. "But the child—"

Before she could finish her terrible thought, there was a clatter of hooves at the far end of the alley. Jerking her gaze toward it, Persephone saw the silhouettes of a half-dozen men on horseback, several of whom were carrying torches.

"You in the alley!" called a commanding voice. "Show yourself!"

Instinctively, Persephone, Azriel and Rachel shrank back into the shadows and stood as still as death. Raising her hand to Cur, Persephone gave him a silent order to stay.

"You would play with *me*?" continued the voice, which was now tinged with barely suppressed rage. "Even though I have *personally* gone to such heroic efforts to rid our fine city of that verminous eyesore you called a home? Even after I *explicitly* warned you and your kind against attempting to run amok through the city offending the sensibilities of your betters? I warn you, whoever you are, come out upon the instant or I shall order my men in there to cut you down without mercy!"

When there was no sign of surrender from the alley, the voice shouted an order. At once, several of the men slid out of their saddles, swords glinting in the torchlight.

As they did so, without even realizing what she was doing—and before Azriel or Rachel could stop her—Persephone took three deliberate steps forward into the flickering light cast by the pitch torches. Looking up, she fixed her eyes upon the man to whom the voice belonged. He was clad entirely in black so that his body seemed to melt into the night, but his ageless face was clearly visible. So handsome that it seemed almost otherworldly, it radiated power, magnetism and . . . something else.

Something terrible.

For a long moment, his fathomless eyes bored into her.

"Who are you?" he finally asked, his tone inscrutable.

To Persephone's horror, she found herself unable to move, unable to speak! Unable to do anything but stand there gaping like an ignorant, ill-bred nobody in disguise waiting for the accusation that would see her facade crumble and her trembling legs give way beneath her.

Then she remembered Azriel looking at her as though it had never occurred to him that she wasn't brave and strong and clever enough to do what had to be done, and her courage returned.

"Who am I?" she echoed in a voice as haughty and cold and noble as could be. Desperately, she tried to remember the noble name that Fayla had used—the one belonging to the living noble-woman who was from such a distant branch of such a minor family as to be unlikely to be recognized—but it eluded her completely, so she latched on to the only other noble name that came to mind, the one Azriel had used with the owner.

"Who am I?" she said again. "I am Lady Bothwell of the Ragorian Prefecture. Who, pray tell, are *you*?"

Head bobbing slightly, the man awkwardly leaned forward in his saddle and hissed, "I am the Regent Mordesius."

Nineteen

STAGGERED THOUGH SHE WAS to discover that she was in the presence of the dreaded Regent Mordesius himself, Persephone did not gasp or cry out or swoon or otherwise exhibit any outward signs of shock and distress.

Instead, she lifted her chin a little higher and dropped into a curtsey as low as befitted a man of such great station.

"Your Grace," she murmured, affecting not to notice the increasingly loud and desperate cries of the nearby slum dwellers. "I am most pleased to make your acquaintance."

"I am most . . . intrigued to make yours, my lady," replied Mordesius, whose eyes had yet to leave her face, "for though I have never personally met the reclusive Lord Bothwell, I had understood him to be determinedly unmarried."

"He was," agreed Persephone smoothly even as she silently cursed herself for not having considered the possibility that Lord Bothwell was a bachelor, "until he met me and—"

"How did you meet?" interrupted the Regent.

Afraid of hesitating even for an instant, Persephone gave the first answer that came to mind. "Hunting," she said.

"Hunting!" exclaimed Mordesius in a voice that told Persephone that she'd made another mistake. "That is interesting indeed, my lady, for I had also understood Lord Bothwell to be of such advanced age that he was hardly able to tend to the call of nature by himself, let alone ride out to bring down game."

"Though you are correct that my husband is of great age, Your Grace," said Persephone, who'd begun to sweat freely, "you have been sadly misinformed as to his health and vigor."

Persephone saw the Regent's eyes narrow. "Is that so?" he said. "But if he is as well as you say, why does he continually plead infirmity as a reason to avoid court?"

Feeling as though she was up to her nostrils in quicksand and not knowing what else to do, Persephone shrugged prettily and curtseyed again—only this time as she dipped down, she inhaled deeply and arched her back ever so slightly, so that the flickering light from the pitch torch might better illuminate her assets.

"As a mere woman, I cannot speak for my dear husband's actions, Your Grace," she murmured as she peeked, wide-eyed and innocent, up through her lashes into the Regent's disturbingly handsome face. "However, I can assure you that he is as loyal a subject as His Majesty could hope for."

The Regent said nothing for so long that Persephone's legs began to shake with the strain of holding her curtsey and she began to fear that her ploy had been too obvious.

Then, all at once, he indicated that she should rise. "Tell me, Lady Bothwell," he said in a voice that sounded almost tender, "how is it that I find a beautiful woman of your great station in such a despicable place on a night like this?"

"I was on my way to the imperial city to . . . uh . . . visit the markets when my cavalcade was set upon by bandits," she explained haltingly, hoping that the Regent would take her hesitation as confirmation that she'd been badly traumatized rather than as proof that she was making up the story as she went along. "Afterward, I was somehow able to make my way to the gates of the city but . . . but by that time, darkness had fallen. The streets were deserted so there was no one from whom to demand directions to respectable lodgings and . . . and then I heard screams and saw soldiers and . . . and I grew frightened and so . . . and so I ducked in here to hide alone until morning."

"Alone?" grunted the Regent, wincing and snatching awkwardly at his horse's mane as the creature shifted beneath him without warning.

Persephone's heart leapt into her throat at the thought of Azriel, Rachel and Cur who were hiding just three steps away. "Of course," she said as she gestured to the darkness around her.

"But why alone?" persisted Mordesius, who was now glaring at his horse with undisguised loathing. "What happened to your attendants?"

For one awful moment, Persephone could think of nothing to say. Then: "Murdered, Your Grace!" she cried in a voice bursting with genuine distress. "Their throats slit! Their bodies dumped where none but the wild beasts would ever find them!"

Mordesius's gaze slid from the despised horse to Persephone. Lifting his bobbing head a little higher, he cocked it to one side and said, "But how did *you* escape, Lady Bothwell? I would have thought that the brutes would have torn the clothes from your ripe young body and used you until you begged for death."

The lust in his voice was so plain to hear that Persephone's fingers itched to reach for her dagger. Instead, she clasped her hands demurely before her, bowed her head and murmured, "Luck, my lord. As it happened, I was some distance away attending to private functions when the bandits descended. I am ashamed to admit that I hid while they went about their terrible business and—"

"Well, what else should you have done?" interrupted Mordesius with more than a trace of impatience. "Seen your noble blood spilled and your virtue destroyed for the sake of a handful of servants that could be replaced as easily as smashed dinner plates?"

"No, of course not," said Persephone hastily. "I only meant—"

"Lady Bothwell, I do not wish to linger here any longer," he announced imperiously. "The routing of the lowborns from the slum is more or less complete. Those that now hide within their hovels in the vain hope that we will forget them shall shortly be in for a very warm surprise. And though I know it will be nothing less than the wretches deserve for defying my personally proclaimed orders to quit that miserable place, I am so tenderhearted that I find the screams of those being burned alive rather . . . interferes with my digestion."

The men around him all guffawed in appreciation.

"I understand," said Persephone, trying not to visibly shudder. Curtseying deeply, and with great dignity, she said, "In that case, I bid you good night, Your Grace."

Mordesius stared at her for a moment before he burst out laughing. "My *dear* Lady Bothwell, you don't actually imagine that I am going to leave you here, do you?" he asked, still chuckling as he gestured toward the alley. "Though my men are doing an admirable job of rounding up the slum's erstwhile inhabitants, there will be some that refuse to meekly accept that they are to be transported to where they can actually be of some use. They will be out this night—seeking to escape my men, yes, but also seeking to wreak vengeance upon anyone who does not share their fate. You escaped ravishment once, my lady. I do not think your luck would hold a second time. Besides, what would you propose to do for the balance of the night? Stand ankle-deep in muck trying to look poised? Lie down upon the vermin-infested filth and attempt to catch up on your beauty sleep?"

"Well, I—"

"No, Lady Bothwell," he said firmly. "You will come with me now. I will find you a suitable suite of rooms at the palace. You will bathe and rest, and in a few days, once you've fully recovered from the various traumas and hardships that you have endured, I will send word to your husband that you are safe and well and ask him to send men to fetch you."

"That won't be necessary," Persephone said quickly. "I can make my own arrangements where my husband is concerned and—"

"As you wish," said Mordesius with a careless wave of his hand. Glancing sourly at the strapping young soldier next to him, he snapped, "You! Get down and assist Lady Bothwell up onto my horse, behind me. I will personally see to her safety during the ride back to the palace."

After a moment of hesitation that betrayed the young soldier's surprise that the Regent would offer to protect anyone—and perhaps his skepticism that the injured man had the ability to do so—the soldier nodded briskly, leapt down off his own horse and held his black-gloved hand out to Persephone. She stepped forward and tentatively took it because, really, what choice did she have? As she could think of no reasonable basis upon which to offer protest, to do so would only have aroused suspicions.

And so, not daring to risk even a glance behind her for fear that the Regent would wonder what—or whom—she was looking at, Persephone followed the soldier out of the alley to where the Regent's horse stood tossing its head with impatience. Aware that all eyes were upon her, she did her very best to take the graceful, mincing steps of a noblewoman and not the long, practical strides of an enslaved girl. She felt that she was putting on a pretty fair show until they reached the Regent's horse and instead of tossing her into the saddle—a prospect she hadn't been looking forward to but which she'd at least been expecting—the soldier laced his fingers together, leaned over and looked up at her with an expectant look on his dirty face.

"What . . . what is the meaning of this?" Persephone blustered, folding her arms tightly across her heaving chest. "I am accustomed to being tossed into the saddle!"

Everyone but the Regent snickered.

"Yes, 'course you are, m'lady!" said the soldier amiably. "Excepting that if I toss you into the saddle while His Grace is still sitting in it, you're as like to knock him to the ground as end up there yourself. This way, see, you can use my hands as a step and throw your leg over the back of the beast without risking life and limb."

"I knew that," muttered Persephone. "I only meant that I am not used to this manner of mounting."

More snickers from the men, this time tinged with lewdness. Persephone glared at them and they quieted at once.

"I am not used to it because it is not seemly for a woman of my station to ride astride like a man or a common wench," she continued coolly. "However, under the circumstances it seems I have no choice but to do so."

"Very good, m'lady," said the soldier, who did not seem to care overly much for Persephone's reasons and explanations. "Up you go, then."

Awkwardly, Persephone placed her foot in the cradle formed by the soldier's laced fingers. Then, having no idea what to do with her hands, she was about to gingerly rest them on the soldier's greasy head when he straightened up without warning, sending her flying into the air. Somehow, she had the presence of mind to fling her right leg sideways, but that only meant that when she landed askew on the horse's back and started to fall, her skirts were in such disarray that they very likely would have ended up around her ears had she not prevented herself from falling by grabbing on to the only thing within reach: the frail body of the Regent. Stifling a gasp of pain, the Regent instinctively flung himself in the opposite direction in order to counterbalance her falling weight. The two of them hung, one on either side of the saddle, for a long, breathless moment before Persephone finally managed to grunt and wriggle her way upright, forcibly hauling the Regent upright as she did so. As soon as they were both out of danger of tumbling to the ground, Persephone tried to make up for how very *un-noble* she'd just looked by rounding angrily on the soldier.

"Clumsy fool!" she said severely. "How dare you treat me so crudely—I could have fallen and been injured! Or worse—I could have injured the Lord Regent! Is that what you were hoping for? Well, is it?"

The strapping young soldier seemed to shrink before her very eyes. "No, m'lady!" he cried, his eyes darting to the Regent in such fear that Persephone suddenly felt guilty for having implied treachery on his part. "No! I swear! I meant no harm to you or to His Grace. I swear! I would never—"

"Oh, enough," muttered the Regent distractedly. Sitting up a little straighter, he grabbed the reins and was about to dig his razor-sharp spurs into the already-bleeding flanks of his mount when there came a loud clatter from the alley. "What was that!" he snapped, wheeling back around.

To Persephone's horror, the strapping young soldier immediately unsheathed his sword and ran toward the alley and those it sheltered. Luckily, he hadn't taken more than three steps when a hundred pounds of hurtling dog flesh violently swept his legs out from under him. As he crashed to the cobblestones, Cur continued running unchecked. He was about to skid to a halt beside the Regent's horse—at Persephone's feet—when he saw the surreptitious but unmistakable order hidden in the flick of her fingers. Veering sharply without breaking stride, he bounded off into the night even as the furious soldier scrambled to his feet and ran for his bow.

"No!" cried Persephone, her entire body stiffening as the first arrow pierced the darkness into which her friend had vanished.

A fraction of a second later, a human shriek from that same direction told them all that the arrow had found a mark, though not the intended one.

Heedless of both the shriek and Persephone's cry, the soldier notched another arrow. Before he could release it, however, the Regent ordered him to leave off and return to his horse so that they could be on their way.

"Lady Bothwell," called the Regent, as they trotted briskly toward the torch-lit chaos of the slum, "I must tell you that I find it odd that you would show concern over the fate of a miserable cur."

"I care about many things, Your Grace," blurted Persephone, who was unable to loosen her death grip on him for fear that she would slide backward off the horse.

The Regent, who was clearly reveling in the feel of her strong, young arms around him, gave a shuddering sigh and said, "That is . . . an unusual attitude for a woman of your station."

"I am an unusual woman," replied Persephone, who could think of nothing else to say.

"Indeed," breathed the Regent Mordesius.

Twenty

AS HE TROTTED ALONG, Mordesius's thoughts harkened back to the day in the dungeon when he'd vowed to Murdock that he'd show the great lords that the king was not the only one who could ride out among the people of Parthania looking like a majestic young god. He'd expected to put on a fine show, yes, but he'd never dreamt that it would be as fine as this! Indeed, he was now bitterly regretting that he'd decided to destroy the slum at night. It was also unfortunate that the good citizens of Parthania felt compelled to stay indoors whilst it was happening for fear of being accidentally added to the lowborn transports. How glorious it would have been for them to see him, their Lord Regent, astride this mighty steed with this beautiful young noblewoman clinging to him like a rescued damsel! Nay, not like a rescued damsel—like a lover. For surely only a lover would cling with such unyielding ferocity. Indeed, his ribs were beginning to ache with the strength of her embrace.

The question was, why? He'd not been the least fooled by the way she'd pouted prettily and referred to herself as "a mere woman," or by the way she'd curtseyed with her breasts thrust upward and her eyelashes fluttering to set a man's loins afire. He'd known in that moment that she'd wanted something from him, and he'd thought that it was mercy for that wretched old husband of hers, Bothwell.

What if he was wrong? What if years of having his tentative advances politely—but categorically—rejected by repulsed noblewomen had blinded him to the face of true desire? What if the thing that Lady Bothwell had wanted was him? It was almost inconceivable and yet . . . and yet . . . dressed in black as he was, he knew that his poor, scarred body was all but hidden by the night. That meant that the only thing she'd really seen of him thus far was his face. And he knew for a certainty that his was the handsomest face in the realm.

I am also the most powerful man in the realm, he thought suddenly as he guided his horse to one side to avoid the body of the man who'd been killed by the soldier's arrow. *Women are attracted to power—power and money. And I have both!*

Mordesius's excitement grew as his thoughts turned to Lady Bothwell's comments that she cared about many things and that she was an unusual woman. What had she been trying to tell him with her strange, cryptic words? Had she been trying to tell him that she might be able to care for him in spite of his cruel injuries? Perhaps her tastes ran in perverse directions—perhaps she *especially* desired men of his ilk. After all, whatever she professed of her husband's health and vigor, Bothwell was unquestionably an old man possessed of an old man's shriveled, shrunken body and sallow, wrinkled skin, an old man's cold hands and bony feet, and an old man's gross noises and disgusting smells. If she could desire *that*, why should she not desire him in his current condition? And if she did, wasn't it entirely possible that she might be willing to lie beneath him that he might get a strong, healthy son upon her noble young body? And if that were to happen—if she were to allow her noble blood to be mingled with his own—wasn't it true that the great lords of the realm would no longer be able to deny that he was a man worthy of being named the heir of His doomed Majesty King Finnius?

It was true. Truly it was!

Of course, he was getting far ahead of himself. Before he could get a son upon Lady Bothwell, he would have to marry her, for though a bastard would prove his virility, it would help him not at all where the great lords were concerned, for they cared only for legitimate heirs. And before he could marry Lady Bothwell, he would have to court her—and see to the death of her husband, of course. Well, no matter. He'd had plans for the old goat anyway, so irritated had he been to discover that a man as decrepit as Bothwell could get such a luscious, loyal young wife while he, himself, had to settle for occasionally groping servant women too terrified to do anything but lie there unmoving and praying for it to be over quickly. He would send Murdock to dispatch Bothwell as soon as the business with Pembleton was finished. In the meantime, he would send a handful of soldiers beyond the city walls to hunt down the scum that had attacked Lady Bothwell. He would give them orders to inflict slow and painful deaths upon the wretches, and while they were at it, to dispatch the strapping young fool who'd dared to hesitate when ordered to assist Lady Bothwell onto his horse. And speaking of the horse, he had half a mind to have the beast destroyed for the way its graceless movements had caused him such jarring pain throughout this long, exhausting evening.

There is always so much to do, thought Mordesius with a sigh as he rode past several dozen grubby-looking children who'd been torn from their lowborn parents that they might be sent onward to toil alongside the Gorgishmen in the Mines of Torodania. *Truly, if I did not have hope that all this would one day be mine to rule, I do not know how I could find the strength to carry on. . . .*

Twenty-One

FOR HER PART, Persephone's mind also began racing the minute the Regent's horse trotted away from the alley, though her thoughts were of a different nature entirely. She knew that Azriel and Rachel's best hope of escaping the city was her in her noble finery, yet she was moving ever farther away from them. She'd saved them by stepping forward into the torchlight but at what price? And to what end? They were safe for the moment, yes, but as the Regent had said, there would be many unfortunates out this night seeking to wreak vengeance upon those who did not share their fate. Would Azriel be able to protect Rachel? Would he be able to protect himself? And what of Cur and Fleet—and what of the child they were meant to rescue? Forcing herself to look upon the horror of what was happening in the slum, Persephone saw black-clad soldiers tearing screaming children from their mothers' arms; she saw unarmed, lowborn men desperately flinging themselves at these same soldiers, only to be struck down again and again until at last they lay unmoving in slowly spreading pools of their own blood. Was the child they were meant to rescue there, among those poor creatures, or was he yet hidden? Or had he been left behind entirely by those who dared not risk the lives of their own children by being seen this night with a child someone might recognize as being a member of the murdered Methusian family?

A sudden vision of little Sabian thus abandoned to a fiery death struck Persephone with the force of a blow to the head. She gasped once, then gasped again as the horse beneath her shifted so abruptly that she nearly lost her balance. Clutching the Regent harder, she looked down to see a spread-eagled man with an arrow through one dead eye. The arrow had been meant for Cur, and while she was grateful that it had not found him, she grieved for this man who'd died in his stead.

The Fates never give but that they take away, she thought bitterly, wishing she were far away from the sights and sounds of this terrible night. To her surprise, she also found herself wishing that it was Azriel's warm, well-muscled body she was clinging to instead of the painfully thin torso of the man who'd caused all this terror and pain. She'd heard the lust in his voice earlier—indeed, out of desperation she'd played to it. Now, however, she feared that she would be trapped by her own game.

For she knew the ways of men well enough to know that when aroused, they could twist the most innocent glance or touch to feed their deluded fantasies. And if those fantasies belonged to a man as powerful as the Regent, she knew it was only a matter of time before he'd find a way to turn them into reality.

And as quick as she was with a dagger, once trapped behind the thick, heavily guarded walls of the imperial palace, Persephone did not see how she'd ever be able to gut him like a fish and escape with her life.

"Your chambers, Lady Bothwell," murmured the Regent with an ungainly bow.

Persephone gave him a strained smile then returned to staring at the beautifully carved door before her. Though not more than half an hour had passed since she'd left Rachel and Azriel hiding in the alley, it felt like an eternity. By the time she, the Regent and his men had reached the moat surrounding the palace, the air had been thick with black smoke and the sound of dry timber going up in flames. As the guard in the watchtower bellowed the order to lift the heavy wrought-iron gate on the far side of the drawbridge and make way for the Lord Regent, they heard the first shrill screams. Persephone had not been able to keep herself from shuddering violently when she heard them, and then shuddering again when she heard the Regent sigh with what sounded like satisfaction. Trying not to think what it said about a man who'd been all but burned alive himself that he would take pleasure in condemning countless others to that same hideous fate, she'd stared straight ahead as they clattered through the watchtower passageway and into the bustling, torch-lit palace courtyard.

There, in addition to drunken young noblemen, milling soldiers, shouting groomsmen and small boys running to and fro underfoot, Persephone had noticed a flock of vulturine old men in black capes and hoods hurrying toward the palace. The grizzled old groomsman who'd deftly lifted her off the Regent's horse had explained that they were physicians come to tend the king, who'd suffered a frightful coughing fit on account of the smoke that billowed thicker with each passing moment. Upon hearing this, the Regent had cursed someone named Moira for being such a fool as to leave His Majesty's windows ajar on a night such as this. Muttering and wincing terribly, he'd lurched off without a backward glance. Persephone had hoped that tending to the needs of the sick king might cause the Regent to forget about her, but he'd returned after only a few minutes and now here they were, standing together at the threshold of "her" chambers.

"Well, Lady Bothwell?" inquired the Regent, who was watching her closely. "Will you not even inspect the rooms to see if they are to your liking?"

At the sound of his voice, Persephone nearly leapt out of her skin.

"Yes—yes, of course I will!" she blurted as she flushed nervously under his inspection. "Forgive me, Your Grace. I am not usually so lacking in graciousness, but it has been a rather long and trying day, and to say that I do not feel like myself right now would be an understatement of rather monumental proportions."

"I understand completely," murmured Mordesius soothingly. "I only pray that you will find some solace in the humble comfort of your accommodations."

With another bow, the Regent flung open the door and stepped back to allow Persephone to be the first to cross the threshold.

Tentatively, she stepped forward . . . and nearly fell over in amazement.

For the room that lay before her was bigger than the owner's entire cottage had been. Perhaps bigger than his entire farm had been!

High-ceilinged and glowing with the soft, clear light of quality candles, it was far and away the finest room Persephone had ever seen. The wood floor was polished so smooth that it gleamed in the firelight, and the dark paneled walls were hung with thickly woven tapestries depicting ancient tales of heroism and love. Against one wall was a canopied bed hung with plum-colored velvet curtains and piled high with pillows—a bed so enormous that Persephone couldn't see how a person would possibly be able to climb into it without the use of a stepladder. Against the opposite wall, beneath a row of shutters that had been closed tight against the smoke outside, lay a table groaning under the weight of more food than Persephone would have been able to eat in half a lifetime. A whole roast pheasant artfully re-dressed in its own brilliant feathers; a joint of meat and a platter of fish; several loaves of bread and an assortment of cheeses; bowls piled high with exotic-looking fruits and candied sweetmeats; three kinds of pastries and a jug of what Persephone presumed to be wine or ale. She stared at the mouth-watering bounty for what was probably an indecent length of time, and when she was finally able to tear her eyes away from it, she noticed a door along the back wall. Even as she wondered where it might lead, it was flung open and a woman and two older girls wordlessly filed into the room.

Startled, Persephone glanced back at Mordesius in mild confusion.

In response, he smiled broadly and said, "I told you that servants could be replaced as easily as smashed dinner plates, did I not, Lady Bothwell?"

Not knowing what to say to this rather horrible statement, Persephone nodded uncomfortably and turned back to continue her examination of the room.

That was when she saw it, partially hidden behind an ornate screen not far from the merrily crackling fire:

A great, claw-footed bathtub half-full of steaming water.

As she gazed upon it in wonder, a scrawny servant girl about eight years of age stumbled into the room lugging yet another pail of steaming water.

"Careful, you!" snarled Mordesius as a wave of water sloshed over the lip of the pail. "That water is meant for the lady's bath, not for washing your filthy lowborn feet!"

"Yes, Your Grace!" squeaked the child. Quaking with terror and grunting with exertion, she somehow managed to hoist the pail high enough to tip the water into the bath. Then, after curtseying to Mordesius and Persephone, she hastily scampered out of the room—presumably to get more hot water.

After she'd gone, Persephone turned to Mordesius. "It is all . . . quite satisfactory," she said, trying not to sound as overwhelmed as she felt.

Eyes gleaming as though he hadn't noticed how lukewarm her praise had been, the Regent took a hitching step forward as if he meant to join her on the other side of the threshold.

"In fact," continued Persephone as she quickly moved to block his way, "when my loving husband and I are reunited, I will be sure to tell him how kindly and respectfully you treated me in my hour of need."

Her words stopped Mordesius in his tracks. Slowly, he lifted his head until his fathomless eyes were once more boring into her.

Once again, she found herself unable to move or speak, unable to do anything but pray that her facade would not crumble and that her trembling legs would not give way beneath her.

"You do that," said the Regent softly. "Also remind him that, one way or another, a careless husband is soon deprived of a beautiful wife."

Hearing an unmistakable threat in his words, Persephone swallowed hard. "And yet . . . I am safe here, under your protection, am I not, Your Grace?" she asked.

"You are indeed," he agreed, smiling as though considering some private joke. "Sleep well, my lady. I shall return upon the morrow that you may accompany me to view a spectacle that I believe you will find most entertaining."

"I shall look forward to it," said Persephone.

Then she curtseyed as modestly as a nun, and carefully closed the door on the Regent's still-smiling face.

After shutting the door, Persephone stood rigid with her hands clenched at her sides, listening intently for the sound of the Regent departing. For an endless moment, she heard nothing except (she imagined) the sound of his heavy breathing. Then, at last, she heard a soft grunt and the uneven rhythm of his gait as he made his way down the hallway.

Closing her eyes, she sighed with relief.

"Bath, m'lady?" came a voice directly behind her.

With a distinctly un-noble yelp, Persephone whirled around to see the woman servant gazing at her with the expressionless eyes of one who'd long since learned how to mask her true feelings.

"Bath, m'lady?" she repeated. "Or would you prefer to dine first?"

Famished though she was, Persephone nearly laughed aloud at the question, for who could possibly eat knowing that there was a tub full of clean, steaming-hot water just waiting to be soaked in? Trying hard to contain her sudden, guilty excitement at the prospect, Persephone calmly informed the woman of her preference to bathe first. The instant she did so, the woman looked over her shoulder at the girl servants, both of whom looked to be about Persephone's age. The taller, skinnier of the two bobbed a hasty curtsey and hurried out the door at the back of the room, while the shorter, plumper one bustled forward with surprising briskness for someone with nothing but a rough-hewn wooden peg where her right leg should be.

"Don't worry, m'lady," she said heartily as she hustled Persephone over to the warmth of the fire and began deftly unlacing her gown. "We'll have you out of these travel-worn things soon enough!"

Feeling acutely embarrassed by the prospect of being stripped naked by a complete stranger, Persephone was nevertheless prepared to submit herself to it until she suddenly remembered that the clothes she was wearing were soaked with sickness.

With a horrified gasp, she wrenched her body away from the nimble fingers of the startled servant girl.

"Get away from me!" she cried, flapping her hand at the girl. "Don't *touch* me!"

Work-worn fingers poised in midair, the girl eyed Persephone cautiously. "Apologies, m'lady, if in some way I have offended—"

"You've not offended," said Persephone quickly. "I just . . . I'm sorry, what is your name?"

"My name?" said the girl blankly.

"You know—the particular handle by which people address you," said Persephone, who could not help smiling slightly as she recalled the words of a certain handsome chicken thief.

The girl gave Persephone the kind of look that she, herself, used to give the owner when she thought he was being an especially thick-headed boor. Insolent, but not so insolent that the fool could be certain she was being insolent. "I know what a name is, m'lady," said the girl with exaggerated patience, "and mine is Neeka."

Persephone nodded as though this was the very answer she'd been hoping for. "Well, Neeka," she said briskly, "the fact is that I should like to undress myself and then I should like to personally bundle my clothes into a clean sheet so that they may be burned to ashes without delay."

Though it was clear that Neeka considered this a bizarre and foolish request, she nodded without offering comment and bustled off to fetch the clean sheet. As soon as she was gone, Persephone hurriedly peeled off her gloves, tugged off her jewels, kicked off her boots, wriggled out of her dusty, mud-splattered gown and petticoats and surreptitiously hid her dagger in its scabbard, the rat tail, the bit of lace and the silky auburn curl beneath a loose floorboard. Then she stepped into the bath, which was so thick with floating rose petals that she felt sure that Neeka and the others would not be able to see her nakedness. Leaning back, she closed her eyes.

"Mmm," she sighed, inhaling deeply. "This doesn't smell at all like rotten eggs."

"Why would it smell like rotten eggs?"

Embarrassed, Persephone opened her eyes to find Neeka staring down at her with a fresh sheet in one hand, a jar of something in the other and a quizzical expression on her face.

"It *shouldn't* smell like rotten eggs," said Persephone loftily, wondering how on earth a girl with a peg for a leg had managed to sneak up on her. "That's exactly my point."

Neeka smiled pleasantly—the way one might smile at a simpleton or a lunatic. Then she went to help the tall, skinny girl and the little scrawny girl, both of whom had just returned with more hot water.

"My older sister, Anya, and my younger sister, Reeta," announced Neeka as she helped little Reeta dump her large pail of water into the tub. "Anya is mute and Reeta only has three toes on her left foot."

The woman servant, who'd disappeared after handing Persephone over to Neeka, now returned carrying several more jars, a fine-toothed comb, four fresh sponges and a cream-colored night-gown and matching robe of such a fine weave that they were almost translucent in the warm light of the fire. After nervously introducing herself as Martha, the woman carefully draped the nightgown and robe over the back of a chair near the fire.

So that they will be warm for me when I emerge from the bath! thought Persephone giddily. She had not forgotten the horrors of this night or the fact that her companions were still out there in the cold, dirty, dangerous darkness, but she knew that there was nothing she could do about that at the moment and nothing to be gained from refusing to enjoy the fulfillment of one of her most cherished childhood dreams.

And so she relaxed and slipped a little lower in the water as Martha and the three sisters quietly took their places around the tub and gently began to bathe her. The jar that Neeka had been holding contained soap—not the slimy brown homemade variety, but a fragrant, creamy cake speckled with petals and herbs; the jars that Martha had brought contained various oils and scrubs. While Neeka and little Reeta each took a hand and began carefully sponging Persephone from bare shoulder to ragged fingertip, Anya wordlessly tended to her embarrassingly grimy, torn feet. Martha, meanwhile, removed the crystal hairpins from her now-disheveled hairdo, combed the tangles out of her thick, luxurious mane and began working richly scented oils through it.

"Scars," murmured little Reeta as she tenderly traced the whip-lash scar on Persephone's forearm.

"And calluses," said Neeka in surprise when she turned Persephone's hand over to sponge the palm.

"Yes," muttered Persephone. "I, uh, like to do my own gardening."

"As does our King Finnius," grinned Reeta.

"How fares the king?" asked Persephone, glad for a change of subject. "I understand that he suffered a frightful coughing fit this night."

"Yes. Sad, isn't it?" said Neeka, without looking up from Persephone's soapy hand. "When the rich and powerful suffer as a result of the terrible things they do to lesser creatures."

"Neeka!" hissed Martha with a wary, darting glance at Persephone. "You've no business criticizing your betters or passing judgment on their actions! And even to imply that you do not pity His Majesty his poor health is to come dangerously close to ill wishing him— which, as you well know, is tantamount to *treason*!"

At this most dread word, Anya's mouth fell open to reveal her gruesomely amputated tongue and little Reeta froze with terror. Persephone stared perplexedly at them, unable to understand why they should be so frightened when there was no one else but her in the room.

They think I am the Regent's creature, she realized with a jolt. *They fear I will report Neeka's words to him!*

Awkwardly, she placed her soapy hand over Reeta's bony little one. "As it happens, I agree with your sister that it was a terrible thing done this night," she confided. Then she smiled as disarmingly as she knew how and said, "Now, enough chatter. Help me finish bathing, so that I may eat my supper without fear of falling asleep with my face in a platter."

Despite her expressed desire to hurry to sup, Persephone lingered in the tub until the water was quite cold. At that point, she earned another odd look from Neeka when, upon remembering that she still had marks on her back from the whipping she'd received at the hands of the owner, she refused assistance getting out of the tub, slipped on a puddle of soapy water and then refused assistance getting up off the floor. When at last she managed to knot her old clothes up in the sheet and slip into the beautiful nightgown and robe, she was delighted to discover that they skimmed her curves as though they'd been made just for her.

Which, of course, they had not.

"I cannot say for a certainty where the Regent found these things, m'lady, but judging by the quality and craftsmanship, I'd guess that they once belonged to the dead queen," said Martha matter-of-factly as she carved another slice of roast pheasant for Persephone.

"The dead queen?" spluttered Persephone, choking on a sip of wine so potent she was already feeling woozy.

"I'd guess the same thing," agreed Neeka, who was gazing at the roast pheasant with ill-disguised longing, "for it is common knowledge that in the days following poor Queen Fey's death, the Regent had her possessions inventoried and thereafter took many of the finer things into his own keeping." She hesitated a moment before sliding her gaze to Persephone's face and deliberately adding, "It is a well-known fact that our Lord Regent has an eye for fine things, m'lady—and a burning desire to possess them at any cost."

Persephone shivered at these last words and tried to finish the food on her plate, but it was no use. A hot bath, a dead woman's clothes, a rich feast, a cup of strong wine, the stress of things past and the dread of things yet to come had all conspired, finally, to sap her of her last vestiges of strength. Waving her hand wearily at the still-heaping platters, she told Martha and the sisters to help themselves.

"Do you mean we've permission to eat from your very own *table*?" squeaked Reeta, who was positively pop-eyed with excitement at the prospect.

Realizing that she'd made a significant blunder but not having the heart to correct it, Persephone nodded. Then she tiredly pushed her chair away from the table and padded across the room to the mountainous canopy bed. Martha and the three sisters hurried after her, intent upon performing their final duties of the evening—Anya to help Persephone out of her robe, Martha to help her into her nightcap, Reeta to fetch the footstool she needed to scale the bed and Neeka to arrange the pillows and blankets to her satisfaction.

When they were done, they all lined up at the foot of the bed and eyed Persephone so expectantly that she began to grow alarmed.

"Are we dismissed then, m'lady?" prompted Neeka at length.

"What?" blurted Persephone. "Oh, uh, yes, of course."

Bobbing curtseys, the four servants eagerly drew the plum-colored curtains around the bed and then scurried over to the table like four little mice that had just discovered a hole in the granary wall.

Persephone smiled to hear their whispered exclamations and giggles, then her smile faded as her thoughts drifted to Azriel and Rachel, Fleet and Cur.

And, of course, the child.

Tomorrow I will find an excuse to go into the city and look for them, she thought drowsily as she drifted off to sleep. *Upon finding them I will do what I can to see them safely beyond the city walls, and then I will turn my thoughts back to escape—and the freedom to live my own life.*

Whatever the risk, whatever the cost.

Twenty-Two

HOURS LATER, in an even more sumptuously appointed chamber, the servants were not giggling or whispering or feasting. They were standing in the cold shadows with their backs pressed against the walls, staring straight ahead and struggling not to yawn or shiver or otherwise do anything to suggest that they were human beings and not pieces of furniture.

In the chair before the fire, the Regent Mordesius slouched unmoving. Though it had been a long, difficult day, he could not sleep for thoughts of Lady Bothwell. Why had she not invited him to dine with her even though one look from him had set her trembling like a bride on her wedding night? Was it because she was embarrassed by her admittedly bedraggled state? Was it out of some misplaced loyalty to that decrepit old husband of hers? And what of the kitchen servants' reports that she'd eaten *every last morsel of food on the table!* The only time he'd ever heard of a noblewoman having such an appetite was when she was with child. But Lady Bothwell couldn't possibly be with child—even an idiot like Bothwell wouldn't be stupid enough to let his wife travel so far in such a delicate condition.

No, Lady Bothwell was not a woman with child—she was simply a woman of strange appetites.

Appetites that he, Mordesius, intended to press to his full advantage.

Twenty-Three

"GOOD MORNING, M'LADY," sang a lilting voice. Feeling none of the apprehension she usually felt when unexpectedly woken from a sound sleep, Persephone lazily opened her eyes to see Reeta's elfin face framed by the velvet bed curtains.

"Good morning, Reeta," she said sleepily. "What time is it?"

"Time to rise," replied Reeta, her face vanishing abruptly.

The next instant, the bed curtains were unceremoniously yanked open. With a yelp, Persephone jerked her head to one side and threw up her arm to shield her eyes from the blinding sunlight.

"'Tis a beautiful day, m'lady," declared Reeta, smiling broadly.

Still squinting, Persephone smiled back. "Where are Neeka, Anya and Martha?" she inquired.

On cue, there was a knock at the door. Persephone nodded to Reeta that she should open the door, and the next thing she knew, a veritable parade of servants—led by Neeka, Anya and Martha— was marching into the room carrying plates of eggs and meat, baskets of sweet buns, silver pots of thick clotted cream, glass bowls of fruit preserves and honey, more pies, more cheeses and more ale.

Blankets pulled up to her chin so that none of these strangers would see her in the dead queen's nightclothes, Persephone stared, wide-eyed, as the table by the now-open shutters was once again loaded down to the point of groaning. She then self-consciously nodded acknowledgment to one servant after another as they respectfully presented themselves at the foot of her bed before filing out of the room.

In the wake of their departure, Persephone cast a rather forlorn look at Martha and asked, "Why are they feeding me so much?"

At this, Neeka, Reeta and even mute Anya dissolved into giggles.

Martha glared at them before clearing her throat and saying, "Well, m'lady, it appears that when last night's platters were returned to the kitchen picked clean, uh, the kitchen servants assumed, that, well . . ."

"That I ate it all by *myself*?" cried Persephone, flopping back onto the goose-down pillows.

The three sisters giggled some more.

"Not to worry, m'lady," soothed Martha as she hurried over to the table to prepare a tray for Persephone. "You just have a bite to eat and then we'll get you dressed for your outing with my Lord Regent."

Persephone's heart plummeted twice—once at the thought of her "outing" with the Regent, and a second time when she recalled that the previous night, she'd ordered burned to ashes every stitch of clothing she had. She did not regret having given the order, for to have done otherwise would have meant having the items taken away to be washed, sprigged, starched, ironed, mended and otherwise restored by untold numbers of servants who would thereby have been exposed to the Great Sickness (which she, luckily, did not appear to have caught). However, a rather distressing consequence of this most considerate and responsible decision was that she now had nothing whatsoever to wear.

Even as she considered this predicament there was another knock at the door and another parade of servants marched into the room. This time, each of them was carrying something fine to wear. In addition to half a dozen richly colored gowns made of the finest cloth and generously embellished with ribbons, lace, embroidery, brocade and gemstones, there were dozens of crisply starched petticoats, an assortment of silk undergarments, two pairs of gloves (one pair made of nothing but fine lace), three riding cloaks (one lined with real cloth of gold and another trimmed in actual ermine!), two pairs of high-heeled dancing slippers, a pair of riding boots (with real silver buckles) and a dazzling array of jeweled hair accessories. Without meaning to, Persephone sighed at the sight of all those beautiful things, none of which—presumably—was soaked with a sickness that could result in hideous death.

"The only thing missing is something sparkly to wear at your throat!" grinned little Reeta, after the last of this batch of servants had been dismissed.

Once again, there was a knock on the door. This time, only a single servant entered the room—an impeccably groomed man who stood as rigid as a statue and stared straight ahead as though he saw nothing of the world around him. Upon his upturned palm lay a dark-blue velvet pillow trimmed with gold tassels, and upon the pillow lay an exquisite silver necklace hung with an amethyst as big as a goose egg. The beautifully cut gemstone was the very color of Persephone's eyes, and there were earrings to match.

"A small token of His Grace's esteem," intoned the manservant.

"It seems our Lord Regent has developed a great fondness for you," observed Neeka neutrally, after the manservant had bowed crisply, turned on one heel and departed.

"Yes," said Persephone, trying not to sound as troubled as she felt, "it seems that he has."

Persephone took breakfast in bed. It was a luxury that rivaled the bath from the night before but she did not let it distract her. Refreshed, restored and having solved the thorny problem of what to wear, she turned her thoughts to coming up with a plan to find and rescue Azriel, Rachel, Fleet and Cur.

If, indeed, rescue was still possible.

"So," she said, waving her half-eaten sweet bun around, "what news of last night's events?"

"Whatever do you mean, m'lady?" asked Neeka, her eyes following the sweet bun as though it were a ball at a royal tennis match.

Persephone took a deliberately dainty bite of the bun. "Well," she said carefully, in between chews, "I mean, was there any report of . . . unusual or unexpected happenings?"

Neeka's gaze drifted away from the bun and settled squarely on Persephone's face. "As m'lady surely knows, official news of great import is rarely reported to the likes of us," she said.

Persephone's mouth flew open and then snapped shut again when she realized that Neeka had not *necessarily* meant to include her in "the likes of us."

"However, we tend to hear a great deal of unofficial news," continued Neeka placidly, "and there was no unofficial news of last night, save the expected: that a handful of notorious criminals were captured or killed, that many families mattering to no one of consequence were torn apart for the greater good of the kingdom, and that the street cleaners will be busy for some days to come clearing away the ruins of the wretched hovels those families once inhabited—and the charred remains of their loved ones who dared to remain behind."

Persephone nodded wordlessly and tried not to imagine sturdy, rosy-cheeked little Sabian as a tiny, blackened corpse lying beneath the rubble. Feeling suddenly as though she might vomit—or even cry—she flung the half-eaten sweet bun down onto the tray and shoved the tray aside. "There was no other . . . unofficial news, then?" she asked in a voice that sounded almost harsh.

"Sometimes no news is the best news," offered Neeka.

And sometimes it isn't, thought Persephone.

"Fetch me the footstool," she said, throwing off the covers. "I wish to get up."

✳

Getting dressed was as much of a production as bathing had been, and there was no way Persephone could hide the marks on her back because she had to have her corsets tightened by someone standing behind her. However, as no one mentioned the marks, Persephone let herself hope that perhaps they hadn't been noticed. Or, if they had been noticed, that it had been assumed that she'd been beaten by her husband, a common enough occurrence among couples of all classes.

After she'd hung onto the bedpost and had Martha haul on the corset strings until she was sure she felt her ribs crack, Neeka helped her into her petticoats and then into a gown of shimmering yellow shot through with silver thread. Its generous overskirt was pinned up into deep swoops along the hem that revealed the thickly pleated ruffles of her underskirt and petticoats, its tight-fitting, lace-trimmed sleeves hung almost to her fingertips, and its bodice was cut so low that Persephone was afraid to breathe too deeply for fear that her dangerously straining bosom would spring free entirely.

Once she was dressed, Anya fetched a pail of warm rose water and gently bathed, oiled and dried Persephone's feet. Meanwhile, little Reeta carefully shaped and polished each of her fingernails, and Neeka combed her hair for a thousand strokes, piled it upon her head, pinned it, perfumed it and pomaded it until it was as hard as marble. When the sisters were done, Martha brought over several jars of cosmetics that she used to powder Persephone's face, rouge her cheeks, paint her lips and draw a fashionable black beauty mark on the left side of her chin. Then she helped Persephone into a pair of beribboned stockings secured high upon her thigh and slipped her feet into a pair of high-heeled dancing slippers before finally securing the amethyst necklace about her neck and hanging the matching earrings from her lobes.

"You look *very* fine," breathed Reeta, clasping her hands beneath her chin.

Martha and Anya nodded their agreement, as did Neeka, who added, "No one would ever know you for anything other than the great noblewoman you are."

Although this statement felt alarmingly close to an accusation, Persephone could think of nothing to do but ignore it.

"Thank you," she said primly.

"You're welcome," replied Neeka. "Now, would you like to do some needlepoint while you wait for my Lord Regent to collect you?"

"Needlepoint?" said Persephone blankly as Anya bobbed a curtsey and hurried off.

"Yes," said Neeka as Anya reappeared carrying an enormous basket full of colorful yarns and fine threads. "Knowing how ladies of your station adore passing the time knitting socks and embroidering cushions and the like, my Lord Regent has kindly provided you with all the tools of your noble craft."

"Oh," said Persephone, whose sewing experience was limited to resentfully stitching up the torn seams of the owner's dirty pants. "Well, uh . . ."

"Oooooh and look!" squealed Reeta, snatching up a square of white silk. "I daresay my Lord Regent has given you one of his very own handkerchiefs to embroider!"

"A great honor," observed Martha with apparent reverence.

"Indeed," said Persephone, who wondered how the Regent was going to like his handkerchief when she gave it back to him covered in great, uneven stitches, ugly knots and loose threads. "In fact, it is such an honor that I believe I shall this very minute go for a walk in the garden that I might find inspiration for a design."

And also a way over the castle walls, she added silently, *for with the Regent so intent upon ensuring that I spend my time engaging in activities appropriate for "my station," it may be harder than I expected to find an excuse to go into the city.*

"Actually, m'lady—" began Martha.

"While I'm gone, why don't you and the others help yourselves to something to eat?" called Persephone as she strode briskly toward the door, her skirts and petticoats swishing deliciously with each step. "After all, I should not like to disappoint the kitchen staff by sending any of the dishes back other than picked clean."

Certain that the prospect of dining from her table would keep Martha and the sisters well occupied while she attempted to flee the palace, Persephone smiled inwardly at her own cleverness, flung open the door and screamed shrilly as a pair of ferocious-looking guards spun around to fill the doorway, the tips of their deadly pole-axes mere inches from the tip of her nose.

"M'lady?" one of them grunted.

Making a noise that sounded very much as though she was leaking air, Persephone smiled weakly and slowly closed the door.

Martha cleared her throat. "What I was going to say just now, m'lady, was that a walk in the garden was likely not possible seeing how my Lord Regent posted guards outside your door. You know," she added hastily, "to ensure that no one enters without permission."

Or leaves without permission, thought Persephone. "That was very kind of him," she said, trying not to sound as anxious as she felt.

"Yes," said Neeka, reaching for another sweet bun. "Wasn't it just?"

While Martha and the others ate their fill of sweet buns and everything else, Persephone paced the chamber trying to think of a way past the guards. By the time the last crust of bread had been drizzled with the final drops of honey, Persephone had developed blisters the size of cockroaches on both heels courtesy of her lovely new high-heeled dancing slippers. Forced to sit down, she thereafter divided her time between listening to the noisy racket of many hammers banging away in a nearby courtyard, wondering aloud when the

Regent would come for her, making excuses as to why she was not indulging in the adored noble pastime of needlework and limping over to the open window to scan the crowded cobblestone streets beyond the palace walls for a glimpse of Azriel and the others. It would not have done them a great deal of good to be seen, but it would have brought Persephone a great deal of comfort to know that they yet lived.

But only once did she see anything that held the hope of comfort—a single, fleeting glimpse of a tall, broad-shouldered man who might have been Azriel. He had his head down as he made his way slowly through a distant market square, and he appeared to be alone. Heart pounding wildly, Persephone leaned halfway out the window and stared so hard that her eyes began to water. As she did so, the man stopped suddenly, lifted his head and seemed to return Persephone's stare. Unfortunately, her eyes were so watery by that point that she could not get a good look at him, and when she blinked to clear her eyes, he was gone.

By midafternoon the hammering outside finally stopped. A short while later, a herald showed up to announce the imminent arrival of the Regent. At once, Martha and the sisters fell upon Persephone—dousing her with perfume, fixing her makeup, checking her hair and helping her on with her gloves. Neeka even offered to stuff some wadding down the backs of her slippers to give some relief to her poor, blistered heels. She was still on her hands and knees making sure that the wadding didn't show when there came another knock at the door.

At the sound, Persephone started so badly that she nearly put the delicate heel of her slipper through Neeka's hand.

"Sorry!" she blurted as Reeta scampered across the room to open the door.

"No worries," whispered Neeka as she maneuvered herself into a standing position with surprising ease for a girl with a missing leg. "Try not to be nervous, m'lady. You look well—just watch the others, do as they do and you'll be fine."

Persephone looked sharply at the girl, but Neeka had already hastened to take her place against the wall next to Martha and Anya.

And then the chamber door was flung open and there stood the Regent Mordesius, resplendent in a long velvet robe trimmed in white fox fur and of a color that would have been called purple if he'd been king.

Head held high with obvious effort, he shuffled into the room.

"Lady Bothwell," he breathed, inclining his head without taking his eyes off her.

"Your Grace," she replied with a deep curtsey.

"You look . . . much improved this day," he said.

"I do not believe that I have ever before so appreciated a hot bath, a fine meal and a good night's sleep in a warm bed," she said truthfully.

Mordesius's dark eyes gleamed. "And I trust that you were not offended that I took the liberty of sending you a few things of my own careful choosing?" he asked, gesturing to her ensemble.

Persephone flushed at the thought that the Regent had personally selected her clothing—probably from among the poor dead queen's pilfered belongings—and that his hands had touched the very undergarments she currently wore next to her skin. "No, of course I wasn't offended that you sent me things," she said, trying not to shudder. "It was . . . most kind of you."

Mordesius smiled broadly, showing his beautiful teeth. Then he shuffled forward some more until he was standing directly before Persephone.

"And this," he said huskily as he reached out and slipped his cold fingers beneath the amethyst that hung about her throat. "You were not offended that I sent you *this*?"

Persephone hesitated, sensing that she was about to make a misstep but not knowing exactly what it was or how to avoid it. "No," she said at last. "I was not offended."

The Regent sighed softly. "Excellent," he breathed. Then, with a quiet grunt of effort, he held out his arm to her and said, "Now we must depart, for the spectacle I promised shall shortly commence, and I would not have you miss a moment of it."

"That is most thoughtful of you," murmured Persephone as she gingerly laid her hand upon his trembling arm.

"Yes," mused Mordesius as he led her from the room. "It is, isn't it?"

Twenty-Four

MORDESIUS WALKED THROUGH the corridors in a calm silence that was at odds with the tumult erupting inside of him. He felt like a boy! Not like the boy he'd been after the fire, of course—that tortured mess of charred flesh and ruined limbs—but like the vital, healthy boy he'd been in the time before. The feel of Lady Bothwell's arm resting lightly upon his own arm was as tender as a caress, and the way she effortlessly moved beside him somehow—miraculously!—made his awkward, uneven gait seem almost graceful. Not only that, but she'd *deliberately* mentioned how warm her bed was, and she'd accepted his gift of jewelry without a single word of protest that it was unseemly for a married woman to accept such intimate gifts from a man other than her husband. Why, it was tantamount to accepting him as a lover—or at least as a potential lover. True, he'd given such gifts to noblewomen in the past only to have his subsequent advances rebuffed, but Lady Bothwell did not seem the type. She was different than those other sows had been. More genuine and at the same time, more mysterious. Certainly more hot-blooded. He'd seen her flush when he'd mentioned having had a hand in choosing her things, as though she, too, had felt the intimacy of the act. He wondered how she'd react if she knew how long he'd spent holding up each item to better picture it hugging her soft, firm flesh. And, of course, the soft, firm flesh of the dead queen to whom it had once belonged.

The thought almost made Mordesius giggle aloud—or might have, if he'd been a man predisposed to giggling.

Glancing sideways at Lady Bothwell now, Mordesius wondered if he should warn her as to the exact nature of the spectacle she was about to witness. If she'd been any other woman, he might have, just to avoid any risk of hysterics, but she wasn't any other woman. In his mind she was already his future queen, the mother of his true-begotten half-noble son. In that great capacity she would need to be able to stand at his side and maintain her composure in all situations, no matter how shocking or gruesome. As it happened, this particular situation would be an excellent test of her abilities in that regard, and he stood ready to judge her accordingly.

Smiling to himself at the thought, Mordesius lifted his aching arm higher and wondered at the possibility that Lady Bothwell might even enjoy the little drama that was about to unfold before her.

After all, she was unquestionably a woman of strange appetites.

There was always the chance that these included an appetite for blood.

Twenty-Five

THERE WAS NO TUMULT erupting inside Persephone as she and the Regent walked silently through the corridors. How could there be when she was concentrating so hard on elegantly matching the Regent step for lurching step? And on trying to ignore the unnatural chill of his fingers against her skin? And on worrying as to the nature of the promised "spectacle"? The Regent had said nothing of it but that she would find it entertaining, and while she fervently hoped that she was about to be treated to a court play or a tournament, somehow, she did not think that was the case.

"Ready, Lady Bothwell?" smiled Mordesius, stopping at last before a set of wide brass doors that were at least twice as tall as Persephone.

"Of course," she replied lightly, in spite of her hammering heart.

The Regent smiled again, then nodded impatiently at the two guards who stood at attention nearby. Soundlessly, they sprang forward and slowly heaved open the heavy doors.

At once, a swell of sound washed over Persephone. Rustling skirts and tapping heels, clinking goblets and courtly music. Deep, self-important voices and throaty, high-pitched ones; laughter that was shrill, grating and as brittle as old bones.

Altogether, it was the sound of wealth and privilege and power, and just as Persephone was thanking the Fates that it had been enough to mask the sound of her entrance—thus sparing her the ordeal of public scrutiny—an infernal, bellowing herald announced the arrival of the Lord Regent Mordesius and his esteemed guest, Lady Bothwell of the Ragorian Prefecture. At once, the room fell silent and all eyes swiveled to fix upon Persephone. Lifting her chin higher to compensate for her badly trembling knees, she held her breath and waited for someone in the glittering crowd to indignantly declare that Bothwell had no wife and to denounce Persephone accordingly, but no one said anything at all.

"They are entranced by you!" whispered the Regent exultantly.

Though it was obvious to Persephone that they were anything *but* entranced, she simply nodded and exhaled as deeply as the constricting corsets would allow. Clearly, reclusive old Bothwell had no friends or family at court—a sad thing for him, perhaps, but an extremely fortunate thing for her.

As the rustling, tapping, clinking, murmuring and laughing slowly resumed, Persephone noticed that although most of the nobles were laughing, not all were. Some stood stiff, tight-lipped and silent, staring at the floor, while others wore the carefully neutral expressions of those intent upon hiding their true feelings. Before Persephone could wonder what to make of this, the Regent began to shuffle forward, bobbing his head in acknowledgment at this person or that. Not knowing what else to do and fearful of being pounced upon by some nobleman who might wish to question her about "her" noble family's long and distinguished history, Persephone clung to his bony arm and shuffled along beside him. As she did so, she surreptitiously gazed about the vast, high-ceilinged room. Directly ahead of her was a set of heavy red curtains billowing gently in the breeze that blew through the massive open double doors behind them. To her left was a dais upon which sat an empty throne with a deep-purple cloth of state draped over it. Lined up on either side of the throne were several low but well-made chairs; before it sat a table covered with white linen trimmed in purple and set with plates and goblets that looked to be made of pure gold. To her right were row upon row of thick-legged tables with matching benches and stools. The tables nearest the dais were covered with linen of plain white and set with plates and goblets made of silver. The rest of the tables were bare of linen and appeared to be set with items of ordinary pewter. About halfway back, the rows of tables bulged outward to accommodate what looked to be a silver fountain. Oddly, it was cast in the shape of a kneeling man with his silver hands clasped beneath his chin and his sorrowful silver eyes cast toward the heavens. For the life of her, Persephone could not imagine why the Erok nobility would favor such a disturbing piece, nor any orifice from which one would wish to see wine pour forth.

Following the direction of her gaze, the Regent craned his head upward to press his cool lips against her ear. "Fear not, Lady Bothwell," he whispered. "The wine will run freely after—"

"My Lord Regent!" cried a voice some distance behind them.

Looking back, Persephone saw a richly dressed but disheveled-looking man bumbling toward them, a frantic expression on his round, red face.

"Who is that?" she asked.

Mordesius neither glanced backward nor slowed his pace. "A minor lord by the name of Pembleton, I believe."

Persephone snuck another look back at the man, who seemed to be having an inordinately difficult time fighting his way through the mostly smirking crowd. "He appears rather . . . upset," she said uncertainly as they came to a halt before the long, heavy red curtains.

"Yes, I expect he does," said Mordesius with more than a hint of satisfaction in his voice. Then he nodded at a pair of nearby servants, who abruptly yanked open the curtains.

For the second time that day, Persephone jerked her head to one side and threw up her arm to shield her eyes until they could become accustomed to the brilliant light.

Even after they did, however, it took several long seconds of blinking and squinting for her to realize what she was looking at:

A freshly built scaffold.

Suddenly, the hammering she'd heard all morning made sickening sense. As she'd feared, the "spectacle" she was about to see wasn't a play or a tournament.

It was an execution.

Persephone had never seen such a thing herself, but her Cookie had had a great-uncle whose second daughter by his third wife had married an executioner, and so she'd heard many a terrible tale. Of men who'd bravely laid their heads down upon blood-drenched blocks to meet their terrible ends, but also of men whose strength or courage had failed them. Men who'd had to be dragged up the scaffold steps, forced to their knees and kicked into position; men who'd been jeered for sobbing and begging for mercy until the very end. And even the end wasn't always the end. Sometimes, if the executioner felt he'd been poorly paid on the previous job, or if he was stupid with drink or sick with flux or too old or too young or hungry or thirsty or simply in a bad mood, it took ten, fifteen, even twenty strokes of the ax to sever the doomed wretch's head.

"Have you ever attended an execution, Lady Bothwell?" asked the Regent, who was watching her intently.

Before she could choke out a suitable answer, an arrogant-looking man with a trim silver beard caught up with them. Introducing himself as Lord Bartok, he gave Persephone a wintry smile and briefly pressed his lips against her gloved hand. As she curtseyed in response, she tried in vain to remember where she'd heard his name before.

"Lady Bothwell is here as my guest," the Regent informed Lord Bartok as he laid a possessive hand over the hand of Persephone's that had just been kissed.

"I gathered as much when you were introduced together," said Lord Bartok, watching Persephone most carefully as he added, "though I must admit that I was *astonished* to learn that old Bothwell had married, for I'd understood him to be both an invalid and a confirmed bachelor."

"Well, you were wrong," said the Regent, clearly savoring the words.

"So it would appear," murmured Lord Bartok, who smiled again before adding, "By the way, Your Grace, I must congratulate you on a fine night's work. I understand that the slum has been reduced to a charred pile of sticks and bones, and that you, yourself, led the men to action."

Mordesius shrugged modestly, but his dark eyes glittered. "As His Majesty is fond of pointing out, I am far more than a skilled administrator," he said, his words heavy with meaning that Persephone did not understand.

The nobleman seemed to understand the meaning, however, because he nodded solemnly and said, "A capable man can rise far in this world."

Pale-faced and tight-lipped, the Regent stared at him for a long moment before replying, "A fool can fall even farther."

"Quite so," agreed Lord Bartok easily. "Now tell me: Are the rumors true? Did your men truly capture another Methusian last night—here, in the very heart of Glyndoria?"

"They did," nodded Mordesius, with a sharp glance at Persephone, who'd begun to sway on her feet.

"And are we about to have the pleasure of seeing—"

"Excuse me, Lord Bartok," said the Regent impatiently, "but as you can plainly see, Lady Bothwell is suffering from the heat and the glare. I must find her a seat in the shade at once, before she faints dead away."

As Persephone was, indeed, on the verge of fainting dead away, she did not see the speculative expression on Lord Bartok's face as the Regent led her away, nor did she feel Mordesius's clawlike fingers as they dug into her lower back, propelling her closer and closer to the scaffold. She hardly heard the boards rattle beneath her feet as she staggered up the steps of the nearby canopied gallery, barely felt the cushion beneath her as she collapsed into a chair in the very front row.

Did your men truly capture another Methusian last night—here, in the very heart of Glyndoria?

They did.

"Shall I have a servant fetch you to your room, Lady Bothwell?" asked the Regent, with more than a trace of irritation.

And are we about to have the pleasure of seeing—?

"No," said Persephone in a faint but determined voice.

If, in fact, it was Azriel they'd captured, and if they meant to force him up the steps of the scaffold to suffer a Methusian's dread death, she would be there for it. She would *not* have his last sight in this world be a crowd of jeering men and women not fit to touch the hem of his silly stolen doublet. As his throat was slit to the bone and he collapsed upon the scattered straw to wait for his life to drain from his terrible wound, she would have him feel the warmth of her steady gaze and take what comfort he could from knowing that there was one in the crowd who cared.

"No," she repeated, with a fierceness that surprised her. "No, I do not wish to return to my room, thank you. It was only the heat and glare, as you said. Already I feel much improved."

Mordesius's expression eased. "You are made of stronger stuff than most noblewomen," he said in an approving voice.

Persephone smiled tightly, then froze as a small band of New Men soldiers rounded the corner of a nearby turret. Led by a weasel of a man in a general's hat, they marched in tight formation. Even so, Persephone could see among their shiny boots the dirty, dragging feet of their doomed prisoner.

Leaning forward in her chair, she gripped the rail before her and prayed for courage.

Suddenly, Lord Pembleton, the disheveled-looking man with the round, red face, broke from the noble crowd that was now assembled upon the green before the scaffold. Stumbling and tripping, he ran at the soldiers with his arms outstretched beseechingly. As soon as he was within range, one of the soldiers stepped out of formation and, holding his poleax chest-high with both hands, shoved the nobleman backward with such force that he fell to the ground. It happened quickly, but before the soldier returned to his place beside his comrades, there was time enough for Persephone to get a glimpse of the prisoner in their midst: an unconscious man with straight brown hair.

Not curly. Not auburn.

Not Azriel!

Her relief was so intense that she didn't even notice Lord Pembleton fight his way back through the crowd to fall at the feet of the Regent.

"Please, Your Grace, *please!*" he cried, gesturing wildly to the young man who was even now being dragged up the steps of the scaffold. "Have mercy on my son! He is a good boy, a father himself! He has been falsely accused. Spare him, I beg you!"

With mounting horror, Persephone stared down at the sobbing father and then up at the son. In addition to being filthy and dressed in rags, the young man had clearly been brutalized. His lips were torn, one eye was nothing but bloody pulp, his limbs were scored with burns and every one of his fingers and toes were swollen and blue and bent in unnatural directions.

Roughly, the soldiers hauled the young man to the front of the scaffold, where they held him aloft. When he failed to lift his head, the hooded executioner shouldered his ax, stomped forward and gave one of the young man's broken fingers a sharp squeeze. Pembleton's son gave a sudden, gasping cry of pain, and his head jerked up as if by the pull of a string. He stared uncomprehendingly at the silent, staring crowd for a long moment before peeling apart his scabbed lips. "Good . . . people," he whispered hoarsely, mindless of the fresh blood that had begun to trickle down his chin. "Know that I did all that I have been accused of and . . . and more. Know that . . . I deserve far worse than this death I am about to receive." Here, he turned his head slowly and fixed his one remaining eye on the Regent—and on Persephone, who sat beside him. "My eternal gratitude," he concluded raggedly, "for the great mercy my Lord Regent and His Majesty the King have shown in not exacting vengeance upon my family as further punishment for my . . . most grievous crimes."

Halfway through this speech, Persephone turned to ask the Regent the nature of the crimes to which the man referred and possibly even to beg mercy for him, if only for the sake of his father, only to see that the Regent was nodding slowly, his eyes alight with obvious pleasure, his lips silently mouthing the young man's words.

No, not the young man's words, realized Persephone with a jolt. Averting her eyes so that she'd not have to look upon the Regent's happy countenance or watch the soldiers maneuver poor Lord Pembleton's son to his knees and force his head down upon the well-used block, she thought, *They were the Regent's words! There is no hope for*—

THUD.

Persephone jumped in her seat and her gaze jerked forward just in time to see the executioner place his heavy boot on young Pembleton's shoulder in order to free the blade of the ax, which had badly missed its mark and was now buried deep in the groaning man's back.

Please, prayed Persephone desperately as she lifted her chin and fixed her warm, steady gaze upon him. *Let him know that there is more than one in this overdressed mob that cares.*

And please, she added, *let him die quickly.*

At least one of Persephone's prayers was not answered.

To the delight and amusement of many in the crowd, it took twelve strokes to sever young Pembleton's head.

"W-what was he accused of?" stammered Persephone, as the executioner snatched up his gory trophy by the hair and held it aloft for all to admire before unceremoniously dumping it into a nearby bucket.

"What does it matter?" shrugged Mordesius, rising to his feet. "As you, yourself, heard, Lady Bothwell, the wretch confessed to everything."

Numbly, Persephone nodded. "And is that all?" she asked, licking her bone-dry lips. "Is there no more . . . entertainment to be had this day?"

Mordesius burst out laughing, a merry sound that contrasted horribly with the noises poor Lord Pembleton was making as he lay atop the headless body of his dead son. "Oh, Lady Bothwell," he chortled, "wasn't that enough?"

Persephone flushed. "I only meant—well, you said that, um, a Methusian had been captured and . . ."

The Regent's eyes gleamed as her voice trailed off. "My, but you are a bloodthirsty little flower, aren't you?" he whispered huskily as he picked up her hand and lifted her to her feet.

Persephone flushed deeper still. "No, I only—"

Reaching out, the Regent pressed a cool finger against her lips, stilling them.

"Shhh," he murmured. "No more talk of blood and vermin. Let us go inside and feed one of your less . . . unorthodox appetites."

Twenty-Six

THE FEAST WAS VAST but nauseating—thin slices of rare beef swimming in their own bloody juices; jellied meats that shivered at the touch; entire hogs' heads boiled to the color of bruises; eggs with yolks like blood blisters; long, pale sausage skins stuffed with some kind of smelly, lumpy curd; lukewarm soup swimming with grinning fish heads; raw oysters served directly from the still-warm body cavities of freshly slaughtered peacocks. And for dessert: rich red velvet cake drizzled with honey the color of old blood. Worst of all was the great silver fountain—still in the shape of a man, but now with its head removed and red wine rhythmically pumping from its neck.

Had the Regent insisted that Persephone sit by his side throughout the meal, she might very well have been undone by her inability—indeed, her stubborn refusal—to let one morsel or drop of that sickening spread pass her lips. However, as luck would have it, upon entering the hall the Regent apologetically informed her that esteemed though she was, regrettably, he could not allow her to sit at the high table with him. He was not *afraid* of giving offense to the great lords of the kingdom, he explained in confidential tones; rather, he felt it would be impolitic to do so until such time as they had given him that which he both desired and deserved.

"Things will be very different then," he promised as he deposited her at a silver-set table and turned away.

Feeling chilled by his cryptic words, Persephone watched him lurch to his own seat at the right hand of the empty throne. Then she turned to see that every other person at her table was a noblewoman about her own age, and that all of them were staring at her with cold distaste, as though they were beautifully plumed carrion birds and she, a verminous carcass unworthy of their sharp little beaks. Instinctively, she tensed and her hand drifted to the place where her dagger should have been. Even as it did, the girls' stony faces melted into simpering smiles. *So, she was Lady Bothwell, was she? Esteemed guest of the Regent, yes? How had this curious thing come to pass? Were the two of them quite as intimate as they looked? What would her husband think if he knew? Where was her husband now? Was he really an old man? Did he smell of death, were his feet quite grotesque to look upon? Was it very horrible to lie with him?*

Well, was he rich, at least?

Though Persephone's nerves were drawn tight as a bowstring, and though it was obvious to her that the young noblewomen were amusing themselves at her expense, she answered every one of their questions. However, she took such care to avoid saying anything that might heap ridicule upon the hapless Lord Bothwell that the noblewomen eventually grew bored and ignored her in favor of discussing in gory detail the execution of Lord Pembleton's son and all the deliciously horrifying rumors they'd ever heard about the dungeon in which he'd passed his final days.

The dungeon in which Azriel might, at this very moment, be languishing in pain and darkness.

After a few moments of this gruesome chatter, the tiny, bright-eyed girl upon whose every word the other noblewomen seemed to hang, chirped, "They say there are only two ways out of the place: in pieces, through one of the trapdoors that opens to the underground river running beneath the castle, or intact, shortly to be chopped *into* pieces."

The other noblewomen screamed with mirth at this witticism and the girl—Lady Aurelia—basked in the glow of their appreciation until she noticed that Persephone was not joining in the fun.

"You do not find my words amusing, Lady Bothwell?" she asked, her sharp little features pinching together in displeasure.

Persephone hesitated. Though she longed to tell this cold-blooded creature exactly what she thought of her and her words, she knew that her own situation was too precarious to risk offending anyone.

"I'm terribly sorry, Lady Aurelia," she mumbled through gritted teeth. "I was so busy admiring your beautiful hat that I'm afraid I didn't hear your words."

Even to Persephone's ears, her reply sounded appallingly insincere, but instead of getting angry, Lady Aurelia laughed shrilly. "Very good, Lady Bothwell, *very* good!" she cried, clapping her little hands in apparent delight. "Oh, do say you'll join us at tomorrow's hunt, for I should like to know what you think of my riding hat."

At this, the other noblewomen twittered behind their gloved fingers.

Persephone smiled thinly and was about to decline when she realized that the invitation would give her the perfect excuse to get past her guards and roam the palace grounds without the Regent stuck to her side, watching her every move. How she would get from roaming freely to finding and rescuing Azriel from a dungeon from which people only ever left in pieces (or intact, shortly to be chopped *into* pieces) she had no idea, but she was a step closer to doing so than she'd been one minute earlier.

It was a start.

Smiling sincerely for the first time since witnessing the execution, Persephone said, "I should like to go hunting with you, Lady Aurelia. Indeed, you cannot know how I shall look forward to it."

※

The thought that she'd made a start sustained Persephone through the long evening of entertainment that followed—through jugglers and jesters, demonstrations of swordplay and wrestling, recitations, singing and dancing. Even so, she was utterly spent by the time she was delivered back to her rooms by one of the Regent's lackeys, the Regent himself having been engaged in serious conversation with an exceptionally obese nobleman whose attention kept drifting to the last of the curd-filled sausage skins. Pushing past the stony-faced guards outside her chamber door, she slipped inside to find Martha and the sisters sitting by the fire, sewing and murmuring quietly together. The warm, companionable sight was in such stark contrast to all that she'd seen and learned and endured over the last hours that it was all Persephone could do not to burst into tears.

Her distress must have been plain to see, however, for Martha and the sisters were by her side at once. They asked no questions—indeed, said not one word—but quickly led her to the warmth of the fire. There, Neeka helped her out of her high-heeled slippers and peeled the bloody wadding from her heels, Martha unlaced her gown and corset, Reeta scampered to fetch her nightgown and robe and Anya thrust a hot poker into the wine jug. Humming softly, the mute girl handed Persephone a goblet of warm spiced wine and then gently began to brush out her stiff curls, pausing once to allow Martha to help Persephone step out of the last of her petticoats, and a second time to allow Neeka to slip the warmed nightgown over her head.

When the last of the heavy pomade had been brushed away and Persephone was snugly wrapped in her robe and comfortably curled in one of the heavy chairs by the fire, she thanked Martha and the girls for their kindness and dismissed them with assurances that she was feeling much improved and would be able to get herself settled in bed in due course.

After they reluctantly departed for their own quarters, Persephone tiptoed over to the loose floorboard and withdrew her dagger and other things. She knew she'd have to hide them again soon enough, but she badly needed to see them now—to touch them and draw strength and courage from the memory of those to whom they'd once belonged. Returning to her chair, she curled her sore bare feet beneath her and, setting the dagger, lace and rat tail in her lap, placed the soft auburn curl in the palm of her open hand.

Azriel's curl, she thought as she stroked it with the very tip of her finger and watched it shimmer and glint in the firelight, *Azriel, who might even now be—*

KNOCK, KNOCK, KNOCK!

Persephone leapt to her feet so fast that the things in her lap fell to the floor. Closing her fingers around the curl, she pressed her fist to her hammering heart and stared at the chamber door. She could think of only one person who would dare to come knocking at such an hour and with such insistence, as though he was owed something for which he hungered and would not be denied.

KNOCK, KNOCK, KNOCK!

Swiftly, Persephone tossed the rat tail, lace and curl into the hole beneath the loose floorboard, slipped her dagger, hilt first, up her sleeve and hurried across the chamber floor. Whatever the consequences might be, she would not allow that monster to force himself upon her, she would not—

KNOCK, KNOCK, KNOCK!

Silently bounding the last few steps to the chamber door, Persephone took a deep breath to steady herself, then threw back her shoulders and flung open the door to find not the Regent, but two filthy, blood-splattered New Men.

And standing between them—shorn, fettered, shirtless, singed, battered, bloody but very much alive:

Azriel.

Twenty-Seven

PERSEPHONE MANAGED NOT TO CRY out or shriek or fall upon him, but only just barely. In an effort not to openly stare at his shorn head—which accentuated his chiseled features to a shocking degree—she fixed her gaze firmly upon the nearer of the two soldiers, a man so hairy that the rank, tangled mess upon his broad chest spilled up over the collar of his dirty black doublet.

"Yes?" she said stiffly.

Hastily, the man removed his cap with his free hand and stared at his feet. "Apologies for disturbing you, Lady Bothwell," he said, "but this ruffian claims to be your slave—"

"My slave?" choked Persephone, whose euphoria at seeing Azriel alive suddenly threatened to unleash itself in the form of loud, uncontrollable giggles.

Upon seeing her strange reaction, the hairy New Man inhaled deeply, mashed his lips together and shot a furious glance at his companion. "I *told* you he was lying!" he hissed.

"I never said he wasn't lying, I said I didn't want to take the chance that he wasn't lying," retorted the other, who looked more like a Latin tutor than a New Man and who was looking everywhere but at Persephone. "I said I didn't think we ought to imprison him or beat him to death until we knew for *certain* that he was lying!"

"*I* knew for certain that he was lying," snarled the enraged hairy one. "Ye gods, what do you think the Regent is going to do to us when he finds out that we not only disturbed Lady Bothwell without cause, but that *we allowed a common criminal to gaze upon her nearly naked body!*"

The desire to giggle abruptly extinguished, Persephone looked down to see that though her body was yet clad in the dead queen's night things, the robe had fallen open and the torchlight from the corridor was shining through the fine weave of the nightgown in a manner that gave anyone who cared to look an exceedingly detailed view of her every curve, hollow and shadow.

Mortified, she snatched her robe shut and looked up to find the New Men and guards all pointedly looking in other directions—and Azriel gazing straight at her with a little lopsided smile on his lips and a heart-stopping expression in his very blue (but rather bloodshot) eyes.

"I hadn't noticed," he said in a rasping voice. "Is she really nearly naked?"

With a cry of outrage, the hairy New Man pulled back his fist as though he meant to smash it into Azriel's face.

"Stop!" ordered Persephone sharply. "Do not strike him!"

"But, m'lady, he—"

"Belongs to me," she said. "And I would have you know that I am most displeased by the condition in which you have returned him to me."

Azriel gazed at the man reproachfully before turning back to Persephone. "They tore my clothes and beat me without restraint, mistress," he offered humbly as he pointed to a nasty gash on his forehead and lifted his arms to put his well-muscled but badly bruised midriff on full display. "They had me halfway to the dungeon before they thought better of it."

Feeling as short of breath as though she were once again trussed up in her corsets, Persephone tore her gaze away from Azriel's bare torso and fixed it upon the now thoroughly alarmed New Men.

"Give me the key to his fetters and be gone," she said coldly. "Go first to the kitchens and tell the servants to send up food enough to satisfy the gnawing hunger in my belly, then go curl up in a corner somewhere and pass this night wondering what punishment the Regent shall inflict upon you should I decide to inform him of your gross trespass against me and mine."

"B-but—"

"And the next time you happen upon a person of unknown provenance, I encourage you to think before you strike, lest misjudgment on your part see you a head shorter before you're a day older."

As soon as the tutorish New Man gave her the key to Azriel's fetters, Persephone grabbed her "slave" by his biceps, pulled him into her chamber and closed the door. Alone with Azriel at last, Persephone was gripped by such an overwhelming urge to pull him close and feel the reassuring warmth of his skin through the thin fabric of her nightclothes that she began to back away. Before she'd gone even one step, however, his powerful arms were around her, sweeping her off her feet and crushing her against him. She made a fleeting, half-hearted attempt to summon feelings of outrage, but the heat of their embrace melted them to nothingness. As sensation collided with sensation, Persephone began to feel reckless and drunk with longing. Sliding her hands up his naked biceps and across his impossibly broad shoulders, she ran her fingers up through his shorn hair until she felt him shudder violently. As he whirled her around and pushed her roughly up against the chamber door, her need for him surged, and when he cupped her head in his hands and leaned in with an expression that told her that the long, hard kiss he was about to give her was only the beginning she—

KNOCK, KNOCK, KNOCK.

"You all right in there, m'lady?" bellowed a gruff voice.

"W-what?" panted Persephone, who felt as though she'd just been yanked back from the edge of a precipice.

"I heard noises," bellowed the voice. "Groaning. Banging. Panting."

Flushing hotly, Persephone gulped down her next pant. "I'm sure I don't know what you mean," she called as she shakily ducked under Azriel's arm and skittered away from him. "Now . . . now, stop listening in at my door. It's rude and I won't have it!"

While the gruff-voiced guard mumbled his apologies, Persephone gestured for Azriel to follow her away from the prying ears on the other side of the door. Upon reaching the fireside, she slid the dagger out of her sleeve, hid it beneath the loose floorboard and warily turned to face Azriel. She didn't know what had gotten into her a moment earlier, but she was back in control of herself now, and she didn't know what she'd do if he wanted to talk about what had just happened—or worse, if he tried to pick up where they'd left off.

But he didn't seem interested in doing either of those things. Acting as if *nothing* had just happened, he collapsed into a chair.

"Among other things, I've come to fulfill my solemn vow to protect you," he announced in a voice so weak and raspy that it was nearly lost in the quiet clinking of his fetters.

Trying not to feel piqued by how easily he'd put their moment of feverish madness behind him, Persephone said, "As ever, your willingness to lay down your life is a tremendous comfort to me."

Azriel's satisfied smile told Persephone that he was well pleased with her words. Rolling her eyes, she poured a second goblet of wine, handed it to him and said, "What is wrong with your voice? Where are Rachel and Fleet? Did you ever find Cur? Were you able to save the child? *What happened to your hair?*"

Azriel drank deeply of the wine.

"I cut my hair," he said in a much-improved voice as she knelt before him to unlock his fetters, "for my disguise would not have borne up under scrutiny otherwise."

"But why disguise yourself as a slave?" she asked, sitting back on her heels. "Why not just call yourself a servant?"

Azriel took another long swallow of wine. "A male servant would never have been allowed to enter a lady's private chambers at night without a chaperone," he explained, wiping his mouth with the back of his sooty hand. "A eunuch slave, on the other hand . . ."

"A eunuch!" squeaked Persephone, her eyes involuntarily flying to Azriel's crotch. "You mean . . . you told them that someone cut off your . . . your . . ."

"Equipment?" he suggested, the corners of his mouth twitching as he followed her gaze. "Yes, that is what I told them, though you needn't look so distressed, Persephone, for I can assure you that my equipment is still intact and in excellent working order." He arched an eyebrow and let one hand hover over the laces of his breeches. "Shall I prove to you that I speak the truth?"

"Not unless you'd like to see your precious equipment go sailing out yonder window," replied Persephone with a scowl that she hoped clearly conveyed to him that she'd put their moment of feverish madness even farther behind her than he'd put it behind him. "Now, where are Rachel and Fleet and Cur?"

"I've not seen Cur alive *or* dead since he saved us with his timely departure from the alley, but after the way he survived his fall into the river, I'd wager he's still alive," said Azriel. "As for Rachel and Fleet, they are safe and on their way back to the Methusian camp, though it took a staggering number of sugarberry branches to persuade Fleet to leave you behind. Oh, and I'm to tell you that Rachel intends to ride hard and return to Parthania as soon as may be in order to save you."

Persephone frowned at the thought of her friend needlessly putting herself in harm's way. "And the child?" she asked, rising from her knees to perch at the edge of her chair.

"With Rachel and Fleet, but—"

"Thank goodness for that, at least," she said. "Last night when I stepped into the light of the soldiers' torches—"

"As I watched helplessly, wondering if I'd ever see you again, that I might have the opportunity to soundly chastise you for your courageous but infuriatingly foolhardy actions," interjected Azriel pointedly.

"And I saw the soldiers herding the people away and setting fire to the slum, I feared that you would be unable to save the child," continued Persephone, as though he hadn't spoken. "For some reason, I could not stop thinking of Sabian and imagining his little body lying beneath the charred ruins. Knowing that your kinsman has been saved makes it easier for me to bear . . . to bear the price paid to rescue him."

"You are very kind to say so, for I know how you loved your hawk," said Azriel. "Unfortunately, your fears were half right."

Persephone stared at him. "What do you mean?"

"The message the pigeon carried was incomplete," he explained, smacking the chair arm in frustration. "There was not one child, but *two*. Two little brothers abandoned to a fiery death by the family into whose care they'd been entrusted. Using the cover of chaos and smoke to slip into the slum, I reached the place we'd been told we'd find the child just ahead of the flames. Upon discovering him hiding behind a sleeping pallet, I scooped him up and ran." Azriel hunched over as though he was about to vomit. After a moment, he sat back up and continued. "I never thought to look for a second child and was halfway to the alley before I realized what the one in my arms was trying to tell me. Of course I turned back at once but by the time I got there it was too late."

Persephone went pale and swayed in her chair. "So . . . you saved one boy but the other is—"

"Not dead," said Azriel quickly. "Not dead—but perhaps wishing he was dead. For you see, when I got back to the place where I'd found the first child, I found the dwelling being consumed by flames. Before I could even begin to despair, however, I saw a New Man running with the child slung over his shoulders like a sack of potatoes. I followed him at a safe distance, hoping that an opportunity to free the second child might present itself, but it did not, and at length I saw the little one being delivered into the hands of the Regent's henchman, General Murdock. Murdock listened as the New Man whispered something into his ear, then he shouted an order to have the Methusian outlaw caged and delivered to the palace dungeon at once."

"So this afternoon when Lord Bartok and the Regent spoke of a Methusian being captured, they were speaking about this *child*?" said Persephone incredulously.

"I imagine so," said Azriel.

Suddenly realizing that someone must have identified the child as a Methusian and had probably done so in order to save himself, Persephone was about to ask what kind of a person would do such a thing when Azriel slid to his knees before her, took her hands in his and said, "Persephone, I mean to rescue the boy or die trying."

Even though she should have known the words were coming, she gasped and snatched her hands away. "You can't—"

"I must," said Azriel, once more reaching for her hands. "I do not know if he is the Methusian king, but I do know that he is where he is because I failed to save him when I had the chance. I cannot turn my back on him now. I won't ask you to help in the rescue itself, but I am on my knees begging you to play the part of a noblewoman a little longer that I may have an excuse to be inside the palace walls, for without that, all hope is lost."

All hope is probably lost anyway, thought Persephone wildly as she recalled what the noblewomen at her table had said about the dungeon. How it was deep within the bowels of the castle; how it had but one well-guarded entrance. How it was a labyrinth so vast that some years past, a servant sent to feed the prisoners had gotten lost and his body had never been found.

And, of course, how there were only two ways out of the place: in pieces, through one of the trapdoors that opened to the underground river running beneath the palace, or intact, shortly to be chopped *into* pieces.

A vision of little Sabian thus dispatched caused Persephone to shudder. She was no Methusian and the child in the dungeon was no one to her. Anyone of consequence would think her a hero for even *considering* the prospect of continuing to play the part of a noblewoman and yet . . .

And yet she could not imagine dancing and feasting in bejeweled finery while Azriel risked his life to descend into hell to rescue the boy.

And so, with a grunt that suggested she was irritated by her own compulsion to involve herself further, Persephone folded her arms across her chest, thrust her chin at Azriel and said, "I have saved your life so many times that I would consider it an affront if you were to undertake your grand rescue attempt by yourself and end up a cornered animal with your guts spilling onto your feet."

At her words, Azriel's heart seemed to leap into his eyes. Nevertheless, his tone was mild—even mildly offended—when he replied, "You paint a rather gruesome picture, madam, and one that has the potential to cause serious damage to my manly pride. As it happens, I am perfectly content to attempt to rescue the child on my own—"

"And yet it would seem to me that two are better than one when it comes to things like rescue attempts."

"That is true," said Azriel carefully, "but I would not have you exposed to danger and—"

"Enough," said Persephone, who could not resist quieting him by pressing her fingertips against his lips. "I have come this far for the sake of your little clansman, Azriel. Come what may, I mean to go all the way."

Without taking his eyes off her, Azriel took her by the wrist, gently pulled her fingers away from his mouth and pressed a long, soft kiss into the palm of her hand. "And when it is over?" he asked softly. "When the child is safe?"

Persephone stared fixedly at his lips against her skin for an endless, breathless moment before abruptly pulling her hand free and saying, "I think we've got enough to worry about right now, don't you?"

A short while later, servants arrived with trays and platters and baskets of food. Azriel stood against the wall in respectful silence while they placed their burdens upon the long table by the shuttered windows. As soon as they were gone, he fell upon the food with such a vengeance that Persephone knew there would be more talk in the kitchens of Lady Bothwell's prodigious appetite. While he ate, Persephone told him everything that had happened to her since departing the alley in the dubious care of the Regent. Later, after Azriel was sated, she fetched a basin of soapy water and once more knelt before him. Trying hard to ignore the way the firelight played across the muscles of his bare chest, the way his eyes followed her every movement, the way he trembled at her touch, and the way she trembled at his, she carefully washed his various wounds while he grimaced and gasped and groaned as though she were hacking off his limbs. By the time she was done, she had gained valuable insight into why Fayla had treated him like a ridiculous overgrown baby that first night in the Methusian camp (namely, because he'd acted like one). Fetching a pillow and several blankets, she fashioned a bed for him on the floor by the fire.

"What!" he exclaimed in mock dismay. "Do you mean to say that you expect me to sleep on this hard, cold floor while you sleep in that great, comfortable bed all by yourself?"

"That is exactly what I expect," said Persephone primly as she clambered up onto the bed.

"But it has been such a difficult few days," murmured Azriel enticingly. "And who knows what the future holds? I, for one, think it would be foolish of us not to take advantage of—"

"Enough!" blurted Persephone, who felt positively *tormented* by the sight of his naked torso glowing in the firelight. "I have fashioned a bed for you and that is where you shall sleep! And if, perchance, you find yourself tempted to crawl in here beside me at any point during the night, I encourage you to imagine yourself a blind, fingerless eunuch."

"If it's all the same to you, I think I'd prefer to imagine myself slit from bow to stern with an old sow feasting on my innards," muttered Azriel.

He sounded so grumpy that Persephone had to bite the inside of her cheek to keep from laughing.

"Suit yourself," she said with a toss of her head.

Then, suddenly fearful of what she might do if she did not stop looking at him, she yanked closed the bed curtains, flopped back and waited fitfully for sleep to come.

The next morning, Persephone awoke late to the sound of loud giggling and even louder shushing. Poking her head out of the bed curtains, she saw Martha fretfully pacing while Neeka, Anya and Reeta gaped at Azriel, who was sitting on the floor by the fire smiling and rubbing his sleepy blue eyes, his lower body swathed in a provocative tangle of blankets beneath his taut, bare midriff.

"That's just, uh, my slave!" called Persephone as she flung back the bed curtains, tumbled out of bed and hurried over to try to explain the presence of a half-naked man in her room. "As it turns out, he also escaped death when the bandits attacked my cavalcade. Last evening, after you'd all retired, two of the Regent's New Men returned him to me."

"And he spent the entire night here alone with you?" breathed little Reeta, her eyes bugging out at the impropriety of it.

"Well, yes, but I can assure you that nothing untoward happened," said Persephone, blushing from the tips of her bare toes to the top of her brow. "After all, I'm a married noblewoman and . . . and Azriel is a slave and . . ."

"And I am also a eunuch," reminded Azriel.

"Are—you—*really*?" said Neeka, looking as though she'd very much like to rip the blankets aside, tear off his breeches and confirm this for herself.

"Absolutely he is!" squeaked Persephone. "Now, uh, I'm to go hunting with Lady Aurelia and the rest of the ladies today. Therefore, after the servants arrive with food—"

"You should hear what they're saying about you in the kitchens!" piped Reeta.

"And I've finished breaking my fast, Martha, I should like you to select a suitable gown and cloak for me," continued Persephone hurriedly. "Reeta, you will find the yeoman of the bowman and ask him to send a bow up to my rooms that I may practice drawing it, for it has been some time since I've gone hunting and I should not like to appear . . . unpracticed. Neeka and Anya, you may help me bathe and dress."

"Perhaps the eunuch could help us," suggested Neeka with a sly, sideways glance at Azriel.

"Well, it would only be appropriate that I do so," he said with a modest shrug. "After all, I *am* Lady Bothwell's Master of the Bath. Trained in the art of sponge and soap, gentle-handed and thorough, I never rush but devote myself entirely to the task before me— tenderly working my way up and down her body, one slow inch at a time, that my lady might eventually step from the water flushed and tingling with the knowledge that she is cleaner than any noblewoman in all the realm." Pretending not to notice the way Neeka was looking at him (like he was a giant sweetmeat), Azriel let his words hang in the air for half a heartbeat before turning his eyes upon Persephone, cocking his head to one side and innocently adding, "Then again, perhaps Lady Bothwell would prefer that I busy myself emptying the chamber pot?"

"Huh?" breathed Persephone, who was flushed and tingling at the very *thought* of submitting herself to Azriel's "gentle hand." "Oh, uh, yes—that is what I would prefer."

"Very good, m'lady," he murmured. "I'll see to it at once."

Twenty-Eight

IN ANOTHER PART of the palace, Mordesius was struggling to control his rising anger. He'd come to the king's chambers under the guise of wanting to discuss the young monarch's upcoming birthday celebrations but with the true purpose of casually mentioning that at the most recent Council meeting there'd been much talk of the many reasons the king ought to name his Regent as his heir. Instead, Mordesius found himself caught up in a discussion regarding a matter as trifling as it was tedious.

"Majesty," he sighed, "I agree that the execution of Lord Pembleton's son was regrettable—"

"It was more than regrettable, Mordesius," interrupted the king, coughing slightly as he shoved his breakfast tray to one side. "It was a grievous misjudgment on your part. I knew the man personally— he was new to court, but I liked his spirit. Just six weeks ago I gave my blessing to his newborn son!"

"That's as may be, Your Majesty," said Mordesius soothingly. "However—"

"Not only that," continued the king, holding his index finger high in the air, "but Moira here tells me that she heard you made an unseemly spectacle of the poor man's execution and caused his bereft father needless pain and suffering in the bargain."

Mordesius turned his dark, glittering gaze upon the insufferable cow who had mothered the king since infancy. She blandly returned his gaze, then settled deeper into her cushioned chair by the king's bedside and resumed shuffling cards.

Promising himself for the thousandth time that someday she would die in agony, Mordesius took a deep breath and turned back to the king. Spreading his scarred hands wide, he murmured, "What you say about the execution is true, Highness, but as we've discussed many times, if you do not show the great lords what will happen to them if they sin against you and this realm, you can never hope to control them."

"I do not believe that Lord Pembleton's son committed any such sins," said the king flatly.

"He confessed—"

"Because you had him tortured!" exclaimed the king.

Gritting his teeth with the strain of keeping his head from bobbing and his rage in check, Mordesius hesitated, trying to figure out how best to handle this most unwelcome development. He had not realized that the increasingly strong-willed young king even knew Pembleton's son, let alone knew him well enough to bestow blessings upon his doomed infant. This, in itself, was cause for concern because it spoke to the fact that he was losing control of the king, a thing that he could not allow to happen until such time as he'd gotten himself named and accepted as heir to the Erok throne.

After that, control of the king would not matter because the king would be dead or as good as.

"Of course I had him tortured," flared Mordesius in a sudden, carefully calculated display of irritation. "Do you think he'd have confessed if I'd brought him a cup of tea and a loaf of fresh bread?"

"No, but—"

"Is this the thanks I get for safeguarding your kingdom lo these many years?" demanded Mordesius, as the cow placidly began to deal the cards into two piles. "For toiling ceaselessly on your behalf, asking nothing for myself?"

At this, the cow snorted quietly.

Mordesius just barely resisted the urge to order her beaten to death on the spot. Stepping closer to the king, he raised his voice a notch and asked, "Do you think I like getting blood on my hands? Do you imagine for one moment that I enjoyed driving scores of your poorest subjects from their pestilent slum or that I took pleasure in the hideous screams of those who chose to burn to death rather than leave their pathetic hovels?"

The already-pale king grew paler at this.

Leaning forward, the Regent twisted the knife a little deeper. "These terrible things were approved *by* you and done *for* you, Majesty. Yet I, alone, willingly carry the burden of responsibility for them. And you show your gratitude by accusing me of—what? Working too diligently? Being too thorough?"

The young king looked at his Lord Regent—not with the eyes of a boy suffering with the sudden knowledge that he'd had a hand in the deaths of innocent people, as Mordesius had hoped, but with the shocked eyes of a young man who'd just gotten his first fleeting glimpse of the way things really were.

"You know that I appreciate all you've done for me and my realm, Your Grace," said King Finnius slowly. "Nevertheless, you erred in your treatment of young Lord Pembleton, and I would not have you do such a thing again without my express permission."

Out of the corner of his eye, Mordesius saw Moira nod approvingly. Clasping his hands together to keep from reaching for her throat, he swallowed his rage at the insults being heaped upon him, staggered to his feet and stiffly bid the king a pleasant day recuperating. Stifling a wet cough with the sleeve of his nightshirt, the king replied that he would not be spending the day recuperating. Mordesius, who always felt most at ease when he could arrange for the king to be beyond the influence of the great lords, tried to convince him that he needed rest in order to fully recover from the fits brought on by the smoke from the burning slum, but the young man would not be dissuaded.

"I am going to make an appearance on the Grand Balcony, and then I am going to spend the afternoon in the garden. Moira thinks the fresh air will be good for me, and also that it is important for those of low and noble birth alike to see for themselves that I am entirely recovered from last night's fit," he explained as he surreptitiously watched his bovine nursemaid pick up one pile of cards, deftly arrange them in her hand and begin studying them. "Besides, Lord Atticus sent word that he has an early birthday surprise for me, and though I am not especially fond of the man himself, I am very fond of surprises."

Mordesius smiled thinly, thinking of the surprise he had in store for the king someday very soon and how he'd like nothing better than to deliver it himself—in the form of a poisoned dagger plunged directly into the boy's royal heart.

"You are smiling, Your Grace," said the king, who was studiously ignoring the pile of cards at his fingertips. "Do you like surprises, too?"

"Oh, yes, Highness," said Mordesius, smiling more broadly still. "I certainly do."

The image of the young king gasping for breath as his life's blood drained away buoyed Mordesius's spirits for a spell, but by the time he was halfway to Lady Bothwell's chambers, he'd sunk into a foul mood once more. At once a soft-hearted fool and a hard-nosed ingrate, the king was getting more difficult to manage by the day. And now he was accepting "surprises" from Atticus? This was even more deeply disturbing than the revelation that young Pembleton had been known to him, for Pembleton was a dead nobody and his father was a broken man, while Atticus was very much a somebody and his father, Lord Bartok, was anything but broken. The Bartok clan coveted the crown almost as much as Mordesius did, and if they were ever to get close enough to the king to start whispering against Mordesius—even if they were to do nothing more than whisper the truth!—there was no doubt in Mordesius's mind that his plan to be named heir would be utterly and completely ruined.

But it is not ruined yet, he thought, smoothing his glossy hair and straightening his robe as he took the final, hitching steps toward the door of Lady Bothwell's chambers. *It is not even close to—*

The sound of laughter from the other side of the door caused all thought to fly from Mordesius's mind and the blood to drain from his face.

Because it wasn't just laughter that he heard—it was rich, seductive, *masculine* laughter.

"Open—that—door," hissed Mordesius, in a voice so terrible that the two poleax-wielding guards nearly knocked heads together in their haste to leap forward and fling it open.

The sight that greeted him was far worse than Mordesius could ever have imagined. Lady Bothwell—*his* Lady Bothwell, future mother of his true-begotten half-noble son, the noblewoman on whose behalf he'd just that morning sent General Murdock on a mission of great import!—was in the arms of a half-naked slave, her back pressed up against his bare chest as though she was nothing more than a common whore. And she wasn't debasing herself with just *any* half-naked slave—this beast was a study in masculine perfection. Broad-shouldered and battle-scarred, long and lean, he was all hard muscle and raw sensuality, the kind of animal that drew females like flies to honey. That, alone, would have been more than enough to make Mordesius want to see him slow-dipped in boiling oil, but one look at the brute's face caused the Regent's displeasure to multiply a thousandfold. For his skin was as smooth and unblemished as Mordesius's own, his features as finely chiseled, his teeth as straight and white. The slave did not resemble the Regent in any way, but there was no denying the fact that he was at least as handsome as Mordesius was. Perhaps . . . perhaps even *more* handsome in his way, for he was much younger than Mordesius, and there was something in his extraordinarily blue eyes, something that seemed somehow familiar—

"Your Grace!" exclaimed Lady Bothwell. Leaping out of the slave's embrace with a haste wholly unbecoming a lady of her station, she dropped into a low curtsey.

The female servants who'd been standing around doing nothing, like the useless drabs they were, likewise curtseyed. The beast bowed deferentially, but with a grace that inflamed Mordesius almost beyond reason.

Wordlessly, the Regent shuffled into the room, indicating to the bumbling guards that they should follow with their poleaxes at the ready.

"Lady Bothwell," he said icily, as the full weight of his stare fell upon the bowed head of the handsome slave. "What is the meaning of this?"

For a moment there was nothing but silence. Then, to Mordesius's utter astonishment, instead of cowering or begging forgiveness for her gross lewdness, Lady Bothwell began to laugh—a lovely, light-hearted sound that caused Mordesius's heart to clench most painfully.

"Forgive me, Your Grace, but I think you are referring to *this*," she giggled, pointing at the beast, "and I think that you thought you'd found me in the embrace of a half-naked man."

"Well, *yes*," spluttered Mordesius, who was so unused to people failing to quail in terror before his towering anger that he hardly knew how to react.

Lady Bothwell laughed again—and again, Mordesius's heart clenched. "Your Grace, this creature is not a *man*, he is a *eunuch*," she explained with a dismissive gesture in the brute's direction. "He has belonged to my dear husband since long before we married, and he was with me when my caravan was attacked outside the city walls. Last night, the two New Men who discovered him trying to return to my service kindly delivered him to me. He slept on the floor by the hearth—far better accommodation than he is used to or deserves. Just now, he was reminding me of the particular technique my husband wishes me to use when drawing a bow."

Mordesius's gaze dropped to the bow in Lady Bothwell's hand, which he hadn't noticed up to that point, then up to Lady's Bothwell's face, then over to the eunuch's face. It was too handsome by far, just as his body was too perfect by far, but where it truly counted, it seemed that he was a mutilated nothing.

Still.

His presence in Lady Bothwell's chambers offended Mordesius, as did the fact that when the bandits attacked her caravan, he'd obviously abandoned his mistress in favor of saving his own worthless hide. That alone was reason enough to have his face carved up like a summer squash, to have his pretty eyes put out, to have one of his hands removed, to have—

"To what do I owe the pleasure of your visit this fine morning, Your Grace?" asked Lady Bothwell.

Mordesius was jolted back to the moment by the sound of Lady Bothwell's voice—and by the thrilling revelation that she found his visit a *pleasure.*

Folding his arms across his withered chest to keep from preening, he said, "As it happens, my lady, I've come to invite you to spend the day with me. I cannot offer you a spectacle such as you enjoyed yesterday. . . ." He paused to chuckle appreciatively at the memory of Lady Bothwell staring at the fresh, headless corpse of young Pembleton and asking if there was more entertainment to be had. "However, I thought we might sit in the garden. You could read to me, and sing and dance and play the lute for me, and speak to me of the many things I should like to know about you."

To his delight, Mordesius saw Lady Bothwell's face flush like a girl being courted for the very first time. His delight was abruptly extinguished, however, when she said, "Oh, Your Grace, I should have enjoyed that very much, but I'm afraid that Lady Aurelia has already invited me to go hunting with her and the other ladies of the court."

"Lady Aurelia? Lord Bartok's daughter?" demanded Mordesius, irritated not only by the fact that the luscious, young Lady Bothwell had been invited to do something that his poor body would never allow him to do, but also by the fact that she'd been invited by a Bartok.

The high-and-mighty bastards were everywhere!

The flicker of surprise that flitted across Lady Bothwell's face at the mention of Bartok's name was immediately replaced by a look of contrition. "I did not think to ask whose daughter Lady Aurelia is, Your Grace," she murmured meekly. "I'm sorry if I have displeased you by accepting her invitation. Shall . . . shall I send word that I'll not be joining her and the others?"

For a long moment, Mordesius said nothing, only savored the fact that Lady Bothwell not only appeared entirely content to miss out on the excitement of the hunt in order to spend quiet time with him but also appeared entirely willing to be ordered about as he saw fit.

Verily, it was as though they were man and wife already!

"You need not send word to Lady Aurelia," announced Mordesius magnanimously, wondering how long it would be before he'd have the pleasure of seeing Lady Bothwell standing before him wearing nothing but the dead queen's silken undergarments. "Take your enjoyment as you will this day, my dear, and this evening, you may join me for supper and . . . amusements in my private chambers."

"Yes, Your Grace," replied Lady Bothwell, who was clearly overcome by the prospect. "I shall look forward to it."

Twenty-Nine

THE MOMENT MORDESIUS and the guards departed, Persephone dropped the bow from her shaking hand and sank into the nearest chair. Neeka swiftly handed her a mug of ale, Anya fanned her face and Martha fussed with her hair while little Reeta, who looked nearly as rattled as Persephone felt and who apparently could think of nothing else to do, ran to fetch her something to eat.

Under the guise of adjusting the cushion behind her back, Azriel leaned close enough to brush his lips against her ear. "You must stop saving my life," he whispered, "for you are starting to make me look bad."

For some reason, Persephone nearly burst into tears at his teasing words. She did not know what had made her laugh in the face of the Regent's rage, nor where she'd found the courage to do so, but she knew for a certainty that if she hadn't, Azriel would have come to terrible harm.

"Go, now. Go hunting with the great ladies of the court," he continued softly, his warm breath tickling her skin. "By the time you return to me, I will have figured out a way for us to save my little clansman—and keep you out of the cold hands of that monstrous old lecher."

Before Persephone could reply, Neeka's face loomed between them.

"While you're gone hunting, m'lady," she said loudly, "shall I teach your eunuch how to promptly adjust a lady's cushion so that in the future you need not suffer having him linger about you so?"

"What? Oh! Yes, uh, thank you," stammered Persephone, wishing she didn't blush so easily. "And . . . and please find him a shirt to wear. It is not . . . seemly for one who serves me in my chambers to be so ill clad, even if he is only a eunuch."

"Indeed," said Neeka, eyes gleaming.

After donning her hat, cloak and gloves and retrieving her bow, Persephone made her way down to the royal stables. By the time she arrived most of the ladies were already mounted, as were a goodly number of dandified gentlemen.

"Lady Bothwell!" cried tiny Lady Aurelia, as she cantered up on a dappled mare. "I'd begun to worry that you'd decided not to join the hunt after all! Do you like my hat?"

"I do," murmured Persephone as she apprehensively watched a scrawny little stable lad hurry toward her doing his best to lead an enormous black mare that was stomping, snorting, tossing its head and glowering at everyone and everything in its path.

"Oh, I'm *so* glad," said Lady Aurelia, her bright eyes shining. "Now, mount up as fast as you can! The Master of the Hunt will sound the horn any moment and I daresay that horse you've been given will join the fray whether you're upon its back or not!"

Persephone smiled weakly at this, then looked uncertainly at the stable lad, who did not look nearly big and strong enough to help her into the saddle.

Lady Aurelia laughed shrilly. "Fear not, Lady Bothwell—you shan't have to fly up into the saddle," she said. "My ne'er-do-well brother Lord Atticus approaches, and if he can hold himself upright for long enough, I daresay he can help you onto your horse."

Aghast, Persephone spun around to find herself face-to-face with the very same Lord Atticus who'd threatened her and Rachel on the road to Parthania three days earlier. Though not as drunk as he'd been then, he'd obviously been drinking, for his doublet was rumpled, he stank of ale and his close-set eyes were bloodshot and watery.

Swallowing hard, Persephone coolly introduced herself as "Lady Bothwell" and held out her hand for him to kiss. For one terrible moment, he scrutinized her face so closely that she was sure he recognized her and was about to denounce her. Then, abruptly, his gaze dropped to her bosom. With a smile that strongly resembled a leer, he then leaned over and pressed his fleshy lips against her glove until his saliva left a mark on the soft leather, just as it had done on poor Fayla's glove. When he lifted his head, Persephone noticed that the vicious scratch Ivan had given him had begun to fester. Though she badly wanted to ask him how he'd come by the scratch—and what had happened to the creature who'd given it to him—she did not dare.

"So," whispered Atticus, still gawking at her bosom as he slipped his hands around her waist and yanked her so close that she could feel the hardness of his codpiece pressed against her, "am I to under-stand that you would like to be mounted?"

Actually, what I would like is to turn the pitiful contents of your oversized codpiece into pig slop, thought Persephone fiercely. Out loud, in a voice as innocent as it was proper, she said, "Yes, my lord. That is what I would like."

Persephone had just managed to crook one knee around the pommel of the sidesaddle and wedge her other foot into the uncomfort-ably tight stirrup when the Master of the Hunt blew his horn and the beaters brought out the hounds. They were the same slit-eyed, gray-black beasts she'd encountered previously, and at the sight of them, Persephone's horse reared and lunged so abruptly that she nearly fell off its back. As soon as she recovered her balance, the horse stopped just as abruptly, causing her to fall forward and bang her nose into its neck so hard that her eyes watered. All the way out of the stable yard and through the palace gates it was the same thing, and whether she yanked on the reins, spoke kindly or issued stern commands, Persephone's horse paid her even less attention than dear old Fleet generally paid Azriel.

By the time they reached the perimeter of the vast imperial parkland in which the hunt was to take place, Persephone, who could usually find something to love in any animal, was convinced that the giant, snorting beast beneath her was pathologically disagreeable, deaf and possibly deranged. She was also convinced that if she attempted to ride it for much longer, it would see that she paid dearly for it. Turning to Lady Aurelia, she was about to ask if there was some way that she could trade in her horse for one that wasn't demonically possessed when she was assailed by a stench so horrible that she began to gag. Quickly covering her mouth with her hand, she looked ahead and saw half a dozen human heads perched on pikes planted in the ground at the entrance to the parkland. Gray and flaccid, with ragged necks, open eyes and dribbles of black blood staining their gaping mouths, they instantly recalled memories from Persephone's brief but terrible time in the Mines of Torodania—and the punishment meted out to anyone caught trying to sneak into or out of the dread place.

"Is something the matter, Lady Bothwell?" inquired a smirking young noblewoman in a gorgeously plumed burgundy hat and matching riding cloak.

Persephone breathed shallowly through her mouth. "No . . . I just . . ." Jerkily, she gestured toward the heads. "Who are—that is to say, uh, who were they?"

"Do you not recognize them?" asked the noblewoman curiously. "They're the bandits who attacked you, of course." She smiled slyly. "I heard the Regent Mordesius was so distressed that your caravan had been attacked that he sent General Murdock out the very next day to hunt down and destroy the lowborn wretches responsible."

Persephone could barely contain her horror that her lie had caused these terrible deaths. "But . . . but how did he know that *these* were the bandits who attacked me?" she gasped.

"Well, weren't they?" twittered another of the young noble-women, a large-nosed, thin-lipped girl in a richly embellished blue velvet dress—a girl who seemed to find terribly amusing the possibility that the General had executed the wrong men.

"Th-they were," stammered Persephone, who had no wish to see more innocent men murdered on account of her lie. "I . . . I only wondered how he knew that they were."

Lady Aurelia rolled her eyes. "Oh, what does it matter, Lady Bothwell?" she asked with sudden impatience. "The deed is done, so let us make haste to get past the stink of it so that we may enjoy the day at hand."

Predictably, Persephone did not enjoy the day at hand. Never in a thousand years could she have imagined that the silly, fumbling lies she'd told the Regent would bear such terrible fruit. Her fateful actions in the alley that night may have saved Azriel, Rachel and one Methusian orphan, but they'd cost six innocent men their lives. Seven, if one included the man brought down by the arrow intended for Cur.

Over the next several hours, while the beaters bellowed and crashed through the underbrush trying to scare up game, Persephone could not stop thinking about the dead men and their families, and about the fact that she was committed to rescuing yet another Methusian orphan.

And she could not stop wondering what price would be paid this time—and by whom it would be paid.

By the time the dinner hour arrived, the beaters had still not managed to scare up so much as a mouse after which the bored nobles might give chase. Complaining loudly (and appearing even drunker than he had that morning), Lord Atticus led the hunting party to a clearing. It was immediately apparent to Persephone that a small army of servants had arrived there long before they, for the clearing was set with ornately carved tables, priceless carpets, billowing canopies and numerous couches upon which weary riders might recline and receive goblets of wine and plates of food. It was as though one of the finer rooms in the palace had been transported in its entirety to the middle of nowhere, and it looked so inviting that Persephone couldn't wait to get out of the saddle.

Just as she was trying to free her foot from the too-tight stirrup, however, a fat hare shot between the legs of her horse, followed closely by two barking, bounding hunting hounds. Squealing loudly, Persephone's horse reared and lunged as it had when it had first seen the dogs. This time, it didn't stop there. Laying its ears flat against its head, it burst into a full gallop directly through the middle of the clearing, kicking clods of dirt all over the beautiful carpets, bringing down snow-white canopies, and dodging couches and shrieking noblewomen before finally jumping clear over a whole hog roasting on a spit over an open fire. The horse's back legs must have landed uncomfortably close to the flames because the instant its hooves touched down, it squealed even more shrilly than before and leapt forward into a gallop once more. Persephone, who had been clinging to the horse's mane like a flea to a shaking dog through it all, now began desperately trying to free her foot from the stirrup. If she was thrown from the saddle, she would almost certainly break her neck, but if she was able to *jump*, she just might be able to control her landing well enough to only suffer broken limbs. Try as she might, however, she could not get free, and before she knew it, the horse had plunged into the thicket of trees at the edge of the clearing. With a gasp, Persephone ducked to avoid being knocked out of the saddle by a low tree limb and then ducked again to avoid being brained by an even lower limb. As the horse continued to pound along, somehow finding a path through the thicket, Persephone's face was whipped by small branches, her hat was torn from her head and she abandoned all thought of trying to jump clear.

Then she saw it.

Directly ahead, beyond the trees, was a cliff—and far below it, the sparkling blue waters of the sea.

The out-of-control beast beneath Persephone did not see the edge of the cliff, did not understand what it meant or did not care. Covered with sweaty foam and breathing raggedly, it continued to gallop as hard as it could. There was nothing Persephone could do. She couldn't make the horse stop, and she couldn't get free of it.

They were going over.

With the fleeting thought that she never imagined that it would end this way, Persephone twined her fingers deeper in the horse's mane, hunkered down and prepared to die.

Thirty

ALL AT ONCE, a fearsome, filthy, four-legged creature with bared teeth and matted fur leapt out of the trees. With a wet snarl, it planted itself directly in the path of the horse's deadly, pounding hooves.

"Cur!" screamed Persephone, her heart bursting with terror and joy.

The deranged horse emitted a shrill squeal, swerved to the left and continued to gallop hard along the crumbling edge of the cliff top. Far below, jagged rocks and a pounding surf promised death to the unlucky, but Persephone was not afraid, for she had never felt luckier in her life. Narrowing her eyes against the biting wind, she tossed her dark hair out of her face and laughed aloud with the happy knowledge that Cur had come back to her.

Eventually, Cur managed to chase the horse away from the edge of the cliff and back into the thicket. There, it thrashed about wildly for some time before finally slowing to a plodding walk and making its way back to the open parkland on the other side. Beyond the trees at last, Persephone was surprised and relieved to see that they'd somehow backtracked nearly the entire distance the hunting party had covered that morning and that the palace gates were close at hand.

"This way," she commanded, trying to lead the horse to a nearby path.

Ignoring her completely, it plowed through a patch of thorny brambles that further shredded the hem of her once-beautiful gown. It then clip-clopped over the drawbridge, through the watchtower passageway and past the open-mouthed, staring guards.

"This way," Persephone commanded again, trying to lead it to the royal stables.

Again ignoring her completely, it turned in the opposite direction, toward the immaculately trimmed hedge that encircled the vast royal garden. Upon reaching it, the horse stood patiently waiting for Persephone to work her boot out of the stirrup. As soon as she'd done so, it tossed her over the hedge and wandered away.

As luck would have it, Persephone landed unhurt in a thick bed of fragrant white lilies. The next moment, Cur emerged from beneath the hedge and was upon her, licking her face and wriggling like a puppy. Hugging him close without a care for who might see, Persephone stroked his matted fur, scratched his smelly ears and thanked him profusely for saving her life.

Then, feeling more like herself than she had in days, she stood up, shook out the tattered skirts of her destroyed gown, ran her fingers through her horribly tangled hair, pinched the cheeks of her branch-whipped, mud-splattered face and began searching for a way out of the deserted garden. Since she couldn't climb back over the thick hedge and had no intention of wriggling beneath it, she turned and followed the path that lay before her.

The carefully tended flower beds on either side of the path were filled with exotic blooms and trees dripping with ivy provided perches for a host of vividly plumed little songbirds. Bushes cunningly shaped into porpoises, sea turtles and mermaids overlooked tiny bridges spanning ponds inhabited by emerald-green frogs and little darting fish whose rainbow scales flashed in the sunlight.

Persephone was enchanted. Deeper and deeper into the garden she strolled with Cur, her purpose entirely forgotten in her delight at the thought of what might be waiting for her around the next bend in the path.

Then she rounded a bend and saw a sight that not only stopped her in her tracks but very nearly caused her heart to stop beating as well.

It was Ivan! Her Ivan—dear, brave, funny Ivan!

And he was alive!

Alive—but tethered and perched on the arm of a tall, dark-haired man. She could not see the man's face, for his back was turned to her, but she could clearly see that he was trying to command Ivan to do something that he did not want to do.

Incensed at the sight of her proud friend alive but enslaved, Persephone all but flew at the man, who was, as yet, blissfully unaware of her presence.

"In the name of the Regent Mordesius, I order you to let that creature alone *this instant!*" she shouted so loudly that she badly startled Ivan, who responded by pecking the man hard in the side of the head. "Are you such a beast that you cannot find other amusements for yourself but that you must torment the poor thing?" continued Persephone, as the man grunted and hopped about in obvious pain. "Can you not see that he is wounded and suffering? Is it not obvious from his bearing that he is not meant for such sport in any event? Stop your tiresome theatrics and show yourself, sir, that I may know what low manner of person has offended me so!"

At this, the man, whose head appeared to be bleeding rather badly, began to laugh so hard that he drove himself into a coughing fit. When it finally subsided, he bravely turned to face Persephone and her wrath.

Luckily for him, her wrath evaporated the instant she laid eyes upon him. About as tall and as old as Azriel, and with eyes nearly as blue, there was something strangely compelling about him—something that made Persephone think she should know him.

"I am the king," he said helpfully, after a moment.

Mortified to the point of horror, Persephone gasped, clapped one hand over her mouth and dropped into a curtsey so low that her legs promptly gave way beneath her.

With Ivan still perched on one carefully outstretched arm, the smiling young king reached out his free hand to help her up. Cur, who was watching from nearby, growled softly.

"Your Majesty!" squeaked Persephone as she staggered to her feet. "I apologize for—"

"Calling me a beast?" he suggested. "Chastising me for my 'tiresome theatrics'? Causing my new bird to peck me in the head?"

Persephone felt herself blush. "I am *terribly* sorry about all of those things, Your Majesty," she mumbled. "It's just that . . . well . . ."

"Yes?" said the king, leaning closer.

Looking up into his blue eyes, Persephone felt a sudden desire to touch his cheek. "Forgive me," she murmured, tucking her hands behind her back, "but you really ought not to use this particular bird for hunting."

King Finnius gaped at her. "You run at me in my own garden—unkempt, unchaperoned, in the company of a flea-bitten mongrel, and now, knowing that I am your king, you *still* seek to correct me?" he said incredulously. "Madam, who *are* you?"

Lifting her chin, Persephone made a fine show of smoothing her filthy, shredded skirts and plumping up her tangled hair. "I am Lady Bothwell of the Ragorian Prefecture," she said with great dignity. "Some weeks past, my dear husband gave his blessing that I might travel to Parthania. There were troubles along the way that I do not wish to dwell upon. This morning, I joined a noble hunting party. For reasons unknown, this 'flea-bitten mongrel' saved my life when the horse I borrowed from Your Majesty's stables went berserk and tried to kill me."

The king's eyes widened at this. "Was this horse you speak of a mare?" he asked, punctuating his inquiry with the touch of his hand to her elbow. "Was she large, black, disagreeable and deaf?"

"Yes," said Persephone, who rather enjoyed the warmth of his touch. "She was also deranged."

The king nodded as though this confirmed his suspicions. "Her name is Lucifer," he said.

"That is a boy's name," said Persephone.

"And yet it suits her remarkably well," said the king. "I've never warmed to her, myself, and had left orders that none should ride her. Rest assured that I shall find out from my Master of Horse how she came to be saddled for you, and that I shall *personally* see to it that Lucifer receives a stern lecture on the subject of her behavior."

"Thank you, Your Majesty," smiled Persephone, thoroughly charmed by the image of this richly dressed young monarch perched atop a weathered milking stool delivering a fiery harangue to a deaf horse.

The king smiled, too. "Now, tell me how you knew that my 'early birthday surprise' was wounded," he said, "for I would hardly have known it myself if Lord Atticus hadn't told me so when he gave it to me."

For a moment, Persephone just gaped at him, cursing herself for a fool. "O-oh," she finally stammered. "Well, uh, I suppose there was just something about the way he was perched upon your arm. You know, as if . . . as if there was something wrong with him."

"There is something wrong with him, all right, and it is his poor attitude," said the king, surreptitiously coughing in the sleeve of his doublet. "Why else would a trained hunting hawk willfully ignore such a fine meal in plain sight?" he asked, gesturing to the dead chick that lay on the ground not far from where Cur was sunning himself.

"Perhaps he is so well trained that he disdains having his meals served to him," suggested Persephone. "Or . . . perhaps he has been brought so low by his tether that he cannot bring himself to eat. Perhaps you would have more luck with him if—"

"I removed the tether?"

Persephone nodded.

"You do not like the idea that this creature should be my captive," observed the king shrewdly.

"I do not," admitted Persephone, with feeling. "Some creatures were meant to be free, Your Majesty, and I think he is one of them."

King Finnius looked at her for a long moment. Then he looked at Ivan. Then, wordlessly—and with infinite gentleness—he unlaced the tether that bound Ivan's leg. Ivan blinked several times, screamed once at Persephone, then exploded into the air with such force that it would, indeed, have been impossible to guess that his wing had been pierced mere days earlier.

As Ivan flew off with an air of great purpose, there came the sound of someone bellowing the name of "Lady Bothwell." As one, Persephone and the king looked around to see Azriel sprinting around the corner of the nearby palace turret. Upon spotting Persephone, he raced toward her—eschewing the path in favor of nimbly leaping over ponds, hedges and flower beds that he might reach her the sooner.

Skidding to a halt before her, Azriel was so obviously relieved to find her safe that for one heart-stopping moment Persephone thought he might sweep her into his arms and crush her against him as he'd done the previous night. Then he noticed her companion and, recognizing him as the king, quickly swept him a low bow.

"Pardon, Your Majesty," he panted, studiously ignoring Cur, who'd begun to growl in earnest at the sight of him, "but when your Master of Horse sent word to my lady's chambers that her mount had returned to the stables by way of the garden and that she'd not returned with it, I feared the worst and came looking for her at once."

"You are a most devoted servant," said the king approvingly.

"His name is Azriel and he is a eunuch," said Persephone, for sheer devilment.

"Really!" said the king, who seemed much pleased by this news. "Well, you needn't have worried, Azriel. Lady Bothwell *did* have a rather harrowing experience with a horse of ill repute but I have assured her that I am going to deal with the brute in a manner she won't soon forget."

He and Persephone shared a private laugh at this. Azriel watched them laugh with the expression of one who'd just swallowed a bug. Then he let out an ear-splitting shriek as Ivan swooped down and dropped a dead rat on his head.

"Ha!" cried the king excitedly, his blue eyes shining with delight. "Look what my hawk has brought me!"

"Congratulations, Sire," said Persephone, smothering a smile at the sight of Azriel's own blue eyes bulging in outrage.

The king hunkered down to get a closer look at his prize. "Of course," he said, wrinkling his nose slightly, "black rats are not *precisely* the kind of game one hopes to bring down with a hawk, and one prefers to have the kill delivered directly to oneself, but *still*. It is a remarkable start, and I have you to thank for it, Lady Bothwell, for it was you who saw that this creature was meant to be free."

Persephone's heart swelled at his words and at the sudden realization that she, a girl enslaved since birth, was standing in the beautiful garden of the imperial palace listening to the king himself thank her for her advice on the subject of freedom.

"Truly," he continued with an enthusiasm that Persephone found inexpressibly appealing, "you are a most uncommon noblewoman and one whom I would like to know better. I will be dining in state this evening so that my subjects may see that I am well, and if it would please you, I should like to have you join me."

Persephone's heart swelled again—the king himself was inviting her to supper! Then she remembered that she'd agreed to share supper and "amusements" in the Regent's private chamber that evening.

"Not to worry," said the king, upon learning of her prior engagement. "I will invite the Regent to join us, and we shall all be merry."

Thirty-One

"I DON'T KNOW WHY you agreed to accompany him to dinner," said Azriel with more than a trace of complaint in his voice.

Persephone sat before the looking glass, admiring the job that Martha and the sisters had done. They'd been frankly horrified when "Lady Bothwell" had returned to her chambers trailing a smelly mongrel and looking like something the cat dragged in, and they'd wasted no time preparing a bath and setting about the business of making her look fit for a king. Persephone flushed hotly as she recalled Azriel's expression as he'd slowly emptied pail after pail of steaming water into the claw-footed tub—half-amused that she'd been unable to entirely ban her Master of the Bath from the process this time, half-ready to explode with desire. Even now, her breath caught at the memory of how close he'd seemed to flinging the pail across the room and sweeping aside the floating rose petals that were the only thing protecting her nakedness from his hungry eyes.

Pinching herself hard to force her thoughts back to the moment, Persephone tugged on the long, puffed sleeves of her silvery gown and said, "I agreed to accompany King Finnius to dinner because he is the king, because I like him and because it gave me a ready excuse not to spend an evening alone with the Regent."

Azriel let out a loud, indignant huff. "I told you that *I* was going to come up with a plan to keep you out of the hands of the Regent."

"And what plan had you come up with?" she asked, twisting around to face him.

Azriel, who was lounging in one of the chairs by the fire, rolled his eyes heavenward and sucked in his cheeks. "I was still working on it," he muttered.

Persephone tried not to smile. "And what of the plan to rescue your little kinsman?" she asked, turning back around and reaching for her wine goblet.

"Figured out down to the last detail."

Persephone choked on her mouthful of wine. "Really?" she said in surprise, after she'd recovered.

"Really," said Azriel smugly. "Today, while you were out gallivanting with your noble friends and making moon-eyes at the king—"

"I was not making *moon-eyes*—"

"I learned that the dungeon is deep underground with a single well-guarded entrance—"

"Everyone knows that," said Persephone, not bothering to hide her smile this time.

Azriel scowled at her before continuing. "I also learned that almost no one is permitted to enter the dungeon save for the prisoners who are condemned to it, the guards who patrol it, the Regent and his general."

Persephone frowned. "But if no one but them enters, how will we get in?" she asked.

"I said *almost* no one," replied Azriel even more smugly than before. "Every second day, a pair of kitchen servants is sent down to distribute bread to the prisoners. They will go down this evening; on the evening of the king's birthday two days hence, we will go down in their stead, carrying their sacks of bread and dressed in their robes."

"Why would they let us do that?"

"Because they dread and fear the task, and because they will be stinking drunk on the fine wine that I will have given to them to drink."

"Where will you get the fine wine?"

"I will steal it," said Azriel with exaggerated patience. "I'm a thief, remember?"

"Oh, I remember," said Persephone, bugging her eyes out at him before reluctantly picking up the amethyst necklace that the Regent had given her.

"Once in the dungeon we will search until we find the child—"

"They say the dungeon is a vast labyrinth," said Persephone as she fumbled with the clasp of the necklace. "We could search forever and not find him."

Azriel, who'd silently come up behind her, lightly ran his hands along hers until he reached the clasp of the necklace, which he deftly closed. Placing his hands on her shoulders, he caught her gaze in the looking glass and said, "We'll just have to hope that doesn't happen, won't we?"

Feeling a little dizzy, Persephone nodded and rather breathlessly asked, "W-what if the guards who patrol the dungeon are familiar with the regular servants? What if one of them notices that we aren't them—or worse, recognizes me as Lady Bothwell?"

Stepping away from her, Azriel began to pace the room. "Most New Men think almost as highly of themselves as noblemen do, therefore I sincerely doubt that any will have lowered themselves to familiarity with dungeon servants. I also doubt their ability to see that which they do not expect to see, which is why I'm not overly concerned that they will recognize 'Lady Bothwell' covered in ashes and dressed in rags. Moreover," he continued, "since the king has insisted that free food and wine be distributed throughout the city in honor of his birthday, and also that processions, contests and entertainments be held both within the palace walls and without, additional soldiers will be needed aboveground to maintain order among the revelers. Therefore, there will be fewer guards on duty in the dungeon than usual—a circumstance that further reduces our risk."

"But what of the risk of waiting two days?" asked Persephone. "The risk to the child, I mean?"

"It concerns me greatly but I can see no help for it," said Azriel. "The palace guards have a separate kitchen with poison testers so there is no way to slip them a draught that will put them to sleep and allow us to sneak past them, and a frontal assault on the dungeon entrance would be suicide for us and certain death for the child. Waiting is a risk, but it is also our best hope."

Persephone nodded. "And what if someone else ends up paying the price of seeing that hope fulfilled?"

Azriel looked at her uncomprehendingly.

"Today I saw the bloody heads of six innocent men who were murdered because of the lies I told, Azriel," she said softly. "Those men's children are fatherless because of me—"

"Those men's children are fatherless because their fathers were murdered by the Regent," said Azriel flatly.

"Because of my lies."

"Because the Regent is evil," insisted Azriel. "Persephone, I am truly sorry those men died but I will not accept responsibility for their deaths, and I will not allow you to do so, either. Two days hence we will rescue the little boy in the dungeon. We will do everything in our power to ensure that no one dies in the process, and then we will leave this place and you will never have to see the Regent again."

Persephone nodded, not wanting to think about who else she might never see again after she left this place. "And what would you have me do between now and then?" she asked.

"Pray for the child and be charming to all," replied Azriel. Then, lifting an index finger high in the air, he solemnly amended his instruction.

"Be charming to all," he repeated, "but not *too* charming."

As agreed, that night Persephone dined with the king, the Regent and all those who'd come to the noisy Great Hall to partake of a royal feast and get a glimpse of their handsome young monarch seated upon his golden chair beneath his purple cloth of state. Kitchen servants, all of whom eagerly watched to see how much the notorious Lady Bothwell would consume, presented dish after dish to the king, who dutifully sampled the contents of each, praised the chef and gallantly offered the choicest morsels to Persephone before sending the dishes onward to be shared among the other tables. He was unfailingly patient and gracious to one and all—why, when a pockmarked servant accidentally dropped the roast-beef platter she was carrying, he waved away the Master of Hall who'd come charging forward to berate the poor woman. He then followed up this kindness by announcing that he liked the smell of roast beef so much that, henceforth, his juice-splattered shoes would be his favorite pair. At this, the Great Hall erupted in sycophantic laughter so loud that Persephone nearly inhaled a mouthful of pheasant.

After she recovered, she cast a sideways glance at the king and asked, "Do they always laugh at your jests, Majesty—even when they aren't especially funny?"

Delighted by her frankness, King Finnius threw back his head and laughed. "Always, Lady Bothwell," he replied. "*Always.*"

To Persephone's relief, the Regent gave no sign that he was angry that his evening alone with her had been usurped, though Persephone was careful not to give him further cause to feel slighted. She conversed with him as often as she conversed with the king and even passed him some of the choicer morsels from her own plate. It sickened her to have to dote upon such a monster, and to have to pretend to be enchanted by all that he said and did, but with two full days of imposture still ahead of her, she dared not risk losing his favor.

When the meal was over, the tables were pushed back against the wall, musicians were summoned and the ladies and gentlemen of the court were called to dance. Persephone, who hadn't seen the traditional dances performed since she was a child living in the merchant's house, declined to join in, giving the excuse that she was still bruised from her fall from the horse. Instead, she sat quietly by the Regent, doing her best to memorize the names and steps of each dance and smiling at the flushed king whenever he glanced her way.

"Are you sure I cannot persuade you to dance, Lady Bothwell?" he asked breathlessly, staggering over to her after one particularly vigorous set.

"I am sure," she said, laughing at his bright-pink cheeks.

The king grinned like the boy he was. "Another time, perhaps," he suggested.

"Another time," she agreed.

"Promise?" he asked, turning his head to cough into the sleeve of his doublet.

Flustered, flattered and pleased, Persephone tucked her clasped hands beneath her chin, smiled and said, "Promise."

The king beamed at her and the next moment was swept back up in the dizzying twirl of dancers. Persephone's eyes trailed him until she felt the Regent's cold black eyes upon her. Turning to him at once, she smiled dazzlingly and shrugged as if to say, *What could I do but humor him? He is the king.* The Regent stared at her for a moment longer before visibly relaxing, patting her hand with his own withered claw and calling for more wine.

Nigh about midnight, the visibly exhausted king formally took his leave of the court. As soon as he was gone, the Great Hall began to clear out—the married ladies retiring to their chambers, their husbands retreating into the shadows to talk business and intrigue, and the drunk and merry young people drifting toward smaller common rooms or out into the night to seek mischief under the cover of darkness.

Bidding the Regent good night before he had a chance to suggest that she do other than retire to her chamber like the proper married lady she was, Persephone quickly made her way toward the back of the Great Hall. About halfway across the room, as she was maneuvering around a silver fountain in the shape of a goddess, she heard several young noblewomen on the other side of the fountain gossiping about the morning's hunt.

". . . I thought I would *die* from laughter. I really did!" giggled one.

"So did I," said another. "Did you see the look on her face when that beast she was riding jumped the spit hog?"

More giggles.

"I'm just sorry the saddle didn't slip," chirped a third, one that Persephone instantly recognized as the tiny, birdlike Lady Aurelia. "I thought you were going to see to it that the half-wit groom loosened the buckle."

"He wouldn't do it," replied the first. "Not for a gold sovereign—not even for a kiss!" Several small screams of unkind laughter. "The fool said that if she were to break her neck in a fall that had been deliberately caused, his life wouldn't be worth two strings of cat gut."

"As if it's worth more than that in any event," said the second.

More laughter.

Then, slyly, "How do you suppose the Regent enjoyed sharing his married lady friend with the king this evening?"

"Not at all, I'm sure, but she played it well."

"Of course she played it well," snapped Lady Aurelia. "She's a whore—that's what whores do. Honestly, did you see the way she simpered at the king?"

"If he's the king," interjected the lady who'd spoken second. "I mean, the *true* king."

"He's the true king," insisted Lady Aurelia. "It is treason to suggest otherwise."

A burble of laughter. "You only say that because your great and powerful father means to marry you to him. My father says that someday a witness to the events in that birthing chamber will be found, and when that happens—"

"It will not happen," said Lady Aurelia flatly.

"Well, then perhaps Lady Bothwell will find some way to free herself from that decrepit old husband of hers so that *she* can marry the king," suggested the second lady slyly.

"That will not happen, either," snapped Lady Aurelia, "for within five minutes of meeting her, my father had dispatched men to the Ragorian Prefecture to find out all that he could about her. If there is dirt, they will find it; if there is not, they will make it up. Either way, if she makes a single serious move toward the king, my father will have what he needs to destroy her utterly."

"Oh, Aurelia, you are *such* a charmer . . ." laughed the first lady as the three of them drifted away, leaving Persephone badly shaken and wondering just how long she had before Lord Bartok's men arrived back with something far more devastating than dirt:

The truth.

Thirty-Two

LATER THAT SAME NIGHT, as he slowly made his way down the weeping, winding stone steps to the dungeon, Mordesius lamented yet again the necessity of having the place so deep beneath the castle. True, it spared him having to listen to the tiresome noises of those being questioned or punished, and true, it utterly crushed the spirits of all but the most resilient prisoners, but *still*. The narrow, slippery stairs were treacherous, Mordesius suffered from the damp, it smelled atrocious and there was always *something* scuttling about in the darkness.

As he continued down the torch-lit staircase, grimacing from time to time as yet another well-fed rat ambled to one side to let him pass, Mordesius thought about the evening that had just passed. *Obviously*, he'd been murderous when the king had informed him that he'd not be dining in private with Lady Bothwell—not only because the king had dared to interfere in his personal life, but also because the royal fool had obviously conceived an affection for the lady, and Mordesius could not imagine how he, scarred and twisted as he was, would ever be able to compete romantically with such a strong and handsome young king.

But then the most extraordinary thing had happened: in a court where ambitious young noblewomen routinely flopped onto their backs if the king so much as looked at them sideways, Lady Bothwell had chosen instead to make it clear that she had *not* conceived such an affection for the king as he had for her. Oh, she'd been polite and attentive enough to the king, Mordesius supposed, but no more polite or attentive than she'd been to him. Less polite and attentive, actually, because she'd gone to special effort to offer him choice morsels off her own plate—something she hadn't bothered to do for the king. Moreover, when the king had gotten up to dance, she had demurred, claiming that she was yet bruised from her fall. Ha! Even now, Mordesius could hardly keep from laughing aloud at the king's gullibility. Of course that was not the reason she'd refused him—obviously, she'd refused him because she knew that it was her duty to sit quietly beside her future husband. And when the king had returned to beg her to reconsider, she'd played the perfect courtier, catering to his vanity and filling his head with empty promises.

Truly, she was a woman without equal.

With that happy thought, Mordesius finally reached the bottom of the stairs. His happiness vanished at the sound of something far bigger than a rat scurrying toward him. Suddenly afraid, he was about to try to lurch back up the stairs when two filthy, hooded servants, each carrying an empty burlap sack, burst out of the mouth of one of the darkened corridors leading away from the place where the Regent now stood.

"Halt!" he barked, panting and clutching his heart. "What do you think you're doing?"

The servants who, an instant earlier, had looked as though they thought Satan himself was after them, now looked considerably more terrified.

"F-f-feeding the p-p-prisoners, Your G-g-grace!" stammered one. "W-we was s-s-sent d-d-down wif s-s-sacks of b-b—"

"Bread, fool," interrupted Mordesius, despising a world that had allowed a useless, babbling moron like *this* to grow to adulthood unscathed while he, himself, had been burned to a scarred husk of the man he should have become. Still breathing heavily, he stared at the man and his companion with undisguised loathing. "Well, what are you waiting for?" he finally snarled. "A cell of your own?"

Without a word, and with the quickness of small animals accustomed to narrow escapes, the two hooded servants darted past Mordesius and disappeared up the stairs.

Sourly, Mordesius watched them go. Then he shuffled into the mouth of the corridor directly ahead of him. After some paces, he came to a wooden door. Ignoring the guard who jumped to attention and reached for the handle, the Regent pulled open the door himself and continued lurching along through the gloom—ignoring other guards and passing through other doors, sometimes turning this way, sometimes turning that way, always humming tunelessly to himself and paying no mind whatsoever to the whispered pleas and promises that issued from the fetid cells lining the corridors, or to the bony hands that poked through the tiny, barred windows to claw after him.

By and by, he arrived at his destination. He was about to order the guard to push open the heavy door when he heard the big Panoraki talking. It had been months since the wretch had done more than laugh like the insolent tribal dog he was—months in which he'd renewed his old game of toying with Mordesius and Murdock. Of smiling knowingly when they asked for the ten thousandth time what healing pool secrets his friend Balthazar had shared with him in the time before the old king turned on them.

Now, Mordesius stood very still and listened to him speak.

". . . How about you just tell me your name, then," he suggested in a voice ragged from disuse.

No answer.

"Come now, lad," he said gruffly. "By my reckoning we've been roommates for somewhere between a day and three. You can't *still* be frightened of me. Is it my hair? Is that what's bothering you? Shall I smooth it down for you?"

Upon hearing the rattle of chains followed by a grunt of apparent satisfaction, Mordesius scowled impatiently. As a race, the dirty, smelly Panoraki placed no stock whatsoever in personal hygiene at the best of times; this particular fool had been shackled to the wall for years, wallowing in his own filth, unable to pick his nose, let alone tend to the matted mess he called hair. What on earth was he doing?

Mordesius heard a faint noise. Then, softly: "My name is Mateo."

"Pleased to meet you, Mateo," grunted the big Panoraki. "My name is Barka. I am a prince of the Panoraki. Do you know who the Panoraki are?"

No answer.

"We are a great warrior people who live high upon the snowy mountains with our wonderful woolly sheep," explained Barka proudly. "I suppose you're a Methusian?"

No answer.

"I tell you, Mateo, I once had a good friend who was a Methusian—name of Balthazar. He was your very own ambassador to Parthania back before it all went bad. Kind of a big-headed fool, if you don't mind me saying, going on as he did about healing waters. Mind you, he died as brave a death as any man I've ever known, and you must always remember that there is great honor in dying well, Mateo. *Great* honor," said Barka, his voice thickening. He paused for a moment, then cleared his throat and cheerfully said, "Would you tell me a story, Mateo?"

To Mordesius's utter amazement, the caged Methusian brat actually laughed. "You're the grown-up," he said in his chalk-soft voice. "You're supposed to tell *me* a story."

"What!" exclaimed the Panoraki. "Who says? I've never heard—"

Irritated by the useless turn the conversation had taken, Mordesius ordered the guard to push open the door so that he could step into the stifling room. At the sight of him, the Panoraki and the child fell silent. The Gorgishman in the hanging cage hissed loudly and bared his crowded teeth. Wordlessly, Mordesius considered his options. He had intended to work on the child tonight, but now he wasn't so sure. After all, although the blood of young Methusians had marvelous rejuvenating properties, he'd more or less concluded that no matter what the formulation, it simply lacked the power to heal his old injuries. As he'd told Murdock, he'd come to believe that finding the Pool of Genezing was his only real hope. And as the Panoraki Barka had so helpfully pointed out, he'd been Balthazar's good friend. If he was in a talkative mood, there was always the chance that, with proper encouragement, he'd finally let something useful slip.

The Methusian could wait.

Decision made, Mordesius shuffled over to the neatly arranged table of implements and picked up a small pair of pliers. His heavy head alive with visions of Lady Bothwell debasing herself for lust of the body he was ever meant to have, he lurched across the room to stand in front of the Panoraki Barka. "Tell me what you know of the location of the Pool of Genezing," he ordered.

For a moment, the big clansman said nothing. Then he began to laugh derisively.

Nodding placidly, Mordesius lifted the pliers and went to work.

Thirty-Three

"I WOULD NOT LIVE the life of a king for all the diamonds in the Mines of Torodania," announced Azriel the next morning, as he stood with his hands on his hips watching Persephone excitedly adjust her plumed hat in anticipation of the arrival of the king, who'd sent word shortly after first light that he wished to spend the day with her.

"Yes," said Persephone, smiling at his reflection in the looking glass. "The life of a king would be a terrible thing, indeed. Beautiful clothes and fine food, courtiers hanging on your every word, attendants leaping to attend your every need—who would want to suffer such a fate?"

"Not me," said Azriel, refusing to rise to the bait, "for I should not like to walk through life pampered and blind, not knowing who loved me and who merely loved my crown." Stepping forward, he leaned down and brought his head so close to hers that their cheeks were nearly touching. Gazing at her reflection in the looking glass, he murmured, "No, the life I'd choose would be a simpler one by far. A plot of land to call my own, a pretty little thatch-roofed cottage, a yard full of scratching chickens. A well-tended garden. A fat pig to slaughter each autumn that I might be kept in bacon and sausages all winter; enough grain to make my bread and beer. Sturdy homespun shirts and a soft, clean bed of feathers. Good candles and plenty of them. An apple orchard, perhaps, and a pond stocked with fish—and an oak tree with a swing hung from a low branch so that on warm summer days I could push my clever wife and later, our babies. Music and laughter each day, and the knowledge that it would all be there tomorrow, and for ten thousand tomorrows thereafter."

The picture he painted was so utterly seductive that for a moment, Persephone could do nothing but stare at his reflection. "But . . . but you're not even a farmer!" she finally spluttered, feeling exasperated for reasons she couldn't quite put her finger on.

"I know," murmured Azriel, his eyes never leaving hers. "That is why I would need a *very* clever wife—one who is good with animals and knows something of the business of farming. And that is why I would like to ask you . . ."

Heart thudding madly, Persephone swiveled to face him.

"To let me know if you ever meet a woman who fits the bill," he concluded with a satisfied smile.

Persephone blinked in surprise, then scowled. "You are a beast," she muttered, giving him a smack in the belly.

Azriel grunted, then laughed. "Enjoy your day with the king, *my lady.*"

After her unsettling conversation with Azriel, Persephone did not think she'd be able to enjoy her day with King Finnius, but she could not have been more wrong, for he was the most perfect companion. He seemed to enjoy the garden almost as much as she did, and they spent several wonderful hours winding their way along the many paths—admiring the colorful blooms, breathing in the heady fragrances and poking little frogs with blades of grass for the fun of seeing them leap from their lily pads and disappear beneath the ponds' sparkling surfaces. With their chaperone, Moira, trailing at a distance that allowed them the illusion of privacy, they tossed crumbs to the fish and birds, and the king entertained Persephone with vivid descriptions of the many wondrous festivities that were being planned in honor of his birthday. When his cough troubled him, the two of them briefly lay down on the thick carpet of grass and watched Ivan perform loop-the-loops overhead. And when they visited the stables, the king did not seem to find it at all strange when "Lady Bothwell" formally forgave Lucifer (the moody mare ignored her), chatted with the chickens and laughed at the goats who tried to chew the bows off the hem of her gown.

"And when Cur tried to bite him, he didn't have a single unkind word to say to him," said Persephone breathlessly when she returned to her chambers in the early afternoon to change into a fresh gown.

"Cur tried to bite him?" said Azriel, gazing fondly at the dog for the first time.

"Yes," said Persephone as Cur snarled and snapped at Azriel. "That is why I'm going to leave him locked in here for the afternoon."

"Perhaps you should stay locked in here as well," suggested Azriel, "for with one notable exception, I have always found Cur to be an excellent judge of character. If he thinks the king is a dastardly rogue—"

"I'm sorry, Azriel, but could you please call Martha and the sisters to help me dress?" interrupted Persephone, who did not appear to be paying very close attention to him. "I know they are busy sewing costumes for the birthday pageant, but the king says he has a surprise for me that I shan't receive unless I return to him promptly."

"A surprise?" sniffed Azriel. "Probably some hideously ugly piece of overpriced jewelry plucked from the royal coffers by one of his lackeys."

"I doubt it," laughed Persephone, "for already this day he has surprised me with a yellow rose to tuck behind my ear, a newborn kitten to hold against my cheek, a waxy comb of fresh honey and a piece of fruit I'd never seen before. Hideously ugly overpriced jewelry does not seem to be his style."

"If you say so," muttered Azriel darkly.

"Martha and the sisters?" reminded Persephone, with a tiny flick of her fingers.

"Oh, very *well*," he huffed.

The afternoon with the king was as enjoyable as the morning had been. With exaggerated care, King Finnius led Persephone down the precariously steep path to the royal docks. There, he gave her a tour of his glittering golden barge and pointed out the treacherous sea caves that dotted the cliff behind them. Together, they explored the rocky beach, marveling at the strange creatures in the salty tidal pools and rescuing the occasional gasping, flopping fish that had been stranded by the low tide. Late in the afternoon, hunger drove them back to the palace garden where they filled their bellies with honeyed pastries and Persephone delighted the king by joining in a game of cards and winning a small fortune in white beans from Moira.

It was nearly time for supper when Persephone finally made it back to her chamber. To her surprise, it appeared empty.

"Azriel?" she called cautiously. "Cur?"

A harsh whisper from behind the screen near the cold fireplace was followed by a vicious snarl.

Silently sidling a few more steps into the room, Persephone picked up a wrought-iron candlestick holder that she judged heavy enough to bash out the brains of any intruder. As she did so, Azriel and Cur suddenly stepped out from behind the screen.

At the sight of them, Persephone's thickly lashed violet eyes grew as wide as trenchers. For Azriel was covered in a host of fresh scratches and bite marks, while Cur . . .

Cur was positively *gleaming*!

There was not a single burr in his ears, not a single tangle in his tail, no evidence whatsoever of ticks and fleas. His long, matted fur had been washed, trimmed and brushed to a luxuriant shine, and it appeared that even his toenails had been cut.

Most remarkable of all, he was wearing a large pink bow around his neck.

Dropping the candlestick holder, Persephone clapped both hands over her mouth and laughed aloud. "Azriel, what on *earth* possessed you to give Cur a *bath*?"

"I don't know," he muttered with a self-conscious shrug. "I thought he did not look the part of a noble hound and . . . and I suppose I wanted to surprise you."

"Well, you certainly did *that*!" said Persephone, laughing even harder as Cur twisted his head in a futile attempt to tear off the bow.

"I used your claw-footed tub," continued Azriel in an embarrassed voice. "I also used your brush, your scissors and the last of your rose-scented bath oil. Oh, and I cut the bow off one of your gowns." Shifting from foot to foot, he said, "Well? What do you think?"

Looking at Azriel, so tall and strong and handsome (and wet and scratched and bitten), Persephone thought that a man like this was almost enough to make a girl like her forget that she had dreams of freedom and a destiny that was not tied to the hopes of a hunted people.

Almost enough—but not quite.

The Fates never give but that they take away.

Feeling a sudden, dull ache in her chest, Persephone walked over to where Azriel stood awaiting her judgment. Laying a hand against his cheek, she said, "What you have done here this day is the sweetest, kindest thing anyone has ever done for me, Azriel, and I swear to you that whatever happens, I shall not forget it."

Smiling like a pirate, Azriel slid his hands around her waist, dipped his head and whispered, "Does this mean that if I find myself tempted to crawl into your bed at some point during this night that I need not imagine myself a blind, fingerless eunuch?"

"No," said Persephone, staring at his beautiful lips, so close to hers.

"How about just blind and fingerless?" suggested Azriel.

Almost without meaning to, Persephone leaned forward and brushed her lips against his. Her body's reaction was instantaneous and explosive. "Blind, fingerless *and* a eunuch," she promised breathlessly, stepping away from him.

"You sound very sure about that," he said with a smile.

"I am," she lied as she forced herself to take another step back. "Now, go away. I need to get ready for supper."

For the second night in a row, Persephone supped in the Great Hall with King Finnius on her left side and the Regent Mordesius on her right. This time, however, though she was once again careful to show the Regent due deference and to pass him some of the choicer morsels from her plate, Persephone could feel the blistering heat of his anger. She could not say if it was directed toward her or toward the laughing young king who ever commanded her attention, but she feared it nonetheless.

After supper, there were pre-birthday entertainments—performances by jugglers, tumblers and fools, recitations by poets and songs sung by rosy-cheeked choirboys. It was very late by the time Persephone finally returned to her chambers. Soundlessly, so as not to disturb the slumbering Azriel, Martha and the sisters helped her out of her silvery gown and into her filmy nightgown, brushed out her stiff curls and tucked her into bed. After they'd tiptoed out of the room, Persephone yawned hugely, snuggled down beneath the covers and closed her eyes.

Exactly one minute later, a loud, petulant voice from the floor by the fire announced, "I don't like him. And what's more, I don't trust him!"

"Who?" mumbled Persephone, who was almost asleep.

"The king," said Azriel darkly. "He knows you have a husband. What game is he playing, wooing you?"

"He's not wooing me," murmured Persephone.

"Of course he is. He's just being especially crafty about it—spending time with you, joining you in simple pleasures, laughing at your jests, treating you with kindness and respect."

"You're right. He's a monster."

"He should not be courting you as if you were a marriageable maid," insisted Azriel.

"He's not courting me," she yawned. "He barely knows me!"

Azriel rolled his eyes. "Don't be naive, Persephone. I see the way he looks at you."

More or less awake by this point, Persephone propped herself up on her elbow so that her dark hair tumbled onto the pillow and her nightdress slipped down to reveal one bare shoulder. "How does he look at me?" she asked, unable to resist the hint of provocation in her voice.

Azriel, who had rolled onto his side to face her, and who was likewise propped up on one elbow, stared at her for so long and with such heat that Persephone's heart began to pound and she began to fear what she had started.

"It is very hard to describe the way he looks at you," Azriel finally said in a low, husky voice, "but I know what I see. And what I see is a great royal fool wooing a beautiful noblewoman who is already spoken for."

"King Finnius is not a fool," said Persephone shakily. "He is sweet, and I think he will be a good ruler."

"Really?" said Azriel, rolling onto his stomach and hunching his broad shoulders in a manner that was all the more provocative for its carelessness. "What makes you think so—the fact that he is handsome and gallant and pays you the kind of attention that is sure to drive the other women at court mad with jealousy? The fact that his kitchens throw away more food in one day than most lowborn families see in a year? The fact that he wears cloth of gold, fills his idle hours with tender amusements and knows nothing of the hardships his subjects suffer? Tell me, Persephone—what has your precious king *ever* said or done to make you think that he will be a good ruler?"

"I . . . have seen him be kind to his servants," she said lamely.

"I do not think the fact that he is not cruel to those few who serve him is the same as being a good ruler to all," said Azriel.

Persephone did not think so, either, but to say so would have felt like a betrayal of the king, whom she liked very much and whom she was certain did not deserve the criticism that Azriel was heaping upon him. And so, leaning forward just enough to torture the one-time chicken thief, she said, "Do you know what I think, Azriel? I think you are *jealous* of King Finnius."

Azriel returned the favor by giving her a smile that sent a ripple of desire through her body. "You are right," he said softly, surprising her. "But so am I."

The conversation with Azriel bothered Persephone for the rest of that night and all the next morning.

"You seem distracted," said the king that afternoon as the two of them sat on a blanket in the garden sharing plates of bread, cheese, fruit and fowl, while Persephone's self-appointed chaperone hovered nearby like a brooding, broad-shouldered specter.

"It is nothing important," she assured the king with a smile.

King Finnius smiled back and gallantly declared, "Lady Bothwell, if something is bothering you, it is important to *me.*"

Out of the corner of her eye, Persephone saw Azriel roll his eyes.

Resisting the urge to stick her tongue out at him, she turned to the king and said, "Nothing is bothering me, Your Majesty. It is just that . . . I have been thinking how dreamlike our lives are and how easy it is to get lost in the dream."

Moira, who was likewise chaperoning, glanced up from her knitting.

"What do you mean?" asked the king interestedly as he took a sip of wine from his golden goblet.

Persephone smiled again. "Only that life within the palace walls is so filled with comfort, beauty and delights that if I'd not seen with my own two eyes the hard, harsh world beyond the walls I would scarcely believe that it exists."

The king made a face. "I cannot believe that the world outside is *that* hard and harsh, Lady Bothwell," he objected, "for it is well-known that peace and prosperity reign within my realm."

"You've borne witness to this peace and prosperity?" asked Persephone innocently.

"Well, not myself, I haven't," replied the king, a trifle impatiently. "I am a young monarch without a named heir, Lady Bothwell. Naturally, my councilors fear my exposure to the dangers posed by ruffians and the diseases of my lesser subjects."

Persephone nodded slowly. "And . . . you are sure that is all they fear your exposure to?"

"What do you mean?" asked the king.

Feeling Moira's eyes upon her, Persephone hesitated. "I mean only that it seems strange to me that your councilors would not encourage you to travel among your people at least *occasionally*, Your Majesty," she said, "for I would think that the very best way to ensure contentment within the realm would be for all subjects to see and know and love their king—"

"I make regular appearances upon the Grand Balcony," put in King Finnius.

"And for their king to *really* see and know and love them, and to make it his business to ensure that justice and mercy are granted to the very least of them."

The king gazed at Persephone in silence for a very long time. "You do not think I can trust my councilors to see to this on my behalf?" he asked at last.

"I do not know if any of them has a heart as good as yours," she said, reaching for his gloved hand. "For you are the sweetest, kindest, most—"

Behind them, Azriel cleared his throat so loudly that it sounded as though he were violently retching.

Turning to him with a raised eyebrow, the king said, "Yes, Azriel? Is something the matter?"

"Forgive me, but I was suddenly seized by a terrible concern for Your Majesty," he mumbled humbly. "You've been up and about for hours already after being desperately ill just a few days ago, and with your delicate constitution, I worried that—"

The king flushed. "I was not 'desperately' ill and I do not have a delicate constitution!" he protested with a darting glance at Persephone.

"Of course you don't, Your Majesty," agreed Azriel in a soothing voice as he subtly rolled his powerful shoulders. "I only meant that you are somewhat frail—"

King Finnius was on his feet in a heartbeat. "You think I am frail?" he cried. "We will wrestle right here and now, you and I, and we shall see who is frail!"

Azriel stepped forward at once.

"Azriel!" said Persephone sharply.

"Do not interfere, Lady Bothwell," said the king quickly, without taking his eyes off his opponent. "Your servant has besmirched my honor and I mean to put him in his place!"

"Your Majesty, how is this a matter of honor?" asked Moira, as her knitting needles continued to click away. "He only said—"

"You shall not interfere, either, Moira," commanded the king in a ringing voice. "This is a matter to be settled between men!"

"But he's not a man—he's a eunuch!" spluttered Persephone in the hope of putting a stop to this ridiculousness.

But it was too late. The king and the "servant" had begun to circle one another. After several feints, they suddenly fell to grappling with a will. Around and around they went, blazing blue eyes locked on blazing blue eyes, while Moira looked on with mild interest and

Persephone inwardly seethed at Azriel and cursed the existence of manly pride in general.

"I . . . should . . . warn you," gasped the king, after some minutes, "I have never . . . before . . . been beaten."

"Well . . . Your Majesty," grunted Azriel, "there is . . . a first time . . . for everything."

With that, he yanked the king forward unexpectedly, pulling him off balance so that he was able to grab him by the front of his doublet, swing him around and trip him using an outstretched leg. With a very surprised look on his face, the king fell backward and slammed to the ground. Azriel promptly dropped on top of him, pinning him like a bug.

For one terrible moment, the king did not move and Persephone thought that Azriel had killed him. Then the king began to laugh. With a look of surprise almost identical to the one the king had worn just moments earlier, Azriel stood up and held out his hand.

The king reached for it. "By the gods, you've beaten me!" he laughed breathlessly as Azriel helped him to his feet. "There's not a nobleman in the realm who'd have dared to humiliate me so!"

"There is no humiliation in being fairly beaten, Your Majesty," said Azriel. "How are you ever to prove yourself a great ruler if you never have to fight for any victory you achieve?"

"Yes! Yes! That is *exactly* what I have told Mordesius!" cried the king excitedly, pounding Azriel on the back in his enthusiasm. Hastily brushing the grass from his royal backside, he coughed into his sleeve, crouched into the ready position and said, "Come, Azriel, let us wrestle again! I am quite sure that I will beat you this time!"

"Your *Majesty*—" began Persephone in dismay.

"Not now, Lady Bothwell," interrupted the king, flapping his hand at her, "for I am about to begin the business of proving myself a great ruler. . . ."

Thirty-Four

"IT IS DONE, Your Grace," said General Murdock.

Mordesius said nothing. For the last quarter hour, he'd been standing at a window watching the king wrestle with Lady Bothwell's eunuch and laugh every time he got thrown. It was an outrage. Worse, even, than when that insufferable cow of a nursemaid taught him to play cards. King though he may be—for now—Finnius was clearly a peasant at heart. Not fit to rule the kingdom and *certainly* not a fit companion for Lady Bothwell. What could he possibly know of her appetites—how could he ever hope to fulfill them? He, Mordesius, was the only one who truly understood and yet . . . and yet . . . however strange her appetites, even Mordesius had a hard time believing that she would prefer him to the king.

"Your Grace?" said General Murdock. "I said—"

"I heard what you said," snapped Mordesius, gripping the window ledge hard. "There were no witnesses?"

"None that lived," replied Murdock, reaching up to give his unusually small head a dainty scratch.

He is repulsive, thought Mordesius with a swell of satisfaction. "Good," he said. "Tomorrow morning, I shall inform poor Lady Bothwell of her change in circumstances."

"I certainly hope she appreciates your taking a personal interest in the matter," murmured General Murdock, pressing his thin lips together.

Mordesius said nothing, only watched as the lady in question was forced to degrade herself by hopping about the grappling pair, cringing, grimacing and shouting words of encouragement to the coughing but still infuriatingly strong and vital young king. "The Panoraki Barka knows something of the Pool of Genezing," said Mordesius abruptly.

Murdock ran his tongue across his long yellow teeth. "Your Grace," he said carefully, "we have questioned that particular prisoner many times over the years—"

"And in your absence, I questioned him again!" bellowed Mordesius, glaring at Murdock over his shoulder before turning his attention back to Lady Bothwell. "Now, more than ever before, I am convinced that he knows something of the pool's secret location. We must do whatever it takes to break him once and for all, and we must do it soon, Murdock, for I swear to you that I shall not suffer my body to be as it is now much longer."

"I understand, Your Grace," said General Murdock impassively. "And what of the Methusian prisoner?"

"I am through playing games with Methusian blood," said Mordesius flatly. "Kill him."

From a different window, in a dirtier, meaner room of the castle by far, a woman smiled as she watched the young king, his sweetheart and her handsome eunuch. She watched the king whenever she could, for she had a special affection for him—an affection born of having been there the night the desperate queen had clung to the sheets tied to the bedposts and strained to expel the contents of her womb. Absently fingering her pockmarks, the woman recalled that though she'd been frightened by the violent, bloody birth, it was nothing compared with the fear she'd felt in the moments that followed. Mute with terror, she'd stood half-hidden behind a tapestry and listened while the enraged Regent ordered everyone else

from the room before making his terrible pronouncement. She'd watched the exhausted queen beg for the life of her child and then weep with grief when, after calmly refusing her, the Regent had left the room to find someone to dispose of it.

It was then, in those few precious moments before he and his strange-eyed henchman returned that she'd somehow found the courage to tiptoe out of her hiding place behind the tapestry. Her intent had been to offer what comfort she could to the queen, but the queen had wanted much more than comfort, and though she'd been shocked by what she'd been asked to do, she'd done it for the love of her beautiful, dying queen—and for the sake of her doomed child.

Feeling the old burn marks at the tips of her fingers, the woman recalled how she'd just barely managed to do what had been asked of her and scurry back to her hiding place before the Regent had returned.

She realized now, of course, that she needn't have worried about hiding.

For the Regent hadn't even noticed her. Both a servant and a child, she'd been twice as much of a nothing as the others in the room had been. To him, it was as though she didn't exist.

But she did.

Thirty-Five

"YOU'RE NOT STILL ANGRY with me, are you?" asked Azriel the next morning as he stood at attention next to Persephone's chair at the head of the long table in her chambers.

"Of course not," she replied, sawing at the ham on her plate so vigorously that she rammed her elbow into his crotch several times before he managed to leap out of range.

Obviously, she was still angry with him. In her considered opinion, the previous afternoon had been a complete fiasco. Azriel and the king had wrestled until the king could wrestle no more. At that point, instead of shooing Azriel back to his spot in the hot sun and once more focusing his full attention upon Persephone, the king had invited Azriel to sit with them—as though he were a person of noble blood and not a lowly eunuch! That he was *not* a lowly eunuch any more than she *was* a person of noble blood was not the point at all. The point was that Azriel had had no business ruining her lovely afternoon with the king!

"I know you probably didn't find it especially interesting listening to the king and me discuss our favorite wrestling moves and compare our sweat stains, m'lady," continued Azriel, his lips twitching with amusement. "But if it helps, I'll have you know that I've come to agree with you that he would be a good ruler. Even though I have exceedingly good reasons to despise him, I find that I cannot help but like him. He is—"

A knock at the door cut him off. Cur barked once. Quieting him with a gesture, Persephone nodded at Reeta, the only servant left to her after the panicked pastry chef had earlier commandeered Martha, Neeka and Anya to help turn out pies for the king's birthday feast that night. Reeta bobbed a curtsey and then scampered over to open the door. She'd hardly done more than turn the knob when the door flew open in response to a hard push from the other side and the Regent Mordesius slouched into the room.

"Lady Bothwell," he said in a sonorous voice.

"Your Grace!" she said, rising to her feet and gliding toward him with a smile in spite of her inward alarm at the chilling looks he was casting toward Azriel. "To what do I owe the pleasure of your visit?"

Flushing at the word "pleasure," Mordesius seemed to forget all about Azriel. Gazing deeply into Persephone's eyes, he rearranged his handsome features into an expression of deepest sympathy and said, "My dear Lady Bothwell, I'm afraid I have most upsetting news."

Persephone pressed her hand against her chest. "It isn't the king, is it?" she blurted without thinking.

The Regent's features hardened to cold marble for just an instant before melting back into oozing sympathy. "No, my dear, it isn't the king," he murmured. "It is your beloved husband."

For half a heartbeat, Persephone had no idea what he was talking about. Then she remembered: "Lord Bothwell?" she said.

The Regent nodded mournfully. "I am terribly sorry to be the one to tell you this but . . . he is dead."

"Dead?" echoed Persephone blankly.

The Regent nodded again. "My reports tell me that the cowardly Panoraki of the mountains perpetrated a sneak attack in the middle of the night," he sighed. "They raided and then set fire to Bothwell Manor and all its outer buildings."

Though Persephone had heard stories of the bloodthirsty Pan-oraki, she didn't believe for an instant that they'd been involved in the attack on Bothwell Manor. Swallowing hard, she whispered, "And my husband—"

"Dead," confirmed the Regent, forgetting to sound sympathetic.

"And what of the others?"

"The others?" said the Regent, not understanding.

"The servants," blurted Persephone. "There would have been dozens of them! What of them?"

The Regent pursed his lips as though in annoyance. "All dead," he said shortly. "But you needn't fret about them, Lady Bothwell. As I've said before, servants are replaced as easily as—"

"Smashed dinner plates. Yes . . . yes, I know," gasped Persephone, who was suddenly having trouble breathing. Clawing at her constricting corsets, she staggered forward that she might sag against the wall instead of falling to the floor.

Dead! All dead—because of her lies! Because of her lies—and because of the Methusians' *preposterous* prophecy. If not for that, Azriel would never have bought her from the owner. She'd never have come to Parthania, never have met the Regent, never have had to lie about who she was.

Once, she'd believed the prophecy of the Methusian king to be nothing more than the wishful thinking of a hunted people.

Now she knew it was a death sentence for all those it touched.

"My dear Lady Bothwell," crooned the Regent now, as he shuffled toward her with his scarred, withered arms extended as though he meant to embrace her. "I am so terribly sorry for your loss. The night we met I warned you that a careless husband is soon deprived of a beautiful wife. Who could have known that it would be his own death that would deprive him of your charms? If there is *anything* I can do to comfort you at this difficult—"

Before he could finish his sentence, the chamber door flew open again and the king bounded into the room. Upon seeing

Persephone—white-faced with shock and horror, on the verge of collapse—he rushed toward her, knocking the Regent aside in his haste to reach her.

"The terrible rumors are true, then!" he cried, snatching up her hands and holding them against his chest as though to warm them. "When Moira told me what was being said in the servants' quarters, I did not want to believe it. Indeed, I could *not* believe it, for I could not imagine that I would hear such news from servants before hearing it from my own trusted councilors." Here, King Finnius paused to glance sharply at the Regent before turning back to Persephone. "But I see from your countenance that it is indeed true—your home is destroyed and your husband is dead!"

"And my servants," said Persephone faintly. "My servants are also dead."

The king nodded in sympathy. Then he released her hands and encircled her with his arms in a gesture that seemed wholly natural. "Lady Bothwell, I swear to you that I will send a delegation to punish the Panoraki for this atrocity," he vowed, leaning down to press his forehead against hers. "Nay, I will send an army to punish them! And I will lead the army myself! By the time I am through with the Panoraki they will—"

"No," said Persephone, twisting out of his arms. "No, Your Majesty, you must promise me you will do no such thing. Whatever has happened, there is nothing to be gained by spilling more blood."

"But—"

"No!" insisted Persephone. "Please! Promise me!"

"All right, I promise," said the king, reaching for her again.

"No," said Persephone for the fourth time, stepping away from him. "I need to be alone. To think and . . . and to grieve," she added, not looking at the Regent for fear that he would see the loathing in her eyes. "Please go. Both of you."

"Certainly, Lady Bothwell," began the Regent in a voice dripping with sympathy. "We will—"

"Go," said the king, cutting off the Regent without appearing to notice that he'd done so. "But if there is anything I can do to ease your suffering. . . ."

"There is not," said Persephone flatly. "Just—go."

Persephone moved not a muscle as the king and the Regent wordlessly filed from the room. Nor did she move when she heard Azriel quietly dismiss Reeta, nor when she sensed (rather than heard) him come up behind her.

Only then did she turn to face him. He was standing near enough to touch, looking almost as distraught as she felt. For a long moment, she said nothing, only studied his beautiful face as though carefully committing each feature to memory. Then, looking past him toward nothing at all, she said, "It is strange, isn't it? I've known for days that there would be a price to pay for continuing with my charade, and yet I dressed up in beautiful gowns, picnicked in the royal garden, played cards with the king and flirted with the Regent as though it was all a merry game. As though the only thing that mattered in the world was that I be charming to all." She brought her gaze back to Azriel's face before adding, "Charming, but not *too* charming."

Azriel blanched. "Persephone, I never meant—"

"I know you didn't," she said, swaying a little for the pleasure of hearing her skirts swish one last time. "Don't worry—I blame myself entirely for getting lost in the dream. For forgetting what is real. For forgetting what matters."

"If you had not stayed, the child's life would be forfeit."

"The child's life is probably forfeit anyway, Azriel," she said, "and ours along with it."

"Not yours," said Azriel swiftly. "For I would gladly die before—"

"Seeing me harmed in any way," she said with a wistful smile. "Yes,

I know. Except I wonder who you would save if you had to choose between me and the child who might be your Methusian king."

"I would not choose," he said stubbornly. "I would save you both."

Persephone nodded a little sadly, as though she knew this was the only answer he could have given and was yet disappointed by it. Then, in the tenderest of voices, she said, "Unfortunately, your willingness to lay down your life is no comfort to me this time, Azriel."

He looked more hurt by this than she could have imagined possible.

"Listen to me, Persephone," he pleaded. "I know you're upset by what happened to the people of Bothwell Manor, but—"

"I do not wish to speak of things we cannot change, Azriel," she said, turning away. "Nor do I wish to hear you speak clever words of reason, for nothing you could say would make me believe that the deaths of those poor people were a fair trade for the lives of two little Methusian orphans. *Nothing.* I do not believe that a Methusian king is coming, Azriel, and I never have. I believe in things that are real."

"The child—" began Azriel.

"Is real," she interrupted, turning back to him. "He is no secret king awaiting his crown but he is real. And that is one of the reasons I will accompany you into the dungeon this night in an attempt to rescue him."

As slowly as if he were approaching a startled fawn, Azriel stepped close enough to slip a tentative hand around her waist. "What are the other reasons you will do so?" he asked.

"If I refuse to help you now, the child is certain to perish. Not only would his death be yet another upon my conscience, but it would mean that the unfortunates of Bothwell Manor died for nothing at all," she explained, trembling with the effort it took to keep from wrapping her arms around him and pressing her cheek against the comforting warmth of his chest. "And besides all that, no one knows better than I what it is to be small and alone in a deep, dark, frightening place."

With his free hand Azriel reached down. With infinite gentleness, he lifted Persephone's chin so that she could not help but gaze
into his eyes. "You are not small anymore, Persephone," he whispered,
"and there is no reason at all that you should ever be alone again."

Trying hard not to think about the pretty little thatch-roofed
cottage with the yard full of scratching chickens, Persephone pressed
the palms of her hands flat against his chest and, after a moment's
hesitation, slowly pushed herself away from him. "Go steal the wine,
Azriel. Get the dungeon servants drunk, take their sacks of bread
and make what other preparations you must," she said in a subdued
voice. "I will spend this day within my chambers playing the grieving
widow. And I will try not to think about the many fates this night
could bring that would be far more terrible than being alone."

Thirty-Six

FOR HIS PART, after leaving Lady Bothwell's chambers, the Regent did not waste another thought on those who'd perished in the fires at Bothwell Manor—unless one counted the thought that he'd profited precious little from the effort and expense that had gone into making Lady Bothwell a widow, and also the thought that the king would pay dearly for having knocked him aside, interrupted him and ignored him as though he were nothing more than a piece of furniture.

Instead, Mordesius's thoughts turned to the forthcoming meeting of the Council. It was his last such meeting as Lord Regent, for at midnight that night, the king would turn eighteen and the ceremony officially transferring to him the power to rule the realm would take place. When that happened, the great Regent Mordesius would become simply Mordesius, just one of many whose existence at court depended entirely upon the king's favor. Simply Mordesius . . . unless he was finally able to persuade the Council to declare him the king's heir, that is. Though the king would have the power to rescind the declaration, Mordesius did not think he would immediately do so, for to have a named heir that had the support of the great lords all but guaranteed the stability of the realm—an important thing for a young king new to power.

And before he could consider reconsidering, he would be dead.

Mordesius knew, of course, that not every nobleman supported his bid to be named heir, but in private conversations over the last few days he'd received the informal assurances of enough of them that he entered the sumptuous Council chamber with high hopes.

Moments later, his hopes were shattered utterly as each nobleman in turn assured him that although he, personally, would like *nothing* better than to see Mordesius named the king's heir, no one had, as yet, been able to find any precedent that would allow a person of the Regent's, well, ahem, somewhat less than noble birth to take the throne. They would keep searching the ancient texts for such a precedent, they all rushed to assure him—they would search just as hard as they possibly could!—but in the meantime, *most* regretfully, there was simply no way they could recommend him to the king.

As he let his murderous gaze slide from one face to the next, Mordesius wondered if he'd be able to get away with having them all hacked to pieces where they sat. The first time they'd balked at supporting him, he'd choked down his rage in the hope that they'd come to see the error of their ways. As he sat listening to them repeat their meaningless assurances now, however, he realized that it had always been hopeless. The trouble he'd gone to over the years to enrich these men in the belief that he was buying loyalty he'd be able to leverage when he made his final leap to the apex of power—well, it had all been a waste.

Worse yet, they insisted upon adding insult to injury by mocking him with these charades of loyalty. It was as though they thought he was too stupid to see that they were merely stringing him along until the reins of power formally passed to the king.

It was as though they thought he was nothing but a pathetic, useless, lowborn *imbecile*!

Shaking with hatred but feeling that, unfortunately, he probably couldn't get away with having them all hacked to pieces where they sat, Mordesius tersely dismissed them with the intention of immediately calling for General Murdock to arrange for at least a few of them to be hacked to death at some point in the very near future.

It was then, as he sat alone at the head of the long table fantasizing about revenge in the form of splatter and gore, that Lord Bartok slipped back into the room and sat down next to him.

"What do you want?" Mordesius practically snarled.

Lord Bartok hesitated, his distaste for Mordesius's unseemly display of temper clear upon his smug noble face. "To propose an arrangement," he finally said. "One that would see both of our deepest desires fulfilled."

"Oh?" muttered Mordesius, who was only half paying attention.

"Before midnight tonight, I will see to it that the great lords declare you the king's heir," said Lord Bartok, as though it were the simplest of matters. "In return, you will this day convince the king to become betrothed to my daughter, Lady Aurelia. When Aurelia eventually bears a child, you will, of course, be required to give up your position in the line of succession, but until then, you will be heir apparent with the full support of the great Bartok Dynasty behind you."

Heart slamming against his thin chest, Mordesius, who was suddenly paying attention with every fiber of his being, stared down the length of the Council table, unable to believe what he was hearing. Was Bartok really such a fool that he did not see the flaw in his plan? Namely, that there was nothing to prevent Mordesius from murdering the king *after* he'd been named heir but *before* the king was able to get a child upon Lady Aurelia? And that even if he was not able to prevent conception, there was nothing to prevent him from murdering Lady Aurelia while she was pregnant? Or to prevent him from murdering the child at birth?

Such things had been known to happen, after all.

One quick look into Bartok's pale eyes told Mordesius that the nobleman knew exactly what he was doing—and that he had no intention of allowing Mordesius to live long enough to make trouble. He would use Mordesius to get what he wanted, eliminate him as soon as he could thereafter and then sit back to await the birth of his royal grandchild. And if by some chance these plans went awry, there was no royal grandchild and the king died without an heir of his body—well, at least Bartok would be able to rightly claim that he was the first and greatest supporter of the new monarch:

King Mordesius.

"I . . . favor this arrangement," said Mordesius in a choked voice.

Smiling coolly, Lord Bartok said, "I thought you might."

Later that afternoon, as he lurched to a halt outside the king's chambers, Mordesius recalled the amazing encounter with Lord Bartok. Feeling a surge of excitement, he breathlessly ordered the idiot guard with the unsightly birthmark to announce him. While he waited for the fool to return, he paced before the door, refining his strategy. Given the mood of the young king these days and the fact that he would very shortly rule in his own right, it wouldn't serve to burst in and order him to marry the Bartok female. However, King Finnius might be convinced to do so if Mordesius were to point out to him that a union with the most powerful family in the realm would go far toward bringing the great lords under his control. Or, better yet, if he were to suggest that the absence of such a union could cause such instability in the realm that the very poorest, most defenseless of the king's subjects would surely suffer terribly for it.

Yes, that is the way I shall approach it, decided Mordesius as he slouched into the king's chamber. *I will tug on the strings of his peasant heart, and after he is betrothed and I am named heir, I will slash those same strings, cut out the heart and—*

"Good afternoon, Your Grace," called the king, who was staring out the window with his feet shoulder width apart and his hands loosely clasped behind his back.

"Good afternoon, Your Majesty," replied Mordesius, who was pleased to see that the insufferable cow was nowhere in sight. "I pray you are well?"

"I am," replied the king without turning around.

"I am glad to hear it," murmured Mordesius. "And are you looking forward to the commencement of your birthday festivities?"

"I am," repeated the king.

"Excellent," said Mordesius. "Majesty, I've come to discuss—"

"Mordesius, do you know what I used to see when I looked out this window?" interrupted the young king, turning his head aside to cough.

"The royal garden?" suggested Mordesius, trying not to sound as impatient as he felt.

"Yes, exactly," replied the king in a tone that informed Mordesius that he'd answered just as the king had expected he would—and that the king was not terribly impressed by his answer. "That is what I *used* to see, Mordesius. Do you know what I see now?"

"No," said Mordesius flatly.

"I see walls, Your Grace. Walls that separate me from my subjects, walls that prevent me from seeing for myself if my kingdom is truly a place where peace and prosperity reign for all people."

Though Mordesius's heart leapt at this perfect opening to begin plucking upon peasant heartstrings, he was nevertheless wary of the odd direction the conversation had taken—and the reasons for it. "What a coincidence, Your Majesty," he said, treading carefully, "for earlier today at the Council meeting I found myself wondering what you might be able to do to ensure stability in the realm, and I think—"

"Lady Bothwell thinks that I should travel among my people at least occasionally," mused the king. "She thinks that the best way to ensure contentment within the realm is for all subjects to see and know and love me, and for me to not only see and know and love them, but also to make it my business to ensure that justice and mercy are granted to the very least of them."

Mordesius felt an instant of white-hot rage toward Lady Bothwell but recovered from it almost immediately. *Obviously*, she had only been telling the king what she thought he wanted to hear, and the fool had been too blind to see it. Taking a deep breath, he said, "Forgive me, Your Majesty, but as we've discussed many times, the risks to your health—"

"Would not be of such concern if I was married and had a child," interrupted the king.

Mordesius blinked in surprise. "That is true," he said cautiously. "And since you are finding yourself giving thought to such matters—"

The king turned to face him. "I am finding myself giving thought to such matters, Your Grace, I *am*," he said, his blue eyes shining. "Before today, I would never have presumed upon my friendship with Lady Bothwell—would never have *dreamt* of dishonoring her in any way but now that—"

"Wait—what are you suggesting?" blurted Mordesius. "Are you suggesting that you are thinking of marrying *Lady Bothwell*?"

"Yes," smiled the king, with a sigh of satisfaction. "Though I've known her only a very short while, I feel as though I've known her my whole life. And though I'd thought that I only cared for her as a friend with whom I had much in common, this morning, upon learning that she'd been widowed, I suddenly realized that I'd been keeping my true feelings at bay. I love her, Your Grace, with all my heart. She is beautiful, spirited, kind and caring—the perfect royal consort. I wish to have her by my side always, and that is why I intend to ask her to marry me."

"*No*," snarled Mordesius, who was so incensed that for an instant he forgot to disguise his tone.

"Excuse me?" said the king, visibly suppressing a cough.

Fearing that he would not be able to mask the hatred in his eyes, Mordesius quickly bowed his head. "Forgive me, Your Majesty," he said through his teeth as his mind raced for a way to avert this disaster. "It . . . it is just that I do not wish to see you humiliated."

"Humiliated?" said the king in surprise.

"By being turned down," clarified Mordesius, cringing to emphasize to the fool just how mortifying such a rejection would be. "Lady Bothwell has only just learned of the violent death of her beloved husband. She is grieving, Your Majesty, and however *flattered* she might be by your proposal, I am quite sure that she is nowhere near ready to share another husband's bed."

Instead of being crushed by this sad news, the king laughed. "Fear not, Mordesius, for I am not such a boor that I would insist upon wedding and bedding the lady while she is still wearing widow's weeds!" he exclaimed. "I shall not propose to her or, indeed, even make her aware of my true feelings, until it is apparent that she has fully recovered from her grief."

"That is most . . . thoughtful of you," said Mordesius, trying not to snarl again. "Even so, Your Majesty—"

"And while I am waiting for her to recover," interrupted the king, "I will be attentive and kind and do all I can to prove to her that I am a good king and a man deserving of her love. Now, what was it that you wished to speak to me about?"

Mutely, Mordesius shook his head, recognizing the futility of even hinting at a match with Lady Aurelia.

"No?" said the king, arching an eyebrow. "Pity—I thought you might have come to inform me about poor Lord Pembleton." When the Regent went very still but did not reply, the king continued. "As I'm sure you're aware, his infant grandson was recently struck down by a mysterious ailment, and grief has reduced the poor man to such a low state that he is unable to speak, bathe or even feed himself," said the king, who paused before quietly adding, "I want you to *personally* see to it that he is tended to by the finest physicians in the realm and that his son's bereaved widow is adequately provided for, Mordesius. I think it would go some way toward atoning for the execution of his son, don't you?"

Mordesius stared at the king, wondering if he realized just how close he was to death.

It did not seem to Mordesius that he did, for the next thing the fool did was *chastise* Mordesius for failing to keep him adequately informed.

"I am quite sure that neglecting to tell me about Lord Pembleton's situation was an oversight on your part, as was neglecting to tell me about the death of Lord Bothwell," said King Finnius. "However, if you wish to continue to serve me in some capacity following the end of your regency this night, I would not have such oversights continue, for much as I like my servants, I do not think it appropriate that I should have to learn of such things from them, do you?"

"No," said Mordesius, the word barely more than a puff of air.

The king nodded. "I appreciate your understanding in these matters, Your Grace," he said as he turned and resumed staring out the window. "You are dismissed."

I am dismissed, raged Mordesius. *I AM DISMISSED?*

"Where is General Murdock?" he screamed, flinging an ink pot at a nearby servant, who had the good sense not to duck but rather to allow the ink pot to hit him squarely on the side of the head. "I summoned him ten minutes ago!"

"I am here," said the General, who'd somehow crept into the room without Mordesius noticing.

Mordesius glared at him. Then he turned to the bleeding, ink-splattered servant and bellowed, "Out!"

After the servant had fled, Mordesius informed Murdock of the king's plans to marry Lady Bothwell.

"I want him *dead*," he spat.

"Of course you do," soothed General Murdock, touching a finger to his thin lip. "And yet, such a thing would not serve your purpose."

"I know it would not serve my purpose," snarled Mordesius. "I said I *want* him dead. I did not order you to kill him!"

General Murdock tilted his small, narrow head in acknowledgment.

"Nevertheless, I shall have my revenge for his ill treatment of me," continued Mordesius raggedly. "And for his lack of gratitude for all that I have done for him, and for his suggestion that I have something to atone for, and for his thinly veiled threat to dismiss me following the end of my regency, and for his plans to coerce Lady Bothwell into marriage with him *even though she has made it abundantly clear that I am her preferred choice!*"

General Murdock, having no interest whatsoever in Lady Bothwell and her romantic inclinations, nodded blandly. "And what form shall your revenge take, Your Grace?" he asked, getting to the important point.

For a long moment, Mordesius said nothing. Then he said, "Is the Methusian prisoner dead?"

General Murdock looked mildly uncomfortable. "Not yet, Your Grace," he admitted, "for I have been busy tying up loose ends relating to several other assignments. However, I had planned to descend into the dungeon tonight in order to finish him."

"Then I will come with you," announced Mordesius, smiling for the first time since his encounter with the king, "that I may be soothed by the sound of the child's screams—and by the knowledge that the smallest, weakest, most helpless of His Majesty's precious subjects died in terror and pain because of him."

Thirty-Seven

PERSEPHONE HAD THOUGHT that a day spent alone in her chambers playing the grieving widow would seem interminable.

Instead, the hours had flown by. After Azriel left to steal wine and make the other preparations, she'd sent word to Martha and the sisters that she did not wish to be disturbed again that day. Then she'd wandered around the room touching and admiring things—the beautiful tapestries, the fine table linen, the polished tabletop, the great, comfortable bed upon which Cur blissfully snoozed and even the needlepoint basket full of brilliantly colored yarns and threads. As she'd wandered, she'd marveled at how much she would miss it all. She, who, not so long ago, would have been overjoyed by the prospect of a bowl of hot hare stew at the end of a hard day's work.

It was astonishing how quickly things could change.

And now they were set to change again, for she and Azriel were about to descend into the dungeon to rescue the child and afterwards, well . . . one way or another, it would all be over.

"How do I look?" she asked, trying not to sound anxious as she plucked at the loose sleeves of the coarse brown robe that Azriel had given her.

"Like a dirty noblewoman dressed as a dungeon servant," smiled Azriel, leaning forward to rub a little more soot on her cheeks.

Ivan, who'd been perched on the windowsill disdainfully observing Persephone's reverse makeover, screamed his agreement with this assessment, then took flight into the dusky skies.

"How do I look?" asked Azriel, pulling the hood of his robe farther forward so that his chiseled features were further accentuated by the shadows and his blue eyes shone like flames in the night.

Gazing up at him, Persephone flinched as though the flames had suddenly leapt out of the shadows and burned her. Then she took a step back and smiled faintly. "You look perfect," she said, hefting one of the burlap sacks full of stale bread onto her back before wryly adding, "but I daresay you already knew that, pompous, overstuffed peacock that you are."

Azriel grinned at this—a dazzling spectacle. "I am very glad to see that you've not lost your sense of humor, Persephone."

"I pray to the gods that I do not lose something more precious this night," she replied grimly. "Come. Let us go."

After checking to make sure that the corridor was empty of witnesses who might wonder why a pair of filthy dungeon servants had been visiting the grieving Lady Bothwell, Azriel and Persephone slipped out the door at the back of the room. Keeping their hoods forward, their heads down and their backs bent in a posture of servility, they shuffled through the dimly lit corridors, rounding this corner and that—past the chambers assigned to the great families, past the chambers assigned to the lesser families, past alcoves and nooks and hallways of indeterminate purpose, until at length they reached one of the wide, winding staircases that led to the ground floor of the palace. Upon reaching the bottom of the stairs, they plunged into the noisy stream of noblemen and noblewomen hurrying toward the Great Hall to partake of the king's birthday feast, which would begin shortly.

If only the corridor wasn't so crowded with those who have dined and sported and spoken with "Lady Bothwell," thought Persephone nervously as she transferred the bag of bread from one sweaty hand to the other. *If only*—

An impatient shove from behind caused her to stumble. She recovered almost immediately, but not before the heavy bag swung forward and knocked into the reeling nobleman in front of her. With a hoarse cry, he spun around, revealing himself to be none other than the drunken, leering Lord Atticus. Horrified at finding herself face-to-face with the only nobleman who'd ever seen her dressed as a servant, Persephone tried to dart away from him but he was too fast for her. Grabbing her by her free arm, he clouted her across the side of the face so hard that her head snapped backward and her hood fell back.

Over the ringing in her ears, Persephone heard Azriel grunt softly, as though suffering from the strain of holding himself back. Most of the hungry, hurrying nobles nearby paid no attention whatsoever to the scene unfolding in their midst—but some did.

Persephone ducked her head in an attempt to hide her face. "Apologies, m'lord—"

"Your useless apologies mean nothing to me!" bellowed Lord Atticus. Lifting his hand high in the air, he was about to clout her again when he froze. Dropping his hand, he grabbed her chin, jerked her head up and studied her face with his close-set, bloodshot eyes. "I've seen you," he announced at length, his brow furrowed with the effort of trying to remember.

"I don't think so, m'lord," gasped Persephone as she tried to jerk her chin out of his grasp. "You . . . you must have me confused with someone else—"

"Confused with someone else?" Lord Atticus screeched in sudden outrage, causing everyone in the vicinity to stop and stare. "Who do you think you are to suggest such a thing to me, you filthy little drab? I ought to have you horsewhipped for your insolence!"

Before Persephone could reply—or someone could realize that the filthy little drab was actually the beautiful Lady Bothwell in disguise—the bugles sounded, heralding the arrival of the king. At once, the drab was forgotten and all eyes turned toward the smiling young monarch. As he swept past on his way into the Great Hall, all the men bowed and all the women curtsied. He looked so excited that Persephone felt a rush of affection for him—and also a pang of regret that this was the last time she'd ever see him, and that he'd never know that her affection for him had been genuine even if she, herself, had not been.

These thoughts were fleeting, however, for almost before she'd finished curtseying—and well before the befuddled Lord Atticus remembered that he wanted to have her horsewhipped—she and Azriel were on the move once more. Ducking into the bustling royal kitchens, they wound their way around bloody butcher blocks, barrels of salted meat and half-empty sacks of flour while at the same time dodging the red-faced cooks, scampering scullery maids and sweaty, sooty little lads who tended the cook fires.

At length they reached a door at the very back of the farthest kitchen. Stepping outside, Persephone was shocked to find herself standing in the same courtyard in which young Pembleton had been executed just days earlier. Licking her suddenly dry lips, she stared at the long shadow cast by the scaffold that had not yet been taken down and tried not to think about the fact that, unlike her and Azriel, the brutalized man had almost certainly been innocent.

"Are you all right?" asked Azriel, who was gazing at her with a calm, expectant expression on his handsome face.

Persephone nodded, not trusting herself to speak.

Turning away from the scaffold, Azriel walked around the outer wall of a nearby turret and up to a small outer building that Persephone would have taken for storage if not for the fierce-looking guards posted outside the door. Pulling the hood of her coarse robe even farther forward, she managed not to flinch or break stride as she and Azriel approached the guards, but her heart began to pound so hard that she was sure the guards would hear it and wonder why.

"We've come—" began Azriel in a mumble.

"To feed the prisoners," said one of the guards, in a voice that made it clear that he thought it was a waste of bread.

The second guard said nothing until Azriel and Persephone were halfway through the heavy door. Then, without warning, he thrust the point of his pike so deep into Persephone's bread sack that she felt the sharp point of it touch her back. Her heart, which had been pounding just moments earlier, abruptly stopped beating. For one forever instant, she thought it was all over.

Then the stinking brute yanked his pike free of the bread sack, gave her a hard shove and laughed. "Just checking to make sure you're not trying to sneak anyone inside to enjoy our hospitality, wretch!"

"No, sir," mumbled Azriel, as Persephone wordlessly shook her still-bowed head. "Who would be such a fool as to do such a thing?"

Thirty-Eight

AS IT HAPPENED, Persephone and Azriel were not the only ones preparing to descend into the darkness just then.

"You're late," said Mordesius as Murdock silently crept into his office.

"My apologies, Your Grace," replied the General blandly. "I had assumed you'd want to wait until after the king's birthday feast."

"Well, you assumed wrong," snapped Mordesius, using one scarred hand to awkwardly knead a painful cramp in his neck. "After the monstrous way the king behaved toward me earlier, I'd sooner see his liver served raw on a golden platter than dine with him."

General Murdock nodded, unconsciously licking his thin lips at the mention of liver.

Mordesius pursed his own lips in distaste. *Murdock really is a disgusting specimen*, he thought. Out loud, he said, "So tell me, Murdock, do you think the Methusian brat we will attend to this night is of an age that he will understand what is happening to him?"

General Murdock's eyes gleamed. "They are always of an age to understand pain, Your Grace."

"Yes," said Mordesius in a satisfied voice as he rose to his feet and began lurching toward the door. "I suppose they are."

Thirty-Nine

DEEP WITHIN THE MAZE of dungeon tunnels, Persephone stifled a scream for the third time. First it had been the filthy, withered hand that had shot out of the tiny, barred window to claw at the air mere inches from her nose. Then it had been the half-rotted corpse crammed into the tiny hanging cage that she'd unexpectedly bumped into. Just now, it was the feel of sharp little teeth sinking into the tender flesh at her heel.

Looking down, Persephone saw what she'd known she would see: a grotesquely fat rat latched on to her foot, blood welling from the corners of its mouth.

Panic rose like a living thing inside of her. "Get it off!" she hissed, shaking her foot. "Get it—"

CRUNCH.

Panting heavily, Persephone stared down at the twitching tail of the rat whose head had just been crushed beneath Azriel's bare heel.

"Come on," said Azriel softly. He paused to mark the wall with charcoal so that they'd be able to keep track of where they'd already been, then started forward once more. "We have to keep moving."

Persephone followed him without speaking. She didn't know how long they'd been wandering around this terrible place already, nor how many glaring guards they'd passed, nor how many corridors they'd explored, nor how many barred windows they'd looked through in the hope of seeing the child, nor how many clutching hands they'd shoved bread into. It seemed as though they'd been down there for an eternity but Persephone knew from experience that places like this did strange things to the mind. . . .

Even as this thought occurred to her, she heard something that did not fit at all with the place she was in.

Stopping abruptly, she cocked her head to one side and listened harder.

And heard it again.

It was the sound of a child—*singing*. It was very far away and she could barely hear it over the sound of another, louder voice singing, but she could definitely hear it.

One look at the electrified expression on Azriel's face told Persephone that he heard it, too. As quickly as they could do so without arousing the suspicion of the guards, they began walking toward the eerie sound of the singing child. The sound grew louder with each step they took and—miraculously!—did not stop until they were directly outside the locked door from behind which it issued.

After quickly looking up and down the corridor to make sure it was truly deserted, Persephone pressed her ear to the door and heard a gravelly-voiced man say, "No, no, Mateo. I know you're doing your best, lad, and I don't like to hurt your feelings, but I must tell you that you're every bit as tone-deaf as your kinsman Balthazar was. Listen to me again, and try to sing as I do."

As the man warbled loudly and tunelessly in an effort to educate the child with the voice of an angel, Persephone turned to Azriel and was about to despair that they had no key when Azriel knelt down, pulled a thin metal file from the folds of his robe and began purposefully poking it into the lock.

"I'm a thief, remember?" he said, grinning up at her.

"I remember," she said, grinning back at him until a noise from a nearby corridor wiped the grin off her face.

As the lock fell open, Azriel, who'd obviously heard the noise, too, jumped to his feet and muttered, "I think it would be a good idea for us to hurry, don't you?"

Persephone did not waste time answering. Shoving open the door, she stepped into a low-ceilinged room that was stiflingly hot and bathed in the glow of a fire that crackled as though fed by the demons of hell itself. Near one wall, in a hanging cage much like the corpse-stuffed one she'd seen earlier, there slumped a painfully thin creature that Persephone immediately recognized as a Gorgishman. Chained to another wall was a gaunt but enormous (and enormously hairy) man who glared at her with such defiance that she immediately guessed him to be one of the mountain-dwelling Panoraki. Pushed into the darkest corner of the room, past a dusty blond skeleton and beyond a bloodstained butcher block, there was a small rectangular cage.

And huddled in the furthest corner of the cage?

A thin, dirty, badly frightened little boy.

Without a word, Persephone crossed the room, grabbed the key from a nearby hook, unlocked the cage and reached for the child, who promptly bit her as hard as he could.

She snatched her hand back with a grunt and a scowl.

"What do you think you're doing?" demanded the Panoraki in alarm, his dark eyes bulging beneath his bushy eyebrows as he watched Azriel fling open the trapdoor in the floor near the butcher block.

"I think we are fetching the boy out of this place," replied Azriel, dumping the last of the bread in his sack into the water below.

"Why?" barked the Panoraki, straining against his chains as he watched Persephone drag the squirming, kicking child out of the cage and hurry across the room with him. "Who is he to you?"

"He is my clansman," replied Azriel, holding wide the mouth of the now-empty bread sack. "What concern is it of yours? Who is he to you?"

"He is my friend," rumbled the Panoraki.

CLANG.

Persephone, Azriel and the Panoraki all jerked their heads toward the sound of a door slamming shut in a distant corridor.

Distant, but not distant enough.

"That would be the Regent, come to play his little games," said the Panoraki with renewed alarm. "If you truly mean to fetch the boy out of this place, Methusian, you'd best do it now." And then, to the child: "Mateo! Mateo, listen to me—you must stop your squirming, lad. You are making an unseemly spectacle of yourself and besides, these two are Methusians come to free you."

"I'm not a Methusian," clarified Persephone, who was struggling to stuff the boy's kicking legs into the mouth of the sack.

In response to this news, Mateo bit her again.

CLANG.

"But I am," said Azriel, with an involuntary glance over his shoulder. Yanking up his robe, he tugged down the waistband of his breeches just enough to reveal a dark-blue, tear-shaped tattoo upon his hip: the Mark of the Methusians.

At the sight of it, the child sagged in Persephone's arms. Quick as a wink, she slipped him into the sack and told him to be as still as he could be and to not make a sound no matter what happened.

"Pretend you are bread," advised Azriel.

With a tiny smile, the child nodded and huddled himself into a loaf.

CLANG.

"*For the love of strong sheep, go!*" begged the Panoraki, frantically jerking his hairy head toward the door as though this encouragement might speed them on their way.

"We will," said Azriel. "Only—we cannot afford to leave behind witnesses."

Persephone's mouth dropped open in horror.

The Panoraki looked surprised and not surprised. "I understand," he said gruffly, lifting his chin.

"I don't think you do," said Azriel. Using his metal file, he swiftly unlocked both the big man's fetters and the door of the hanging cage.

CLANG!

TAP, TAP, TAP. . . .

"Those would be the footfalls of the henchman Murdock, who must have come along for the fun," said the Panoraki, falling away from the wall and stumbling only briefly before finding his footing. "And unless I'm very much mistaken—and I'm not, for we Panoraki never are—he and his master are almost here!"

"Can you make it through the trapdoor?" asked Azriel, swinging the "bread" sack over his shoulder, grabbing Persephone by the hand, and heading for the door.

"Aye," nodded the big man as he unsteadily pulled open the door of the hanging cage, reached inside and grabbed the hissing creature by the scruff of his neck. "And I'll take this surly little sneak with me when I go. Good luck, Methusian."

"And to you," said Azriel over his shoulder.

TAP! TAP! TAP!

"Go!"

Forty

PERSEPHONE AND AZRIEL made it out of the stifling room but were too late to escape the corridor.

As luck would have it, however, the big Panoraki had been mistaken after all. Rather than the Regent and his henchman, Persephone and Azriel found themselves shuffling past a pair of guards who took no notice of them except to shout at them to get on with their miserable task. Bobbing their hooded heads in compliance, Azriel shuffled faster, with Persephone right behind him, shielding the "loaf of bread" lest one of the guards decide to use his pike to check the contents of the sack.

Neither of them did.

Nor did any of the other guards they encountered as they made their way back through the dank, dark corridors. And with each step she took, Persephone found herself feeling a little more hopeful that she, Azriel and the child might actually escape with their lives.

Then, as they turned the final corner and were headed for the winding staircase that would lead them back up into the land of the living, Persephone saw the legs of two men who were descending the staircase toward them.

The legs of one man were strong and sturdy.

The legs of the other were withered and crooked.

The Regent and his henchman had come to play their little games, after all.

Realizing that she, Azriel and the "loaf of bread" stood directly in the path the two monsters would take as they made their way to the stifling—but now-empty—room, Persephone grabbed Azriel's arm and dragged him into the shadowed doorway of a nearby cell. As she shrank against the ancient iron door, it suddenly gave way. Hastily, she and Azriel ducked inside and eased the door shut behind them.

Barely a moment later, the Regent and his general were in the corridor.

And then they were walking past the spot where Persephone and Azriel stood as silent and still as death in the flickering torchlight that shone through the tiny, barred window.

And then they were gone.

Weak with relief and unable to believe that they'd actually escaped undetected, Persephone stepped back to give Azriel space to open the door. Instead of meeting up with solid ground, however, her foot met with nothing at all. With a gasp, she started to fall. Luckily, she didn't have far to go, and by the time she'd twisted around so that she could use her hands to break her fall, she'd already landed with a grunt in a shallow puddle of evil-smelling water.

"Are you all right?" whispered Azriel as he carefully set down the burlap sack and hurried over to her.

"Yes," she replied.

Pushing herself to her knees, she rolled up her dripping sleeves and dried her hands off on the front of her smock. She was about to get to her feet when her eyes, having adjusted to the deeper gloom, caught sight of a propped-up corpse not three feet from where she knelt.

The corpse had been an old woman in life; or at least, this place had made her old. Her filthy body was a mess of sores, her dead lips puckered grotesquely around a toothless hole of a mouth and what was left of her thin, gray hair hung limply around her cadaverous face.

Heart pounding, Persephone was about to turn away when the corpse blinked.

Then, without warning, it lunged forward and clamped its cold, bony hand around Persephone's damp wrist. Persephone opened her mouth to scream but before she could, Azriel put his hand over her mouth.

"*She's alive,*" he hissed.

The corpse—or rather, the woman—blinked at Persephone again. Then she smiled broadly—a gruesome sight given that all she had to show were blackened gums. "The old Methusian Seer told me . . ." she began faintly, before stopping as though she was too exhausted to go on.

At these words, Persephone felt a jolt of superstitious dread so powerful that she tore her wrist from the old woman's grip and would have bolted from the room if Azriel hadn't been crouched behind her, blocking her way.

"What did the old Methusian Seer tell you?" he asked urgently. Leaning forward, he picked up the poor woman's skeletal hand and gave it a squeeze in the hope of reviving her. "*What did she tell you?*"

Slowly, her milky eyes shifted to Azriel's blue ones. "That I would lay eyes upon the true heir to the Erok throne one last time before I died," she whispered.

Persephone recoiled in disbelief at what she was hearing but Azriel leaned even farther forward, so far forward that Persephone could feel his full weight upon her back.

His handsome face was only inches from the old woman's ruined one. "What do you mean?" he asked breathlessly. "*What are you saying?*"

Jerking her withered hand from Azriel's grasp, she clutched his arm and whispered, "I am saying that the lost royal twin has come home at last."

Then, as though the desire to set eyes upon the true heir of the Erok throne was the only thing that had kept her soul tethered to this world, her eyes rolled into the back of her head, her hand slipped from Azriel's arm and she slumped over into the fetid pile of straw.

Dead.

Forty-One

NEITHER PERSEPHONE NOR AZRIEL spoke until they were out of the dungeon and back in the relative safety of her chambers, where they planned to quickly change into disguises that would offer them a better chance of escaping the city unmolested.

"What do you think she meant by her words?" asked Azriel excitedly as he helped Mateo out of the burlap sack.

"Nothing," lied Persephone.

With trembling hands, she poured a goblet of watered wine for the boy and filled a plate with food while Azriel set an embroidered cushion upon one of the great dining chairs and hoisted Mateo up to sit upon it.

"Eat," he told the boy, ruffling his hair.

Wordlessly, the traumatized, half-starved child picked up a piece of cold roast venison with one grimy hand and a hunk of soft cheese with the other, crammed them both into his mouth and then reached for the watered wine.

After distractedly admonishing him to slow down, Azriel took Persephone by the elbow and propelled her over to a spot by the fire so that they could speak privately.

"The old woman spoke of a lost royal twin, Persephone," he said eagerly. "She spoke of the rightful heir to the Erok throne!"

"Words," she said with an airy wave of her hand.

"Words spoken by a Methusian Seer," said Azriel.

"*Maybe* spoken by a Methusian Seer," corrected Persephone.

She turned away from him then, so that she would not have to see the look in his eyes. She knew what he was thinking. He was thinking that it was no coincidence that he couldn't remember his life before the Methusian camp, no coincidence that Ivan had swooped down with the dead pigeon clutched in his talons at the very moment the Methusians all looked up, no coincidence that the message the dead pigeon had carried had directed them to Parthania, no coincidence that Azriel had seen Mateo captured but had been unable to save him out on the street. He was thinking that the Fates had led them down into that dungeon not so that they could rescue Mateo, but so that they could find the old woman.

And he was thinking that if the old woman's remarkable dying utterances were to be believed, then little Mateo was not the Methusian king—

He was.

Persephone watched him now as he strode back and forth before the fire, trying so hard to be objective about what he already believed in his heart to be true.

"I mean, everyone knows that something untoward happened the night the queen gave birth," he reasoned, half to himself. "People thought that perhaps her child had been strangled or born dead and replaced with a changeling of the Regent's choosing, but what if they had it wrong? What if the queen's son—King Finnius— was born alive and . . . and—"

"And so had his elder twin?" broke in Persephone. "Because to be the rightful heir to the Erok throne, you'd have to have been born first, you know."

"I know," said Azriel, flushing to hear her give voice to his outrageous thoughts. "I also know that you think I'm grasping at straws, and perhaps you are right. After all, even if the old woman *had* been told by a Seer that she would lay eyes upon the rightful heir to the throne, how could she possibly have known that I am he?"

Though Persephone wanted to slap him and shout that there was no way she could have known, she knew that if she did that, he would think her so stubbornly single-minded that any hope she might have of eventually making him listen to reason would be lost.

So instead of slapping and shouting, she shrugged and said, "I suppose you resemble the king. You are both tall, you both have blue eyes and you are both of a similar build."

"Yes, but there must be a thousand men who have those same features," said Azriel.

"That is true," said Persephone quickly.

"Of course, there *is* this," said Azriel, holding aloft his partially amputated finger. "The old woman mentioned the Methusian Seer and the twin only after I clamped my hand over your mouth to keep you from screaming."

Persephone stared at his finger for a long moment before reaching up and touching the scarred tip of it. "I . . . suppose it is *possible* that someone cut off your finger to mark you so that those who knew of your existence would be able to recognize you as the lost twin," she said reluctantly, knowing that this was what he was thinking.

"Yes," agreed Azriel with feigned indifference. "But the wound was still bleeding when I arrived at the Methusian camp all those years ago."

"Perhaps they'd only just mutilated you," said Persephone, stating the obvious. "Perhaps someone had kept you hidden in the years following your birth and had to get rid of you in a hurry."

"But why leave me with Methusians?"

"Can you imagine a better place to hide an unwanted royal twin than among the Methusians?" snorted Persephone. "Who would ever think of looking for you there?"

"But why get rid of me in the first place?" pressed Azriel. "If I was, indeed, the first-born twin, why not keep me and get rid of the younger twin? Why get rid of either of us?"

"I don't know!" said Persephone impatiently. "Perhaps the Regent chose to keep the weaker twin in the hope that he would die in infancy. Perhaps he believed that if the weaker twin died, he'd be able to step in and fill the power vacuum created by the empty throne."

"But if—"

"Enough 'buts,' Azriel!" exclaimed Persephone. She'd shown herself to be reasonable enough to at least entertain the possibility that he was the Methusian king; now it was time to make him listen to reason.

"You are right," he agreed with sudden fire, before she could speak a single word of reason. "The time for talk—and action— will come later, once we've reunited with Cairn and the others and shared with them what has been revealed to us this night. As planned, we must leave Parthania at once and—"

"No," said Persephone before she could stop herself. "Not 'we.'"

Azriel went very still. "What do you mean 'not we'?" he asked.

Though Persephone should have been prepared for this moment, she was not. Looking up into Azriel's beautiful blue eyes, she felt the weight of the decision she was about to make pressing down upon her heart. "I followed the path you and your people put before me, Azriel, and . . . it would appear that I have found the Methusian king," she said faintly. "Now I must find my own path."

"No."

"Yes."

"*No.*"

"Why not?" asked Persephone in a half-joking voice. "Because I am your slave?"

"My slave?" said Azriel incredulously. "My *slave?*" he repeated. With fumbling fingers, he reached inside his robe, pulled out the key to her old fetters and pressed it into the palm of her hand. Wrapping his fingers tight around hers, he forced her fingers to close around the key and then pressed her closed hand against his beating heart.

"Don't you know?" he asked hoarsely. "Don't you *know*? You've never been my slave, but by the gods, since the first moment I laid eyes upon you, I have been yours. I haven't just fallen for you, Persephone, I have fallen in love with you."

"Don't say that," she whispered.

"I *will* say it, and do you know why? Because my love for you is the truest thing I have ever known."

And then, before she could utter another word, he pulled her into his arms and kissed her so deeply and with such passion that her knees turned to water, her head began to spin and she felt as though she were falling into an abyss from which there was no escape.

Slowly, her fingers uncurled and the key to the fetters dropped to the ground with a clink. When the kiss finally ended, Azriel pulled his head back just far enough to look into her eyes.

"I would never ask you to forgo the search for your own path if I did not believe that you'd already found it," he whispered. "Our paths are as one, Persephone, I *know* they are. I cannot say what the future holds or if I am, in fact, the prophesied one, but I *know* that we are meant to be together. Please say you feel it, too. Tell me we will walk the path before us together and I will dedicate my life to yours in very truth."

Persephone said nothing for a long moment. Then she bowed her head and whispered, "Do you promise?"

"I promise," he said fervently. "Will you come with me?"

Persephone bit her lip and nodded wordlessly.

"Do *you* promise?" he asked.

With a tremulous smile, she looked up, leaned forward and gently pressed her mouth against his. "I promise," she lied.

If anyone had pointed out to Persephone the irony of the fact that she knew Azriel intended to hold to his promise when she had no intention of holding to hers, she'd have once again told them she had no choice in the matter.

For she knew that as soon as Cairn and the other Methusians learned of the old woman's dying utterances, they would cleave to the notion that Azriel was the lost royal twin. They would excitedly point out that he had the look of the king, that he knew not from whence he came, and that the Fates had not only guided him to the dungeon but had also seen to it that he escaped. Not in pieces (or shortly to be chopped into pieces) but very much alive. Fueled by his clansmen's enthusiasm, she knew that Azriel would become even more convinced that he was the Methusian king—and she knew that his belief in this destiny would spell his doom.

For even if it *were* true, there would never be any way to prove to the Erok people that he was the lost twin, and any attempt to forcibly take the throne from poor King Finnius would be treason. The punishment for treason was death, and though Persephone had once steeled herself to watch what she'd thought would be Azriel's grim execution, she could not do it if he was going to run toward it.

And since she'd feared that she would not have been able to resist his enticements if she'd told him that she meant to leave him, she'd had no choice but to lie.

"Hurry and prepare yourself and the child to leave at once," Azriel was saying now as he strode purposefully toward the door at the back of the room. "I'll be back before you know it. I didn't 'borrow' a sword earlier for fear that its disappearance would arouse suspicion, but I intend to do so now. There's not a nobleman in the palace sober enough to notice the disappearance of his sword right now, and I wish to be properly armed to defend you and Mateo, come what may." He stopped suddenly, ran back to Persephone, swept her into his arms and kissed her hard. "You won't regret this," he promised, kissing her again.

I'm not so sure about that, she thought. But all she said was "Go."

✳

The instant the door closed behind Azriel, Persephone forced him from her thoughts and focused on the task at hand. Flying to the washbasin, she scrubbed her hands and face clean of the soot that had been part of her dungeon-servant disguise. Then, after brusquely ordering the child Mateo to shut his eyes, she cast off her coarse brown robe and pulled on her favorite gown. Without the help of Martha and the sisters, she could not tighten the corsets or properly fasten the bodice but her traveling cloak would hide that. Throwing it about her shoulders, she pulled up the loose floorboard and tossed the auburn curl, the bit of lace and the rat tail into one pocket. Then, studiously ignoring the way Mateo's eyes were following her every move, she slipped her dagger into the other pocket and snatched up the empty bread sack. Hurrying over to her wardrobe, she began throwing into the sack everything she thought she'd be able to carry—crystal hairpins and dancing slippers, silk stockings and lace gloves. A single, snow-white petticoat; what was left of the cake of fine soap. The necklace the Regent had given her that first day went around her neck for safekeeping.

Once I am clear of the imperial capital, I will trade the vile thing for coin, she thought, and *perhaps . . . perhaps someday I will use some of the money to buy myself a pretty little thatch-roofed cottage. . . .*

Her preparations complete, Persephone lastly wrapped several days' worth of bread and cheese in a linen napkin and laid this on top of the other things in the sack. Then she hefted the sack and whistled for Cur. Mateo, who'd slid from his perch at the table to kneel on the floor and hug the dog, made a soft noise of protest as Cur pulled away from him. Persephone was about to tell the child not to be afraid because Azriel would be back shortly when the servants' door opened and Neeka walked into the room.

Persephone froze as the servant girl slowly took in the bulging bread sack on her back, the traveling cloak about her shoulders and the grubby little child on the floor at her feet.

"You're finished, then?" asked Neeka curiously.

"Finished what?" asked Persephone, hedging.

"Pretending to be Lady Bothwell," said Neeka.

Even though some part of her had known the words were coming, Persephone could not keep from gasping aloud.

"We've known from the start, you know," continued Neeka. "No lady in the realm would be caught dead with feet as calloused and dirty as yours were the night you first arrived. Nor would a lady praise a bath that did not smell of rotten eggs, nor trouble herself to learn the names of her servants, nor invite those same servants to eat from her own table, nor show such an appalling lack of interest in needlepoint." She shrugged. "You're beautiful enough to be noble, and the airs come natural enough to you, but to those of us who've emptied your chamber pot each morning, you've given yourself away a hundred times over."

Nodding at the fact that Neeka and the others had figured out what she, herself, would have figured out in a trice if she'd been the one emptying the chamber pot, Persephone said, "You've known from the beginning and yet you never denounced me. Why?"

"Besides the fact that you treated us with kindness and respect, it was clear to us that you were playing with the Regent. It was not important to us what your game was, only that it caused him to suffer pain, frustration and humiliation. For you see, it was he who cut out Anya's tongue," explained Neeka, who paused before adding, "She was eight years old at the time."

"I'm sorry," said Persephone, not knowing what else to say.

"Sorry won't bring back her tongue," said Neeka matter-of-factly. "May I ask you a question?"

Persephone nodded.

"He's not a eunuch, is he?"

Persephone smiled faintly. "No."

Neeka nodded as though Persephone's answer agreed with her own careful study of the matter. Then, eyeing the bulging burlap sack on Persephone's back once more, she said, "When he returns for the child, is there some message you'd like me to give to him?"

Tell him I love him, thought Persephone suddenly and with a fierceness that frightened her.

"Bid him good luck," she murmured, pulling up the hood of her traveling cloak. "And tell him I'm sorry."

Forty-Two

MEANWHILE, IN HIS SUMPTUOUSLY appointed private chambers, soon-to-be Simply Mordesius was raging over the fact that the little Methusian, the big Panoraki and the Gorgishman had somehow escaped the dungeon.

"I want the drawbridge raised and the gates shut," he frothed. "I want the watch doubled—no, tripled. No one leaves the palace grounds this night under any circumstances. Do you understand me, Murdock? Well, do you?"

"Yes, Your Grace," said General Murdock impassively.

"Don't you 'yes, Your Grace' me, you useless imbecile!" shrieked Mordesius, hurling a perfect golden pear at the General's unusually small head. "My prisoners did not escape by themselves! Someone helped them do so and when I catch the Methusian wretch, I am going to make him wish he'd never been born. And so help me, Murdock, if you let the culprit escape, I will make you wish the same thing!"

"What makes you think a Methusian was behind the escape, Your Grace?" asked General Murdock, who did not seem the least ruffled by either the flying pear or Mordesius's threat. "The Panoraki and the Gorgishman are also gone."

"Yes, but they have been my guests from the beginning. Who would take such risks to rescue them now?" snarled Mordesius, wondering why he always had to think of *everything*. "The Methusian prisoner was a new addition, Murdock, and that is why I *know* that this was the work of a Methusian."

Murdock nodded thoughtfully. "But if the prisoners escaped through the trapdoor—"

"Don't be an idiot. A child would never survive a fall into the cold, fast-moving water that runs beneath the dungeon," said Mordesius scathingly. "Why rescue the brat only to see him battered and drowned? No. Somehow, his rescuers found a way out of the dungeon and—"

"Excuse me, Your Grace."

Eyes bulging in outrage, Mordesius snatched up another piece of fruit and was about to fling it at the intruder when he saw that it was none other than Lord Bartok.

Breathing raggedly, Mordesius looked askance at him and muttered, "If you have come to discuss the betrothal of your daughter to the king, I can assure you that this is *not* a good time."

"I understand, Your Grace," said the greatest of the great lords with a graciousness that made Mordesius want to scream. "As it happens, however, I have come because I have information that I thought you might find . . . interesting."

Thin chest heaving, Mordesius wiped some flecks of frothy spittle off his chin with the back of his hand. "What information?" he asked rudely.

"Some days ago, I sent several of my men to the Ragorian Prefecture to make inquiries with regard to the Lady Bothwell," said Lord Bartok.

Mordesius's dark eyes bulged in their sockets. "How . . . how *dare* you," he said, stammering with rage. "Lady Bothwell is—"

"Not who she says she is."

There was a moment of stunned silence. And then:

"What do you mean?" breathed Mordesius.

Lord Bartok shrugged elegantly. "Your Grace, there is no Lady Bothwell and hasn't been since the recently deceased Lord Bothwell's mother died in childbirth fifty-three years ago."

Another silence.

"But . . . but that is *impossible*," spluttered Mordesius, whose thin chest had begun to heave once more. "If that was so, General Murdock and his men would have discovered it when—"

"They burned Bothwell Manor to the ground?" said Lord Bartok, wincing as though pained by Mordesius's inability to grasp the facts. "Unfortunately, Your Grace, my men inform me that the General and his men did not think to make inquiries before they set the fires."

Mordesius went pale beneath his lovely olive complexion. "Is this true, Murdock?" he demanded.

"You ordered us not to make inquiries, Your Grace. You said that such inquiries would start unwelcome rumors," reminded Murdock, taking care to leave unsaid the humiliating fact that Mordesius had not wanted rumors started because he'd feared they might harm his burgeoning romantic relationship with the lovely Lady Bothwell.

"Not making inquiries . . . that was an unfortunate decision," said Lord Bartok, wincing again, "for it has given the woman who calls herself Lady Bothwell and the man who calls himself her eunuch much time to make mischief."

"But he is probably not even a eunuch!" gasped Mordesius in sudden horror.

"Probably not," agreed Lord Bartok solemnly. "He is probably her lover."

A vivid image of *his* Lady Bothwell writhing naked in the arms of the handsome wretch who was not a eunuch made Mordesius want to vomit up his guts. She had played him *and* the king for fools—but he, Mordesius, was sure to bear the brunt of the ridicule, once the truth got out. For it was he who'd brought her to the palace, he who'd escorted her so proudly, he who'd—

A thought struck Mordesius so hard and so suddenly that he stiffened abruptly, causing his poor body to shriek in protest.

. . . It has given the woman who calls herself Lady Bothwell and the man who calls himself her eunuch much time to make mischief. . . .

Indeed, what greater mischief could there be than to steal a Methusian out from under Mordesius's very nose? And who would steal a Methusian but another Methusian—or two?

The whore had shown up the same night the child had been captured; her lover, the day after. The two Methusian cockroaches were probably lying together right now, celebrating their great victory over him and *laughing*.

The place in Mordesius's chest that had turned cold grew colder still, so cold that it felt as though it would never be warm again. Clenching his beautiful teeth, he ordered General Murdock to set every soldier at his disposal to the task of finding the so-called eunuch, the Methusian brat and the woman who called herself Lady Bothwell.

"And what shall we do when we find them?" asked General Murdock, sucking at a piece of food caught between his long front teeth.

"Bring them to the Great Hall where the king is even now enjoying his birthday feast," ordered Mordesius. "Let his first task as true, ruling monarch be to order and preside over the immediate execution of the handsome nobody, the defenseless child and the whore who tricked us all."

Forty-Three

PERSEPHONE AND CUR made it down to the main floor of the palace and out into the moonlit courtyard without running into Azriel or any courtiers who might wonder why Lady Bothwell was going riding at this time of night when she was supposed to be sitting quietly in her rooms mourning the death of her husband.

Halfway to the stables, however, Persephone noticed something that made her wonder if her luck had run out.

Pairs of torch-bearing armed soldiers—and lots of them—were hurriedly entering and exiting outer buildings, looking behind trees and stabbing their deadly pikes into bushes too thick to otherwise penetrate.

All of them appeared to be looking for something . . . or someone.

Well, I suppose that makes sense, thought Persephone uneasily as she slowed to a halt. *By now the Regent will have discovered that his prisoners have escaped from the dungeon and he will be looking for . . .*

"There she is!" boomed a voice.

Persephone jerked her head toward the sound, and her heart leapt into her throat when she saw that the huge, hairy, pike-wielding soldier who'd bellowed was running straight for her. . . .

And that there were half a dozen others just like him at his heels.

Ordering Cur away from her, Persephone dropped the bulging bread sack, whirled about and began to run. If she could make it to the palace gate and across the drawbridge, she just might be able to disappear into the crowds of revelers enjoying free meat and drink in celebration of the king's birthday. As she ran, she could hear the pounding footfalls of the guards close behind her. They were bigger and stronger than she was, but she was swifter and stronger than she looked, and no matter how hard they ran, they were unable to close the gap. Casting one final, frantic glance over her shoulder, Persephone was about to plunge into the shadowy watchtower passageway that led to the drawbridge when two things happened. The first was that she saw that the drawbridge was up. The second was that another half-dozen soldiers poured out of the watchtower passageway toward her, their pikes at the ready.

Without slowing down, Persephone veered left, burst through the wooden door by the guards' barracks and barreled down the gentle hill that led to the deep and treacherous water of the filthy moat.

I'll swim if I have to! she thought desperately as she fumbled for the clasp of her traveling cloak. *I'd rather drown than—*

Before she could finish her thought she saw it:

An ancient rowboat floating nearby.

Gathering up her heavy skirts in both hands, she leapt for it, landed and nearly capsized. Instinctively hunkering down to find her balance, she pulled out her dagger and began frantically sawing at the rope that tethered the boat to the shore.

She got a quarter of the way through the rope . . . halfway through . . . three-quarters—

"Gotcha!"

Several pairs of rough hands dragged her, spitting and snarling, out of the boat. There was a cry as Persephone bit one soldier hard enough to draw blood and another cry as she elbowed a second soldier in the face. Yanking her dagger hand free, she slashed the air wildly, causing the others to leap back in alarm.

Breathing hard, Persephone panted, "Stay back! I w-warn you, I'll . . . I'll—"

A high-pitched drunken laugh cut her off.

Lord Atticus.

Shouldering aside the nearest soldier, he stepped close enough to slit from bow to stern. Before Persephone could have the satisfaction of doing so, however, the young lord shoved his leering face into hers and whispered, "*We've got your lover and the brat.*"

Persephone was so horrified that she froze, the blade in her hand momentarily forgotten. The next instant they were upon her, pinning her dagger arm behind her back. One of the soldiers pressed the point of his pike between her shoulder blades, forcing her back to arch and her chest to be pushed forward.

Lord Atticus grinned and licked his lips. "According to the Regent, your lover and the brat shall shortly be executed for the king's entertainment," he informed Persephone as he unsteadily leaned forward to inhale the perfumed skin of her bosom. "You will, too, of course, but not before I've had my own entertainment." Reaching out, he abruptly tore one of the sleeves from Persephone's gown, exposing the bare flesh of her arm to the chill of the night. "That is why I am out here instead of inside drinking my fill of the king's fine wine," he explained, breathing his sour breath in her face. "For you see, when my father told me you were nothing but a Methusian whore in disguise, I suddenly remembered where I'd seen you before. You were one of the twins." He grinned again. "We met on the road outside Parthania, remember?"

In response, Persephone stopped struggling for just long enough to lift her chin and spit in his face.

Bellowing in outrage, Lord Atticus gave her a vicious backhand.

"You'll pay for that, you stupid cow!" he shrieked.

Persephone struggled harder, twisting and kicking with all her might, but it was no use.

There were too many of them and they were too strong.

I am lost, she thought despairingly, *and Azriel and the child along with me.*

Then she heard it.

The wonderful, beloved sound of salvation.

CLIP, CLOP, CLIP, CLOP, CLIP, CLOP.

Persephone craned her head, and her heart leapt at the sight of Fleet galloping down the hill on the other side of the moat—a look of horsey determination on his face, Rachel clinging to his back and a horde of shouting soldiers at his rear.

"Fleet!" screamed Persephone hoarsely. "Rachel! Over here! I'm over here!"

Without slowing or even hesitating, Fleet—the broken-down old gelding with the pathological fear of water who'd never liked getting his feet wet—leapt high in the air and landed with a splash in the very middle of the moat. Whinnying at the top of his lungs, he thrashed his way to shore, scattering and trampling the soldiers before rearing up on his hind legs and clobbering Lord Atticus in the side of the head with a pawing hoof.

The drunken nobleman crumpled to the ground without a sound.

"Quick!" cried Rachel, who was clutching Fleet's mane with one hand and reaching out to Persephone with the other. "Up!"

Backing up three paces to give herself a running start, Persephone dashed forward and, using the crumpled body of Lord Atticus to give herself a boost, scrambled up behind Rachel and looked around for a means of escape.

One quick glance at the swarming soldiers on the other side of the moat told her they could not go back the way Fleet and Rachel had come.

"That way!" she urged, pointing to the door in the castle wall. "Go!"

"Stop!" cried a voice.

As one, Persephone and Rachel looked around to see that a very young soldier was poised to hurl his deadly pike—and that the weapon was aimed directly at Fleet's big heart. Persephone opened her mouth to scream, but even as she did so, she heard a wet snarl and saw a flash of glossy fur and the tattered remains of a pink bow. As Cur knocked the surprised soldier to the ground, Ivan arrived from above to scratch out the eyes of anyone left standing. Fleet wheeled around and Persephone drove her heels into his sweaty flank. He leapt forward through the open door as planned, but once inside the palace walls, he completely ignored Persephone's frantic pleas that he head for the deserted garden. Instead, he galloped straight toward the royal stables.

He probably smells turnips! thought Persephone in despair as she heard several soldiers in the courtyard give a cry of recognition and begin running toward them.

Sliding to the ground before Fleet was halfway through the stable door, Persephone dragged Rachel out of the saddle, grabbed a brimming bucket of cut turnips and ran through the side door that led to the corral. Hastily scanning the several dozen high-strung thoroughbreds that were snorting and pawing the ground in agitation at the noisy goings-on beyond the corral fence, Persephone saw what she'd hoped to see.

Giving Fleet a quick kiss on the muzzle, she shoved the bucket of turnips at Rachel, pointed at Lucifer and said, "Do you see that enormous, ill-tempered black beast over there?"

"Yes, but—"

"The instant I open the corral gate, I want you to fling these turnips in the direction of the beast and then step aside. With luck, Fleet will chase after his snack with such gusto that he'll start a stampede and I'll be able to use the ensuing chaos to reach the palace and find the king."

"Why do you need to find the king?" asked Rachel, wide-eyed at the prospect.

"So that I can get down on my knees and beg," said the girl who'd never begged for anything in her life. "Beg for the lives of Azriel and the child we rescued from the dungeon."

"And if the king refuses?" asked Rachel, who did not know what on earth was going on but who knew enough to know this was the important question. "If he orders you arrested, too?"

"I cannot believe he would do that," said Persephone, edging toward the gate of the corral. "Anyway, I have no choice. Find somewhere to hide but be ready, Rachel, for if the king fails us and we somehow manage to fight our way out, we'll be running for our lives."

Persephone's plan to start a stampede worked better than she could have hoped. Dodging trampling hooves and bellowing soldiers, she dashed through the dust-filled chaos of the courtyard, into the palace and through the doors of the Great Hall, where the king's birthday festivities were well underway. Azriel and the child were nowhere in sight.

What if I am too late? Persephone thought wildly. *What if they are already dead?*

Forcibly choking down her rising panic, she scanned the crowded hall until she spotted the king on the far side. He was sitting upon his throne looking pleasantly disheveled—his sleeves rolled up, his hair slightly mussed, a lopsided grin on his handsome face. Even as she watched, he rose to his feet and joined the dance.

Heedless of the stares and whispers and giggles of those who'd taken note of the recently arrived Lady Bothwell's bedraggled appearance, Persephone plunged into the crowd, elbowing and shoving her way toward the dancing king. When she was close enough to touch him, some instinct made her glance over her shoulder.

Her blood ran cold at the sight of the Regent Mordesius entering the Great Hall with a broad smile on his face—and Azriel, held between two vicious-looking soldiers, at his side.

Azriel, but not the child.

Frantically, Persephone reached out and tugged on the back of the king's shirt.

"Your Majesty—"

"Lady Bothwell!" he cried a little drunkenly, his handsome face shining with delight at the sight of her. "I had thought you would not feel up to joining the festivities but I see that I was wrong!"

"You were not wrong, Your Majesty—" began Persephone.

"You're missing a sleeve!" coughed the king, his slightly bleary blue eyes widening as though in amazement.

"Yes," said Persephone. "Majesty, I must speak with you—"

"Very well," said the king, sweeping her into his arms, "but first you will *dance* with me."

Persephone tried to extricate herself from his arms that she might fall down on her knees and start to beg, but his grip on her was too firm and he was spinning her too fast. There was nothing she could do but follow his lead and try not to stomp on his toes. With every spin, the music seemed to play louder and faster, and then the great lords and ladies of court were falling back to encircle the spinning pair, stomping their feet and clapping their hands and shrilly crying out that they'd never before seen such a dancer as the king, never!

"Your Majesty!" shouted Persephone, desperately trying to make herself heard above the din. "Please, Your Majesty! I *must* speak with you."

The king stopped spinning so abruptly that Persephone nearly fell over. It wasn't her words that had caused him to stop, however. It was the sight of the "eunuch" Azriel being kicked to his knees.

And the sight of the gleaming knife in the hand of the soldier who stood ready to slit his throat.

"Mordesius," panted the king, who still had Persephone clasped tightly in his arms as if he might take her for another spin at any moment. "What . . . what is the meaning of this?"

Before the Regent could reply, a crash and a scream caused every person in the Great Hall to jump.

It was the pockmarked servant who'd dropped the roast beef platter at the king's feet a few days earlier. This time, however, instead of looking flustered or terrified, she was staring at Persephone as though she'd just seen a ghost.

Which, in a way, she had.

For what she'd seen was that Persephone's whiplash scar—the one that crisscrossed the outside of her left arm almost to the elbow—exactly matched the scar that the king carried on his bare right arm. Wherever the scar ended on Persephone's flesh, it began on the king's; wherever it ended on the king's flesh, it began on Persephone's.

There was only one possible explanation for why their scars matched so perfectly.

And the clumsy, pockmarked servant knew exactly what it was.

Forty-Four

MOVING WITH SURPRISING SPEED and agility for one so clumsy, the pockmarked servant spun around and started running from the Great Hall as though her life depended on it.

Which, indeed, it did, for she was not the only one who'd seen the matching scars. Her scream had drawn everyone's attention to them—the king, the woman who was not Lady Bothwell, the great lords and ladies of the land.

And, of course, the Regent. "Stop!" he bellowed.

But the pockmarked servant paid no heed, for she knew that to stop was death.

For her part, Persephone only dimly heard the Regent's shout, so transfixed was she by the sight of the matching scars. Logic told her that she and the king must have been scarred at the very same time, in the very same way.

But I've had this scar for as long as I can remember! she thought wildly, looking up at the king, who looked equally stunned. *That could only mean—*

CRACK!

Jerking her head away from the sight of her arm pressed against the king's arm, Persephone saw that Azriel had used the distraction to jump to his feet, yank his arms free of the soldiers who held him and elbow them both in the face. Blood from their mangled noses had splattered nearby noblewomen, who were shrieking and fainting and adding to the general chaos of the situation. Even as Persephone watched, Azriel shoved the Regent so hard that he fell to the floor. Then he ran over to her, snatched up her hand and began dragging her through the crowd in pursuit of the pockmarked servant.

Mordesius slammed against the blood-flecked marble floor hard enough to knock out of him what little breath had been left in his lungs.

It is impossible! he thought as he frantically tugged his robe down over his thin, scarred legs and awkwardly pushed himself to his hands and knees. *Impossible! I was so careful—so thorough. I was sure I'd tied up all loose ends! I used trusted men, I ordered the disposal of the queen, the midwives, the attendants, all those of consequence who might have sought to cause trouble with the truth. And then, of course, there was the matter of the child—*

"Mordesius, what is the meaning of this?" demanded the king, who looked very pale and more sober than he'd ever looked in his life. "W-why does Lady Bothwell share the scar I've borne since infancy?"

Mordesius thought quickly as he staggered to his feet, for he knew that he would lose more than the title "Regent" if the king and the court were ever to learn the truth.

He would lose everything.

"I do not know why that woman shares your scar, Majesty," he said tersely, "but I do know that she is not a lady at all. She is an imposter!"

"An imposter!" exclaimed the king, with a harsh, wet cough. "No, I don't believe it—"

"It is true," insisted Mordesius. Brusquely, he ordered two of his soldiers to escort the king back to his rooms and to let no one enter or exit, upon pain of death. "It is for your own safety, Majesty," he assured King Finnius, "for I have reason to fear that the entire palace is riddled with Methusians and that they intend to murder you this very night."

The coughing king looked aghast. "But how do you know—"

"It is my business to know," said Mordesius.

Then, after ordering everyone in the Great Hall to stay where they were, he turned to the two bleeding soldiers, pointed in the direction that the pockmarked servant, Persephone and Azriel had fled and said, "After them."

The pockmarked servant was fast, but in her terror, she made a mistake. Instead of turning left down a passageway that would have led her out of the palace, she turned right down a passageway that ended in what appeared to be the office of a minor clerk.

It was a dead end.

Whirling around as Azriel and Persephone came bursting into the room after her, the terrified woman threw up her hands as though to ward off a blow. "Please don't kill me!" she cried.

"No one is going to kill you," said Azriel as he swiftly barred the door. "We only want to talk to you."

"Azriel, where is Mateo?" asked Persephone. "Atticus told me that the Regent had you both!"

"Like you, he lied," said Azriel, flashing her a look that plainly showed his hurt and anger that she'd lied and run away from him—again. "Mateo is safe with Neeka."

"Thank the gods, I—"

"Don't thank them yet," said Azriel curtly. Striding over to where the servant stood trembling with her back against the wall, he pointed to Persephone's scarred, bare arm and said, "Tell us what you know about this."

As the woman opened her mouth to reply, someone hammered hard on the other side of the barred door.

"In the name of the Regent Mordesius, I order you to open the door at once!" bellowed a voice.

"Forget that," ordered Azriel. Jabbing his finger toward Persephone's scarred arm once more, he said, "*Tell us what you know about this!*"

The woman's eyes darted from Persephone to Azriel and back again. Then she thrust her clasped hands at Persephone. "Forgive me, I did not want to do it!" she sobbed. "I was only a frightened child and the poor queen begged so piteously!"

"OPEN THE DOOR!"

"What did the queen beg you to do?" asked Azriel, blocking Persephone's way so that she could not back away.

"There was so little time," panted the woman, who'd suddenly begun to speak so rapidly that she was tripping over her own words. "The Regent had gone to fetch someone to murder and dispose of the infant, but the queen had hope. Hope that her firstborn might survive to someday return and claim her inheritance. But for that to happen, the infant had to be marked in some way." The woman's eyes widened at the memory. "So the queen took off the necklace that had been a gift from her own mother and asked me to dangle it in the heat of the fire. And when she deemed it hot enough, she had me bring it to her side, where her two babies lay nestled. And . . . and . . . may the gods forgive me, while she held your tiny arms together, I looped the necklace around and held it in place until the air was filled with the smell of your newborn flesh burning. And then the soldier with the mismatched eyes came and took you away."

THUD, THUD, THUD. . . .

Ignoring the sound of something ponderous being pounded against the door, Persephone grabbed the pockmarked servant by the arms. "But I don't understand!" she exclaimed. "Why did the Regent want to get rid of one of the babies?"

The woman smiled hollowly. "The Methusian Seer had promised the king a son and Mordesius had been named Regent of the unborn boy child. But the clever Seer had said nothing about a girl child—and certainly nothing of a girl child born first. Regent of the second born is Regent of nothing."

Her mind reeling, Persephone asked the question she knew Azriel wanted to ask but would not. "And . . . and did the Seer perchance mention what any of this had to do with the coming of a great Methusian king?"

THUD, THUD, THUD. . . .

Out of the corner of her eye, Persephone could see the heavy bar across the door beginning to splinter, but the pockmarked servant paid no heed. Dropping to one knee, she looked up at Persephone with a reverence bordering on awe and said, "I know nothing of what the Seer may have said about any Methusian king, Your Highness. I know only that you are the lost royal twin and rightful heir to the Erok throne."

M.L. FERGUS's many books for young people have been translated into more than a dozen languages, optioned for television, adapted for stage, and won or been shortlisted for numerous prestigious awards. She writes illustrated books for young readers under the name Maureen Fergus. She lives in Winnipeg, Canada with her family.

More information about M.L. Fergus can be found on her website www.maureenfergus.com.